SILVER
SHOES

Published June 19, 2018
Printed in the United States of America
Print ISBN: 978-1-63152-353-3
E-ISBN: 978-1-63152-354-0
Library of Congress Control Number: 2018932576

Book design by Stacey Aaronson

For information, address:
She Writes Press
1563 Solano Ave #546
Berkeley, CA 94707

She Writes Press is a division of SparkPoint Studio, LLC.

The Silver Shoes

A Novel

JILL G. HALL

SHE WRITES PRESS

This book is dedicated to my grandmothers,
Mabel Greenbaum and Grace Todd,
who came of age during the 1920s
and showed me how to love unconditionally.

I

Anne loved New York this time of year, when maple trees began to sprout emerald leaves but it was still cool enough to bundle up. If only she could stay here forever with Sergio and not go back to San Francisco.

A black-and-white-striped awning graced the storefront of Timely Treasures, listed as a "top ten New York City best bargain shop." A bell jingled as she stepped inside. She closed the door behind her, blocking out the city noise, and was greeted by the scent of beeswax and lemon. She waited for her eyes to adjust to the dim light. Perhaps the owners kept them low to save money.

She pulled off her knit cap and put it in her backpack. Ducking her five-foot-eight frame to see into the nearest mirror, she squinted at her sorrel-colored hair. What a frizzy mess! She fluffed it upside down and secured it atop her head with a scrunchie.

She wandered the aisles stuffed with buffed antique furniture, Erté sculptures, knickknacks, and gewgaws. This shop was too upscale for thrifting, the wares too high-end. She'd only come in search of found-object inspiration for her artwork.

Turning to leave, she caught sparkly reflections from a back table—as if lit by a spotlight on a stage, pulling her toward them. As she drew closer to the satin-clothed table, an interesting display revealed itself: a pair of silver shoes rested atop a box, surrounded by a rope of pearls, a pair of cream-colored gloves, an enameled cigarette case, and a white marabou-feather boa.

She ran her fingers over the shimmery rhinestones that graced the shoe's two-inch heels. In vintage times, women didn't wear the soaring stilt heels of today. She picked them up. These shoes were made for dancing and might even fit her. The woman who had owned them must have had big feet, too.

Ha! Maybe a Rockette had even owned them. After all, they were in New York. Anne searched for the size but couldn't find one.

Sergio would get a kick out of them. Since he worked in the shoe business and was very generous with samples, the last thing she needed was another pair, but these really spoke to her. And Sergio might think they were sexy. He loved it when she wore sensuous footwear. They were so fancy, though. Where would she ever wear them?

All of a sudden the shoes grew warm, as if kissed by the sun, tempting her to try them on. A salesperson still hadn't appeared, so Anne pulled off her boots, slid her feet inside the shoes, and clasped the T-straps. Shifting her feet side to side, she admired how the leather moved, soft and supple. The best thing about buying used shoes was that someone else had worn them in for you. As she stepped along the aisle, a warm glow ran from the soles of her feet up to her heart and swirled there. Maybe they were magic!

She closed her eyes and clicked her heels three times, chanting, "There's no place like home. There's no place like home. There's no place like home."

"Are you planning to buy those?" A man stood before her.

"Oh!" She jumped. "You scared me!" She bent to unclasp the T-straps and slipped off the shoes, waiting for her racing heartbeat to subside. "How much are they?"

He took them from her and spoke dramatically. "They're in *perfect* condition. I'd say seventy-five smackeroos." In his suspenders, bow tie, and slicked-back hair, he reminded her of the emcee character in the *Cabaret* revival Sergio had taken her to last year.

She sighed and shook her head. "That's too much."

The man's sad eyes penetrated hers. "Make me an offer."

She glanced at the shoes again. She shouldn't buy them, but she had to follow her instincts—they'd been right before. From the wallet in her backpack she offered him a bill. "How about twenty dollars?"

He paused for a moment and studied her. "Thirty and they're yours."

"Deal." She took out a ten, picked up her boots, and started toward the counter. There went the rest of her bus money.

"I have more things from the same estate if you're interested." His hand swept over the other items on the table.

"No, thanks." She shook her head, tugging her boots back on.

He wrapped the shoes in tissue and placed them carefully in the vintage box.

"May I have a bag instead?" she asked, placing the money on the counter.

"You must store them in the original box. The shoes are very valuable."

If they were so valuable, why did he take thirty bucks for them? "I'm traveling and the box will be in the way."

"Even so, I insist." He held up the box. "Promise to never throw away the box."

It didn't look like much—a shoebox with barely legible Italian words handwritten on its side. Sergio could translate it this evening. She loved when he spoke Italian to her.

"Okay. I promise." She shrugged and opened her backpack.

The man gently laid the box inside. "You'll be glad to have it." He eked out a thin smile and escorted her to the door. "Are you going on a trip?"

"No, heading home."

"Where's that?"

"San Francisco."

The man nodded and put his hand on her shoulder. "That's a stunning coat. Dior, correct?"

"Yes." She stepped back.

"Lovely brooch, too. How much for both?"

The breath caught in her throat, and she clasped her hand over the rhinestone snowflake pin. It had been the connection between her and her dear friend Sylvia. When Anne wore the brooch and coat, she could still sense Sylvia's presence.

"I'll give you a good price."

"They're not for sale. Goodbye." She fingered the key in the pocket of her black velvet coat and stepped out onto the sidewalk, relieved to get away.

She'd better hurry or she'd be late to meet Sergio. She skirted a construction barrier. A he-man type with bulging muscles threw debris out a top window and she had to duck. Dust particles flew into her hair as the mess fell into a dumpster on the sidewalk. Since she started visiting Sergio two years before, the economy had surged and New York developers were investing in renovations like mad. Housing costs had skyrocketed. She could never afford to rent an apartment here.

San Francisco was expensive enough. Without rent control, she'd never have been able to stay in her studio apartment the six years since she'd moved there. Hopefully, Sergio would invite her to move in with him. After all, this bicoastal romance had been going on for two years, and things were still hot and heavy. The lease on her San Francisco apartment had almost expired, and the landlady wanted her to sign another.

If Sergio didn't ask Anne soon, she would need to broach the subject herself. They couldn't keep up this long-distance relationship forever. If he told her no, she'd be mortified, and it might push her to break up with him. But she couldn't imagine living without him.

2

1929

Spring warmth filled the air. The New York sidewalks teemed with sailors, shoppers, and businessmen, all hurrying along in a noisy symphony of purpose. An automobile honked, shooing a horse-drawn carriage out of its way. A bicyclist zipped by. Skyscrapers towered overhead like urban cliffs.

Clair saw the Chrysler building glinting in the distance. Its rounded tiers reminded her of a wedding cake.

Clair had the good fortune to be out on her own this sunny afternoon—Mrs. Schmidt, her chaperone, had come down with a cold. The sense of freedom put a song in her heart. She'd return home before her father did, and he'd never know the difference.

She tugged down her cloche hat, afraid it might spring off. Since she'd turned eighteen a few weeks ago, he'd made her wear it over her updo. "Your strands seem to have a mind of their own. Someone might imagine you're on fire!"

Aunt June said Clair's hair was the same color her mother's had been. Maybe that's why her father insisted she wear it up and covered, so as not to bring back memories of his beloved wife. "Your hair's your glory, never to be cut," he'd said. "And only for your husband to ever see down."

She shook her head and gazed at a pair of rhinestone shoes displayed in a shop window. Imagine dancing in them! Too bad her father wouldn't allow her to wear them to her ball. He'd say they were too garish. A pair of *peau de soie* Mary Janes would suffice—at six feet, she towered over most folks already. Clair used to be able to talk her father into anything, but recently he had become downright particular, even grumpy. She had no idea why.

As she spun into Macy's through the revolving door, the store exploded with a plethora of color. She passed a perfume display, lace handkerchiefs in a glass case, and umbrellas in a stand. Hopefully, the department store would have some gloves that fit. Her ball was coming up fast, and neither Bergdorf nor Saks had ones large enough.

A snooty saleswoman at Saks had peered down at Clair's large hands and sniffed. "Try Macy's." Clair held back embarrassed tears. She tapped her fingers across her thighs, playing an imaginary keyboard. She had to look her best on her special night.

She studied the candy display, filled with lemon drops, peppermints, and licorice. Aunt June used to bring her here and let her pick a sweet. Clair always chose her favorite nonpareils, chocolate circles coated with white sprinkles, and ate each of them a different way.

The first one she'd crunch and chew for an immediate burst of pleasure. The next she would hold in her mouth, making it last as long as possible. Once she even held a piece in her palm until it melted, made sure no one was watching, and licked it off. She wasn't a naughty girl, but she couldn't help herself.

Things were much easier then. The only decisions she had to make were which candies to choose. But she was no longer a child. Soon she would be a part of society, so she had to play the part of a perfect young lady.

"Miss, may I help you?" The man behind the counter broke her reverie. She couldn't resist buying a bag of nonpareils and nibbled on one as she wandered toward the back of the store.

A short, round salesgirl approached her. "That looks delicious!"

Taken aback, Clair held out the bag. "Want one?"

"I couldn't." The blonde's curls bounced as she shook her head. "Well, maybe one." She took a candy from the bag, popped it in her mouth, and held it closed as her Wedgwood-blue eyes lit up. "Mmm."

She must be the *savor in your mouth as long as possible* type.

No, the girl chewed and swallowed. "My favorite!"

"Mine, too." Clair smiled.

The girl eyed her. "Nice hat. I could make one bigger to fit over your hair better."

Clair didn't know how to respond. "Where would I find the gloves?"

"I'll show you!" The girl swayed across the store to a long cabinet against the wall. "Cream or white?"

"Cream."

She pulled out a long drawer, set it on a nearby table, and held a pair of gloves to Clair's raised hand. "Much too small." The girl shook her head.

Clair sensed her face turning red. She had heard that so many times before.

"What lovely long fingers you have!" The girl took Clair's raised hand. "They fit your body so well. Sometimes a person's hands will be really small, and their bodies look too big for them. Sometimes it's the opposite—too big of hands on a small body." She looked Clair up and down. "But your hands suit you just right."

"Thank you." Clair had never thought of it that way.

"My gloves are short and wide. See, short hands. Short body." The girl wiggled her fingers and drew her hand down toward the ground.

Clair smiled. "Interesting."

The girl returned to the drawer and rummaged through it, making an absolute mess. She handed another pair of gloves to Clair. "These should do."

The rich cream color would match her pearls exactly. Clair

slipped the gloves on and ran the smooth texture along her cheek. "Satin." She easily pulled them up to her elbows.

The girl rubbed Clair's fingers to check for size. "Perfect. They fit like gloves." The girl giggled. "Isn't that funny? They *are* gloves!"

Clair laughed, too. They were so comfortable she hated to take them off.

"Where are you going to wear them?" the girl asked.

"My coming-out ball."

"How exciting! Your own ball." She gazed at Clair as if she were a princess.

A man approached them, and the salesgirl stood erect. "Hello, Mr. Smithers."

"Winifred." He nodded through his wire-rimmed glasses, owl-ish eyes magnified.

Clair swallowed and smiled at him. She'd hate for Winifred to get into trouble.

Winifred waited a few seconds until he walked away. "That's the manager," she whispered. "He's told us not to fraternize with the customers."

"Your name is Winifred?" What a stuffy old lady's name, it didn't fit her.

"Yes, god-awful, isn't it? My friends call me Winnie."

She probably had a lot of friends. Clair rolled off the gloves and handed them to her. "Thanks for your help. Send the bill to my father, Leland Devereaux at the Waldorf."

"Ooh. That fancy-schmancy hotel?"

Clair nodded.

"Shall I have them delivered?"

"I'll take them." Clair couldn't wait to slip them on again when she got home.

Winnie wrapped the gloves in tissue and put them in a box. "You know my name now. What's yours?"

"Clair. Clair Devereaux."

Winnie shook Clair's hand as if she were a man. "Enchanted." Winnie giggled.

Clair had to learn more about the girl. She didn't seem to have a care in the world. "How long have you worked here?"

"Six months." Winnie lowered her voice. "But it's only temporary."

Clair glanced around to make sure Mr. Smithers wasn't near. "Temporary?"

"Yes, I'm really a performer."

"You are?" Clair had never met one before.

"I dance."

"You do?"

"Yes, look how limber I am!" Winnie leaned over and touched her toes.

Clair couldn't believe Winnie had actually done that in public!

Winnie rolled back up. "I sing, too. My boyfriend Rudy says I'm talented." She paused. "Well, to tell you the truth, he's not really my boyfriend, but someday he will be. He's planning a big show, and I'll be his shining star."

"You don't say." Clair wished she had as much confidence as this warm, funny, vivacious girl, not always keeping her thoughts bottled up inside. Maybe if she had someone to talk to. She'd always had trouble making friends. At finishing school, the other girls made fun of her for being so tall, studious, and focused on her piano playing.

Winnie smiled at her. "Do you have a beau?"

Clair tapped her fingers against her thighs and shook her head.

"Don't worry! You're so pretty you will soon. I've had boyfriends since I was thirteen."

"You have?" What did Winnie's parents think about that?

"Sure." Winnie handed her the package.

Clair looked at her watch. "I'd better be going. Thanks for your help."

Winnie put her hands on her hips and wiggled them up and down in Mae West fashion. "Why don't you come back and see me sometime?"

Clair covered her mouth to hide her laugh. She picked up the candy from the counter and noticed Winnie staring at the treats.

"Another?" Clair offered. Winnie helped herself. Clair had a good feeling about her, as if they had known each other for a long time.

3

Out of breath from rushing, Anne spotted Sergio in front of The Om yoga studio. He was as handsome as ever, with a strong nose and dark eyes, his shoulder-length hair pulled up into a magnificent man bun. As he kissed her cheeks, she caught a whiff of his tangy honeysuckle scent.

"*Fretta*! I thought you'd gotten lost." He opened the door, ushered her inside, and helped her slip off her coat.

She hung it on a hook. "I did. My cell phone ran out of juice, and I couldn't use the GPS."

She stuffed her boots under a bench. In her socks, she followed him into the dimly lit studio where Indian flute music played. Supine bodies were spread throughout the space, and a candle flickered on a corner table. The instructor, a silk scarf adorning her head, sat cross-legged at the front of the room on a platform. Anne sat on the mat Sergio had prepared for her.

The instructor smiled. "It's time to begin. Knees to your chests."

Sergio did as instructed, and Anne followed suit.

"Inhale and let it out. Inhale and let it out. Inhale and let it out." The teacher's voice hummed low and mellow.

Anxiety kicked in as Anne tried to slow her breathing. Before she'd met Sergio, she'd tried yoga many times but had never been able to get the hang of it. She'd always been a klutz. Since he was crazy about it, for the last few months in San Francisco she'd been going to the Y for sessions, and she felt as if she had gotten pretty good at it.

Last night, when he told her he had a surprise and that they would finally get to go to a class together, she smiled and said, "*Fantastico!*" She hoped she could impress him.

"Lift your right leg, and hold on to your foot or the back of your calf."

Anne raised her leg. See? Easy as pie.

"Your right leg," the instructor repeated. "*Right* leg."

Embarrassed, Anne quickly switched legs. Sergio grinned at her with a wink, his leg straight above his head, his hand hooked over his heel. He could pull it almost all the way to the ground. For a guy, he sure was limber.

She closed her eyes and pretended not to notice. Continuing to follow the teacher's words, she gradually got the hang of it, and her mind began to wander. She hadn't told Sergio she lived on a shoestring, but he'd probably figured it out. Luckily, he didn't know that two years ago she'd almost moved back in with her mother in Michigan.

However, since her solo show at Gallery Noir in San Francisco, her pieces were selling. With that and her valet parking job, she got by pretty well. She didn't need much to live on, but money management had never been one of her life skills. Flying back and forth to visit Sergio didn't help her income, either. The worst of it was, she'd been so distracted, there hadn't been time or energy to focus on creating new art.

She was past thirty—it was time to get serious about life. And Sergio was the one. They got along so well. Since they didn't get to spend enough time together, they didn't waste time arguing. Besides, Sergio, with his easygoing, fun-loving personality, wasn't the type to fight. The only thing they ever squabbled about was who would visit whom next, and when. No fights like she'd had with her previous boyfriend, Karl.

She'd thought Karl had been the one, but after being together for months, he'd confessed he hadn't filed for divorce after all—his wife and their baby still lived with him. How stupid Anne had been! But Sergio was different, and she sensed she could trust him. His cross-country texts were romantic and liquid with love. Their Skype dates were hysterical. And she was gaga over him. Her body reacted every time her mind drifted to him: the touch of his hand on her back, the curl of his hair on the nape of his neck, his smoldering bedroom eyes. This traveling back and forth wasn't practical, though.

"Stand in mountain pose. Hands in prayer position. Flat back. Arms to the side, leg out behind you, and lean over." The instructor raised her voice and the class stood.

Anne pulled off her socks, stretched her leg out behind her, and raised it high. This airplane one was easy. But then her leg began to wobble, and she lost her balance and fell to the mat. Sergio glanced down at her, but seeing she was fine, he continued to retain his perfect 747. Everyone else was in perfect form, too.

She stood with the group in prayer position as they started to do something called a Sun Salutation. The teacher's voice droned on and on, and Anne tried to follow the woman in front of her as best she could. Being led through the poses, she felt more wimp than warrior.

The momentum picked up. The scrunchie popped out of her hair and flew to the other side of Sergio. She didn't want to stop to get it, so her hair kept falling in her eyes.

She ran out of breath, her muscles shook, and it was all she could do not to collapse on her mat. She was in good shape from hiking the San Francisco hills, but this was a different type of exertion.

"Get ready for *shavasana*. Lie on your backs." The instructor's voice soothed.

Anne had never been so relieved. She pulled her socks on, lay back, and Sergio spread a light blanket over her.

"Arms out, palms up, and close your eyes." The instructor paused. Her smooth voice murmured, "Feel your heels on the ground. Feel your ankles, feel your calves . . ."

Anne peeked, just like she always did as a girl, stealing a look in church during prayers. The calming sound of a singing bowl rang, and her thoughts flew away.

Would Sergio invite her to move in with him? She didn't expect him to take care of her. She'd get a job, so long as she had time for her art. With all the techies moving into San Francisco, Mrs. Landenheim, her landlady, would love for Anne to leave.

Those techies were ruining the San Francisco art scene, pushing creative types out into Oakland and other suburbs. Her work had taken off in San Francisco, but New York was naturally the next step for her art career. Yes, New York would be stimulating and what she needed. She'd also be closer to her family in Michigan and could visit them more often. Plus she could be with Sergio all the time.

He gently nudged her. "You're snoring."

"I am not!" she whispered back.

"Thank you for your excellent effort and attention. Namaste." The instructor bowed to the class.

Anne bowed, too. "Namaste." At least she knew how to do that.

They stood and she rolled up her mat.

"Want to stay for Zumba?" Sergio teased.

"No, *grazie*."

4

In Sergio's co-op twenty stories high, Anne felt part of the clouds. It was not quite sunset. Using the telescope, she spied children playing on boulders in Central Park and the horse-drawn carriages lining up for evening rides.

Sergio set down a glass of wine for her, then lifted the hair off the nape of her neck and nuzzled there. She turned and kissed him, hoping he'd forgotten about her disastrous yoga performance.

"*Mia bella*, why were you so late to yoga?"

"Shopping."

"I worried you weren't going to show. Did you enjoy the class?"

She took a sip of her wine, crossed to the leather couch, and sat with a sigh. "I promise I've been practicing. I hope I didn't embarrass you in front of your teacher."

He laughed and sat beside her. "It's taken me years to be able to do some of those poses. It's not a competition. Go at your own pace."

"Are you sure?"

He nodded and kissed her again. "Now show me what you bought today."

She unzipped her backpack sitting on the granite countertop and took the shoes out of the box. "Look." She carried them over to him. "I believe they were dance shoes!"

He flipped them upside down and examined the soles. "You're

right. See these tiny holes?" He pointed to a shoe's ball and heel. "There used to be taps screwed in."

Taking the shoes, she studied the barely visible holes. "Cool."

"Looks like they're from the 1920s or '30s."

"Double cool."

"Model them for me."

She slipped them on, clasped the buckles, and stood up, feeling a warm glow rise through her feet all the way to the top of her head. Imitating a sophisticated model, she walked back and forth on the hardwood floor. Shuffling her feet back and forth, waving her arms wildly, she tried to imitate Bruno Mars' moves.

"*Cause uptown funk's goin' to give it to ya!*" She sang off-key and faux-tapped across the floor. "*Say my name, you know who I am. I'm too hot!*"

Sergio grabbed her hands and joined in dancing until they both fell onto the couch in hysterics.

Trying to catch her breath she said, "I bought them at Timely Treasures in the village."

"Never heard of it." He shook his head and took a drink of his wine.

"The strange man running the shop insisted I keep the box."

"He's right. It can be important to keep a box to authenticate the item as it increases in value."

"I saw that on *The Big Bang Theory*. Did you see the one where Sherman played with that Dr. Spock doll and broke it?" Anne asked. "He'd taken it out of the box."

Sergio laughed. "Mr. Spock, not Dr."

"Yes, Mr. Spock."

"It's like a Rolex, too."

Happy with the Timex her mother had given her for her sixteenth birthday, Anne had never paid much attention to watches. She glanced at Sergio's wrist, surprised she had never noticed he wore a classic Rolex like the one in magazine ads. After all this time, she wondered what else she didn't know about him.

Sergio went over to her backpack and took out the shoebox, a rattling sound emanating from inside it. "I hear something." Pushing yellowed tissue paper aside, he pulled out a strand of pearls.

"Oh my gosh!" Anne's hands flew to her cheeks. "Those were displayed on the table beside the shoes. How did they get in there?"

"The shopkeeper must have been sweet on you and slipped them in there as a gift."

"Ha. Ha." She took the pearls and rubbed them along her teeth.

"*Cosa stai facendo?*" Sergio's eyebrows shot up, and he grabbed the pearls.

Anne laughed. "It's a trick Sylvia taught me. I didn't mark them, so they're real. See?" She pointed to the pearls.

He rolled his eyes and draped the pearls over her head. She turned to the plate-glass window, a mirror in the darkened sky. The strand's knot hit her chest at the heart chakra and looped down to over her belly button. "This is mysterious. Maybe that's why he told me to keep the box."

"Perhaps."

Anne took off the pearls. "How strange. I wonder how they got in there. I should take them back. Would the shop still be open?"

Sergio checked his watch. "Probably not, and it's rush hour."

"I have to go home tomorrow. Please take them back for me. They're probably worth a fortune."

"Stay another night and return them yourself. Visit your boyfriend again."

She grinned. "Can't expect Howard to cover my valet shifts by himself much longer. I gotta get back to the St. Francis."

Sergio shook his head. "When are you going to quit that job?"

She shrugged. "Tips are good." She hadn't told him how much she needed the money to make ends meet.

Standing, she grabbed his hand and pulled. "Let's not waste any more time. Come to bed."

"Hold on." He let go and patted the seat next to him. "We need to talk."

"What is it?" She brushed her hand over her hair. Maybe he was going to ask.

He paused, then looked into her eyes with his brown ones. "We've been together for quite a while. Next summer in Italy, you'll be meeting my nonna."

Anne nodded and hoped nothing would get in the way of this trip. She'd had to cancel once before because her solo show had been scheduled for the same time.

"It's time I met your family, too."

Her breath caught in her throat. Her family was quirky, to say the least. He was sophisticated and well, they were not. Her beloved hometown, Oscoda, was the opposite of New York.

She frowned.

"What's wrong?" He put his hand on her knee.

She swallowed. "I hoped you were going to invite me to move here with you."

"Of course. That should come next. I miss you so much when you aren't here. But first I need to meet your family."

Oh boy! What if he didn't like them or the town she loved so much?

5

In the mansion's courtyard, clouds shifted in the marbled sky. A slight breeze rustled the edge of Clair's chiffon dress, tickling her ankle, and she kicked that leg out.

"Miss Devereaux!" Mr. LeRue fingered the thinning strands that tried to cover his shiny dome.

"I'm sorry."

He stuck the paintbrush between his teeth, stepped forward, and pushed a red curl behind her ear. "Relaxed smile and upright posture, please."

"Yes, sir." It wasn't the first time she'd been told to sit up straight.

He returned to the canvas, pointed the brush, and swirled it in a circle. "Eyes that way. Gently down. Not on me."

Clair repositioned her head and admired the way the morning clouds reflected among the floating water lilies in the rectangular pond. Like a butterfly alighted, her hands rested motionless on her lap. She had no interest in sitting for a portrait, but her father had insisted, and she desired to please him.

Most New York girls in 1929 had their photographs taken for their coming-out balls, but her father commissioned John Singer Sargent, the best portrait painter in the world. With his special talent, each and every one of his subjects looked beautiful. Unfortunately, Mr. Sargent had passed away and Mr. Andre LeRue, recently returned from Paris, came with high recommendations. This would be his New York debut.

The new gloves felt smooth on her hands and she resisted the urge to run them over her cheek. Her gown she adored—blush pink, like the baby roses blooming on the courtyard arbor. Most girls wore white for their coming out, but she had been able to convince her father otherwise. The pearls, a gift from him, had been too long, almost to her thighs. The jeweler had suggested resetting some of the beads into a tiara.

"Please, Father!" Clair had begged.

He nixed the idea. "Too ostentatious."

Instead, he had a single band made for her to weave through her hair. The jeweler had knotted between each pearl on the headband but had been too busy to do so with the necklace. She'd take it back after the party to have it restrung correctly.

Her fingers began to practice scales, her knees serving as piano keys. She played her favorite song, "The Man on the Flying Trapeze," and sang the words in her head. She loved to play the piano, but not how the maestro her father had hired required. The instructor insisted she slow down the tempo and play boring pieces. Those Brahms lullabies would put anyone to sleep, not just babies. When alone, she even played boogie-woogie music. Her father would be furious if he knew. This fall at Juilliard, she'd be able to meet other musicians and learn to play all types of new music.

A dove landed on the stone tiles and began to coo. Clair turned her head.

"Miss Devereaux!" Mr. LeRue stomped his foot and tugged on his Dalí-esque mustache, its ends as pointy as his paintbrush. "I must insist."

She clasped her hands tightly and reset the relaxed smile. "Sorry!"

Father would be disappointed if she ruined the portrait. He'd said that her future children would want to see how lovely she'd been at eighteen. Too bad her mama hadn't sat for at least one photograph. There were no pictures of her in their suite, not even a wedding portrait. He claimed they had all disappeared in a fire. Clair had been six when her mama died, and couldn't recall much except that she rarely smiled, but when she did, the whole room shone as if a bright light had been turned on in the middle of the night.

Mr. LeRue began to hum, breaking Clair's reverie. She recognized the tune, a Viennese waltz, but resisted the urge to join in. Would anyone besides her father dance with her at the ball? Maybe some nice boy would attend who was even taller than she. The chance of that was about the same as a circus elephant bouncing into the ballroom.

She doubted she was the beauty her father claimed, but she had tried her best to look pretty for the sitting today. Most girls had their mother to guide them. She had considered asking Aunt June, her mama's sister, but decided against it.

They spent time together on afternoon outings. If her father happened to be home when she came by the suite, he never seemed to welcome her. Somewhat outspoken Aunt June had once suggested Clair stay with her occasionally for female companionship. Clair's father wouldn't hear of it.

He had said, "I'm her father *and* mother. Besides, there's Mrs. Schmidt." The old lady with the chin hair in the suite next door tutored Clair for a few hours in the morning and chaperoned her as needed.

Clair had overheard Aunt June raise her voice. "Leland, for goodness sake, at least move into a real home and send her to school."

On Monday and Wednesday afternoons, the maestro came over for piano lessons. Tuesdays and Fridays, after teaching all day, Aunt June visited, and if the weather cooperated they would walk to the park or visit the library. Clair loved to pet Patience and Fortitude, the lion statues that guarded the entrance to the massive building, and to explore all the shelves of books contained inside.

Her family was different than others she'd read about in books, with rambling houses and dining room tables filled with relatives celebrating together. Instead she ate with her father in the suite or downstairs in the restaurant where the conversation remained stilted but polite.

"The Waldorf is just fine, and Mrs. Schmidt is, too," her father's deep voice had boomed at Aunt June's suggestion.

"I mean a home with a garden and friends to play with."

"Balderdash! I'm fun!"

"What did you say?" Mr. LeRue asked.

Clair hadn't realized she'd spoken out loud. "Nothing. Sorry."

Her father and Aunt June had always had friction between them. Clair sensed it had to do with her mother. She had heard them mention her once not long after she died.

"What about Mama?" Clair had asked.

"Nothing, dear." Her aunt pulled Clair onto her lap.

"Am I like her?"

Aunt June and her father had glanced at each other.

"Was she tall, too? With lots of energy?"

"Yes, dear." Her aunt stroked Clair's hair.

"Your sister, right?"

"That's right."

"Where is she, Father?" Clair had asked him this a hundred times.

He sighed and raised his bushy eyebrows. "In heaven."

"Is it far away?"

"Farther away than you can imagine."

Her mother hadn't seemed ill and had died suddenly. When her father told Clair, he seemed distant and didn't even shed a tear. That seemed strange, thinking back on it.

Clair fingered Aunt June's cameo pinned to her high lace collar. Clair tried to picture her mama up there in the fluffy clouds like the angels on the brooch playing harps. God had a long beard and hopefully was being nice to her.

She knew her father had done his best to fill the gap. Whenever she'd start to cry for her mama, he'd hush her and say, "Good girls never cry." And she would hold back her tears to please him, even though they would drip out the sides of her eyes. She soon learned not to ask about her mother, and to cry only when she was alone.

"How's it coming?" Without moving her head, Clair slid her gaze sideways as Mr. LeRue dipped his brush onto the palette and dabbed a few short strokes on the canvas.

"I'll be done soon." His brow furrowed in concentration.

The hardest time was the dead of night when loneliness came stalking, taking her by the throat and not letting her breathe. That's when Clair missed her mama the most, the smell of rose water, her smooth skin and soft lullabies. It had been years since she'd been gone, but the memories continued to haunt Clair when all was quiet but the ticking of the mantle clock, and she wondered how different her life would be if her mama were still alive.

"Okay. You can relax." Mr. LeRue put his paintbrush down.

Clair rolled her shoulders and stood. "May I see it?"

"Not until the ball." He shook out a cloth to cover it as she rushed over.

"Okay. Just a peek." The artist raised his head proudly and stepped back.

Her hand flew to her face to disguise her horror. *Genius, my foot!*

"Do I really look like that?"

"To me you do. Isn't it marvelous?"

It was ghastly! She didn't dare hurt his feelings, so she held back tears and tried to sound enthusiastic. "It's *colorful*."

Her body appeared elongated like Alice in the *Adventures in Wonderland* after she tasted the "EAT ME" cake. In the painting, Clair's head touched the top of the canvas and appeared humongous. Worst of all were her arms, a tangled mess of string.

How horrible. And the ball was next week! She would be humiliated when her father unveiled this portrait.

6

Their suite on the ninth floor of the Waldorf had two bedrooms, one on either side of the parlor. A fire warmed the book-filled parlor where Clair sat near her father's desk.

"Goodbye, Clair. See you tonight." He patted her head and left for the office.

She tried to find his newspaper, but he must have taken it with him. He had no idea that each day, as soon as he left for Wall Street, she took his newspaper from the receptacle and read it front to back. She perused fashion magazines, but she found current events and business concepts intriguing, too, and tried to learn as much as possible about market trends.

She opened the sash and perched on the window seat. A morning breeze drifted into the suite. Below, autos drove by and people pounded the pavement on their way to hustle-bustle lives. A nursemaid pushing a pram walked slowly.

Unless suitors came to call after her upcoming ball, the summer would tick on endlessly, like the hands of her metronome—back and forth, with no purpose or end in sight. She looked forward to school starting in the fall but had no idea what she would do with her life once she graduated. She longed to do more than go to church bazaars, teas, and balls. At her age, Aunt June had been teaching and working to get women the right to vote. Clair knew she would not have been brave enough to be a suffragette. But what could she do? She knew what she dreamed of was impossible.

Clair drifted to the piano. Her fingers touched the keys. Melancholy slow, like the beat of her heart. She longed to pick up the pace. The remnants of Victorian constraints felt corset-tight.

When Clair once mentioned to her father that she wanted to work after college, he scoffed, "What would you do?"

"I could teach piano to children, help with the church choir, maybe even direct a choir someday."

"No need. I'll take care of you until you get married, then it will be your husband's responsibility." As if she were a doll to pass on. "Only hussies work! I knew this would happen when ladies got the vote. What's next? A woman stockbroker?"

"But Aunt June works."

He frowned. "She's different."

"What do you mean?"

He looked down. "Oh, nothing. She's always been industrious."

Hearing Winnie's dream of being a performer had stirred up Clair's own childhood desire, the one she hadn't dared tell anyone about. More than anything in the world, she yearned to be a dancer. Dancing was similar to playing the piano, but with her whole body. Her mama had once held her while she danced around the suite, singing. Clair remembered her voice as captivating.

Clair would never forget her tenth birthday when Aunt June took her to see the Russian Ballet Company, agile in their pointe shoes and frilly costumes. Clair's heart had reeled when the tutu-wearing dancers turned around and around, spinning and spinning. She craved being up there on the stage. One tall dancer, the Sugar Plum Fairy, had been quite stunning, and as graceful as a leaf floating from a tree.

Later that night, alone in her room, Tchaikovsky still resonated in Clair's chest. In front of the mirror, she tilted her head up and lifted one arm, then the other. Pointing her toes, she raised each leg as high as it would go, picturing the tall dancer who had raised one leg very high above her head. Clair's body tingled. She could grow up to be a dancer.

That same year, her father had taken her to the circus. Clair had also fantasized about performing under the big top: the beat of the drums, the high-stepping ponies, their shiny manes braided with pink ribbons. When the girl rode in standing on the back of a big horse, she looked as tall as a skyscraper. Her silver-sequined costume shone in the lights, and the feather on her head bounced to the music.

As the rider let go of the reins and raised both hands above her head, Clair's heart galloped, frightened the girl would fall. Clair looked to her father for reassurance, but his eyes were wide, too. After a few more circuits, the horse slowed to kneel and the girl gracefully stepped to the ground, curtsying to the crowd. Clair wondered how it would feel to perform in front of a crowd and make their hearts beat fast.

That girl Winnie wanted to be a performer, too, and she shouted it to the world. Clair knew she never would be able to tell anyone about her dream. First of all, her father would be mortified. Besides, Clair didn't have Winnie's pizzazz.

Clair wished she had someone to talk to, a friend who would understand. Perhaps Winnie would lend a kind ear. Her bubbly, uninhibited personality made her seem as if she didn't have a care in the world.

Hurriedly dressing, Clair resolved to go back to Macy's and find Winnie. She rode the Otis down and slipped out of the hotel. She tossed a penny to the little newsboy on the sidewalk. He jumped up and pecked her on the cheek.

"Oh, my!" She rubbed her face with a suede-gloved hand. "That wasn't necessary. I only wanted a paper.

"Sorry, miss. I didn't mean nothin' by it." He twitched his nose like a rabbit's.

"A kiss should be saved for someone special," she scolded, trying not to smile. It was impossible to resist his freckled face, despite it being smudged with dirt. He looked to be about eight years old.

"I'm Clair. Now shake like a gentleman." She held out her hand.

He reached out and jiggled it. "Nook."

"Nook? How did you get a name like that?"

"The police call me that cuz I hide from them in nooks and holes." He glanced up the busy street.

She frowned. "Why do you hide?"

"Tried to put me back in that nasty orphanage with stinky food and whippins. I's never going back there." He nodded his head once.

"What about school?"

"What do I need that for? I ken read."

"Really?" She doubted it.

He flipped a newspaper to the front page and read it aloud. "Man falls off building to his death." Nook looked up with a smug, missing-tooth grin until his eyes gaped at something behind her.

"Here comes a copper!" He dropped his papers, rushed down the street, dodged a truck, and climbed up a fire escape on the side of a building. At the top he did a handstand, holding on to the metal rails.

Clair hoped he would get away.

She strolled down the street and studied the silver shoes again in the small shop window with a sigh. The rhinestones sparkled in the morning light.

Macy's bustled with afternoon shoppers as Clair bought a bag of nonpareils. Walking the perimeter of the ground floor looking for Winnie, she scanned the shoe, handbag, and dry good sections. Disappointed, Clair nibbled a candy and rode the wooden elevator up to the second floor. In the dress department, she spotted Winnie's blonde curls.

Winnie caught sight of Clair and her face brightened. "Hiya, toots!"

Clair handed her the bag of sweets. "In thanks for helping me find those gloves."

Winnie opened the bag with a squeal, "You're the bee's knees, the cat's pajamas, the glitter to my gold!"

Her expression shifted to a frown, and she hid the bag behind her back. "Good afternoon, Mr. Smithers."

"Is everything okay here?" The manager moved toward them, staring through his owlish glasses.

"Just grand." Clair smiled at him. "This salesgirl is most helpful."

"I'm just going to show her the corsets."

Clair blushed. She couldn't believe Winnie would mention personal undergarments in front of a man.

"All right, Winifred. Get to it." He nodded at Clair and walked on.

Winnie reopened the bag. "That was a close one." She popped a candy in her mouth and munched on it as she led Clair behind a screen to the lingerie section. She picked up a small corset and started giggling. "This one would fit a baby."

"Do babies wear corsets?" Clair asked, putting on her best straight face.

Winnie pursed her heart-shaped lips. "I was only teasing."

Clair paused. "Me, too!"

Winnie's blue eyes opened wide. She giggled infectiously, and Clair joined in. It had been a long time since she'd made someone laugh.

Winnie held up another corset, in Clair's favorite rose pink, with lace trimmings.

"This would fit you perfectly." Winnie held it up to Clair for size.

"I couldn't." She shook her head. It was much too fancy.

"It would be beautiful on you. Try it. No one will see you behind the screen."

"No, but thank you." Clair couldn't imagine undressing in such a public place.

"Then take it home. You'll be glad you did."

Clair fingered the smooth silk. It would be much more comfortable than the scratchy white one she usually wore. "I'll take it."

Winnie nodded and started to wrap it up. "Hey, what are you doing tonight—want to come hear some music with me?"

Spending an evening with Winnie sounded terrific. "Carnegie Hall? I love the philharmonic." Clair had read that Toscanini would be conducting *Boléro*.

"Something like that."

"Who will escort us?"

"No one." Winnie shrugged. "We'll go by ourselves."

Clair frowned. Her father would never allow her to go out at night without a chaperone. "But isn't that dangerous?"

"Aw. Nothing'll happen. Please come." Winnie grabbed Clair's hand. "We'd have such fun."

Clair's father had an Odd Fellows lodge meeting tonight and wouldn't be home until late. "What time would we be back?"

"Early." Winnie smiled, handing her the box.

"Okay." Clair nodded slowly.

"Goody!" Winnie clapped her hands. "Where shall we meet?"

"How about the clock at the Waldorf?" Clair spied Mr. Smithers approaching and stepped away with her package.

"I've had a hankering to see the inside." Winnie smiled. "Seven thirty."

As Clair rode the wooden escalator down, she was tempted to return and tell Winnie she couldn't go after all. If Clair's father found out, he'd be livid.

7

The milky morning fog was so thick, Anne's plane circled San Francisco International Airport several times. After half an hour it descended, bumped along the runway, and finally came to a stop. Red-eyed and jetlagged, Anne pulled her suitcase through the terminal and climbed onto the shuttle into the city. This back and forth had been getting to her.

By the time she arrived at her stop at the corner of California and Polk, the morning sky had cleared to a gray wash. She hopped off and walked uphill toward her apartment, passing Lady Goldfinger's Complete Nail Care and Waxing Salon, Hair Future, and Creative Custom Tailoring. Below her apartment building, Pizza Pino's first offering of the day smelled enticing.

Anne unlocked the wrought iron security gate, stepped into the foyer, and froze as Mrs. Landenheim's apartment door opened and her Siamese cat skittered out.

Mrs. Landenheim poked her curler-covered head out the door. "Rent's due."

"I'll get right to it." Anne kept going up the stairs and almost tripped on the torn carpet.

For years they'd played the same game. The landlady reminded her the rent was due, and a few days later Anne would finally slip it under the mat, the last of it in cash tips. It used to be because Anne didn't have the money, but lately, what with all her travel and distractions, she would lose track and forget. According to Mrs. Landenheim, she couldn't do anything right. She complained about Anne's tardiness with the rent, her clomping up and down the stairs, and had even recently accused her of feeding her cat. Anne couldn't wait to move out of the place.

She trudged up the stairs to her third-floor studio apartment. It was its usual cyclonic mess—clothes tossed on the floor, dishes in the sink, newspapers strewn throughout. With no more space in her tiny closet, shoes lined the edges of the room.

Setting down her suitcase, she dropped her backpack on the daybed. On her wealth and prosperity altar, she lit a gardenia candle, rubbed the Buddha's tummy, and fingered the amber pendant hanging over it, bequeathed to her by Sylvia. Anne smiled as she touched her father's dog tags and heard Aunt Tootie's voice saying, "These are for you. They symbolize bravery. You're courageous like him—you followed your dreams all the way to California."

From the cupboard Anne grabbed a bag of Chips Ahoy!, got a Diet Coke from the fridge, and with a yawn, sat on her dinky daybed, already missing Sergio's luxurious king. She couldn't wait to be there full-time.

She had loved big-city living in San Francisco, and New York would be even better. Cities were as different as people. When she first drove cross-country to California in Tweety, her yellow Karmann Ghia, she'd stopped in Los Angeles first. She'd bought a map to the stars' homes and drove around looking for famous actors, but the only ones she saw were in the wax museum. Everything was so spread out, the freeways were ghastly, and public transportation was practically nonexistent. With all that traffic, the Botoxed lips, and its high prices, LA felt more like the city of devils than angels.

After that, San Francisco felt like a breath of fresh air. Strong winds blew out any semblance of smog, and she could get anywhere by walking or taking the bus.

If she moved to New York, what would she do with Tweety? Nobody in the Big Apple owned cars, not even Sergio. With the price of gas she didn't drive the Karmann Ghia often, but it had sentimental value. To earn money to buy it, in high school she had sold collaged boxes at Oscoda's Annual Souper Bowl Supper & Art Show and also set up a table on Route 23 during Paul Bunyan Days for the passing tourists. It took her two years to save up enough, but she'd done it.

What would she take with her to New York? Sergio's place was completely furnished, so she wouldn't need to take much. Her kitchenette certainly wasn't his style. She had traded three of her paintings for the red Formica table and pleather chairs at the flea market. The seats were torn, but fortunately they made red duct tape. She'd stuffed the table and chairs in the back of Tweety and lugged them upstairs one at a time. The coffee table came from her mother's house. The cigarette burns gave it a "vintage" look. With her Avon business going well, her mother had been happy to let it go to California and buy a new one.

It would take her a while to sort through her art supplies. She pulled her journal from her backpack and started a list.

Sort through:

- *ceramic figurines*
- *vintage magazines*
- *lace remnants*
- *postcard collection*
- *paints and brushes*

At Sergio's, where would she do her art? No way could she take over a corner of his pristine living room or set up in his gourmet kitchen. Maybe she could use his guest room. Renting a loft studio with such astronomical rents would be out of the question.

She pushed a pile of newspapers aside on the coffee table, pulled the shoebox from her backpack, and set it down. Carefully lifting the shoes from the box, she caressed the rhinestones. If these shoes could speak, what stories would they tell? Who had been the dancer that owned them? And what about those pearls? Were they hers, too?

Anne's phone buzzed. "'Lo."

"Hiya, love." Fay's British accent was bawdy.

"How're you doing?" Anne sat on the daybed.

"Hunky-dory. In town?"

"Just got in." Anne slipped on the shoes, lifting her feet to admire them. "I bought some very cool shoes at an antique shop. Sergio says they're from the 1920s."

"Were they expensive?"

"Naw. Thirty bucks."

"Have you checked ebay and Pinterest for comparisons?"

"No, but that's a great idea." Anne took off the shoes and displayed them on the counter. "How's Gallery Noir?"

"Things have picked up."

"It's paid off for Freddy to have you curate." Anne sipped her Diet Coke.

"Righto. I have such great taste." Fay guffawed.

"You do." Fay had always believed in Anne's work and kept putting it in front of Mr. Block, the former owner. He had disparaged Anne's collages and called them kindergarten art. She had never been so embarrassed in all her life.

Fay had told him, "Running a gallery is not always about what a curator loves, but what others might." After months he finally relented and let her show a few of Anne's pieces. Soon they started to sell. Later, after much wrangling, he had agreed to let Fay mount a solo show of Anne's work, to rave reviews and more sales.

"How *is* Mr. Blockhead?" Anne asked.

"Seems happier lately."

"The financial strain of keeping the gallery going must have made him so mean."

"I think there's more to it. He's been wearing a barmy grin. Something's up."

"What do you think it is?" Anne made her way back to the daybed.

"I have no bloody idea. What are you working on?"

"Nothing."

"I'm not surprised with you flitting back and forth to visit Sergio all the time. You've been diverted by love."

"That's no excuse." Since Sylvia's death last year, Anne had been at a complete loss. She'd visited galleries, scrounged junk shops, and looked through vintage magazines, but nothing had called to her. With the "Sylvia Series," the mojo had flowed so hot and fast she hadn't even been able to get all of her ideas down.

"Stop beating yourself up, love. You've been in a fallow time, it happens. Now get back to it. I have wall space waiting. Remember, use your heart, not your brain."

"Pep talk mania!" Anne laughed.

"Gotta run. Ta-ta! Call when you have some pieces for me."

Anne stepped out onto the private rooftop garden. The recently renovated Victorian Painted Ladies across the street, each a different pastel shade, had been sold for a mint. It was only a matter of time until Mrs. Landenheim decided to fix up their building, too, and Anne got kicked out.

She studied her planter box with the seeds she'd sown—herbs, strawberries, tomatoes, carrots, and peppers. Sylvia up in heaven would have been pleased, and Anne had imagined her friend's voice pontificate, "Choose nutritious. That's delicious." They should have sprouted by now but they hadn't. Nothing had taken root except a jumble of weeds in the muddy soil. Anne knew she should pull them out but wasn't in the mood.

Back inside, she made coffee and ate more cookies.

On her computer, she typed into Pinterest: *1920s rhinestone shoes.* Scrolling through the photos, she perused the shoes: satin pumps with vamp edges, bead-embroidered heels from Harrods, and stunning brocade evening shoes. She almost clicked off but then froze on a pair of shoes identical to her own, T-strapped with tons of rhinestones. They were from the Met Collection, the frickin' Metropolitan Museum of Art! She couldn't believe it. She'd actually bought a pair of museum-quality shoes. She found her coat where she'd dropped it on a chair, grabbed the lucky key from the pocket, and kissed it.

8

Anne woke from a deep sleep. Raindrops exploded on the roof like a tap dancer's feet, then tapered off into a soft consistent rhythm. Layers of a dream wavered in her brain, colors shifting into a blend of sparkling rhinestones. Perhaps a new series had started to reveal itself. She tried to return to the dream, but it eluded her.

In the kitchen, she opened a cupboard. Darn it! She was out of coffee. As she clattered down the stairs, Mrs. Landenheim's door opened, the Siamese slipped out—and following it, a man.

Aghast, Anne blurted out, "Mr. Block!"

He turned and stared at her, his Andy Warhol–inspired hair a shambles, his eyes wide, his mouth hanging open.

Mrs. Landenheim came out the door, blue peignoir set on, the usual dark circles gone from her droopy basset-hound eyes. "Dear, don't forget your glasses." She cooed at Mr. Block, slid them on his nose, and kissed his cheek. "Have a nice day, darling," she said before he raised an umbrella and dashed out into the rain.

Anne suppressed a grin. An unlikely couple—they must have struck up a romance the night of Anne's art reception. Anne had been a matchmaker without even realizing it and couldn't wait to tell Fay she'd discovered the mystery to Mr. Block's elated mood.

"Rent's due." Mrs. Landenheim picked up the cat and stroked its back.

"Fine." It had only been a day.

"You haven't signed the new lease yet, either." Mrs. Landenheim went back inside her apartment.

Anne still had thirty days. Maybe Mrs. Landenheim would agree to let Anne go month-to-month without a lease. At the entrance door, Anne opened her umbrella, but raindrops as big as water balloons burst from the sky. El Niño must be here at last! Pulling her umbrella back in, she walked up the stairs to her apartment.

She grabbed the rest of her flat Diet Coke from the fridge and crawled back into bed. Her valet shift didn't start until the afternoon, and she resolved to use her time wisely.

Sparkles from her dream flashed in her mind, and she tried to summon it up. If you write down your dreams, you have a better chance of remembering them. A little late now, but she'd try her best. She wrote in her journal: *Colors, rhinestone sparkles. The Met. I smelled lemons looking into a glass display case at the shoes.*

That's all she could recall. She sipped her Coke from a cup and continued jotting stream of consciousness thoughts:

Moving to New York! Get to be with Sergio all the time! Wonderful to sleep with him every night, visit my favorite museums, and have tea at The Plaza whenever I wish. Lots of culture. More opportunities for doing and selling art. But what if I pack up and move there and he dumps me? He wouldn't do that. He loves me.

She texted Sergio: *Any luck returning the pearls?*

Sergio wrote back: *The shop was closed, in the middle of the day. I'll try again.*

Anne replied: *Good luck and thanks!*

Her phone buzzed with FaceTime. "Hello, Cousin Pootie."

As a toddler, Anne couldn't say "Trudy," so she called her aunt "Tootie." The nickname caught on with the whole family. Tootie's daughter Prudence was born a year later, and everyone called her "Pootie" for consistency.

"How's the California weather?" Her cousin's blonde hair was pulled up in a ponytail. Without any makeup at all, she was cute.

Anne glanced out the window. "Rainy. How's Michigan?"

"Getting spring snow!"

A baby's wail could be heard behind Pootie. "Wait a sec." She moved off-screen, allowing her Hummel figurine collection to come into view on her knickknack shelf. Anne had been with her when Pootie found most of them in thrift stores. Pootie returned and set her son on her lap.

"Baby Brian's gotten so big!" Anne longed to hold him. He was adorable with his father's quarterback body mass.

Pootie draped a blue knit cap over the baby's peach-fuzz scalp. "Show Anne how sweet this looks on you!" The hat drooped down, covering his blue eyes. His angry lips scrunched up. Pootie pulled off the cap and bounced him up and down until he smiled.

"I didn't know how big to make it. I had only knit for adults before," Anne apologized.

"Don't worry. He'll grow into it."

"How's Brian?" Anne still couldn't believe that the guy she'd had a crush on in high school had married her cousin.

"Wonderful. He's watching the game." Pootie glanced over her shoulder, picked up the baby's hands, and moved them back and forth, saying in a deep voice, "Air conditioner broken down? Don't start cryin', just call Brian."

The girls laughed at the imitation of Pootie's husband's TV commercial for the family business, the same script his own father had used.

"I can't wait to see you at the christening." Pootie rubbed Baby Brian's back.

"Are you sure I should be his godmother? You know I'm not a traditional Christian."

"You'll teach him how to fish, won't you?"

Anne nodded. "Of course."

"Then you're it. Please, please, *please* bring Sergio with you when you come."

"Maybe." Anne pictured foodie Sergio eating meat and potatoes on TV trays watching *Hoarders* with her mom, Tootie, Pootie, and both Brians. She wouldn't tell Pootie about her plans to move to New York yet. It would be all over Oscoda in no time. "If I bring him, do you promise not to give him the third degree?"

"I can promise, but I can't guarantee our moms won't grill him."

"I'm not sure he'll appreciate Michigan. He's pretty cosmopolitan."

"Like the drink?" Pootie grinned.

"Ha. Ha."

Pootie held up her outstretched left hand. "I'm sure he'll be smitten with the mitten."

The baby began to cry. "Gotta go! Bye-bye!" Pootie waved Brian's little hands.

"Over and out."

Anne took another sip of her Coke and lounged back on a pillow. She should call Sylvia's husband, Paul, today and schedule a visit to Bay Breeze soon. But she didn't want to tell Paul yet she was going to move to New York. It would be hard to live so far away from him. They'd grown close over the past few years. Past eighty, it was difficult to know how many years he had left. And she'd heard when a partner passed away, many times the other did soon after.

She got up and dumped Scrabble tiles on the table and sorted through them in search of the perfect word. She picked a letter, *B*, then another. *B-E-G-I-N*. "Yes, that's it!" she said aloud and placed the word on the wooden holder. She needed to start. She carried the word to her altar, lit the gardenia candle, and rang her Tibetan chimes.

Maybe she had been using her brain too much, as Fay had said.

The shoes displayed on the counter sparkled. She picked them up, and they warmed to her touch again for a second. She felt the urge to paint them, so she put them back on the counter and set a canvas on her easel. It was all about faith. She needed to let go of the inner voice that nagged that no one would like the result.

Sure, she could paint round fruit, but could she recreate these shoes with their ins and outs and all those brilliant faceted rhinestones? She'd need to figure out how to get them to sparkle and shine on the canvas. Shading and shadows would be important. She usually preferred collage and assemblage, but maybe painting would be a good direction.

Her acrylics dumped on the counter, she shuffled through them in search of the right colors. She squished a blob of Graphite and another of Titanium White directly on the canvas from the tubes. Then she filled a jar with water, found her favorite big brush, put it in the water, and swirled the colors together, covering the entire canvas for a unifying background, clean and fresh. She'd forgotten how good it felt to paint.

With the rain, it would take ages for the canvas to dry. She tossed her cup in the sink, picked up her clothes from the floor, and finally unpacked her rolling bag, cramming all the dirty clothes into the hamper. No way would she go up the street to the Laundromat in this weather.

Straightening the coffee table, she stared at the dang shoebox and regretted her promise not to throw it away. Oh well, it might be good to store found objects in. She pulled all the tissue paper out and glimpsed at something hidden in the bottom of the box. Her fingers gently picked up the photo, brittle as a fall leaf, yellow and curled with age.

Two girls dolled up like flappers, smiling brightly, their arms hooked together. The full-figured girl wore an outrageous feather hat and a beaded dress. The tall, slim one wore a fringed number and a string of pearls. Could that necklace be the same one sitting in the bowl on Sergio's counter? Last time he went by the shop, it was still closed. Maybe one of the girls had owned the shoes, too. Anne peered closely at the photo but couldn't quite make out what they had on their feet.

What an era! Anne had always found the Roaring Twenties fascinating—speakeasies, bootlegged booze, the Charleston. What would it have been like to live back then? The man in the shop told her he had more items from the same estate sale. She wished she'd paid more attention to what he had to offer. What else had been on that table? She closed her eyes, as if playing the concentration game. Shoes, pearls, a statue . . .

Anne propped the photo up against a book on the coffee table, then sat back and studied the photo. Were the girls at a costume party, or could they have been real flappers?

9

"There you are!" Winnie waved from in front of the clock outside the Waldorf's Peacock Court. Her beaded chemise was so sheer, her slip showed through. An extraordinarily tall ostrich feather stuck straight up out of her turban.

"Sorry I'm late. I had to wait until Father had left." Clair grimaced.

Beside Winnie, Clair felt like a fuddy-duddy in her pastel Sunday dress and lace evening cap. What concert were they going to that Winnie would wear such an outfit and all that makeup? Even so, she looked smashing.

"I almost gave up." Winnie kissed her on the cheek. "That man over there keeps glancing at me. I think he has a crush."

Clair glanced at Mr. O'Shaughnessy. A big, strapping man with a kind heart, he'd probably wondered why flamboyant Winnie was there. The hotel manager had worked at the Waldorf for many years. Clair knew his wife and his children, all ten of them. "I'm sure he meant nothing by it. Let's go." She grabbed Winnie's arm and steered her toward the exit. If Mr. O'Shaughnessy spotted them, he'd certainly tell Clair's father.

Winnie stopped. "Wait! Aren't you going to show me around?"

"Another time." Clair quickly led her across the lobby's mosaic floor. She ducked down the steps while the doorman had his back turned.

"Where's your driver?" she asked.

"Driver?" Winnie laughed. "We're taking a cab."

"A cab?" Clair had never ridden in one before.

Winnie raised her arm and whistled shrilly. A checkered cab pulled over. As she climbed in, her feather got stuck, and she had to draw back and reenter. Clair slid in behind her.

"Ninth Avenue and Forty-fourth," Winnie ordered.

The driver nodded and raced away from the curb going north. Clair peered out the back window as the doorman turned with arms akimbo and a confused expression. Clair doubted he could recognize her at this distance. She sat back while an unexpected rush of freedom surged through her body.

"Winnie, how do your parents feel about you going out unescorted?"

Winnie gazed down at her gloved hands. "My folks? I don't have any."

"I'm sorry."

"Pa might still be alive back in Mississippi. I left there a long time ago."

Clair couldn't imagine ever abandoning her father. "Whom do you live with?"

"I'm at a women's boardinghouse."

"That sounds fun." It wouldn't be as boring as the hotel.

Winnie shook her head. "Yeah. If having fun is living with a bunch of old geese."

Clair nodded. The sky had darkened to a faded lavender blue. Streetlights flickered on as they drove uptown. People dressed for an evening out walked along the sidewalks. Bicyclists and a packed electric bus whizzed by. Clair looked forward to hearing some good music. It had been ages since she'd been to a concert. The girls continued to converse as the moonless sky grew darker.

Finally, the driver pulled over, then turned and studied them. "Are you sure this is it?"

"Yep." Winnie giggled.

Clair stared at the two-story brick building with the windows boarded up. A fire escape cascaded down its side. "This can't be it!"

"Sure is." Winnie winked at the cab driver.

He held out a hand. "That'll be two smackeroos."

Winnie dug in her bag and paid him. They got out of the taxi, and it drove off. No other cars were on the street. An assortment of deserted structures surrounded them. Shadows shifted at the sky's edge, and from overhead came a shrill scream. Clair yelped and grabbed Winnie's arm.

Winnie laughed. "It's only a crow, silly."

The almost-invisible bird swirled in a circle above them and landed on a spindly pine tree. If Clair had stayed home, she'd be safe in bed by now.

"Don't worry, honey. Come on." Winnie led a trembling Clair along the gritty sidewalk toward the building.

A bum carrying his bindle on a stick turned a corner and staggered toward them, his filthy clothes reeking. "Hey, girlie." He slurred his words and started to reach for Winnie's feather.

"Go away!" Winnie shoved him.

He tottered back and fell on his behind. "You're one tough broad," he slurred.

"You're right, mister!" Winnie yelled, as he scrambled up and scuttled away.

Clair would never have the nerve to defend herself so bravely. In the distance, she heard the shattering of glass and a dog's howl. Clair hadn't ever been anywhere so dark before, except maybe at the beach cottage in the summer. Nights there could be jet black, though stars dotted the heavens. Here in Manhattan, the dark, sooty air was suffocating.

"It's right here." Winnie guided Clair down the few short steps below street level and knocked on a large wooden door. What on earth kind of music would be played here?

A slit opened, a cacophony of noise escaped, and a pair of eyes peered out. "Password!" the man yelled.

"Rudy Moody," Winnie drawled.

The slit slammed shut. Clair's eyes opened wide.

"Oops!" Winnie giggled and rapped on the door again.

The slat reopened. "Yeah?"

"I meant Moody Rudy."

This time, the door swung open. The girls stepped inside the low-ceilinged space, and the door closed behind them. Clair's eyes soon adjusted to the dark, smoky haze, but she still felt disoriented. What was this place, and who were all these people?

Men in dapper suits and women in short fringed attire with glasses and cigarettes in their hands talked and laughed. Two women wearing tuxedos, with short black hair shining bright as shoe polish, strode by arm in arm. Clair knew she looked out of place.

A stocky man, his hair parted off-center and sporting a dark double-breasted suit, came toward them, a white carnation in his lapel. "Hey, Win!" His flat nose looked as if it'd been broken in a fight. He pointed to his cheek. "Put one here."

"No, Rudy." Winnie shook her head but batted her eyelashes at him.

He leaned closer to her. "Come on!"

She pecked his pockmarked cheek and smiled as if he were a nonpareil.

"'Atta girl." He gazed at her. "What a getup!"

She stood back and wiggled her hips. "Made it myself, and the hat, too."

Rudy nodded. "Swanky! And that feather."

"*Merci beaucoup!*" Winnie's perfect French accent surprised Clair.

Rudy smiled. "Who's your gal pal?"

"This is Clair. She's a lot of fun."

No one had ever described her as fun before. "Charmed." Clair resisted the urge to curtsy.

"Welcome!" Rudy didn't seem moody at all, only a bit gruff. "Glad you made it tonight. The joint's really gonna jump."

That sounded enthralling and maybe even dangerous. He led them to a table next to the dance floor. The small stage held a piano.

"Be right back." On his way to the carved wooden bar, Rudy clapped one man on the back and nodded at another. The room was filling up.

"Isn't he dreamy?" Winnie twisted a curl sticking out from under her hat.

She must consider him handsome in a rugged sort of way. Clair nodded. "What exactly is this place?" It felt as foreign as the moon.

"Rudy's Roost. It is *the* place! Last week a talent agent from Hollywood came in with Gary Cooper."

Clair couldn't believe it. She had seen him in *Wings*. How divine it would have been to see him in person!

Rudy wove back through the crowd toward them carrying glasses.

"And look at that Rudy. He's my Cooper." Winnie stared at him. "He seems rough on the outside, but inside he's a marshmallow."

Winnie removed her gloves and lit a cigarette. "Want one?"

Clair shook her head.

Rudy pulled up a chair and set down their drinks. "Here you go. Wet your whistles."

"I'm parched." Clair peered into the dark liquid. "Oh, good. Sarsaparilla." She took a sip, swallowed, and banged her glass down, then started to cough. It burned her throat. Probably that was what turpentine tasted like. "It must have gone bad."

Winnie and Rudy stared at her, then each other, and laughed.

He put his hand on Clair's shoulder. "No, doll, it's hootch."

"I'm not familiar with that brand." She shook her head.

Rudy explained. "Booze, rotgut."

"Moonshine." Winnie giggled.

Clair couldn't breathe. "You mean alcohol?"

Winnie nodded with a smile.

Clair's body grew hot. This must be a speakeasy! Her father would be devastated if he found out. The other night he'd railed against them. How they were ruining the country and should be destroyed. She might now be considered a wanton woman.

Winnie chugged down her whole glass, smacked her lips and burped.

"You slay me, Win." Rudy opened his mouth and tried to burp, too.

Clair stood. "I shouldn't be here."

"Why not?" Winnie frowned.

"Isn't this place illegal?"

Winnie and Rudy guffawed.

Tuxedoed musicians jumped onto the stage and began to play a lively jazz tune on piano, bass, and saxophone. Whenever this type of music came from the radio, her father made her turn it off. He called it "the devil's music."

"I need to go home," Clair whispered into Winnie's ear.

Winnie took Clair's arm and pulled her back down. "Give it a chance."

"What?" Clair couldn't hear Winnie because the trumpet blared so loudly.

A lone woman in a short red dress appeared on the dance floor and began kicking her legs out sideways, spinning and wiggling her body. A skinny man soon joined her, leaping back and forth. That was no Foxtrot! Clair couldn't take her eyes off them and realized they must be doing the Charleston, or maybe even the Black Bottom. She'd read about these scandalous dances in the newspapers. Soon, other dancers joined in. Winnie and Rudy ran onto the dance floor, too. Clair understood what he'd meant when he said the joint would be jumping. It literally was.

She grew hot and cautiously took another sip of the drink. It went down a smidge easier this time. She closed her eyes to get her bearings. The "devil" music was jarring but irresistible. The sounds engulfed her, and soon she began to nod her head in rhythm. Holding the sides of her chair, she resisted the urge to get up and dance.

She hoped her father was wrong, because if the devil liked it and she did, too, that meant she was evil. The music penetrated her whole body. She couldn't help herself—she leaped up onto the dance floor. Copying Winnie, Clair crisscrossed her hands above her knees. Her arms flew and her Mary Janes stepped back and forth, and forth and back. Somehow she knew exactly how to do this.

Rudy shouted at Clair, "Hey gal pal! You've got great rhythm!"

Her long legs soon mastered the dance. Out of breath, she ran back to the table, took another sip of the magic potion, and danced back onto the floor.

Winnie leaned over and yelled into her friend's ear, "Glad you stayed?"

Clair smiled and nodded. This was fun. She felt as if she'd been friends with Winnie forever.

A loud blast from the trumpet surprised her. What would happen if her father ever found out? But as the trumpet note slid down the scale and she spun around again, she really didn't care.

10

Anne's phone woke her with a buzz. She yawned, tired from a late night valeting at the St. Francis. Eyes closed, assuming it was Sergio, she answered, "*Ciao, grande uomo.*"

"What?"

Anne didn't want to tell her mom it meant "Hello, big man." Instead she said, "Hello, in Italian."

"You are so clever."

"Hi, Mom." Anne sat up envisioning her mother in Oscoda, in their yellow Craftsman cottage, sitting at her vanity as she smoothed her auburn hair, a shade lighter than Anne's own, and applied Lava Love Glimmersticks Lip Liner by Avon.

Her mom constantly experimented with her beauty wares. "I've got to be familiar with what I'm selling," she'd say.

"At a yard sale I bought you that collection of thimbles of women's heads you admired in the Avon catalog."

One of the heads reminded Anne of the tall girl in the shoebox photo. "The ones from the '20s and '30s? You are the best mom in the whole world."

"I know! You can get them at the christening. I hear Sergio's coming."

"I'm not sure. Is all of Oscoda gossiping about us now?"

"Not me. I can't wait to meet him. Has he popped the question yet?"

"You'll be the first person I tell." Anne rolled her eyes. "If I bring him, promise not to tease me about being an old maid." Since her thirtieth birthday, her mom and Aunt Tootie brought it up every chance they got. Anne had read in a recent copy of *The Sun* that the average age of marriage had recently trended upward. Even if a woman reached forty without a husband, she likely would still get married during her lifetime.

"Cross my heart. Okay, I've got to get to my next appointment. More than a pretty face." Her mom practiced one of the Avon sales slogans.

Anne brushed her teeth, put her bountiful hair in a scrunchie, and made coffee. She lit the altar candle, then stood back and studied the shoes on the counter, shining even in the dim morning light. She twisted them from side to side to get the right angle.

Drawing a quick sketch in her journal, she copied it onto her canvas with charcoal. Darn! The proportions weren't quite right. She dampened a paper towel, wiped off the charcoal, and restarted. This time she worked extra slow, constantly glancing at the shoes. The second try seemed pretty good, and she decided to let it sit before painting it.

She reexamined the photo of the girls, wanting to make a transfer. It was definitely too fragile to put in the scanner. Instead she took a picture of the photo with her cell phone. It was pretty faded, but she texted it to Sergio anyway.

Look what else was in the shoebox!

She e-mailed the photo to her computer, enlarged it as much as possible, and printed it. Too blurry. She pressed a few editing buttons, and a more detailed image appeared. She printed it out on thick watercolor paper.

At her kitchen table, she traced the girls' outlines with a fine-tip marker. Using a teeny brush, she mixed a bit of red and white together. She held her breath as she daubed pink paint on each of the girls' lips. The scent of roses wafted in the air. Anne sniffed the paintbrush and the paper but couldn't smell anything.

To work on more details, she carefully picked up the original photo from the coffee table and started to prop it onto the table, but it slipped from her fingers and flew to the ground facedown. On the back was extremely faded writing she hadn't noticed before. She picked up the photo and squinted at it.

Clair & Winnie at Rudy's, 1929.

Wow! Those were the girls' names, Clair and Winnie, 1929. They must really have been flappers. Where was Rudy's?

At her computer, Anne googled "Rudy's" and added "New York."

A long list of pizza joints and even several Mexican restaurants across the country appeared. Scrolling through the list, she spotted a Rudy's Bar & Grill located in Hell's Kitchen. The site even had a dropdown tab that provided details about its history.

Dive into New York's most famous dive bar, right through the original wood door. Feels like you've stepped back in time, doesn't it? Maybe even as far back as the rumor that this joint was first a speakeasy in 1919, frequented by the likes of Al Capone.

One of their slogans was "Less talkin' and more drinkin'!" The article included pictures of other famous people besides Capone who'd partied there: Frank Sinatra, Sir Paul McCartney, Julia Roberts, and others. Drew Barrymore had even been kicked out once for being underage. Anne scrolled down further and found a critique by Peter Landau in "New York Nightlife." He highly recommended it as a Critic's Pick. *It has dirt-cheap booze, red leather booths, and free hot dogs.*

Cool! It could be the same Rudy's where the photo had been taken.

She texted Sergio: *What do you think of the photo?*

He got right back to her: *Yes. Lovely.*

Anne: *Do you know Rudy's?*

Sergio: *Rudy who?*

Anne: *Rudy's Bar & Grill in Manhattan.*

Sergio: *In Hell's Kitchen? Hell, yes!*

Anne: *The photo was taken at Rudy's. Could it be the same one?*

Sergio: *Sure.*

She shook her head in disbelief. Could Clair be the one who owned the pearls and the shoes, or was it Winnie? How wild! This must be a sign Anne really was supposed to move to New York. In order for that to happen, she needed to take Sergio home.

This time, she called him. "Hi. Want to meet me in Michigan in May?"

"*Ovviamente.* I can't wait."

She hoped she'd be ready by then to expose him to her family. "I'm warning you. It will be an experience you'll never forget."

11

Anne smelled freshly mown grass as the Lyft driver pulled into Bay Breeze's circular drive. The rose garden was filled with blooms. A blue jay doused himself in the birdbath, his blue Mohawk waving. The birch tree had begun to sprout green leaves.

In the rhinestone shoes, Anne carefully navigated the steep front steps, and stopped on the top landing to admire the sun as it began to dip into the bay, releasing an explosion of violet, fuchsia, and orange on feathery clouds. The effect was humbling, more stunning than any painting she could ever create.

She looked forward to spending time with Paul but didn't want to see his face when she told him she was moving to New York. She pushed the doorbell, and the Westminster chimes rang. Last time she stepped inside Bay Breeze, Lucky had dashed out the door and it had taken forever to get him back inside. This evening though, Anne had come prepared. She slowly opened the door as the roly-poly hot dog of a beagle-basset skidded toward her on the marble floor and lunged between her feet. She blocked his way, quickly pushed him back inside, and closed the door behind her.

Anne grabbed a bit of Bacon Bark from her coat pocket and bent over. "Lucky, sit!"

He wiggled his fanny.

"Lucky, sit."

He sat down, and Anne gave him the treat. "Good boy." She patted his smooth head.

Anne stood and her breath caught in her throat. The foyer smelled of gardenias, Sylvia's scent, and a wave of longing swept over her.

Paul, leaning on his cane, ambled toward her. "Look who's here. The prodigal artist!" The light from the chandelier above revealed his welcoming smile.

Anne half expected to see Sylvia there beside her husband, but of course she wasn't. It had only been a few months since she had last seen Paul, but he had aged. He was more stooped over, his bald head appeared to have more spots on it, his once sky-blue eyes seemed filmier. Anne hugged him, blinking back tears as Lucky nipped at her heels.

"Sorry! Hi! Long time no see." Smoothing down his pompadour, Paul's caregiver, George, rushed in from the kitchen, slipped the leash on Lucky, and led him out the door. Or perhaps Lucky led him?

Anne took Paul's elbow, and they made their way into the library. Helping him into his chair, she sat across from him on the couch and fingered the key in her pocket. The first time she visited Bay Breeze, it had been to deliver the portrait collage she'd made of Sylvia that still hung above the desk. The same Asian rug graced the floor beside the blazing hearth, and the couch was just as cozy. The floor-to-ceiling bookcases, filled with more volumes than one could ever read in a lifetime, surrounded the room.

"Paul. Sergio has . . ."

Fay entered the room, her multicolored caftan billowing. "Blimey! It's been ages," Fay said in her broad London accent.

Anne jumped up and gave the Gallery Noir curator a hug. "What are you doing here?"

"I'm living with George." Fay smoothed down her blonde bob. Last time Anne had met with her, it had been short with red spikes.

"Here in Bay Breeze?"

"Where else? Alcatraz?" Fay guffawed and dropped onto the couch.

"But we talked the other day. Why didn't you tell me?"

"I wanted it to be a surprise."

"I am surprised!" Anne couldn't believe it. George, a widower, had always been a grump-meister. George and Fay had met at Anne's gallery reception last year, too, and within minutes Fay literally had him eating grapes right out of her hand. She'd been with Sergio longer. How'd Fay make that happen so fast?

"I'm happy for you." Anne looked at Paul. "How do you feel about this?"

"The more the merrier. George can use the extra help, anyway. I'm so hard to take care of." Paul chuckled.

"That's for sure!" Fay checked out Anne. "Don't you look fancy."

Anne jumped up and posed. She had worn her hair in an updo for a dramatic effect and of course had on the black velvet coat with the snowflake pin, too.

"Crikey!" Fay hooted. "Those must be your new shoes."

Anne pointed each foot. "I looked them up on Pinterest as you suggested. They're museum quality, from the Met Collection." She sashayed across the library, did a few klutzy turns, some phony tap steps, and demurely curtsied.

Fay laughed, snorting through her nose. "You're a nutter!"

"There are tiny holes here where taps used to be." Anne sat and pulled up a foot and pointed to the heels.

Fay squinted with a nod.

"Sylvia and I loved to watch tap dancers in Broadway shows." Paul sighed.

Lucky ran into the room as fast as his little legs would carry him. He leaped up onto the hassock, jumped onto the sofa, and walked along it toward Paul's chair.

"What a circus dog!" Anne laughed.

Paul picked up Lucky, let him lick his chin, and set him on his lap.

George set a tray on the desk.

"I want mine shaken, not stirred." Fay said with a deep voice.

"Of course." George prepared martinis and handed one to each. Then he sat beside Fay, on the couch's arm, and kissed her on her cheek.

Paul raised his glass. "To our gorgeous artiste."

"Cheers!" Fay clinked her glass to Anne's, and everyone took a sip.

Anne told the group about finding the shoes in the antique shop, and the man insisting she keep the box with the pearls in the bottom.

Paul blinked. "Are they real?"

"They sure are. I checked them with my teeth like Sylvia taught me."

Paul laughed. "Women love their pearls."

"I asked Sergio to return them to the shop for me. But when he got there, the curtains were closed and a sign in the window said: *Closed until further notice.*"

George offered a plate of canapés to Anne, and she took a baby quiche.

"Look what else I found in the bottom of the box! I'm making a collage with it." She handed her phone with the flapper photo to Fay and popped the quiche in her mouth.

Fay put on her cat-eye glasses. "Quite the lookers!"

"Writing on the back said they were at Rudy's. I googled it. It was a speakeasy, and it's still there."

Paul smiled wistfully. "Sylvia and I went there once. It was dark and romantic."

"I'll go there next time I visit Sergio."

"What did you want to tell me about him?" Paul asked.

"It's a long story. I'll tell you later." She didn't want to spoil the evening and would wait and share her moving plans right before she left tonight.

"How's it going with him?" Fay blinked dramatically at Anne.

"Since we aren't together very often, it's always electrifying." Anne grinned.

"Oooh! Naughty."

Anne felt her face turn red.

Fay continued. "It must be love. You can't deny it."

"Jeez! I guess so."

"There's nothing like love." George walked toward the kitchen. "I need to finish dinner. Anne, sure you can't stay?"

"No, I've got a late shift."

"Do you need help, hon?" Fay smiled at George.

He turned and gazed at her with goo-goo eyes. "No, you chat with Anne."

"Too bad you can't stay. Next time have dinner and let's play Scrabble afterward. I miss our game nights." Paul rubbed behind Lucky's long, droopy ears. "Still parking cars?" he asked Anne.

She nodded.

"I wish you'd let me help you. Sylvia would want that." He closed his eyes.

"Thanks, but I need to be independent."

Paul's head nodded back on the chair's headrest.

"Paul!" Fay hollered. "Wake up!"

"Sorry! I was just resting my eyes."

"Tell Anne about the doctor."

"He wants me to have cataract surgery." Paul scowled.

Anne smiled at him. "That might be good."

His brow furrowed. "I haven't had surgery in all my eighty-some years. I'm certainly not going to start now!"

Fay tipped her head toward Anne.

Anne took another stab at it. "Wouldn't it be great to be able to read more easily?"

"Never stopped." Paul shrugged. "I listen to books on tape with my headphones. Much more relaxing than holding a heavy old book anyway."

"I understand. But don't they use lasers now? Haven't any of your friends at the club had it done?" Anne asked, and nibbled on her martini olive.

"Maybe. But the doctor told me to have my knees done, too. *That* is out of the question. With Sylvia gone, I'm not dancing much anyway."

Anne sighed.

George came to the door. "Dinner in fifteen minutes."

"I've gotta go." Anne jumped up.

Fay gave her a hug. "Ta-ta! Coffee soon?"

"Next week?"

"Of course."

Paul stood with help from Anne. "It's good to have you here, Anne. I've missed you. What was it about Sergio?"

"About the shoes was all." She did a little jig and hugged Paul. She would wait and tell him about her move when her plans were firm. No reason to make him sad earlier than needed.

12

This certainly wasn't Rudy's. Everything shone. Chandeliers glowed onto round cloth-covered tables where silver bowls of sweet pea blossoms rested on mirrored glass. Gold-trimmed place cards had been set at every seat, adorned with the guest's names in elegant penmanship. The dance floor had been polished to perfection.

Clair's heart rapped rapidly in her chest. Her father was counting on her to make a good impression on this, her first introduction to society, which included eligible bachelors and their families.

The gloves felt smooth on her hands, and her blush-pink gown flowed softly over her body. Fortunately, a coconut-oil shampoo had made her hair more manageable. She had wound the never-cut mass of curls atop her head and slid the pearl band through her tresses. Still, she wished her father had let the jeweler make her a tiara.

For the thousandth time, Clair wondered if she had anything else in common with her mother besides their height and hair. Too bad her mother couldn't be here tonight to celebrate her coming out. Perhaps the evening wouldn't be a disaster after all. But then she caught sight of Mr. LeRue on the stage setting up his covered canvas and lost all faith.

He waved to her and hollered across the dance floor, "Can't wait to reveal this to the world!" A ridiculous beret sat askew on his balding head, and he had draped a white-fringed scarf over his tuxedoed shoulders.

She found her father in conference with the caterers. He was clean-shaven and handsome, his wavy brown hair beginning to recede, which made him look even more distinguished.

"I hate to interrupt, but Father, I need to speak with you."

"But I'm . . ."

"It's urgent." She tugged on her father's arm and stuck out her lower lip, an expression she knew he never could resist.

His unusual eyes—one brown and one blue—softened, and he nodded. "If you insist."

"It's about Mr. LeRue's painting." She led him up the stage steps, rushing to pull the cloth off the portrait, but Mr. LeRue stepped in front of the easel with crossed arms. "Don't spoil the surprise."

Her father laughed. "What's the harm?"

"The harm?" Mr. LeRue raised his hands. "The element of drama, the moment when the crowd applauds in astonishment and amazement at my talent."

"Father, I beg you! Please look."

He nodded at Mr. LeRue, who threw his hands in the air and removed the cloth.

Clair cringed. The painting was even more hideous than she had recollected! Puffs of salmon-colored swirls dominated the foreground, and black lines ran every which way into an oblong sphere, the head, which resembled a Macy's parade balloon.

Her father's eyes grew wide, and he started to cough. Mr. LeRue patted him on the back. "Yes! It is a masterpiece. Miss Devereaux has been such an inspiration."

Aunt June climbed the stairs and joined them. Lovely in her midnight-blue gown, a halo of copper-colored hair surrounding her face, she reminded Clair of the angel paintings on display at the Met.

"I got here early in case you needed any help." Aunt June ran her hand over Clair's coiffed head and kissed her on the cheek. As her aunt turned, her eyes took in the picture. "Oh, my land!"

"*Ultra moderne*." Mr. LeRue smiled with pride.

"*Oui, très moderne*." Aunt June turned her large brown eyes to Clair's father. "Leland, what do you think?"

His face turned red. "It's, it's . . ."

She smiled at Mr. LeRue. "Yes, it's beyond words. So magnificent we should keep it all to ourselves. Don't you agree, Leland?"

"But—"

"What a wonderful idea!" Clair chimed in with a nod and slipped her arm through her aunt's.

Her father finally caught on. "Yes, of course. We'll hang it in a place of honor."

Mr. LeRue frowned. "But it requires a public exhibition."

Her father pulled a roll of cash from his pocket, peeled off some bills, and handed them to the so-called artist. "Here's extra for us to keep it private."

"I couldn't." Mr. LeRue shook his head. "We should go on as planned."

"It's better this way," her father said in a firm voice, holding out the entire handful of bills. "I insist."

With lowered eyes, Mr. LeRue accepted the cash and slithered off the stage. He crossed the dance floor and slipped out the ballroom doors. Clair sighed with relief.

"Leland, you handled that very well." Aunt June nodded at him.

"With your help." He grunted and checked his pocket watch. "Clair and I had better get out of sight. The guests will be arriving soon."

"This is a special night." Aunt June looked into Clair's eyes. "Be not afraid of greatness." She stepped down the stairs and crossed the dance floor, ready to greet the guests as they arrived.

Clair smiled at her aunt's Shakespearean advice and picked up the cloth that had covered the picture. "Father, thank you. I would have been embarrassed."

"It looks like you."

Tears sprang to her eyes. "Really?"

"I'm teasing, Raffie." He winked at her.

He hadn't called her "Raffie" for a very long time. The nickname had started years ago when he used to take her on outings to the zoo. She had yelled, "Hey, Daddy, that animal is tall like me!" From then on, he had called her "Raffie," short for "giraffe."

"You look so grown-up."

Clair hoped it was true.

Taking the cloth from her, her father covered the portrait and carried it offstage. Then he pulled the thick velvet curtains closed and returned to her.

"I have another surprise for you."

Maybe the jeweler had made the pearl tiara for her after all. "What, Father?"

"I've chosen a fellow for you."

"For what?"

"To marry."

Clair laughed. "You are funny!"

Her father knitted his bushy eyebrows. "I'm not joking. I thought you'd be pleased."

Clair couldn't believe his words. "There's plenty of time for that. Besides, the term starts in September."

Her father paused and scratched his chin. "We'll talk about college after you're married."

"But you've promised I could go. I'm already enrolled." She tried not to cry.

He shook his head. "I've changed my mind. If you are too educated, no man will ever marry you." He patted her arm. "He's a fine chap. You will meet him tonight."

Clair sensed there was no more to say on the matter. Seething, she wondered what kind of boy her father had chosen for her. She sang "Clair de Lune" in her head to help her calm down.

The two stayed hidden behind the curtain, listening to the guests' voices as they entered the ballroom.

As the lights lowered, Mayor Walker slipped through the curtains, shook her father's hand, and grinned at her. "Ready?"

"Yes, sir." Feeling weak, Clair pulled the satin gloves toward her elbows.

"This is it." Her father hooked his arm through hers.

The mayor stepped though the curtains out onto the stage and spoke into the microphone. "May I have your attention, please?"

The crowd continued to talk. Mayor Walker cleared his voice and spoke louder. "Your attention, *please*."

The noise died down. "Ladies and gentlemen." He paused. "It gives me great pleasure to welcome you here this evening. Don't forget at the next election to vote for your favorite mayor!"

The crowd chortled.

He waited for the room to quiet down once more. "First, allow me to introduce DAR member, former head of the Lady's Auxiliary for the Vote, and the debutante's aunt, Miss June Dudley. Please stand and show everyone that lovely face."

Soft applause ensued. Clair peeked through the curtains to see Aunt June stand from the front table with a wave.

"And now I give you Leland Devereaux—broker extraordinaire, cultural and commercial juggernaut, Grand Poobah of the Odd Fellows Section Number 25, and deacon at Grace Church—with his charming daughter, Clair April Devereaux."

As if by magic, the curtains opened and the orchestra began to play "The Blue Danube" waltz. With a measured gait, her father guided her across to center stage. The blinding lights hit her, and the room fell silent. She froze as if she were a Macy's mannequin. Unlike a mannequin, her real heart beat faster than ever.

"Smile," her father said under his breath. A polite applause began, which gradually grew louder. "Hear that? They think you're beautiful."

She managed a smile. He paraded her down the stairs, across the dance floor, and down the aisle through the standing guests to the receiving line area. She towered over most guests as they shook hands.

"What a pretty gown," she must have heard fifty times. In preparation for their balls, all young girls were taught how to behave properly—how to curtsy, what to say.

"Hello, Bea." Beatrice Beach Bernard had debuted last year. Her beady eyes reminded Clair of the buttons on Aunt June's boots. "So kind of you and your parents to come."

"Hello, Clair." Bea held her head high. She always acted as if she was better than Clair.

Mr. and Mrs. Jefferies and Johnny came by next. Both Beatrice and Johnny attended Clair's church. She had known them since childhood. He had always been kind to her. With his neatly combed hair, he looked rather dapper, even though he was quite a bit shorter than she. She doubted her father would have selected him for her.

The line dwindled as guests began to find their tables. Someone handed her a silver goblet. She took a sip of the too-sweet punch and handed it back. Despite prohibition, she'd heard at some of these affairs the punch was laced with alcohol. Wouldn't that be fun? But with her teetotaler father, she knew that wouldn't happen this evening. No one would dare.

Her stomach growled; she hadn't eaten a thing all day. She wondered what Winnie would say if she were here. "Hey doll! Great dress. When are we gonna eat?" Her giggle would sure liven up this stuffy crowd.

Her father touched Clair's back. "Dear, please meet Farley Parker, a client of mine."

The stocky man seemed about thirty. His hair had been parted in the center, and he wore an outdated walrus mustache. His eyes were an eerie hurricane gray.

She curtsied, took the man's hand, and stood erect. "Pleased." Feeling his sweaty grip through her gloves, she tried to loosen her hand.

"I'm sure your father has spoken of me." His eyes shifted from side to side.

Clair couldn't recall if she had heard his name. "Yes, of course, Mr. Parker."

"Dazzling. Simply dazzling." He was staring at her.

Managing a smile, she finally pulled her glove away, rubbed it on her lace handkerchief, and proffered it to the last person in line.

By the time she reached her table, the centerpieces had begun to wilt. The mayor stood, pulled her chair out for her, and took his seat between her and Aunt June. Her father sat beside her on the other side. Dr. Johnson, with his small pointy nose, sat on the other side of her aunt. An empty chair stood at Mrs. Schmidt's place. Her cold had turned into bronchitis. Surprisingly, Mr. Parker had been assigned to their table, too.

The orchestra played softly. White-gloved waiters offered round bread rolls along to the right. Clair spread one with a scalloped pad of butter. Though a few moments before she had been starving, she could barely take a bite. She studied the room wondering which boy her father had picked for her. She couldn't believe he wouldn't let her go to college in the fall.

The salad was served, a strange combination of apples, celery, and walnuts. She declined the creamy white dressing offered.

"Do you have an automobile?" Mr. Parker asked no one in particular. "I recently bought one of those Lincoln Town Cars. It cost me an arm and leg. I tried to get the price down, but . . ."

Clair and Aunt June exchanged glances. Her aunt tried to cut off Mr. Parker's monologue. "Leland, this is a dish fit for the gods."

Clair's father smiled at her aunt and drew a figure eight with his fork over the salad. "It looks quite the newfangled mess, but yes, it's delicious. The chef highly recommended it as his own recent creation."

"Oh, dear. It's going to be quite a year for influenza." Dr. Johnson fretted. Some salad dressing dripped off of his muttonchop sideburns.

"You don't say? I had it once so bad I couldn't get out of bed for a month." Mr. Parker finished his salad and wiped his mouth with his napkin.

The next course was escargot, small dots of wonder that still sizzled in a ceramic plate's petals. Clair stabbed her tiny fork into one, delicately lifting it to her mouth. They had lobster thermidor for the main course, and red velvet cake for dessert.

The orchestra began to repeat "The Blue Danube" waltz, and her father led her onto the dance floor and took her in his arms. All eyes were on them, which was thrilling because she knew she could dance well.

"Who is he, Father?" she asked as he guided her to the right.

"Can't you guess?"

"I have no idea."

"You'll know soon enough."

Next she danced with the mayor and then Dr. Johnson, who kept tripping over her. Even after she counted aloud, "One, two, three—one, two, three," he still couldn't get the rhythm.

Johnny Jefferies asked her next. He didn't seem to mind that she was taller. She enjoyed being waltzed around the dance floor by him.

As the evening progressed, she had danced with practically every man, young and old, in attendance. This was completely different than her night at Rudy's dancing with Winnie. She grinned at the notion of asking the orchestra to play a jazz piece and all the guests jumping up to do the Charleston.

Finally, Mr. Parker swaggered toward her. "Let's dance." He put one arm on her shoulder and another around her waist, holding her more tightly than called for. He smelled of the petroleum jelly he'd used in his hair.

His strong arms led her decisively around the floor, making her feel lighter than air until he said, "You remind me of a summer swan," and he eyed her as if he were Valentino and then turned his gaze away.

Why would he say something so inane to her? He acted like he wanted to court her. The song finished and another began. Instead of letting Johnny Jefferies tap in, Farley ignored him and continued to guide her through the next song.

She glanced at her father, sitting at the table, in hopes he might save her, but he smiled at her as if she had found a prince.

Farley escorted her back to their table, and his hand skipped down her derriere. She hoped it had been by accident. Her face turned fiery, and she promptly sat down. Everyone had left the ballroom except Mr. Parker and her father. "Clair, you were the belle of the ball."

Yes, she'd been the center of attention, every debutante's dream, but she longed for home. Her feet were killing her, and she desperately wanted to take off her shoes.

"I'm tired." She yawned and stood, but Mr. Parker wouldn't take the hint.

"Might I call on you some evening?"

Her father perked up and patted him on the back. "Certainly, son. Anytime."

She had a moment of panic. This old man couldn't be the one her father had chosen for her. He couldn't be!

13

As Anne crossed Union Square, she waved at the Goddess of Victory atop the soaring pillar. American flags flapped in the wind in front of the St. Francis Hotel, and cedars lined the square near fuchsia blossoms. A pandemonium of chattering, like monkeys in a tree, came from above. She gazed up at the flock of chartreuse parrots, like small winged limes shooting through the sky. She loved seeing them.

In dress slacks and men's resale wing tips, sporting Austin Powers ruffles on her work uniform blouse, Anne sprinted into the parking garage and clocked in. She applied lipstick by looking in a truck mirror and stuck the beefeater-style hat on her head. She feared it was because of her frizzy, out-of-control hair that management had recently added the odd toppers to their outfits.

Howard pulled up and hopped out of a BMW. He managed to look cute in the uniform; his wisps of blond curly hair escaping the hat reminded her of Little Lord Fauntleroy.

"Girlfriend!" His eyes lit up when he saw her. "How *was* the Big Apple and that scrumptious Sergio?"

"Great! I found some killer shoes."

"Of course you did."

A customer exited the hotel. Howard accepted the ticket and opened the BMW's door. "Thank you, Mr. Hoffman."

The man handed Howard a tip and drove off.

"Check these out." Anne showed Howard the shoe photo on her cell.

"Ooooh. You'll need to wear them to Disco Night at Rhinestone Ruby's."

"Oh, yeah, sure." Last time she had joined him, she couldn't even follow the crowd doing the Electric Slide. "Also, look at this!" Scrolling through her phone, she showed him the flappers' photo and the beginnings of her collage.

"Nice."

A yellow Hummer's horn blasted. "Hello!" The driver's voice boomed as big as his vehicle. "Does anyone work here?"

Howard waved with a smile and said under his breath to Anne, "Busy today. The National Association of Donut Makers is in town. They all drive big fat cars." He moved toward the Hummer.

Anne and Howard parked cars for the next hour or so. After pulling into a nearby spot, Howard shook his head. "Lot's full."

Anne groaned. She hated when they had to park on the street. "And it's trash day, too!"

A Mercedes SUV rolled in. The buxom blonde carrying her fluffy, diminutive dog got out. "I'll be here a few days."

Anne gave her a ticket, then drove the Mercedes up the hill and around several blocks until she spotted an open space. It would work if that trash barrel weren't in the way. She turned on the blinkers, put the car in park, jumped out, and moved the can as far over as possible, next to a turquoise T-bird. She slowly backed into the space but couldn't get close enough to the curb.

Honking their horns, a parade of cars lined up behind her. She pulled back in, closer this time, and nudged the rear bumper gently onto the bin. She tried again, and this time, the wheels made contact with the curb, but not without tipping the bin over onto its side, spewing garbage onto the road.

She waved at the still-honking motorists with an embarrassed smile. Not her most shining hour. She rolled the barrel sideways back to the curb. Before she could decide whether to try and clean up the garbage, a truck sped up the hill, mashing the trash onto the road. She jogged back down the hill to the parking garage, a good mile away.

After work that night, hiking up California Street, Anne huddled against the wind in her coat and tugged a knit cap down over her head. At the top of Nob Hill, the last cable car rumbled by. Behind the Mark Hopkins Hotel, an Ansel Adams moon had begun to rise. Across the street, limos lined the Fairmont's entrance. A valet opened a shiny Cadillac's door. A woman in a sequined formal stepped out as her date in black tie accepted the receipt. Anne identified with the valet; he must be as bone-tired as she was.

Illuminated from within, Grace Cathedral's rose window romanced vivid colors. At the bottom of the hill, she spied Mata Hari huddled in a doorway.

The homeless woman sat up. "Hey, girlie. Long time no see." Her voice squeaked like a rusty chain.

"Hello! How've you been?"

"Can't complain." Mata tugged on the gold cap Anne had knitted for her last year. "It's late. Where've you been?"

"Working."

"You're an artist. Don't you do that at home?"

"I am, but I also park cars to pay the bills."

"I don't have bills. All I've got is right here." Her hand swept over her bedroll as if it were a divan in a maharaja's tent. "Do you love parking cars?"

"I hate it."

"Then quit! Life's too short."

"How do I live?"

"Trust the universe." Mata Hari raised her arms to the heavens and licked her chapped lips. "Everything will work out."

Anne said good night and strode on, mulling over whether to really quit. At home, she threw the danged beefeater hat on the floor and jumped on it.

She called Howard. "I can't do it anymore. I'm not cut out for this."

"I was waiting for that."

"You were?"

"Yes, you're too good for this job."

"But how am I going to pay my bills?"

"Trust the universe," he said.

Hadn't she just heard that? If only it could be so easy.

14

As usual, Fay was looking hip. She wore a tunic over leggings, with tall boots to finish off her ensemble. "'Lo, mate. Nab a table. I'll buy us drinks."

Diana Krall's version of "Fly Me to the Moon" played in the background as Anne wove through the packed Coffee Cup Café looking for a spot to sit. A young couple rose to go. Anne quickly snagged their bay window table overlooking Sutter Street, settled into her chair, and watched the fog ooze by.

Fay soon joined her with their drinks.

Anne licked whipped cream off her mocha. "Guess what? I quit my job."

"Bloody good. It's about time."

"I'm not sure how I'll be able to pay the rent, not to mention buy food. I don't want to go back to selling art at the farmers market."

"How about sitting the gallery again when I need you?" Fay dunked her tea bag up and down.

That wouldn't be so bad, though it could be boring. "I appreciate that, thanks."

"There's an instructor opening at the SFMOMA coming up."

"But I'm not a teacher." Anne shrugged and drank some of her mocha.

"You could try. It would be consistent income for you."

A baby started to cry, and its mother picked it up and made her way out the door trying to juggle her coffee, too.

Fay glanced at Anne's paint-splattered sweatshirt. "You've been working."

"Yep." Anne looked at her phone, scrolling down to show Fay the beginning of her flapper piece. Anne had added more color to it that morning.

Fay put on her glasses. "Blimey! That's going to be marvelous. Can't you finish it soon? I'm hanging another show next week and would love to include it."

"I'll let you know. I'm also doing a painting of the rhinestone shoes."

"Do you have it on your phone? Show me."

"No. It's not very far along." Still too raw to share.

"You're back, then. I'm proud of you!" Fay took the tea bag out of her cup and set it on a napkin.

"I've been trying to use my intuition and not my head like you recommended."

"Glad I could be of help. Did Sergio return the pearls?"

"Nope. The shop is still closed." Anne peered at Fay. "I have something else to talk to you about. I'm thinking of moving to New York."

Fay raised her voice. "Are you daft? Last year you told me you loved it here and San Francisco is where you belong. Why can't he just move here?"

"Because of his job."

"Can't you keep commuting back and forth?"

"I miss him too much."

Fay frowned. "I can appreciate that, but your career has recently started going gangbusters here."

"You do such a good job selling. I'll send my work out to you."

Fay shook her head, blew on her tea, and took a sip. "Freddie has decided to only represent local artists."

Anne's chest felt tight. "Are you kidding me? Why?"

"Several reasons." Fay counted on her fingers. "Freddie feels we should be more specialized. Our clients and tourists love to buy local artists' work. And shipping costs are horrendous."

That plan just went down the drain.

Fay studied Anne. "Sergio and you are serious, then."

Anne nodded with a smile. "Yep."

"Has he asked you to marry him?"

"No, we've talked about it in general."

Fay frowned. "That's tosh. So you'll move all that way without a commitment?"

"Sure! People live together all the time without being married. Look at you and George."

"But isn't it risky? What if things don't work out between you?"

Of course things will work out. "I'm willing to take that chance."

"Do you get along with his family?"

"I'm meeting them in Italy this summer, remember?"

"That's right." Fay nodded. "How does he get along with yours?"

"He's going with me to Michigan next month. Which will really be a test."

Fay sighed. "I'll support you no matter what, but I'll miss you—and miss representing your work."

The words tugged at Anne's heart.

They left the café together, but then Fay stepped into the gallery next door as Anne walked up the hill toward her apartment.

Later at home, Anne rolled out a yoga mat, started the Rodney Yee CD, and lay on her back. She took deep breaths, and soon her body felt as if it were floating in blue skies. Swirls of clouds caressed her. She sank into one and it supported her like God's hands. Soon the crashing waves on the beach and Yee's calm voice made her sleepy, and she began to nod off. A trolley clanged by, waking her up.

She turned over and gazed at the flapper collage—using her heart, she sensed what to do next. Mixing red and orange hues together, she lightly painted the tall girl's hair and used zinc white to color in the feather.

Romance must have been much simpler then: no cell phones, e-mail, or Facebook. No airplane travel, long-distance relationships, or living together before marriage. Anything goes now. Fay was ridiculous to think Anne needed a commitment before moving to New York.

15

As the last glimpse of sun disappeared behind a skyscraper, Clair opened a parlor window and tried to catch an evening breeze. Automobiles, taxis, and pedestrians crowded the street below. There had been no relief from the heat. If only those small clouds overhead would produce rain and clear the air.

Someone rapped on the suite's door. "I'll get it," her father called from his bedroom, and hurried to the foyer.

"Evening, Leland," Farley's voice boomed.

A dull ache filled Clair's stomach. Lordy, not again! This was the third evening he had come to call since the ball the previous week. Every time he had talked nonstop, stared at her moon-eyed, and never sensed when he should leave. His greasy hair had permanently stained the sofa doilies.

Clair wondered why Farley was such a good match, but she couldn't figure out how to ask her father without being disrespectful. And what had happened to the other boys at the ball? Hadn't any of them been interested in her? She suspected her father had told them to stay away.

Her father escorted Farley into the parlor. As he removed his bowler hat, a cowlick sprung up from the back of his head. "You look handsome this evening, Miss Clair." He handed her a nosegay of daisies.

She sat on the damask-covered divan and sniffed the bouquet. The flowers brought on a sneeze.

"*Gesundheit*!" Her father offered Farley a cigar. "Here, son."

He stuffed it between his sow-like lips, parked himself across from her in a chair, and lit a match. "I hear the market did well today."

Puffing, he lit the cigar, and Clair imagined his mustache catching fire. "Did it?"

Her father sat in his easy chair and frowned at her. "Yes, AT&T is up. Glad I bought you all those shares."

Farley handed her father a fat envelope. "How about buying me more?"

He opened the envelope and peeked inside with a smile. "Are you sure?"

"Yes, is investing all your funds in the stock market prudent?" Clair couldn't help herself. Aunt June had been wary of it.

Farley squinted. "What do you know about it?"

She shrugged and batted her eyes demurely. Her father had warned her not to appear too intellectual. Setting the flowers on the end table, she picked up her fan and waved it back and forth, staring at the striped wallpaper.

Farley smiled at her father. "Leland, you always pick winners. What about Ford?"

"Yes, it's definitely slated to go up, too." The men continued to converse, and the room filled with smoke.

She wished she could go to her room, strip down to her slip, and read *Sense and Sensibility*.

She picked up a *Vogue* and thumbed through it as the men continued to talk. A tall model in a beaded dress had been posed with dramatic flair, one long arm outstretched. Clair wished she could wear something that *au courant,* maybe even to Rudy's. Too afraid her father would find out, she had so far resisted the urge to return, though she yearned to move to those jazz rhythms again.

She couldn't take it anymore and stood up. "Good night. I'll leave you men to your important business."

"Don't go." Her father raised his eyebrows at her.

She reluctantly sat back down and flapped her fan.

Farley moved near her on the divan. "Please continue to grace us with your presence."

Her father tried, too. "Let's talk about something you're interested in."

"Isn't my bow tie keen? I bought it this afternoon." Farley moved closer to her so she could inspect it.

She scooted back away from him. "Jolly." The yellow with red polka dots resembled a circus clown's tie.

"It cost me an arm and a leg. My haberdasher tells me I'm quite the dapper dresser."

She nodded. That's the last thing he was.

"Clair. Why don't you play the piano for Farley?"

"Please do." He grinned at her.

Glad of any diversion, she leaped up, strode to the baby grand, and slid onto the bench. She lifted the cover and began to play Chopin's "Raindrop" prelude. Maybe it would bring the much-needed rain showers. She kept the tempo slow as the maestro had insisted. Soon, the music carried Clair far away, and she closed her eyes and began to sway back and forth.

"Clair, you play divinely." Farley broke the spell. "Can you play something a little more snappy?"

"How about 'The Man on the Flying Trapeze'?" her father suggested.

Clair ran her fingers over the piano keys and picked out the notes to the familiar song. It had been a while. She had forgotten the lyrics, but as she played, they came back to her. Her father moved and stood beside her. His tenor voice blended smoothly with her soprano. Singing duets with him had always been one of her life's pleasures.

"*He floats through the air with the greatest of ease,*

the daring young man on the flying trapeze."

Farley slid next to her on the piano bench and joined in, croaking like a bullfrog, destroying the father-daughter harmonies. Her fingers continued to hit the keys, but she had stopped singing and soon her father did, too. Farley continued with gusto. She would never care to play that song again.

At the conclusion, her father applauded. "Bravo!"

Farley grinned. "Didn't we sound fine together?"

Clair stared at him in amazement.

"Oh, yes." Her father rose and shook Farley's hand. "I'm going to turn in. You two sit awhile and converse."

"Without a chaperone?" She was as stunned as a bird that had flown into a window. "But, Father!"

"You kids will be fine." He kissed her forehead, went down the hall to his bedroom, and closed the door.

Farley was no kid. It hurt that her father had left her alone with this odious man. He didn't feel she was worthy of someone more cultured. She started to play the "Raindrop" prelude again. Farley lumbered over to the desk and helped himself to another cigar.

She yawned. "I'd better turn in, too."

"What's the rush?"

"I have to prepare early for the church bazaar."

Sticking his cigar in an ashtray, he sat next to her on the piano bench again. "Only a while longer." He enclosed her in his arms.

She jumped up. "Mr. Parker!"

"What? You know you want to kiss me." Farley stood and reached for her again. "Don't worry, I won't tell your father."

She pushed Farley back and raised her voice. "You'd better *go*."

"Shhh!" He looked toward her father's bedroom.

She strode to the foyer and opened the front door. "Goodbye."

"Well, I can take a hint."

"Can you?"

"May I call on you tomorrow?"

She shook her head. "I'm busy."

"How about Sunday?"

"Then, too." Even with those big ears, he didn't seem to grasp what she was saying.

"When, then?" He stood there.

They stared at each other. She wouldn't give in. "I'm not sure." She pushed him out the door and swiftly closed it behind him.

She should have told him to drop dead. But young ladies of her standing always had to be polite. Next time she would shove him like Winnie did to that bum and say, "Scram. And don't ever come back!"

16

The morning after Farley's visit, Clair sat at the table, running her fingers in a hidden rhythm over the folds of her dressing gown. Room service had delivered and laid out poached eggs, bacon, and toast, but she couldn't eat a thing. She hated to be disrespectful but had to confront her father.

Her father put down his newspaper, cracked open an egg, and took a bite. He had slicked back his hair neatly, and a striped tie lay knotted over his white shirt.

She sipped her juice and put down the glass. "How could you leave me alone with Mr. Parker?"

Her father looked up from his plate. "Don't you like him?"

"Do *you?*"

Her father smiled. "He's a fine young man."

"He's not young at all."

"He's only thirty-five."

She tried to keep her voice calm. "Only? He's twice my age."

"You two have a lot in common."

"We do? What?"

"Music." Her father nodded.

"But he can't even carry a tune." Her hands pleaded with him.

Her father frowned and spread marmalade on his toast. "He tries."

"He's not very smart."

"Nonsense, he has promise." Her father used his knife for emphasis.

"Yes, promise to bore me to death."

"Clair!"

"What do you mean by *promise*?"

"He's very wealthy."

"What's that got to do with it? You've always said we have plenty."

Her father paused and studied her. "He could take care of you if anything ever happened to me."

Her hand went to her chest, and tears filled her eyes. "Nothing will happen to you." She had a strong desire to put her arms around him.

He shrugged. "Life is full of the unexpected."

She knew this was true. She paused. "But I'm too young to marry."

"Balderdash! Plenty of girls your age have wed."

"Maybe I would rather be a spinster like Aunt June."

He blinked and looked down at his plate. "June is different."

"In what way?"

"Never mind." He shook his head.

"But I'm not ready."

He raised his voice. "You will be ready when I *say* you will. He has requested to escort you out tomorrow evening, and you'll go."

She tried to reply, but the words wouldn't come. How could her father force her to step out with such a nincompoop, let alone marry him? It cut her to the core.

"Give him a chance." His eyes softened. "For me."

She clenched her hands together in her lap and bowed her head as if in prayer, but inside she roiled. "Yes, Father."

When she was young, he'd take her to the park and say, "Stay close." Even though she longed to run to the top of the rocks or along the grassy slopes to the other end of the verdant open spaces, she always obeyed. Flying kites, he'd let her hold the ball of string and tug on it. She'd wish it could go all the way to the moon or maybe up to heaven to see her mama.

Now he wiped his mouth with a napkin, walked over, and kissed her on her head. "There's a good Raffie. I'll be home early today."

Clair was glad she was meeting Aunt June for tea that afternoon. They hadn't seen each other since the ball and had a lot to talk about. Hopefully Aunt June would be able to give Clair some guidance. She took her time getting ready in a pale-pink frock with a hat to match and walked over to The Plaza.

The opulent tearoom surrounded her in marigold-and-French-blue damask. A stained-glass ceiling swirled above. Clair spotted her aunt at a corner table next to a giant bouquet of roses, freesia, and baby's breath. Waving off the maître d', Clair crossed the room in a gaited rhythm with the pianist playing a Strauss waltz. A waiter carrying a tray laden with sweet-smelling confections passed by her, and she resisted the urge to reach out for a meringue and pop it in her mouth.

Aunt June stood. Her bi-corner hat with the bow on the side folded up in front to reveal her lovely face. "It's been ages." She gave Clair a hug and they both sat.

Though considered an old maid at almost forty, Aunt June still had a charm about her. Not glamorous, but attractive, with a healthy figure. A thousand suitors had probably proposed to her in her day. She stayed active in civic events, and seemed contented with that and her teaching, but Clair always wondered why she'd never married.

A waiter delivered a teapot to their table and left. Clair listened to the pianist's étude for a few moments. "I need your help . . ."

"What is it, darling?"

"Father has decided I should marry Farley."

Aunt June opened her brown doe eyes wide. "That big talker from the ball?"

"Yes." Clair nodded.

"That's preposterous!" her aunt blurted out, then clasped a hand over her mouth.

A large woman sitting behind Aunt June in a pheasant-feather hat turned and stared, then leaned and whispered to the others at her table. The hat had a bird's nest with robins' eggs in it. Winnie would love it, but Clair wondered what the Audubon Society would think of all that plumage. They had recently helped pass laws for bird protection.

The waiter returned, lifted the teapot lid, peeked inside, poured a cup for each of them, and stepped away. Clair absentmindedly dropped three sugar cubes into her cup instead of her usual one and stirred, the spoon rattling against the dainty white porcelain.

"I don't want to marry anyone now, let alone Farley. Remember Father had agreed I could go to Juilliard in the fall? But now he has said no, that I should wait until after I get married. What if my husband won't let me? Will you please talk to Father?"

"He probably won't listen to me."

"But you've always told me how important your Barnard degree was."

"Yes, without it I couldn't teach. Which was my calling."

"I just have to go to college, too, and be the best musician I can be. Please try to help me convince him."

"You know him. Once he's made up his mind, it's hard to change it. I'll try, though."

Clair fingered the edges of her cup and found the nerve to ask, "Why don't you get along with Father?"

Aunt June hesitated. "Long ago we seemed to agree on everything. But now we don't agree on much. Take, for instance, the

Volstead Act. I'm working hard to repeal it. It's made the whole country more dangerous."

"But Father says alcohol is the devil's drink."

"Pshaw!" Aunt June blew air out. "I've had a few nips in my time, dear, and the devil hasn't gotten me and I'm still going to heaven."

Shocked, Clair paused, then whispered. "I confess, I've had a few, too."

Aunt June smiled. "And?"

"After a while I felt as if all my troubles had gone away."

"And did you dance, too?"

Clair nodded and took a sip of tea.

Aunt June laughed, "Good for you! Did you enjoy it?"

The relief of sharing this secret made Clair's whole body relax. "I guess so."

Aunt June tilted her head. "Not sure?"

"It was wonderful!" Clair raised her hands and shook them in a Charleston rhythm. She caught herself when the ladies at the next table turned to stare.

"Be careful though. It sounds as if you've been to a speakeasy, and they can be dangerous places."

"Don't worry, I've decided never to go back."

"That's probably for the best." Aunt June frowned. "Now to the problem at hand, Farley. Why does your father want you to marry him?"

"Father says he'll provide for me." Clair pulled an embroidered handkerchief from her purse and dabbed at tears.

Aunt June squinted. "How does he make his money?"

"He only says 'industry.' I'm not sure what kind."

"I only met him that one night, but he sure does blow his own horn. We must find a way for you to go to college before marrying."

"Father seems so down lately. I hate to disappoint him."

Aunt June sat back. "It's the market, dear. Soothsayers are predicting a dive."

Clair looked around at the exquisitely dressed diners eating luscious food in the lavish setting. It seemed as if money grew on trees and would never go away.

"He must be worried." Clair frowned.

"Even so, you need to be brave and convince him you aren't ready to marry."

The waiter delivered the sandwiches, scones, and sweets—all artistically arranged on a tiered tray. Aunt June helped herself to a cucumber sandwich. Clair started to reach for a cookie but then stopped herself. She had to follow the correct protocol. One must eat from the top to the bottom: sandwiches, scones, then sweets.

Clair nibbled on a quail-egg sandwich. "I agree."

Aunt June smiled at her. "When you're ready, you should marry for love."

"How can you say that if you've never loved a man?"

Her aunt looked into her teacup as if reading the leaves. "I did once, long ago."

Clair saw her aunt with fresh eyes. "I never knew that."

"The course of true love never did run smooth." Aunt June sighed.

"What happened?" Clair hated to pry, but she couldn't help it.

"I believed he loved me, too." Her aunt paused. "But . . . something happened, and I realized he never had."

"That's so sad."

"Yes. Very." Aunt June nodded and looked down to spread lemon curd on a scone. "But it was a long time ago."

Clair leaned toward her. "Tell me more."

"My beau became . . ." Aunt June paused. "Let me say, distracted."

"How?"

"I had been busy with the suffragist movement. I helped get women the right to vote, but lost my beloved in the process."

"But if you lost him, was he really your true love?"

"Probably not." Her aunt shook her head with downcast eyes. "But I do regret never being wed or having children of my own."

"You've always seemed happy." Clair reached for her aunt's hand.

"Thank you. You are so kind." Her aunt gazed at Clair. "I've been blessed to have you in my life."

"And I've been blessed to have you, too." Clair nodded. "I need more of a purpose in life than kowtowing to a man. You did it, and so can I."

She folded her hands demurely in her lap, then grabbed a meringue with her fingers instead of using the tongs and gobbled it down.

17

Anne had rendezvoused with Sergio at the Detroit airport and rented a car. After three hours heading north on US-23, she came to her favorite part of the drive. Beach cabins dotted the roadsides, and glimpses of Lake Huron showed between breaks in the pines and sycamores. She glanced over to see if Sergio had noticed the change in scenery, but he had drifted off to sleep.

She let him snooze a while longer, then touched his shoulder gently. "We'll be there in less than an hour."

He yawned, opened his eyes, and smiled. "I can't wait to meet your family."

She hoped he'd like them and they wouldn't be too hard on him. "I'm so happy you're here with me. Look to your right—that's Lake Huron. Keep your eyes peeled for a great blue heron." She wished he'd begin to appreciate the natural setting.

Sergio turned his head. "What do they look like?"

"They're very tall with gray feathers and a question-mark neck."

"I'll spot one for us." He rolled up his hands and put them over his eyes like binoculars. "If you love it so much here, why did you move away?"

"It's not reality. I need big-city energy to do my work."

"I'd think it would be the opposite."

"I know. Strange, huh?" She shrugged.

"Maybe you should journal about that."

"I think I will." She liked that Sergio appreciated her journaling. Karl, her last boyfriend, had teased her about it.

The sun began to slowly shift toward the west. "We're almost there. Please don't mention anything about moving in together."

Sergio gaped at her. "You haven't told them?"

"I'd rather wait until our plans are firm." Anne eyed him for a reaction.

He nodded and pulled down the visor, tying his hair back into a neat ponytail.

In their last phone conversation, she'd told him she quit her job and reminded him that she had a new lease to sign. But he hadn't bitten.

It was eight o'clock and beginning to grow dark when she turned onto Maple Lane, cruised two blocks, and parked in front of the two-story Craftsman. Hydrangeas bloomed in the garden, and the maple tree in front of Anne's gable window upstairs had sprouted bright-green leaves. Her mother's sign—"Avon's Skin So Soft Sold Here"—had been stuck in the freshly mowed lawn.

Her mom came out onto the porch and greeted them dressed in her baby-blue "power" pantsuit, with full-on makeup and freshly blow-dried hair. Anne liked that she was trying her best to impress and gave her a big hug. Every time Anne came home, she realized how much she loved and missed her mom.

Her hands on Sergio's shoulders, her mom looked up into his eyes. "I'm delighted to finally meet you."

"Me, too, Mrs. McFarland." He kissed both her cheeks.

She hesitated, then kissed him on both cheeks, too.

He handed her the bouquet they had picked up at a party store on the highway.

"You are so *sweet*!" She took the flowers and kissed him again.

So far, so good.

"Come on in," she said as they followed her through the screen door and into the kitchen. "Wash up, I've got a snack ready. Anne, get yourselves some pop in the fridge."

Anne handed Sergio a cherry cola and took a Diet Coke for herself. They sat while her mother put the flowers in a vase.

He mouthed to Anne, *Any wine?*

She shook her head no. *Sorry.*

He opened the cherry-cola can, took a sip, and grimaced. She traded him for her diet cola and he smiled at her.

Her mother pulled a giant platter out of the fridge, took off the Saran Wrap, and set it in the center of the table, then handed out paper plates and sat down. Anne observed his reaction to the baloney and Velveeta cheese sandwiches.

He chewed slowly, swallowed, and drank some pop as her mother pelted him with a gazillion questions. "Where are you from? Tell me about your family. Is Anne your first serious girlfriend? Tomorrow morning Anne can take you on the nickel tour. Afterward we're meeting the family at her favorite fine-dining establishment."

Anne laughed. "Tait's Bill of Fare is the *only* fine dining in town." Not wanting her mother to feel bad about forgetting Anne didn't eat meat, she took the baloney out of her bread and hid it under the potato chips on her plate.

Sergio stretched his shoulders and rolled his head. "Let's take a yoga class, too."

"I'm surprised you didn't bring your mat with you on the plane," Anne teased.

Her mother stretched her arms overhead. "I've been thinking of trying it, too. There's a new studio in the old yogurt place."

Anne smiled in relief. There hadn't been a yoga studio in town before. "We'll check it out tomorrow."

Sergio nodded. "Sounds good."

"I could stay up and visit all night, but you must be tired." Anne's mother led them into the living room and handed Sergio an armload of linens with a small wrapped present on top. "Here you go, and this is an Avon gentleman's guest gift for you, too. It's a best-seller."

"Thanks!" He gave Anne a look that asked, *We don't get to sleep together?*

She just smiled at him.

"Nighty night. Sleep tight. Don't let the bedbugs bite." Her mother gave each of them a hug and kiss, and gazed at them. "I'm so glad you're here. Feel free to watch the idiot box, but please keep the volume down." She turned and climbed the stairs.

"The what?" Sergio whispered as they sat on the plaid couch.

"Idiot box. TV," Anne said. "Open it." She pointed to his gift.

He removed the wrapping and read the label: "Musk Marine for Men. Bonus Size Roll-On Antiperspirant Deodorant. This should last me for the rest of my life." He pulled off the cap and sniffed. "Have you complained about my BO to your mother?"

"A little." Anne leaned over and smelled his neck, then kissed it.

He put his arm around her. "Your mom is sweet."

"Yes, she is."

"Inquisitive."

"That, too. Wait until you meet the whole fam-damily."

He pointed to the pair of ducks mounted on the wall. "Quite the decor."

"Uncle Robert was a taxidermist." Anne tried to see the living room how Sergio must, as outdated Midwestern.

"Look how they're staring at us."

Anne tossed a pillowcase over them. "You'll sleep better this way."

Sergio laughed. "Thank you. Let's check the yoga schedule." He typed into his cell, then frowned. "I don't seem to have cell service."

"It doesn't always work here."

"What's the Wi-Fi password?"

"What Wi-Fi?" Anne smiled and shrugged.

His eyes grew wide.

"Let's get your bed made." They pulled out the hide-a-bed, making it up with sheets and a pink blanket.

"It can be quite comfortable and cozy."

"Can't you sleep here with me and get up early and run upstairs?

She eyed the staircase. "Better not. I think Mom's still awake."

He ran his hands over the bumpy surface with a grimace. She pulled him close and whispered, "See you later, alligator," then clambered up the stairs to her bedroom.

18

The next morning after a pancake breakfast, Anne pulled her mom's Ford Fairlane out of the garage.

"Why aren't we using the rental car?" Sergio asked.

"I learned to drive in this baby and made a lot of memories in it."

"Did it in the back seat, huh?" he teased.

She laughed. "Noooo!"

He yawned and put his hand on her leg. "I slept pretty well considering the foldout and the fact you didn't sneak down to visit me as promised."

The last time Anne peeked out of her room, her mom's light had still been on. "Hopefully tonight." Anne wiggled her eyebrows at him.

They located Yoga and Yogurt on Main Street, but the windows were shuttered and the sign in the window said: *Gone fishing. Namaste!*

"Sorry. We can push back the living room furniture and practice there."

"It's not the same without an instructor."

She pulled the car away from the curb and continued down the street. "Here's where my favorite thrift shop was, but it closed two years ago."

He read the new sign. "Beach Monkey. Looks like an interesting place."

"Yes, they repaint old furniture and resell it. Pricey though."

She drove out to River Road. "On the right, we have Richardson Elementary School."

Sergio intoned, "Where the famous Anne McFarland, artist extraordinaire, began her illustrious illustrating career."

"With Play-Doh, fat crayons, and tempera paints."

They cruised further up the road. "And here we have Oscoda High." Anne pulled over and parked.

Sergio read the sign. "Home of the Owls!"

"Hoot! Hoot!" she cheered, raising a hand above her head for each cry.

Since it was Sunday, the school was quiet. Spread out over a couple of acres, the low blue buildings were trimmed in white. Pines, sycamores, and maples shaded their way as they walked across the campus. A gray squirrel nibbled a morsel and ran up a tree.

"Tell me about your high school," Anne said, taking his hand.

"My parents sent me to an all-boys boarding school outside Boston when I was twelve. They wanted me to learn the American way."

She was surprised she hadn't heard this before. They sure had different upbringings. "So young? Weren't you homesick?"

"Desperately," he whispered. "My parents were working their tails off at the factory keeping the business going. They planned for me to take over the business and someday expand it overseas."

"Have you accomplished that?"

"Yes." He nodded, putting his arm around her and kissing the top of her head. "We've gone global, as they say."

"What's this?" He stopped in front of a graffitied boulder with a smattering of unidentifiable words.

"Senior Rock! I'd sneak over here with Pootie at night and paint satirical cartoons of students who'd been mean to me."

"Who would ever be mean to you?"

"You'd be surprised." She'd never told him what a nerdy misfit she'd been. Always wearing resale-shop clothes. Sketching in her notebook. He wouldn't understand. "Let's go. I have something else to show you."

They drove back up the highway and crossed the Astoria Bridge, the river a blue ribbon flowing beneath them. She continued up the road, pulled over, and pointed to a massive display behind a chain-link fence.

"And here we have Paul Bunyan and his ox, Babe." Anne felt nostalgic whenever she visited these humungous kitschy statues. "When I was little, you could walk right up to them, push a button, and hear a narrator tell the tall tale through a speaker."

Sergio nodded. "Really?" She could tell he wasn't impressed.

Anne took on the persona of a deep male voice. "Growing up, Paul Bunyan was too big. Too big for the furniture. Too big for regular clothes. Too big to play with the other kids. But out among the tall trees in the great northern forests, Paul felt at home. So he set out with his big blue ox, Babe, to live the life of a lumberjack. Blah, blah, blah. And that ends the grand tour."

They returned to the car, and Sergio said, "You act very different here."

"What do you mean?"

"You seem more quirky." He ran his hand over her hair.

"Is that good or bad?" She frowned.

"I'm not sure." He shrugged. "I haven't decided yet."

What an odd thing to say. She held back tears and looked at her phone. "Time to go to the restaurant."

"*Fantastico*! I'm starving and can't wait to meet the rest of your family."

"They're gonna love you." She tried to remain positive. "Just don't bring up politics or ask about our family tree and you'll be fine."

"What's left?"

"The weather."

~

Outside Tait's Bill of Fare, noon church bells rang in the distance and white petals drifted from the ornamental pear tree. Anne grabbed Sergio's hand and guided him through the door. It was packed—good thing they had a reservation.

Her family waved as Sergio and Anne wove their way to the table. She tried not be too nervous, but prayed they wouldn't tease Sergio too much. She introduced him and they sat. Cousin Pootie handed adorable Baby Brian over to Anne. She held onto his soft, tiny hands. He wore the knit cap and had almost grown into it.

She loved this restaurant, from the tin ceilings with the brass chandeliers, to the red tablecloths and old oak bar. She glanced at Sergio. Compared to the tony New York restaurants he frequented, this must seem like the Podunkville Express.

A vivacious waitress in a white lace apron dropped off their drinks and took their orders. Anne's mother, Aunt Tootie, and Pootie gabbed away. The two guys sitting across the table from her were as different as night and day—one dark, the other fair—but each handsome in his own way. Sophisticated Sergio in his white linen shirt and rugged Brian, Pootie's husband, in his black T-shirt with the bald eagle on it. He picked up his stein and tipped it toward Sergio, who clinked his back at him. Anne hoped they would get along.

"Why don't you order the ribs, Anne?" Pootie teased, and the whole family laughed. They couldn't accept that she was a pescatarian.

"What business are you in?" Brian asked. "Shoes?"

"Yes . . ."

The waitress did another drive-by, dropping off a bread basket.

"I'm in heating and air." Brian sat up straight.

The women all mimicked his ad. "Air conditioner broken down? Don't start cryin', just call Brian."

On cue, Baby Brian began to cry. The couple at the table next to them peered over with a glower. Pootie took the baby from Anne and jiggled him up and down.

Brian continued. "I'm going to expand."

Anne gooped some honey butter on the hot bread and took a bite. "Another van?"

"No, he's getting into solar," Aunt Tootie answered, and took a sip of her pop.

"Isn't that a *bright* idea?" Pootie's blonde ponytail shook as she laughed.

Everyone at the table laughed except Brian.

"Do you get enough sun here for that?" Sergio asked.

"Certain times of the year. The economy is improving, and people are looking for ways to spend their money. Maybe you could open up a shoe store here, too."

Anne's mother piped up. "You could move here and run it."

Anne caught Sergio's eye. "You'd need to carry Birkenstocks, though."

"Yes, give Millican's some competition," Pootie smiled. "It's been the *only* shoe store here for forever."

"But I don't do sales," Sergio said.

The family looked at him quizzically, and Brian asked, "Then what do you do?"

"Design and manufacturing. We *make* shoes." To change the subject, Sergio looked at Aunt Tootie. "Tell me about the McFarlands." He smiled at Anne teasingly.

"Of course you've heard Anne's father was my brother. We were from the South, and Ma had been fickle. Had five husbands."

"I've never heard that before." Anne hit Pootie on the shoulder. "Did you know that?" Pootie, still bouncing Baby Brian, nodded her head.

Tootie continued. "We called her the black widow. She'd always say, 'Honey, they just keep on dying.' At least she married Daddy for love. The others she said she married out of habit."

Anne gaped. "Grandma McFarland? But she was such a sweet lady."

"She'd been a fireball." Tootie raised her voice.

The waitress delivered their meals. Sergio stared at his pan-fried perch smothered in pickle-infused tartar sauce. He forced himself to take a bite and swallow. Then he put down his fork.

Anne had warned him Michigan wasn't exactly a culinary mecca. "Here, I'll trade meals with you." She pulled his plate toward her and handed him her bowl. "You'll love the Swiss onion soup."

"Thanks." He took a spoonful and smiled.

Tootie dug into her Chicken Especiale. "Uncle Robert's a bit of a mystery man. I met him once at Daddy's funeral."

"Is he even still alive?" Anne's mother asked.

"I suppose so." Tootie shrugged.

"Did he ever marry?" Pootie handed Baby Brian to Brian so that she could dig into her burger.

"God, no! He wasn't marriage material, stubborn and ornery. Mama told me that he once proposed to a pretty young thing, out of good will, but she'd already been married to a Yankee. The older you get, the harder it is."

Pootie cleared her throat and stared at Anne.

"Thirty-something isn't that old!" Anne defended herself.

"Mama's sisters, Dixie and Trixie, were a kick. Dixie moved to California and married a surfer. Trixie married a preacher, and they drove an old station wagon around the country, doing revival shows. She sang and played the tambourine. She wore her hair as tall as the Empire State Building, and he had the most god-awful comb-over."

"Just like the Donald!" Sergio exclaimed. Everyone at their table and the one next to them stopped eating and stared at him. Anne had forgotten to warn him Michigan teemed with Trumpsters, even in her own family.

Pootie fed the last of her mashed potatoes to Baby Brian, then picked him up from Brian and handed him to Anne again. "What are you doin' tomorrow?"

"Let's go for a hike," Sergio said.

Anne laughed. "No, sir. You're in my territory. I'm taking you fishin'!"

"Fishing? Do you want to take me hunting, too?"

"Not this time."

"You mean you've shot a gun?"

"Of course she has." Pootie punched Anne on the arm. "Tell him about the time we were shooting beer cans at Danny's farm." She turned to Sergio. "She didn't realize there would be a kickback, and the bullet casing jumped out and went down her top!"

Anne's face turned red.

Sergio grimaced. "You're kidding."

"That was so funny!" Pootie said, and everyone at the table laughed except Anne.

"No, it wasn't. I still have the scar." Anne fingered the spot in her cleavage.

"Has she shown it to you?" Pootie asked Sergio with a wry smile.

"Not yet." He leaned over as if to get a peek.

"Anne. Remember when you let Danny take you hunting? He was crazy about hunting, and you were crazy about him. Tell Sergio."

"No, that's okay." Anne couldn't believe Pootie brought this up.

Pootie continued. "She tried to impress him with her sense of adventure. Even bought herself an Elmer Fudd cap and full camo outfit. You were so upset when he made you wear that ugly orange vest over it. Tell it, Anne. No one can tell it like you."

Anne sighed. The cat had come out of the bag anyway. "We were in the woods waiting behind a blind."

"A what?" Sergio asked.

"A little hut where you hide to watch for deer. After waiting for an hour, a doe strides into the clearing. It had white spotted fur and such a sweet face. I held my breath as Danny raised his rifle and cocked it. The doe froze and stared at us. I couldn't help myself—I clapped my hands and yelled, 'Run!'"

Pootie laughed. "That was the end of that romance. She decided to stick with fishing after that."

Sergio frowned. "Did that really happen?"

Brian nodded. "Sure did. I heard it from Danny myself. He was pissed. I prefer duck hunting. Can you come back in October? Join us for a guy weekend. We get up at sunrise, row boats out into the lake, and wait for the ducks to fly overhead. At night we eat chili, swap stories, and smoke cigars. I'll let you use the AeroBed."

"Would be more comfortable than the . . ." Sergio coughed to catch himself before he said *foldout*. "Sorry, October is a very busy time for me at work." He hadn't eaten any more of his soup.

Brian drank the rest of his beer. "Let's go over to the Edelwiess Tavern for another brewski."

"That's okay. Maybe some other time." Sergio looked as if he might run out the door, grab a bus, and head back to the airport.

19

Before dawn, Anne shook Sergio's shoulder. "Get up!"

He rolled over. "*Mamma mia*! It's not even light yet. Let me sleep a little longer."

"We need to get there while the fish are still jumping." She couldn't wait to show him Lake Tawas, one of the most romantic places ever. Once he got there, he'd love it. "Come on!"

He got up and threw on his jeans and white dress shirt from the night before.

"That might get ruined. Here." She handed him a T-shirt she'd bought especially for this day. He pulled it over his head without noticing the openmouthed fish, the dangling hook, and the *Bite Me!* caption. She smiled, handing him a mug of coffee to go.

Her mother's garage was filled with gardening equipment, Avon boxes, and the family's old snowblower. She handed Sergio two fishing poles and her pink tackle box. Then she draped binoculars around her neck and donned her hat with the hooks pinned onto it.

Sergio squinted. "Really?"

"Yes, really. It's my lucky hat. If I don't wear it, I won't catch a thing."

"But you look like an old man."

"Don't worry. No one you know will see us."

He smirked and chuckled.

She looked up at the cloudless apricot-colored dawn as she closed the car's trunk. "I sure hope the weather holds."

Sergio yawned. "The news last night said sunny skies predicted."

"In Michigan, there's no such thing as a long-range weather forecast. It can be clear and seventy-five degrees, but then, within no time, the nimbostratus will rush in and ruin it all. Besides, the lake can get breezy. Better grab a jacket."

"I'll be fine." He sipped his coffee.

She headed back into the garage and grabbed a fluorescent-green windbreaker from the rack. "Let's take this just in case."

"But it's an XXXL."

She threw it in the back. "Want to stop at Walmart and get you one that fits?" She glanced at his frowning face. "You've probably never even *been* to a Walmart."

He didn't answer.

They drove south and within a half hour arrived at the lake. Purple hyacinth lined the beach beside the dock. A frog jumped on the sandy shore. A goose led her five goslings single file on a morning swim.

"Isn't it beautiful here?"

"It's a big lake." He didn't sound very happy. "I can barely see all the way to the other side."

"Yes, and it goes down that way for miles." She hopped off the dock into the boat and set down the cooler. Sergio handed her the life vests, tackle box, and fishing poles. Then she reached for his outstretched hand. He grasped it with tight lips and climbed aboard, the boat rocking to and fro.

"You can swim, can't you?" she teased, and sat on the back-bench seat near the motor.

"Of course." He landed on the seat facing her.

"Ready?"

He saluted her. "Aye, aye, captain."

She tightened the hat strap under her chin, revved the motor, and took off across the gray-green lake, trying to avoid the blooming water lilies. Cattails rose above the water like Chippewa spears.

Along the bank, maple tree branches waved goodbye to them in the gentle breeze. The leaves blew upside down, which meant a storm was on its way. She wouldn't mention that to Sergio, though. He wouldn't believe her.

In the center of the lake, she cut the motor and smiled. "This is a good spot."

"What makes you say so?"

"No reeds and deep water."

He looked down into the depths.

"Want me to show you how to bait your hook and cast?" she asked.

"Sure." He grimaced as she opened the cooler, took from the baggie a wiggly worm, and wove it back and forth onto the hook.

"Watch." Pulling her arm back, she threw the line into the rippling water several yards away and handed him the pole.

"Hold it like this." She placed his hands on the rod.

"I've got it." Something splashed near the boat, getting him wet. "What was that?"

"A fish." She baited her own hook and cast it out. "Now all we do is wait."

After a minute or two he yelled, "I've got one!" and started to reel it in.

She looked at the top of his pole. "Might just be the current tugging on it."

He kept reeling until the hook and the worm popped out of the water. "Nothing."

"Too bad." She sure hoped he'd catch a fish.

He reeled the line in all the way, pulled back, and let it go. He'd forgotten to loosen the gripper though, so it plopped back into the water in front of him. He pulled his arm way back, and this time he cast perfectly a few yards off.

"Wow! Babe Ruth. Hit it out of the park, baby." The line was slack. "Reel it in a bit."

Holding their poles, they sat in silence for a while. Purple dragonflies hovered overhead like miniature helicopters. To the west, white clouds began to billow on the other side of the lake. Anne smiled at Sergio. His mouth responded with half a grin, his foot bouncing up and down.

She needed to keep him entertained to help pass the time. "Last time Pootie and I were out here, she caught the ugliest fish ever. It resembled a catfish, but it had a hairy mustache and a beard, had to google to identify it. It was a dogfish! I swear I had heard it bark when she pulled the hook out of its mouth."

Sergio laughed.

Anne's line had slackened. She reeled it in and recast.

He did, too, but his hook got stuck in some reeds, and when he tried to roll the line back in, it snapped and broke. "*Porca vacca!*"

"Don't worry, that happens all the time." She fixed his line up, added another worm, and he recast.

"Fishing is similar to doing art. You gather up your materials: paints, brushes, found objects, canvas, tray or box. To fish you also have to gather the equipment: rod, reel, and bait. You can fish off the shore or a pier, or take the boat out into the middle of a lake or even into the ocean. To do art, you can dive in, sign up for a class, or find a mentor to guide you.

"With both you just need to go for it—get started, cast the line—but then wait and be patient. Maybe that day you will catch a fish or create a masterpiece, but maybe not. Either way, you showed up and tried. That's what matters. You can always try again another day."

"Look!" Sergio yelled. "Is that one of your great blue herons?" He pointed to a sandbar about half a mile away.

She raised her binoculars. A giant long-necked crane foraged in the reeds, feathered in pale gray, a bright-red marking on its head.

She whispered, "Oh my God, I think it's a sandhill crane! I've always wanted to see one. They're very rare here. I'd love to get closer, but we might scare it away."

She handed the glasses to Sergio.

"*Magnifico*. Now what's going on?" He handed the binoculars back to Anne.

Tiny black birds were dive-bombing the crane. "The little birds are trying to protect their eggs, but they're no match for the big bird. Survival of the fittest."

"Gross." Sergio grimaced.

After a while, the crane unfurled its wide wingspan and majestically flew away.

"Wow." Anne smiled.

"*Interessante*."

Clouds began to gather and darken, moving toward them across the lake. The smell of rain filled the air.

Anne frowned. "We should go. Sorry we got skunked."

"That's okay." He shrugged.

"Maybe next time." She doubted there would be a next time.

She pulled the string on the motor, but it wouldn't turn over. She kept at it a few times. "I'd better stop or the engine will flood."

Light flashed on the far-off shore. "Was that lightning?" Sergio ducked as thunder pounded the sky.

The next time she pulled the engine's string, it snapped off. "Oh, God! We'll have to row back." She looked down on the floorboards near the bow, but the oars weren't there. Darn it! Mr. Halston had reminded her to grab them from the pole barn when she got the life jackets, but she forgot. She searched the water for another craft that might give them a tow, but the lake was deserted.

Within a few minutes, the clouds burst open, dropping raindrops the size of acorns. She pulled her jacket's hood over her hat and handed Sergio the giant windbreaker, and he tugged it on.

"We'll need to wait until someone comes and tows us in. It could be a while." She hoped they wouldn't need to spend the night out there.

20

Farley escorted Clair to his bottle-green Lincoln. She slid onto the passenger seat and looked up toward the suite's window. She couldn't see him, but she knew her father was looking down with a smile on his face. To make him happy she had dressed with care, donning a powder-blue skirt and jacket, clasping the opal brooch he'd given her for Christmas onto her high-laced collar. She had pinned her hair up neatly and topped it off with her cloche.

As Aunt June had suggested, she'd confronted her father again, but he insisted she go out with Farley. Since she loved her father, she decided to truly try. Still it stung. Since he had married for love, she had always assumed he would encourage her to also. They were going to a movie house. She'd heard them called "petting pantries," and she hoped he wouldn't try anything tawdry with her. *Sunrise: A Song of Two Humans,* hailed by the *Times* as a masterpiece, was playing.

Farley stopped to inspect the front of his car, took a handkerchief from the pocket of his three-piece suit, and rubbed a spot on the Lincoln's hood. He nodded his head and put the handkerchief back in his pocket. "Let's go."

He jumped in, revved the motor, and maneuvered the car away from the curb.

"Watch out!" a man yelled as a double-decker bus swerved at the last second, missing them by an inch.

Clair put her hands on the dashboard. "Careful!"

Farley laughed, racing the car down the street into dense traffic. He honked the shiny bulb horn at a horse-drawn carriage. *A-oo-gah!*

He patted the steering wheel and started to brag about every little detail of his town car. "Yes, this baby cost me $4,800. Worth every penny. With aluminum pistons, it's guaranteed to go at least seventy miles per hour."

"Keep your eyes on the road!" Clair's heart raced faster than the car.

He navigated between other automobiles, passing a policeman on a motorbike and another horse-drawn carriage.

He continued, "On our honeymoon, we'll take this for a spin in the country and test that guarantee."

"Our *what?*"

He eyed her. "Our honeymoon. Your father has agreed we'll be married this spring."

How could he make such plans behind her back? "But I haven't agreed—you never even asked me."

"Sorry." He glanced at her. "Wanna get married?" He put his hand on her knee.

She pulled her leg away. "No."

He kept right on blathering. "The 384-cubic-inch flathead V8 engine . . ."

Yes, like your own flat head. She examined him more closely. Actually, his head did look flat, even on all four sides, like a square, a blockhead, an ignoramus. Except for his god-awful cowlick. She had an urge to reach over and tamp it down but didn't want to get grease on her gloves.

The Times Square traffic was thick, but Farley found a parking space, and they rushed into the movie palace. They squeezed into their seats right before the lights went down. The theater smelled of body odor and cheap cigars. She pulled her rose water–spritzed hankie from her clutch and held it to her nose.

A newsreel showed the invention of bumpers on the front of cars to decrease injuries and fatalities from accidents. First, they threw a dummy in front of a moving car, and then a man jumped in front of a moving truck. Both times the bodies glided along gently. Farley could sure use one of those on the front of his car.

He put his paw on her knee, but she pushed it away. Her mind went back to his words: her father had agreed they'd marry in the spring. She needed to convince him otherwise.

The movie's title scrolled across the screen. Though talkies were becoming popular, this was a silent film—but instead of an orchestra, synchronized music emanated from speakers, a nice touch. The film flickered on. George O'Brien. She had seen him in *The Silver Treasure* and *Paid to Love*.

Farley groped for her fingers, and momentarily she let him hold on. His rough skin reminded her of a wet potato and she let go, rubbing the moisture on her hankie. Farley frowned and slumped with crossed arms.

As O'Brien rowed Janet Gaynor out onto the lake, Clair became captivated by the movie, and she wondered if he would really kill his wife. Later in the film, grief-stricken over what he had almost done to her, he asked for her forgiveness and plied her with flowers and gifts. What wonderful acting! Their bodies close, O'Brien gazed at Gaynor as if he truly loved her. Her large expressive eyes reminded Clair of Winnie.

Could her friend really have *it*? Clair wished she was with Winnie instead of Farley and wondered what was happening at Rudy's. Clair bet the joint was jumping.

~

On the sidewalk after the movie, Farley suggested they go out for a bite to eat.

She yawned. "I'm not hungry, and besides, I'm tired."

"We can sit for a while in the parlor."

That's the last thing she wanted to do.

"Mr. F!" a large man called, hurrying toward them.

Farley glanced at the man, took her arm, and rushed her toward his car. He turned on the motor and screeched away from the curb.

"Please try to drive slowly. Who was that?" she asked.

"No one." He shook his head with a frown.

"No one?"

"I mean, no one I want to talk to tonight." He turned and looked behind him.

"You sure?"

"Yes." In silence for once, he drove along with the traffic.

"Have you ever been to a speakeasy?" She smiled at him.

"Clair!" He looked shocked. "Of course not. What would your father say if he knew you asked me that?" Farley snorted a laugh.

"He might not mind if I went with you."

"Clair." He shook his head. "Perhaps you aren't the girl I thought you were."

She grinned at him.

"Are you pulling my leg?"

"Of course." What a fuddy-duddy.

He sped up his pace. This time, she closed her eyes and pretended to be on a roller coaster. At the hotel, he walked her up to the suite.

"Good night." She stood with her back to the closed door.

"You're so pretty." His eyes scanned sideways, and he put his hand on her arm.

She gently pushed it away.

"May I come in?"

"We might wake Father," she whispered. "You'd better go home."

He closed his eyes and leaned toward her for a kiss. She considered it for a very brief moment. That way, she could tell her father she'd tried. Plus, she'd never been kissed before, and she was curious. She studied his straggly, untrimmed mustache, clotted with wax, and her stomach roiled. She leaned back and pushed him away. He stopped, confused, and she quickly said good night and slipped inside.

Her first kiss should be something special. To make that happen, she might need to push Farley away several more times. She would never be able to kiss him. But would he always take no for an answer?

21

The ghastly dates with Farley and evenings in the suite continued for weeks. His boorish nature still gnawed at her craw. He had fallen asleep and snored loudly at the philharmonic, he ogled passing women, and, night after night, at the end of the evening he tried to kiss her, but she kept pushing him away.

Tonight she bid Farley and her father adieu as they left for the Odd Fellows meeting. Then she ran to the window and used her opera glasses to watch them climb into the Lincoln. Finally, an evening alone! She turned the radio dial until she found some jazz. "Yes Sir, That's My Baby," one of her favorites, came on. Giving in to wild abandon, she did the Charleston, keeping an eye on the door in case the men returned for some unexplained reason.

For two months Clair had resisted her craving for Rudy's, but as she danced, her desire began to overpower her. Clair looked at the clock on the mantel. The men wouldn't be back for hours. Did she dare escape and go to Rudy's? No, she couldn't. Or maybe she could, if she promised to behave—no hooch or even dancing. She would only listen, tap her feet, and observe the others. Winnie could give her some advice about Farley, too.

Clair rushed to her dressing room. Feet bare on the black-and-white tiles, she slipped on her pale-pink gown and examined her body in the full-length mirror. She sighed and her shoulders sagged.

The debutante dress made her look dowdy, and her copper-colored hair was too full. She had to look more in vogue. Foraging in her jewelry box, she pulled out her pearls and placed them around her neck.

She paused for another look and sighed again.

Replacing the pearls in the jewelry box, she picked out two large brooches. Looking in the mirror, she gathered a handful of material at each hip and pinned up the sides. She hoped her legs didn't still look like the toothpicks the kids at church had teased her about.

Winnie's turban had been so striking. Clair wound her hair as tightly as she could and donned one herself. Instead of a feather, she attached her opal pin to it for a little sparkle. Because of her thick hair, the turban poofed up in a tall mound, looking very dramatic.

Her father had never allowed her to wear makeup, but she had a stash hidden, and when he was at work she sometimes applied some and made faces at herself in the mirror. She considered putting on a little lipstick, but that would be going too far.

Throwing on her coat with the fur-shawl collar, she stealthily hurried out the back of the hotel through the kitchen.

When the cab pulled up to the speakeasy, it looked dark and the block was empty. Rudy's might not even be open.

"Let's sit here for a moment," she told the driver.

A few minutes later a limo arrived, and a couple climbed out, went down the steps, and entered the building.

Clair paid the cabbie and marched down the steps herself, hoping the password hadn't been changed. "Moody Rudy," she said when the slit opened. The door swung ajar and she slid inside. The smoky place was packed to the gills, and it took a moment for her eyes to adjust. The band could be heard over the sound of laughter and voices.

"Hey, gal pal—what a surprise! Long time no see." Rudy handed her coat to the doorman, took Clair's arm, and led her to Winnie's table next to the crowded dance floor. "Be right back with your drink."

"No booze," she called after him, and put her hand on Winnie's shoulder. "Am I ever happy to see you."

Winnie jumped up, smiled brightly, and yelled into Clair's ear. "Hiya, toots! Afraid you'd dropped off the ends of the earth." She tugged on Clair's turban. "This is spiffy, but it could use a few feathers. How was the ball? Bet you looked like a movie star." Winnie wiggled her hips.

Clair shook her head. It felt great the way the turban kept her hair in place. "Not really, but I did dance a lot."

"I'm sure you did." Winnie sat and pulled Clair down next to her.

Clair frowned. "I'm glad to see you. I could sure use someone to talk to."

"What's wrong?"

"There's this fellow my father is encouraging me to marry, but I can't stand him."

"Why not?"

"He's old and stinky, and talks a blue streak."

Winnie scrunched up her nose. "Does he have money?"

"I suppose so. He brags about all the things he buys."

"Could you fall for him over time?"

Clair removed her gloves. "No!"

"Sounds like a bluenose, a killjoy. Follow your heart. If you don't care for him, don't take him." Winnie shimmied her shoulders as the feathers on her hat shook.

Good advice. Clair never wanted to take Farley anywhere. "They're planning a spring wedding for us. How do I get out of it?"

"Play it cool. That's ages away. Maybe he'll disappear over time."

"I doubt that." It wouldn't be that easy. "Why is it so packed tonight?"

"Got a new performer. She's supposedly quite the vamp."

Clair noticed a man in a pompadour staring at her from across the dance floor. He looked familiar, but she couldn't quite place him. Beatrice Beach Bernard rested her arm on his. Clair hadn't seen Bea since the ball and barely recognized her. She wore plenty of makeup; her hair had been bobbed and bleached blonde. A short yellow dress clung to her body like a lemon rind.

Bea's parents probably had no idea Bea was here, either. The man leaned over, said something to her, and they both laughed. Bea waved at Clair and pulled him across the dance floor toward her.

"Hi, Clairy!" Bea squealed, her voice high-pitched, and leaned down to hug Clair. Clair was taken aback; they'd never been close friends.

"I see you two know each other." Winnie giggled. "And who is this looker?"

"Andre, Andre LeRue." The man straightened the scarlet ascot at his neck.

It was that darned artist, the one who had painted the horrendous portrait! He must be wearing one of those Hollywood toupees advertised in the magazines. At least he had shaved off that atrocious mustache. She hadn't seen him either since the night of her ball, and she said a grateful prayer to her father and Aunt June for saving her from humiliation that night.

"Word out is that you're a genius," Winnie gushed.

Mr. LeRue nodded. "I've heard that word bandied about. Hello, Miss Devereaux."

"You've met?" Winnie smiled.

"Ooh, Clair! Andre is so mad at you." Bea's voice grated on Clair.

"Yes, if it wasn't for you, I'd be famous by now."

Bea howled a laugh, her overbite even more pronounced with all that lipstick on. "You are so funny, Andre!"

Clair could feel her face turning as red as his ascot. Thanks goodness the lights were low.

Mr. LeRue studied her turban. "Trying to be a flapper? I don't think you're the type."

A rock sat in the middle of Clair's chest.

"Come on, Bea, let's dance." Without a goodbye, LeRue pulled Beatrice away and onto the dance floor.

Winnie put her arm through Clair's. "Don't worry, honey, you'll be fine. They're just teasing you."

Rudy joined them with their drinks.

"Do you know Mr. LeRue?" Clair asked Rudy, and nodded her head in the artist's direction as he did the Black Bottom with Beatrice.

"Who?" Rudy shrugged. "Oh, him. He's looking for a job."

"Doing what?"

"I plan to step it up and move to a real theater. He says he can do the costume and set design."

Oh, geez! He'd probably put the women in shredded frocks, and the sets would be painted in colors that clashed. "Are you going to hire him?"

"I might. He's a nice enough guy, even though he's a little fruity," Rudy chortled.

Clair frowned. She would be too embarrassed to tell them the whole tawdry tale of the painting. From across the floor, Mr. LeRue stared at her with a sly grin. Clair's pulse beat in her ears like a kettledrum. Mr. LeRue had been so angry, he might tell her father about her being here just for spite.

"I'd better go." Clair started to stand.

Winnie grabbed her arm. "But you just got here."

"You can't miss the floor show." Rudy pushed her drink toward her.

The band started playing an upbeat version of "Someone to Watch Over Me." Winnie jumped up and grabbed Clair's hand.

Clair pulled her hand away and shook her head. "I'm only going to listen tonight."

"Sure?"

Clair nodded.

"Suit yourself." Winnie pulled Rudy onto the dance floor.

Clair sipped her drink. Drat! It was filled with booze. She surreptitiously spit it back into her glass.

Winnie tangled her arms around Rudy's neck, and he tugged her in closer. He closed his eyes, and his tough-looking face softened. A moony grin rested on his lips. Would anyone ever hold Clair like that?

The song ended, but Rudy and Winnie remained on the dance floor as the band played "The Man on the Flying Trapeze," reminding Clair of Farley's horrible singing. She'd take Winnie's advice to follow her heart, and find a way to not take him. Clair played the melody along on her thighs and soon forgot about Farley.

Next the band struck up "Yes Sir, That's My Baby," the same song she had danced to on the radio at home. The floor soon filled with folks rollicking to the Charleston. In her seat, she moved her feet forward and back on the wood floor.

Soon though, she got swept up in the music, and she jumped up and joined in the dance, doing the steps beside Rudy and Winnie.

Her turban popped off, so she ran over and tossed it on the table next to her glass. Darn thirsty, she gave in, took a sip, and swallowed a gulp. With the rough taste of hooch in her mouth, she took the pins out of her hair and let it fall down her back. If her father knew, he'd be fuming that all could see her glory. He might lock her up in her room forever, but at that moment, she didn't care. All she cared about was the bump, pump, pump of the band.

At the end of the dance, out of breath, she took another sip of her drink. "I've really got to go," she told Winnie and Rudy.

The band began to pick up their instruments and vacate the stage.

"But the floor show's about to start." Winnie pulled Clair down onto a chair.

"Don't worry, my driver will take you home afterward." Rudy smiled at Clair.

Winnie asked, "When are you gonna give me a chance to be onstage?"

He leaned down and kissed her cheek. "After I have bigger digs is all." He walked across the dance floor, inviting people to take their seats.

"I can't wait to see this. There's supposed to be a talent scout from Hollywood here tonight." Winnie tugged down her hat and studied the room.

Suddenly the lights blinked out, and the room grew black and quiet.

"Ladies and gentlemen!" Rudy's voice echoed from the microphone. "Straight from the distant lands of eastern Europe, for your entertainment pleasure, I give you Varinska!"

A spotlight flipped on, illuminating a lone woman onstage. Dreamlike, her eyes focused above the crowd as if casting a spell. A chill ran up Clair's spine. This must be the most beautiful woman on earth. Straight ebony hair parted in the center cascaded down over her shoulders and fell over her pale arms. Gold chains strung with coins and rubies fell over her bohemian blouse and into the crevice between her rounded breasts. A crimson skirt stopped above her ankles, revealing bare feet.

A far-off violin began to play, and Varinska slowly swirled her hips in a figure eight. Clair recognized "Hungarian Dance No. 5," but had never imagined it performed this way, sultry and sensual. She had asked to learn to play it on the piano, but her maestro had claimed it wasn't decent.

Varinska's husky voice was as deep as a baritone's, but dark and tangy like licorice. Clair couldn't place the exotic guttural language that resonated into her own chest with a longing filled with loneliness. The singer hit all the notes exactly on pitch and stepped forward, one eyebrow raised, holding a mystery. Even though Clair didn't understand the lyrics, it was obvious what they meant. "Come back to me, darling. Wrap me in your arms always."

Varinska slowly shook a tambourine above her head, its cymbals shimmering in the light. Then she bumped the instrument back and forth across her hip in rhythm to the music, jumped off the stage onto the dance floor, and sprinted in a circle, taking big leaps. As the music sped up, her voice quickened and grew louder.

Clair held her breath until the end when Varinska twirled, arms upraised. Varinska yipped a few times like a lone wolf and suddenly crashed to the floor. The lights went out, and in the blackness, there was a stunned pause from the crowd.

Clair rose to her feet with the audience. They clapped for what seemed like an eternity until Varinska sprinted back into view to the wild Hungarian rhythm. She turned in a circle and landed with one foot pointed forward, bending to a low bow. Through her whole routine she never smiled, not once, but Clair sensed that behind those sad eyes the performer knew she had enraptured everyone in the room. As if struck by lightning, Clair recognized she'd never be the same again.

22

Clair finished her second drink and followed Rudy and Winnie out the door, where Rudy's black Cadillac waited. It was past midnight. Shadows shifted in the sky, a brisk wind shook the pine tree in front of the building, and a murder of crows circled above, cawing. The driver opened the Cadillac's door, and the girls slid in.

"Get them home in one piece," Rudy ordered.

"Yes, sir." The driver nodded, got in, and turned on the motor.

Rudy leaned in, kissed Winnie's cheek, and pounded on the top of the car twice.

As they drove away, Winnie waved goodbye to him. "The Waldorf, please and thank you. I'm spifflicated," she slurred from her lipstick-smeared mouth. Then she laid her head on Clair's shoulder, closed her eyes, and promptly fell asleep.

The wind blew a spruce tree back and forth like an ocean wave in a storm. Clair's head spun from booze, thrills, and possibilities. She shouldn't have stayed so long. Her father would be home already, waiting up for her. No matter what happened though, she wouldn't regret it. To see Varinska's act made it worth it. Clair's body tingled all over reviewing the performance in her mind as she played the Hungarian waltz on her thighs.

As they reached the hotel, Mr. O'Shaughnessy stepped out the front door and down the steps to the sidewalk to greet them. The doorman must have gone home. Clair slid down in her seat. "Drop me at the back!"

"Sure thing." The driver blasted away from the curb as Mr. O'Shaughnessy turned with a frown.

Winnie awoke. "Here, let me help you." She stuffed Clair's hair back into the turban and patted the top of her head. "Don't take any wooden nickels." Winnie kissed her on the cheek and popped a peppermint drop into her mouth. "This should conceal the liquor's odor."

Clair slid out of the car, almost fell, and quickly pulled her body erect. She entered through the kitchen, made certain the lobby was deserted, and rode up in the elevator. She sucked on the candy and paused at the door to brace herself.

"Shhh!" she whispered to herself as she almost tripped getting into the suite.

To her surprise, the lights were out in the foyer and parlor. Her father snored behind his bedroom door, a deep French horn. She sighed with relief.

She thought she would fall asleep right away under the smooth sheets, but her body felt as if it were still dancing. Like every night, Clair tried to recall her mother's sweet voice singing a lullaby to her, but it was drowned out by Varinska's performance running through her mind. She turned over and fluffed her pillow.

A spark inside her had been lit—so deep and disturbing that it frightened her to acknowledge it. The flint had been there for years but had never fully been a reality until tonight. It burned so bright that she realized it wouldn't ever flicker out and turn to ash, no matter how hard she, or anyone else, tried to extinguish it.

Deep inside, she'd always known about her desire but had never believed she would be able to act on it. She had a desire to entertain, to enrapture a crowd, and to hear that applause, too. Onstage, she would help take people's minds off their worries and make them happy. But her father said performers were hussies. He had seethed that women embarrassed their families by going onstage.

Aunt June would take Clair to theater matinees, and whenever he started to complain about it, Aunt June said sweetly, "Leland, you are welcome to join us." She gave him that look, as if she was holding something over him. He harrumphed and stayed home, smoking cigars and waiting for the ticker tapes to come in.

Ballets, operas, Shakespeare plays—Aunt June had taken her to them all. In the theater, Clair felt as if she was in another world, a magical world, viewing the well-lit stage. Graceful dancers *en pointe*, a mezzo-soprano's voice resonating, the poetry of an actor emoting—she adored them all. But Varinska was different. She had that something Clair couldn't quite place.

Once, Aunt June had taken her to an eccentric modern dancer's studio. She also had that *something*. Some reviewers said she must be crazy, and others called her a genius. Mesmerizing and red-lipped, with wide, dark eyes in a full-length hooded dress, the dancer had squirmed and fought in staccato shapes and sometimes into hideous contortions, as if trying to release the demons inside her. Clair yearned to move like that, too.

She now got out of bed, donned her funeral dress, wrapped a shawl over her head, and moved in front of the dressing room mirror, imitating the performer trying to escape the fires of hell. Clair widened her eyes and twisted her lips. She raised one Varinska-esque eyebrow and moved her hips in a figure eight, imagining what it might be like to entertain a crowd. But it was useless. No girl with a father like hers could ever perform onstage.

And so she returned to bed, considering once again how to break her habit of dreaming of the stage.

23

Her first morning back from Michigan, Anne lounged in her daybed and summoned up their afternoon stuck on the lake. Even though the rain had cleared and they'd witnessed the most beautiful purple-and-pink-hued sunset ever, Sergio wasn't pleased. He shivered with cold and didn't say a word, but she sensed the whole experience scared him. She had been stuck out there before and assumed someone would eventually come along. And she had been right. Before it was completely dark, a boat came along and towed them back to the dock.

She sighed and thought of the conversation she'd had with Sergio as they headed south back to the airport.

"I'm sorry the trip was a bust. I'd hoped you'd be smitten with the mitten."

"I liked it." He put his hand on her knee.

"No, you didn't."

"To be honest, I felt like a fish out of water."

They both laughed at his unintentional joke.

"Will you ever want to go back?"

He shrugged. "*Sicuro.*"

"How about Perchville in February?" She smiled but kept her eyes on the road.

"What's that?"

"Fishing tournament and Polar Bear Swim. They cut a hole in the ice, and people dive into Lake Huron."

"You're kidding."

"Nope. I've done it before, but I know it's not for you. You didn't care for my family, either."

"Your mom is nice, but the rest of the family is pretty . . . unusual. It was hard to get a word in edgewise. I'm sure they are good people. They love you, and over time I'll probably love them, too." He leaned over and kissed her on the cheek.

Anne's eyes moistened. "You're so sweet. Are you certain we're meant for each other?"

"Why not?"

"You're rich and I'm poor. You're sophisticated and I'm not."

"I don't care about any of that. I've told you before, you're different than the women I meet in the fashion industry. You're wholesome and down to earth. One of the things I love about you is that you take me out of my comfort zone and encourage me to try things I'd never even imagined doing before."

"Like the Polar Bear Swim?"

He laughed. "No, I'm not doing that! Like fishing, thrifting, and eating terribly gross food."

She laughed. "What else?"

"Carrying a woman in my arms in a subway station, shipping Ferragamos across the country to get her attention."

"And?" Her voice took on a sultry timbre.

"I'm not going to say any more." He smiled a smile that had warmed her all the way home.

Anne laughed and popped out of bed, poured some coffee and lit her gardenia candle. Since quitting her valet job, she loved having hours on end to do her art. She pulled her hair up and twisted a scrunchie into it, then started back in on the flapper collage, adding more color and depth to the girls' clothes.

While the collage dried, Anne moved to her shoe painting. The shading and darks and lights of the rhinestones were still challenging her. She needed inspiration.

From her stash, she grabbed an old tackle box about the same size and shape as the shoebox, screwed off the lid, and removed the inset, setting it aside. To the mermaid-blue paint left over on her palette she added a little oxide green and stirred it together to make a delicious turquoise. She painted the entire box, inside and out.

In front of her found-object shelf, she closed her eyes, inhaling deeply and letting her breath out slowly. After a minute or so, she opened her eyes and scanned the ceramics. She skipped over the Goldilocks with braids, a blue-and-white Chinese fisherman, and a white poodle, but reached for the Lladró knockoff, a teen in a flowing gown. Anne ran her fingers over the smooth texture and set it on the table. She picked a few other things that appealed to her: a dollhouse-sized old-fashioned telephone, a cameo charm, a dove in flight, a faux diamond ring, and a starburst pendant.

Anne's phone buzzed. "Hi, Mom. I'm back safe and sound. What did you think of Sergio?"

"He's nice, dear. But are you sure he's really for you?"

"What do you mean?"

"He's so *foreign*."

Anne cringed. "That's one of the things I love about him. Yes, dark and handsome, too."

"If you're sure, then when can we start planning the wedding?"

Anne laughed and sat on a kitchen chair. "We haven't even lived together yet."

"These are modern times, but is that really necessary? What would Aunt Tootie say?"

"Probably something like 'shacking it up with the Italian'? But how else can I tell if Sergio and I are compatible?"

"Don't you know that by now? Maybe you should give him the 'old tomato'?"

"Like Suzi?" Their neighbor had given her then-boyfriend, Tom, an ultimatum, and now she was stuck with three kids, a yard full of knee-deep weeds, and a husband carousing at Barnacle Bill's every night.

Anne believed in the romance of a proposal. Not a videotaped Facebook posting, but a one-of-a-kind, private candlelit dinner. She didn't expect him to get down on his knee at the beach and propose like Brian did with Pootie. Sergio wasn't the type, more the diamond-ring-in-a-champagne-glass type. "I want him to love me enough to ask me himself."

"I'm sure he does and is just waiting for that special moment." Her mom always had such a positive attitude. "Gotta go. Big Avon party this afternoon."

"Good luck!" Anne hung up, musing over what her mother had said about living together. She'd read in *The Sun* that for the first time in the modern era, the majority of couples lived together before marriage. It made perfect sense for her to live with him.

With the painted box dry, she twisted eyelet screws in the top of the inside; tied fishing line to the starburst, ring, and dove; and attached them, making sure they were all at different lengths, as if flying. She glued the ceramic girl to the back of the box underneath the ring, the telephone next to the girl, and the cameo in the forefront. The outside needed one more thing, so she decoupaged a strip of antique lace along each side. Standing back, she studied the assemblage with a smile and felt that rush of proud happiness. Her piece resembled one by Joseph Cornell, one of her favorite artists.

She touched the telephone and pushed the diamond ring back and forth as if it were a swing. "I'm going to call it *Waiting for a Ring*," she said aloud with a laugh.

Then it hit her. Fay and her mother were right. Anne needed a commitment before moving all the way across the country. Sergio hadn't mentioned anything about marriage lately, and they'd really only discussed it in broad terms. Mrs. Landenheim wanted her to sign the new lease, and Anne needed to move forward with her life and make plans. She hated to do it, but she'd have to bring it up to him herself.

She scrolled through her music, located her favorite Beyoncé hit, and shook her booty around the room, singing at the top of her lungs. "'Cause if you liked it, then you should put a ring on it!"

24

The next morning, Clair awoke with a strong desire to see Varinska perform again, to go back to Rudy's in a new outfit so in fashion that even Mr. LeRue would be impressed. As soon as her father left for the office, she went straight to the shop with the rhinestone shoes and stared at them in the window.

She'd love to make them sparkle while she danced, not hide them in her trunk. She shook her head. No, either way, her father would get the bill and realize she'd made an extravagant purchase. He might even get angry. For the first time, he'd recently complained to her about spending too much money. She looked at the shoes with a sigh.

A woman strutted out of the barbershop next door with a striking short haircut. What a dream it would be to have a bob, too! Clair had never been in a barbershop before. Several years ago when women started frequenting them, Clair read in the paper that men had complained. Most barbers now welcomed women.

Clair took a deep breath and entered the shop. The barber gave her a wide smile and nodded to a bench. "*Un momento.*"

She sat on the padded seat while he lathered shaving cream over a reclined customer's face. A sweet lime scent sprang into the air.

The barber had neatly trimmed slicked-back hair and seemed to be only a few years older than Clair. His dark eyes glistened in the light as he stropped a razor on a piece of leather. Like a sculptor, he shaved the customer's face and wrapped a steaming towel around it, reminding her of King Tut's mummy inside his golden sarcophagus. She had read all about him in *National Geographic*.

Soon the barber unwound the towel, put tonic on the man's blond hair, and slicked it back. The dapper man paid and nodded at her as he left the shop.

"Next?" The barber pointed to the empty chair with a smile.

She wished Farley's smile was that kind. Her heart started to beat fast and she contemplated running for the door, but instead she made her way to the vacated chair. She removed her cloche hat and the barber took it from her, hanging it up. He whipped out a cloth like a sail and draped it over her. In the mirror, she watched him take the pins from her hair and set them on the counter. There was no ring on his finger. It felt odd to have a man touch her hair.

"Unusual color, *autunno* leaves. *Bellissimo*." He continued to remove the pins until her hair tumbled down the back of the chair.

"A little trim? Even up the ends, no?" he asked.

She stared at herself in the mirror. It was her hair, not her father's! "A bob, please."

"Are you certain?" Their eyes met. A tingle sputtered in her belly. She yearned to run her hands over his smooth face.

"Yes, thank you." She nodded, closed her eyes tightly, and listened to the *snip, snip, snip* of the scissors. Titillated and terrified at the same time, she tried to breathe and hoped she wouldn't be sorry.

He began to sing "O Sole Mio," one of Clair's favorite Italian arias. She yearned to sing along, but instead simply let herself relax into the music.

It seemed like hours until he said, "*Perfetto*!"

Opening her eyes, she barely recognized the girl in the mirror. The barber dropped Brilliantine on his hands and gently ran his fingers through her locks, wavy now that the weight had been lifted. She turned her head back and forth. Her eyes seemed a lighter brown, her cheekbones more pronounced, her lips brighter.

The barber kissed his fingers. "*Splendido!*"

His voice and manner were so alluring, she wished she could ask him to call. But her father would never approve of her seeing an Italian, let alone a barber.

She checked her watch. "I've got to go!"

"Here, you'll need this. *Complimenti della casa.*" He slipped a bottle of hair oil into a paper bag.

"*Grazie.*" She took it, paid him, and rushed out the door. The air on the back of her neck was cool, the lightness of her head felt fancy-free. She had to get to Rudy's tonight. She couldn't wait to dance in her new hairdo. She hadn't had time to buy a new outfit, but this was even better!

Clair pulled her cloche down over her head and tried to walk nonchalantly into the parlor. Her father worked at his desk.

"Where have you been?" He eyed her.

"Purchasing music." She pointed to the bag.

"Did you do something to your hair? Take off your hat."

She doffed it slowly.

He jumped up and dropped the account book with a gasp. "You've cut your glory! How could you?"

"It's simpler this way."

He stared at her. "But what will Farley say?"

"Farley? Father, I've tried, but he's not for me."

"I disagree." He pulled a handkerchief from his smoking jacket pocket and wiped his brow.

To change the subject she said, "Aren't you home early?"

"I'm not well," he said slowly.

"I'm sorry. Maybe you should lie down for a while?" There was a knock. "I'll get it." Clair walked into the foyer and opened the door.

Mr. O'Shaughnessy stood there, holding a dress box. "Special delivery, Miss Clair."

She took it. "Thank you."

"Good day." He blinked at her new do with a stern face and closed the door.

She lifted the box lid and peeked at the note card resting on tissue paper:

Gal pal,

Made it myself, just for you. Wear it tonight.

There's big doings.

Winnie

"Who was that?"

"Something from the tailor, Father." Clair couldn't wait to see what it was.

"More clothes. Don't you have enough?"

"A girl can never have too many dresses."

He shook his head with a frown. "I don't have the energy to argue with you now. Anyway, what's done is done. I'm skipping dinner and going to bed."

"May I at least order you some tea and toast?"

"No." He coughed and ambled to his room.

Clair was surprised he didn't give her a harder time about her hair. She hurried to her bedroom, opened the box, and pulled out a fringed dress in her favorite color—a deep rose with a sequined headband to match, with feathers, of course. Winnie knew just what she needed. Clair put it all on and studied herself in the mirror. She sure looked the bee's knees.

~

That night as Clair stepped out of the elevator, she tugged her coat closely about her, but Mr. O'Shaughnessy stood in her path.

"Miss Devereaux, your father called down. You must return to the suite."

She had knocked on his bedroom door before leaving, but he didn't answer. She had been certain the coast was clear. But no such luck.

Clenching her fists, she rode the elevator back up. She would tell her father she wasn't a baby anymore. Before opening the door, she straightened up to her full height, and then stomped inside the suite.

He stood in the foyer with arms crossed. "And where did you think you were going, young lady?" His hoarse voice rasped just above a whisper.

She followed him into the parlor. "To a concert."

"With whom?" He sat in his chair.

"Friends."

The line between his eyes deepened to a crease. "Take off your coat."

She hesitated. The tangled knots in her stomach twisted tighter. Her heart beat so loudly she believed he might hear it.

"Remove it." He kept his voice calm, but she could tell he was ready to explode.

With her head down, she took off her coat and laid it on the back of the divan, exposing her new dress.

"Stand there." He pointed.

As she walked backward away from him, the fringe tickled the back of her knees.

"You're going out in that? Where did you get such a horrendous outfit?"

"I bought it."

"Go to your room and take it off. That blasted headpiece, too."

Clair looked him in the eye and put a hand on her hip. "Why?"

He raised his voice. "Because you look like a floozy."

"But it's all the rage." She pursed her lips.

"Not for you, it isn't. Go to your room!"

"But my friends are waiting."

"Who? That shopgirl you've been gadabouting with? I know what you've been up to."

Clair shook her head in disbelief. Who had alerted her father? Had it been Mr. LeRue, or perhaps Mr. O'Shaughnessy?

"You're not to associate with her type."

"What type?"

He raised his voice. "Full of shenanigans! Up to no good."

Clair rolled her eyes. Frustration seethed below her placid surface. "Winifred is a sweet girl."

"Where does she live?"

"Nearby." Clair couldn't tell him Winnie lived in a boardinghouse. She put her coat back on and moved to the window seat. The street had filled with folks who had the freedom to come and go as they pleased.

"Girls these days think they can do whatever they want," he growled.

She turned toward him. "Perhaps you haven't noticed, but it's 1929, and girls *get to do* what they want now."

"You don't mean that, dear." Her father gave a grunt. "Go change."

"But it's the fashion!"

Suddenly he jumped up, raised his hand, and stepped toward her. "No sass, missy, or I'll—!"

Frightened, Clair pulled back. He had never threatened to harm her. His voice was so loud, everyone in the building might hear.

He put his hands in his pockets. "You're acting just like your mother."

"My mother? What do you mean?"

"A tramp, that's all." Then his eyes clouded over. He slowly returned to his chair and put his head in his hands.

"What about Mama?"

"I'm not going to say anything else, except don't follow in her footsteps."

"What footsteps?" Clair moved to him.

"Darling, you're not a hussy. So don't act like one." He shook his head slowly and gazed into her eyes. "You need to keep your reputation intact. We need to hold onto Farley. If he finds out you've been gallivanting about . . ."

"Farley!" She stamped her foot. "Is he all you can think about?"

"What's wrong with him?"

"I don't love him."

"Love? What do you know about love?"

"Not much, but I'd like to learn." She wanted to remind him he'd married for love, but now she was confused.

"Go change, bring that monstrosity to me, and I'll throw it in the trash can where it belongs. You're no tramp."

"First tell me what you meant about Mama."

"I'll speak of her no more. You are no tramp, that's all."

"Maybe I am!" She ran to her room, slammed the door, dropped onto the bed, and sobbed into her pillow. She had really wanted to go to Rudy's.

A reputation wasn't so important in this day and age. Many girls from the speakeasy had been known to be out dancing with a man, and that didn't seem to harm them. Winnie wasn't like that. Clair wouldn't even consider having relations before marriage. As a good girl, all she did was dance. And maybe sip a little hooch.

She cried again, perplexed by his comment about her mother.

Had she really been a tramp? Clair had always been certain her father had loved her mother, but now she wasn't so sure.

The next morning, Clair begged her father to tell her what he had meant by his harsh words about her mother, but he refused to talk about it. As soon as he left for work, Clair snatched her wadded dress out of the trash can by his desk and hid it in the bottom of the trunk in her bedroom.

That afternoon she called Aunt June, hoping she would shed some light. "Father accused me of being a tramp like my mother. I don't understand. I thought he loved her."

Aunt June paused. "My sister was a handful."

"What do you mean?"

"She had a wild streak."

Clair sat up straight. "No one ever told me that." She probed Aunt June for more details, but she was tightlipped and hung up quickly, pleading a headache.

Her mother had been wild. No wonder Clair's father had been so angry.

25

That evening, Anne resolved to bring up the topic of commitment with Sergio. Writing on a sticky note, she wrote a new affirmation: *I am worthy*. She stuck it on the bathroom mirror and closed the bathroom door to practice in the full-length mirror.

Hand on her head, she leaned in a bit and raised her eyebrows. "Hey, big boy, how about a proposal?"

She clasped her hands in front of her. "Please ask me to marry you?"

Too blatant, better to start more subtly. "Are we in a committed relationship?"

That sounded about right. When they FaceTimed later, she'd ask him.

She filled the tub, tossed in a pink bubble bath bomb, stripped, and climbed in. On the edge of the tub, she lit two candles, one for herself and one for Sergio, and practiced her line, "Are we in a committed relationship?"

Where they would get married would be a challenge. With his family in Italy, hers in Michigan, and friends in San Francisco and New York, it could get quite complicated. Anne didn't crave a giant Bridezilla affair. She imagined herself in a vintage lace minidress and a short flyaway veil. Pootie, of course, would be her maid of honor, and Baby Brian could hold the pillow with the rings on it. He'd look so cute in a tux. Ha! Here was Anne planning her wedding and they weren't even engaged yet.

Out of the tub, she dolled up—in a lace nightgown with her hair zhuzhed. She sent Sergio a photo of *Waiting for a Ring* and tried to relax.

He called ten minutes later. "*Buona sera*." He smiled, handsome in his tank top, his hair pulled into a sleek ponytail.

"*Si. Buona sera*." She tried a sexy voice and shimmied her shoulders.

"*Sei bellissima*."

"*Grazie*."

He held his hands up toward the screen. "I wish I could jump through the phone and be there with you."

"Me, too. Thanks again for coming to Michigan. I feel bad you didn't have a better time."

He nodded. "I did learn a lot about you."

"Good or bad?"

"Both." He laughed.

She decided to change the subject. "What do you think of my new piece?"

"It's hard to see the details in the photo. But from what I could tell, I like it. What are you calling it?"

"*Waiting for a Ring*." Hint, hint.

"Do you mean ring as in call or ring as in diamond?"

"Either or both."

"*Magnifico*. Double meaning." He nodded his head.

Anne inhaled and let it out. "Sergio, are we in a committed relationship?"

He frowned. "Of course."

"We are? But we never discussed it."

"I told you I love you."

"But does that mean commitment? Since we live so far from each other, how can we have a commitment until I move there?"

He frowned. "Do you mean you want to go out with other guys?"

"No, not at all!" She shook her head.

"What is it, then?"

She hesitated. "Well . . . a ring." There went her subtle hint.

His eyes opened wide. "An engagement ring?"

"Yes. I think—"

"I'll be there next month. We'll talk about it in person then."

"I can't wait!"

They said good night, and she hung up and did a fist pump. "Yes!" He had heard her, and he would propose.

Too excited to sleep, she tossed an old paint shirt on over her nightie, turned on some Enya, and started another piece. When you're on a roll, you're on a roll. From her found-object shelf she grabbed a ceramic bust of a girl wearing a pink dress with a lace-embroidered collar, hair in an updo. For some reason it reminded Anne of the tall girl in the photo. The figurine's eyes were closed, hands in prayer position. As Anne held the piece in her hand, she ran her fingers over the details, and a fresh rose scent filled the air. The intoxicating aroma drifted through the room, and the girl seemed to wink at her. Dizzy, Anne sat on the daybed until the scent diminished. She rubbed the figurine, but the scent didn't come alive again and neither did the girl.

I must have imagined it.

She located a silver tray with ornate edges and fancy handles in her goody cupboard, put it on the table, and set the girl in the middle. Then she rifled though a shoebox full of random objects, picking out items and placing them on the tray: a rusty key, a plastic rose, a tram token, a rhinestone star from a hair clip, a pair of doll-sized sunglasses, a refrigerator magnet with a vintage pair of robins, an old wristwatch, dance shoes from a charm bracelet, and a compass.

Anne's chest began to hum, and she held her breath as she manipulated the objects surrounding the girl. Losing track of time and space, it was all about making art. She found a pair of *milagro* wings almost two inches across and put them behind the girl. She added a tiny plate from a miniature tea set behind the girl's head for a halo. Now the girl resembled an angel. Anne's hands moved fast as she glued down the pieces.

She pulled jars out of boxes until she found black tiles and periwinkle-blue florist gems, then glued them to the tray's border for a finishing edge. To fill the gaps between them she took up a chipped floral plate, put it in a paper bag on her cutting board, broke it with a hammer, and glued the pieces in between the tiles and the colorful gems.

Even though Anne had taken a mosaic course in college, mosaics had never been her thing. At least not until now! She was handling the pieces gently, but one moved under her finger. She'd better let them dry before filling in the space between pieces.

The class had used grout, the same kind used in kitchen and bathrooms, but she hated the gritty texture, so she searched for a neater solution. She squished glue between the spaces and used a teeny paintbrush to fill in the gaps. Dumping faux pearls from a Michael's sale into a bowl, she added the pearls to the edge one at a time using needle-nose pliers. After a while she got into a meditative rhythm. Time flew by until she finished, and she stepped back and studied it. The pearls gave it an exquisite unifying effect.

Finding Her Way, that's what she'd call it! She clapped her hands. In the 1920s, girls certainly didn't have a lot of decisions to make in life. They were probably all virgins when they got married, too. Anne wished her life could be so simple.

26

Since the day of Clair's haircut, her father had kept an eagle eye on her, and boring Farley had continued to come over. To lull them into complacency, she had put every effort into appearing demure and sweet. Three weeks later to the day, she couldn't stand it any longer. After her father left for a meeting, she slipped on the fringed dress, threw on her pearls, put a dab of rose water behind each ear, and snuck out through the kitchen.

By the time the cab dropped her off, the band had already struck up and the dance floor was filled with revelers. Rudy hadn't greeted her at the door, so she looked around on her own. She spotted Bea shimmying, but fortunately Mr. LeRue wasn't anywhere to be seen.

The energy of the speakeasy ignited Clair's senses. Readjusting the beaded headband, she wiggled the fringe on her dress and stood up tall. This was where she truly belonged.

She tracked Winnie down at their usual table. Her rhinestone-studded headpiece was stunning, reminding Clair of the shoes in the shop window. She slid into a seat beside her friend and asked, "Is that your newest creation?"

Winnie's eyes lit up, and she gave her friend a squeeze. "Yes, doll! Ooh, I knew that color would be perfect!"

"It's my favorite. Thanks for the gift."

Winnie smiled proudly. "Made the headband, too. Those pearls are to die for." She fingered the necklace and moved to Clair's hair. "And that bob! It so suits you. Where've you been?"

Clair frowned. "In prison."

"That big talker still panting?"

"A date's been set for the spring."

"You're not going to marry him, are you?"

Clair shrugged. "I have no choice. If not, I'll never be able to get out."

"Don't be silly. You're here tonight. You must protest. If he insists, run away."

"Where would I go?"

"You could stay with me in the boardinghouse."

"That's very kind of you." Clair would keep that in mind. "How's it going with Rudy?"

"He's stuck on me." Winnie giggled, looking past her.

"Did you ever doubt it?" Clair laughed.

Rudy came toward them with a grin and put their glasses on the table. "Hi, gal pal!" He grabbed another chair and sat down.

"Boy, the joint's jumping tonight." Clair took a sip of her drink.

Rudy nodded. "Varinska is reeling them in. She just finished her set."

"You mean I missed it?" Clair asked. Darn.

"Don't worry, she'll be on again." He waved across the room. "Want to meet her?"

"Would I ever!" Clair had never been near anyone so exotic before.

Varinska sauntered toward them in her gypsy regalia, ignoring the man who reached toward her to try and get her to sit with him.

"Darlink!" She smiled at Rudy.

"Have a seat." He stood, and she settled into his chair.

"Can I have a drink?" she asked.

"You know the rules." He frowned at her.

Varinska tilted her head dramatically to the sky. "Performers no *drink* when *work*." Her heavily accented voice resonated in a slow cadence. "Cigarette me, Rudy." She smoothed down her hair and leaned over toward him, exposing her décolletage, which was covered in coin necklaces. He didn't even seem to notice.

Rudy removed a Lucky from an enameled case in his coat pocket, lit it, and handed it to her.

"*Danke*." Varinska gave him a wry smile, stuck the cigarette in an ivory holder, and took a drag, leaving a tinge of crimson lipstick on it.

The barman motioned to Rudy. "Excuse me," he said, walking away.

"Varinska, this is our friend Clair Devereaux," Winnie said.

The singer put out her hand. "'Ello." With one eyebrow raised, she gazed at Clair.

Starstruck, Clair had a thousand things to say, but all she managed was, "You perform so freely."

"I came to America for freedom. Free is vhat's important. Keep no matter vhat!"

"We were just discussin' that!" Winnie said.

Clair looked at Winnie with a grin.

Varinska forced a bleak smile and sipped from Winnie's glass. "Must rest before go back to stage. Show takes all strength." She rested an arm over her brow, stood, and dramatically wandered through the crowd and out of sight.

"Wow!" Clair smiled.

The band began to play "Yes Sir, That's My Baby." Winnie grabbed Clair's arm and pulled her onto the dance floor.

Clair shimmied to the rhythm, enthralled by the exhilarating feeling of fringe moving on her body. She stepped one foot out and then the other, eventually swinging her arms back and forth, too. As she became one with the music, the force of her movements grew wilder. She leaned forward, whipping the pearls around her neck with glee, but her hand got caught in them, and they broke and flew off onto the wooden floor in all directions.

"Oh, no!" Down on her hands and knees, the crowd continued to dance around her. Afraid someone might step on a pearl and slip, she rapidly gathered up beads and called for Winnie to help, but she was dancing and couldn't hear her over the music. Clair scooted over to their table and tossed them into her bag. A man knelt beside her, scooped up a handful of pearls, and dropped them into her bag, too.

She looked over at him and smiled a thank-you. He was a stranger. In the dim light, all she could make out were his eyes, radiant with laughter. Her heart pumped rapidly. She didn't know if it was from the dancing, the excitement of the necklace breaking, or from being shoulder to shoulder with this young man. Together they followed the trail of pearls to a table, picking up beads as they crawled underneath it.

They continued to fill her purse with the pearls until they could find no more.

"Thanks!" she yelled over the music.

Curtained by the tablecloth, the man pulled her to him for a kiss. He tasted good, salty and tart like olives. She knew she should push him away, but unable to help herself, she closed her eyes and kissed him back.

A loud, shrill whistle shrieked twice. Not bells and whistles, but just a whistle. The band stopped playing and there were screams.

"You're all under arrest!" a man's voice shouted.

Clair started to lift up the tablecloth, but the young man pulled her back and shook his head at her.

She heard Rudy's voice. "Run! Don't give them your real names."

"What's happening?" Clair's hands began to shake.

The man spoke close to her ear, "A raid."

"I've got to get to Winnie." Clair tried to scoot out from under the table, but the man grabbed her foot and pulled her back to him. Sounds like stampeding horses ravaged her ears, and she held him tight. Then more screams, the smashing of glass, and the roar of angry voices.

Clair put her hands over her ears and closed her eyes as the man held her in his arms. After what seemed like an eon, the speakeasy became pitch-black. Loud footfalls and a beam of light from an electric torch streaked around their table, then disappeared.

When it grew quiet, the man put a finger to his lips, lifted the cloth, and looked out. "Stay here," he whispered.

She peeked out while he walked the speakeasy's perimeter.

"The coast seems clear." He picked up her purse and helped her crawl out from under the table. The floor was sticky beneath her shoes, and the speakeasy smelled of smoke, hooch, and danger. She looked up at him. He was half a foot taller than she was.

"Where is everyone?" she asked.

"Those that got caught are probably in jail."

"Rudy and Winnie? Varinska?" Clair couldn't even imagine what her father's reaction would have been if she'd gotten arrested. "I need to go."

"It's not safe yet. The police will be keeping an eye on the building. Come with me."

His hand on the small of her back, he guided her, avoiding the broken glass. Winnie's hat lay trampled on the dance floor, and Clair's stomach clenched. Behind the bar, the young man's hand groped, searching for something. A moment later he pulled a lever and a door flew open.

"What's this?" she asked, ducking to follow him through into a dark hallway.

"Probably where they hide the stash."

She realized the crates lining the hall must be filled with liquor.

They continued along until the path emptied into a back room. He lit a candle on the desk with a match. She could make out his face, his visage more handsome than she'd originally seen in the dim light of the club—wavy hair, a strong nose, clean-shaven face. He gazed at her with sapphire-blue eyes.

Sitting beside her on a red velvet chaise, he asked, "Who taught you to dance like that?"

"No one."

"You must be a natural." His voice was rich, with a touch of an accent she couldn't quite place. He kissed her again. This was it—heart-pounding, magnetic, full-body desire. Love! This was the way she had always dreamed it would be.

He pushed her down onto the chaise. His lips on hers, his arms wrapped her up in an erotic heat that she couldn't resist. His hands roamed and she let them. Furnace-hot, she encouraged him to remove her dress, revealing the lacy corset.

"Oh!" He smiled and kept going, kept going, and kept going. The fever drew her to him on the velvet chaise. She wasn't a bit afraid. She had never wanted anything more in her whole life.

Afterward, he pulled a shawl from the back of the chaise over their naked bodies, and she drifted off to sleep.

A clock chimed in the distance, waking her. The candle had gone out. She had no idea how long she had slept, but she knew her life had been transformed. The man continued to sleep, his breathing soft and slow. She inhaled the manly scent of him: tangy hair oil, sweet sweat, and sex.

Gray light seeped into the room through a grimy window. The man slept on his back. His hair was the color of wet beach sand, and his lips formed a slight smile. A few lines creased the corner of his eyes. He might be a few years older than she'd imagined, but not too old for her. She couldn't wait to get to know him better. Still asleep, he rolled toward her and put his hand on her arm.

She noticed a shiny glint on his left ring finger, a band of gold.

He must be married! How could he have made love to her if he was already married? Her recently ignited heart flickered and grew cold. What had she done?

In silence, she dressed quickly, picked up her clutch, and slipped down the hallway back out into the bar area. She found her coat in the cloakroom, pulled open the heavy front door, and stepped into the fresh air.

A quarter moon hovered in the western sky like a white parachute. Not a soul was in sight. She hurried up the stairs to the street. The man's sensuous scent still surrounded her. How could she have been so naive?

27

Before Clair entered the suite, she ran her fingers through her hair and braced herself for a confrontation. To her relief, her father's bedroom door was closed. In her room she looked in the mirror. Her red hair still bounced about her face; her eyes were still brown. Her cheeks were still milky white, and she touched them, their smooth softness reassuring. The outside visage remained the same, but everything else about her was different.

The realization that sexual relations could be so wonderful suffused her with regret. She was so mixed-up. Lust, fear, and disappointment mingled with shame, guilt, and sorrow.

But the man had been so beautiful. And now she had experienced what it was to have a lover. My God, she could never do that with Farley!

She dumped the pearls from the clutch onto her satin feather pillow and deposited them into an envelope. Slipping out of the dress, she hid it deep in her trunk. She washed her face but opted not to take a shower.

Under the sheets she closed her eyes, taking pleasure in his scent and replaying the night's images in her mind. The jazz, the pearls flying, the threatening police whistles, the man holding her safe under the table with his kisses and caresses, the velvet chaise below her body—and the ring.

Questions tumbled in Clair's mind like ocean rocks. How could she face her father across the breakfast table? Would he be able to tell what she'd done? How could she get away, and to where?

Their vacation cottage called to her, the one place in the world where she always felt at peace. It sat on a promontory where a sandy beach met lapping waves that darkened rounded stones. This time of year, the off-season enclave would be deserted and would provide the perfect respite.

She pulled her valise from the armoire and started to pack. It wasn't necessary to take much. Her dresser drawers were filled with swimsuits, blouses, stockings, and such. A favorite sun hat hung on the hall tree at the entry.

Clair sat on her bed with tears in her eyes. Her father would be furious if she left the city without telling him. But she needed to be alone and consider her options. She had no idea how much time he would allow her. A month would be heavenly, but she couldn't imagine her father would let her stay away that long. She grabbed the valise, threw some essentials into it, and tossed the envelope of pearls on top.

She dipped her pen in blue ink and started to jot a quick message. It was so quiet she could hear the nib scratch across the page.

Gone to cottage. Need time to think about Farley.

Love, Clair

She quietly closed her bedroom door. Glad for the thick carpets, she tiptoed down the hall, propped the note on his desk, ruffled through a drawer for his spare cash, and helped herself. Stealing out of the suite, she rode the elevator to the lobby and rushed outside. The street had already filled with folks hurrying on their way to work. A smokestack puffed soot, wilting the reddish-orange morning sky to a dingy brown.

"Extra! Extra!" Nook stepped in front of Clair, his freckled face endearing. "Mornin', miss. Paper?"

Clair shook her head. "Not today."

He flipped it over and called, "Speakeasy Raided!"

"I've changed my mind." She handed him a coin and took a paper.

"Penny for my thoughts?" He smiled his missing-tooth grin.

"Sorry, Nook. No time today, but here's another penny."

He caught it, jumped high in the air, twirled, and landed squarely on his feet. "Thank you, miss!"

Clair's eyes grew wide as she studied a photo. Police were piling folks into the back of a paddy wagon. Prominently displayed, Beatrice's face looked out the back. Her poor parents would be scandalized. Clair imagined them in church next Sunday—her mother's tearstained face lifted to the altar, her father's head gazing down.

Someone bumped into Clair.

"Sorry!" the woman said, and kept on walking.

Clair stowed the paper under her arm and started down the street. A vendor unpacking colorful fruit into his stall held an apple toward her. She wasn't hungry but knew she might be later, so she accepted it and paid him. Fortunately the jeweler had just opened up, so she dropped off the pearls to be restrung.

She walked the few blocks to Grand Central. The turquoise constellation ceiling rose high above her, and she couldn't wait to be at the cottage under a real canopy of stars. She stood in line to buy a ticket and then waited restlessly on a bench for her train to be called. Wanting to keep an eye out for her father, she resisted the urge to go back to her paper.

Finally she boarded the train, tossed her bag in the overhead rack, and settled into a window seat, making sure to sit on the east side for a better view of the Atlantic. Unrolling the paper, she searched for photos of Rudy, Winnie, and Varinska, but couldn't identify them.

SPEAKEASY RAIDED!

Beatrice Beach Bernard arrested for assaulting an officer with her handbag. Glasses filled with alcohol were found on the premises, but no hidden liquor was discovered.

Clair read the rest of the article but didn't recognize any of the other names. As the train whistle blew, she relaxed back on the leather seat, watching the city disappear. She felt gratitude to the nameless man. If he hadn't saved her, she might have been in the paper, too—or even in jail.

Miles out of town, the scenery changed from sooty darkness and skyscrapers to acres and acres of farmland, and trees in the midst of changing to fiery fall colors. A cow grazed beside a large red barn, and chickens scattered as the train chugged past. Dust swirled around a pair of horses in a pasture as they kicked up their hooves. Her mother and aunt had grown up on a farm. Clair had always wondered what it would be like to live with rows of corn or wheat as neighbors instead of other hotel patrons.

Her mother, the farm girl. Her mother, the tramp. Now that Clair was a sullied woman, was she a tramp, too?

Her mind drifted to the previous night, and she relived each moment. Those deep kisses, his warm hands, and her desire-filled body beneath his. His strong shoulders above her. The tangy taste of his tongue, the velvet chaise beneath her, all of him—inside her.

Had he known the raid was coming? Was that why he helped her, or was it preordained destiny for them to be under the table at the moment the police arrived? Chances were she'd never find out or even see him again. Did he live in New York City? Perhaps she'd pass him on the street or in Central Park pushing a pram for his pretty wife. Inside would be a darling baby resembling him, with blue eyes and wavy hair, too.

She wished she had at least asked the man his name. She'd call him "Mr. X." It would be better than thinking of him as "him" or "that man." If she had waited, she might have even inquired why he made love to her when he had a wife waiting at home. Clair already knew the answer, though. Why does any man have affairs or mistresses?

Her father was different than most men and hadn't stepped out with a woman since her mother died. Clair always believed it was because he had loved her mother so much. But now Clair wasn't so sure. Once she had asked him if he wished for another sweetheart, but he said, "No, you're my best girl." It suddenly dawned on her that he could have been with other women without her knowledge.

A marriage to Farley was out of the question now that she knew the thrill of true attraction. She tried to reprehend herself for letting go and submitting to temptation. In fact, now she understood what the priest had meant when he said that lust was a sin. But she couldn't have pulled herself away even if she had wanted to.

28

Wind whipped Anne's apartment, whistling as loud as a jet plane. She snuggled back into her cozy bed, glad she could sleep in. Sergio wouldn't be there until the next day, so she had plenty of time to clean up her place. Being on such a creative roll lately, it had been impossible to keep it neat.

The buzzer rang. Who would come by in this weather? She got up and threw on a big T-shirt.

"Yes?" she yelled into the intercom.

"Surprise!"

"Sergio?" Her heart cartwheeled. *Oh my God!* He was a day early.

"*Si*, it's me."

"Come on up!" She buzzed him in, raced to brush her teeth, and ran her hands over her hair. Hearing his feet tromp up the stairs, she tossed a towel over the dishes in the sink and kicked a pile of clothes under the bed. When he knocked, she sauntered over and opened the door. With his windblown hair he looked as handsome as ever. It had been a month since their Michigan trip.

He stepped inside, embraced her, and closed the door with his foot. Pushing her straight back onto the daybed, he gave her a long and luscious kiss.

"Hello, big boy," she murmured. "I'm glad to . . ."

"Shhh." He kissed her neck and kept going.

Afterward, Anne smiled. "You don't waste any time, do you?"

"*Perché dovrei?*" He shrugged with a wicked smile.

"How'd you get here a day early?" she asked.

"A meeting got canceled, and I thought I'd surprise you."

"You sure did." Maybe he couldn't wait to propose.

Despite the noise of the wind, Sergio soon fell back to sleep. Mrs. Landenheim's Siamese mewed outside the door. Anne knew she never should have started placing scraps there. That scallywag would pester her forever. Anne pulled on a robe, filled a bowl for the cat, and set it out for him. She made a pot of coffee, then crawled back into bed.

Sergio looked so sweet asleep, his curly hair soft on the pillow. He was the one. She'd known it even on the first night they met at her friend's gallery opening in New York. When Anne had doubted whether she was a real artist, he had said: *If you pick up a paintbrush, therefore, you are an artist.* He wasn't an artist himself but had an interest in the arts and listened attentively whenever she talked about her work. He always viewed her new pieces and gave her positive feedback, boosting her confidence in the process.

As if reading her thoughts, he opened his eyes, stretched, and smiled, saying, "Show them to me."

"I already have! But I'll do it again." She jumped up on the bed, opened her robe, and flashed him.

He laughed. "Not that! Your newest inspirations."

She giggled, closed her robe, and leaped off the bed—just catching herself from tripping. She had hoped they'd talk about their relationship, but she wanted him to bring it up first.

She picked up the photo from the altar and handed it to him. "Careful, it's fragile."

He studied it for a moment. "These do look like the pearls." He flipped it over and read the back.

"Aren't the girls lovely?"

He nodded and set the photo on the coffee table.

She picked up *Finding Her Way* by the handles and presented it to him as if it were a sacred relic.

"Look at all those pearls. You've got a theme going." His fingers caressed the pearls she'd used instead of grout. One popped off and fell onto the sheets. "Oops, sorry."

She scooped it up. "No problem. It happens all the time. Have you been by the shop lately?" She leaned the mosaic against the wall so they could view it.

"Every week, but it's still closed."

"That is so weird." The aroma of coffee dripping into the carafe roused her. She poured them each a cup.

"Here's *Waiting for a Ring*." She placed the assemblage on the coffee table beside him.

He rolled over and propped himself up on his hand.

She hoped he'd understand the significance, but he didn't seem to. "You study it and I'll fix us breakfast!" In anticipation of his visit, she had even bought groceries.

"Uh-oh." He cringed with a laugh.

"You'll live." Last time she tried to cook oatmeal for him, it boiled over and stuck to the pot and stove.

Whenever she stayed with him, while she wiled away the mornings in bed reading the *New York Times*, he'd prepare extravagant morning feasts: eggs Benedict, French toast, vegetable frittata. At night he usually took her to the most delicious gourmet restaurants. It was a wonder she hadn't gained fifty pounds.

From the fridge she took out the egg carton, but it slipped from her fingers and all but one of the eggs broke on the floor.

"Need some help?" He glanced her way.

"No, thanks. I've got it." Scrunching up her nose, she wiped up the mess as the eggs slipped and slid. She threw it all in a baggie and tossed it in the trash.

She nuked some leftover pizza, put it on a floral antique plate from her stash, and joined him in bed. "Not what I'd planned, but I did heat it up."

"Thanks, Martha Stewart." He took a bite with a smile.

Anne rolled her eyes.

They ate their pizza and lolled the afternoon away reading, napping, and chatting. She waited for him to bring up the topic of marriage, but he didn't.

In the late afternoon he said, "I know it's early, but I'm getting hungry. Put on your green dress, baby. Where's somewhere romantic you'd like to go?"

"Top of the Mark. Best place in the city to view the sunset, eat tapas, and drink martinis."

"Let's get this party started! Wear your rhinestone shoes, and we'll take the cable car up the hill." Sergio made his way into the bathroom and turned on the shower.

Anne twirled around the room. *Tonight's the night!*

29

Anne put her hair in an updo, donned the sexy silver shoes, and did a quick rumba—or what she thought was a rumba. She couldn't help it, every time she put on the glittery shoes, she felt like dancing. Glancing in the mirror, she hoped she looked pretty enough to propose to.

Freshly shaven, Sergio came out of the bathroom, ponytailed hair still damp, tight jeans and white dress shirt on.

"Looking hot." She smiled at him.

He checked her out. "You, too."

The green dress, a favorite secondhand-shop find, was the one she'd worn on the night she met him. She had been embarrassed because everyone else in the New York gallery had worn black. Sergio had admired her dress and said she appealed to him precisely because she didn't fit in with that crowd.

He threw on a sports jacket, and Anne donned her velvet coat. They trekked down the stairs and stepped outside. The sky had filled with dark clouds. Bouncing on a gust of wind, a seagull squealed above them. Sergio took Anne's hand as they crossed the street, walked half a block, and waited for a cable car on the corner. One soon stopped, packed to the brim.

The conductor raised two fingers and yelled, "Two, room for two. Jump on, rear to rear and cheek to cheek."

Sergio helped Anne climb aboard and jumped on. They sardined themselves into the back and held onto a pole. As the car rose up California Street, buildings passed by: the Painted Ladies, the local Laundromat, Nob Hill Hardware. They hopped off at the top of the rise in front of the Mark Hopkins Hotel. A tony couple got out of a limo, and a bellman piled their luggage from the trunk onto a cart. Anne and Sergio followed the couple into the lobby and took the elevator up to the nineteenth floor. At the Top of the Mark, the line for a table snaked all the way back to the elevator.

"The view is worth waiting for. Can you hold off for a while to eat?" Anne asked. It would be the perfect place for a proposal.

"Even though that breakfast pizza was very filling, I don't think so. I'm hungry now."

Anne tried not to be too disappointed as they rode the elevator back down.

They hiked around the corner just in time to catch the sunset. She snuggled up close to him, his body shielding her from the wind, while clouds reflected over the bay, bursting like pink-and-violet-paint-filled balloons.

As the blush shades faded, she turned, kissed him, and raised her eyebrows expectantly. *Hey, handsome, propose already.*

Sergio said, "Where to now? I'm starving!"

She paused with a sigh. "Let's go to the Fairmont's Tonga Room across the street? It might be a little touristy, but it's been recently restored and got good write-ups." *Yes, dimly lit and romantic!*

They crossed the street and entered the Fairmont's side door. Down a hallway, they found the tiki-laden entrance, where a group of tourists waited behind a plastic vine used to rope them off.

"How long is the wait?" Sergio asked the hostess at the podium.

"I can take you now. Follow me." Her dark hair was swept up in a vintage movie-star style with a Polynesian sari wrapped tightly around her frame.

Anne and Sergio followed her across the wooden dance floor and through the Hurricane Bar, which resembled a pirate ship. The bar was crowded, but there were plenty of empty tables in the restaurant—never a good sign.

They were seated next to an Olympic-sized pool. Plastic bromeliads and ferns were draped on pillars. A palm-fronded bandstand stood on one end. Anne studied the room. *Uh-oh.* It was more tacky than kitschy. Would Sergio hate it?

She gazed at the pool. "I should have brought my fishing pole." On second thought, maybe she shouldn't have brought that up.

Sergio laughed and reached for her hands. "You are *fantastico*."

"You, too." *Here it comes.*

He looked into her eyes and said, "Will you—"

A loud whooshing noise was followed by a blast of wet air on her shoulders. She screamed, then giggled as a cascade of water fell at the far end of the pool. Lights flashed and thunder boomed. A cheesy recording of African jungle drums played.

"This place is more like Disneyland than Disneyland." Sergio grimaced.

"It's a combination of the Tiki Room and *Pirates of the Caribbean*."

They read the names off the drink menu aloud.

"Tonga Kong!" Sergio raised his arms like King Kong.

"Fog Cutter." She swam her arms in front of her. "Hurry Kane." She raised and swirled them above her head.

A tattooed Hawaiian-shirted waiter asked, "What'll you have?"

"I'll have a Mai Tai," she said. *Why not?*

"A Sapporo for me. Waters, too."

The waiter nodded and moved away.

They studied their menus.

"What looks good to you, Big Foot?"

She loved it when he called her that. He'd called her that since the first night they met when he noticed how big her feet were. "You're the foodie. Why don't you choose?"

"Okay." Tracing the columns with his finger, he perused the entire menu.

The waiter set down their drinks and started to leave.

Sergio called out, and the waiter turned back. "We're ready to order. We'll have pot stickers, the Royal Pu Pu Platter, and coconut-encrusted shrimp."

"Coming right up." The waiter moved over to a table at the other side of the room.

Anne removed the paper umbrella from her drink and took a sip. "Ew. It's all rum and no juice."

Sergio gulped some of his beer and nearly spit it out. "It's warm!" He looked for some water.

"The food is supposed to be good, though."

"Let's hope so."

After two more cycles of thunderstorms, it wasn't funny anymore. After twenty-five minutes, the waiter tossed their food on their table and left.

"What a mess! I can't eat this."

"It'll taste fine." She stabbed into a piece of smothered-in-sauce crab, and tried to chew it. It took some effort to swallow the conglomeration. She put down her fork. "Real poo-poo is more like it." Tears of disappointment stung her eyes.

"Let's go." Sergio tried to get the waiter's attention, but unable to do so, he stood and threw some cash on top of their food.

Outside in the hallway he asked, "Have any more of that pizza at home?"

"No. The restaurant upstairs is supposed to be great, but a bit pricey."

They rode the elevator up to the lobby and entered the elegant

Laurel Court, a marble-pillared room with lovely hand-painted trompe l'oeil murals of tall junipers and European architecture. However, a sign said that it was closed for a private party.

The noisy bar beside it, stuffed with formally dressed patrons likely ditching the ballroom's fundraiser, didn't have any seats available.

Sergio and Anne shimmied up to the bar. He ordered potato skins, shrimp skewers, and olives to go. Her heels hurt her feet as they walked down the hill toward her place. At Grace Cathedral, Anne spotted Mata Hari curled up in a side doorway.

The homeless woman sat up when they approached. "Who's the hottie?"

Anne smiled. "My boyfriend, Sergio."

"The New Yorker. I've heard about you." Mata Hari grinned her toothless smile and eyed the food.

Sergio handed her a potato skin. "All good, I'm sure. Anne's told me all about you, too."

Mata Hari sniffed it. "Are you being good to Missy?"

"Of course." He nodded.

"Got any cash to spare?"

"Sure." He pulled out his wallet and handed her a few bills.

Mata Hari hid the money between her saggy breasts and curled back up. "He's a keeper, darling! Run along. I've got to get my beauty rest." She pulled a satin sleeping mask over her eyes.

"Sweet dreams," Anne's voice sang as they continued down the hill.

"So sad." Sergio shook his head.

"The homeless population here has gotten out of control. Pretty soon all of the artists will be homeless, too. This city has become so expensive."

"Speaking of that, have you signed your lease yet?"

"No, I thought we'd better talk first."

He nodded but didn't say a word.

Upstairs, they ate and listened to music and went to bed early. The subject never came back up.

The next morning, with Sergio beside her, Anne pulled Tweety out of the parking garage and cruised to Golden Gate Park. Before the crowds arrived, they rode the elevator up to the de Young's observation deck. It would be the perfect place for a proposal. But foggy weather made the usually spectacular view invisible. They took in the museum and afterward walked the gardens.

Faded by a dreary sun, the sky seemed to be covered in a matte wash. Geraniums in brilliant jewel tones lined the walkway while juniper branches twisted in the wind. Her skirt kept lifting like an umbrella, and she kept pushing it down to her boots.

Finally, Sergio led her to a concrete bench next to a secluded pond where giant lilies floated. Anne huddled inside the black coat and fingered the key in her pocket.

He looked into her eyes and sighed. "You know I'm crazy about you. I call you all the time. I laugh at your silly antics. When we're together, I can't keep my hands off you."

"That's lust, not love."

"Is that all you think this is?" He crossed his arms.

"No." She shook her head.

"And when we aren't together, I miss you. Please come live with me." He took her hand.

She needed to stick to her decision. "But I can't move to New York yet."

"Why not?" He dropped her hand.

She hesitated and swallowed back tears. "You don't love me enough."

"What do you mean? I love you!" His words drifted in the air and flew away.

"I love you, too, but I need a commitment before I give up everything I have here and move all that way." Tears welled up in her eyes.

"But we are committed."

"Don't you want to marry me?" Anne grabbed a Kleenex from her backpack and dried the tears streaming down her face.

"Of course, probably, someday."

Anne swallowed. "That's not a for-sure, then. When will you know?"

"It's hard to say. We should live together awhile to make sure."

"Aren't you sure by now?" She blew her nose.

"Sort of. But I need to be one hundred percent certain. An engagement to be married is a forever commitment, no matter what." He paused.

"Is it because I'm a slob? Are you worried I'll make a mess of your place?"

"I have a maid, and besides, you promised to keep your things in their place."

"Is it my cooking skills?"

He smiled. "That doesn't matter. I love to cook."

"Then what is it?"

He shrugged.

"I don't need to get married now, just to know we're planning to."

"I'm sorry, Anne. I guess I'm just not ready."

She dried her tears and wadded up the tissue.

He looked away. "Since we want different things, maybe we should break up."

She twisted the Kleenex in her hand. "Break up? But I love you, and you love me, too. If that's true, why don't you want to marry me?"

He looked down. "I'm not sure. I guess because marriage is more than just loving someone." He pulled out his phone and pressed a button. "I should go home today."

"But you still have two more days with me." A rock sat in her stomach.

"There's a flight in three hours. Let's swing by your place so I can get my luggage. I'll get a ride from there."

As they walked back toward the car, she reached for his hand, but he pulled it away. "Let's talk more about this," she implored him.

"There's nothing more to talk about now. I need some space."

Maybe she shouldn't have given him an ultimatum. The thought of losing him forever made her feel as if she might suffocate behind a flickering screen of sadness.

30

By the time Clair arrived in the small beach town, her heart felt as blue and fragile as a robin's egg. She stepped off the train, and the fresh salt smell of the Atlantic cleared her senses. She searched for Mr. Nelson, their caretaker, surprised that her father hadn't alerted him to pick her up.

The warm Indian summer weather was inviting, and she toted her valise down the long dirt road toward the cottage. Blooming hydrangeas decorated the gray wood shingle walls. She found the key under the flowerpot and let herself in the pale-green back door.

Unlacing her shoes, she slipped them off and dropped them on the mudroom's hardwood floor. She raced down to the beach, where a gentle wind blew in the gray-blue sky. The rippling sea sparkled, reminding her of the shoes in the window and Winnie's trampled cap. Clair cringed inside. Her friend might be sitting in jail right now.

Clair strolled along the shore, savoring the soft sand between her toes, gingerly avoiding the golden seaweed with its scalloped lacy edges and orange bulbs. It took her mind back to the summer before her mama died. What ever happened to that good-looking Mr. Benny? Clair hadn't thought of him in years. He had teased her, pretending he planned to munch down on one of the seaweed bulbs like a carrot, but instead exploding one in his big palm with a loud pop. She'd tried to smash one, too, but at six she wasn't strong enough.

Now she picked one up and easily crushed it in her hand with a puncturing burst of power. With her clean hand, she held up her skirt and waded into the icy water, rinsing the mess off her hand in the cold current and drying it off on her hem.

She wandered farther up the beach and perched on a rock. Mr. Benny had seemed much younger than her father, with a striped swimsuit that exposed big muscles and a funny anchor tattoo on his arm. Her beautiful red-haired mama had laughed at his jokes. Clair laughed, too, even though she had no idea what they were all about. It must have been a weekday, because her father wasn't there. He only came up on weekends.

"Honey, go down and make drip castles, why don't cha?" Mr. Benny had suggested to Clair.

"Yes, make one as tall as you can, darling." Mama gave her a hug.

Clair obeyed and went to work. She looked up for approval and saw Mr. Benny put his hand on Mama's leg from underneath the parasol. Father got angry when her face got too ruddy. But when Mr. Benny was near, it turned red anyway.

Clair now put her hand on her own hot face as Mr. Benny and Mama's behavior became clearer. Had her father ever found out?

That same summer night, after her bedtime story, her mama said, "Don't tell your father Mr. Benny was here."

"Why not?"

"It'll be our little secret." Her mother kissed her forehead. "That's a good girl."

When her father came up that Friday night and Mama wasn't in the room, he asked Clair if any strangers had visited during the week. She kept the secret but had been confused. She always obeyed her mother, but she had also been told never to lie.

Now that Clair had lost her own innocence, she understood that Mr. Benny and her mama had been attracted to each other. Maybe her father *had* found out, and that's why he had called her mother a tramp. If he knew about Clair's own tryst, he would certainly call her a tramp, too.

Back at the cottage, she wiped her feet in the mudroom as the phone rang twice in the kitchen. It must be her father. She considered not answering it, but decided she'd better.

"Farley will be there to pick you up this afternoon." Her father's voice was filled with rage.

She hoped nobody was listening in on the party telephone line.

Clair's stomach clenched as she sat on a straight-backed chair. "Father. I need some time. Please allow me to stay for another few days."

"What's going on with you?"

"I'm considering your request that I marry Farley."

"That's good, but it's not right for a young lady to be out there all alone!" She wanted to ask him if he worried she might have a Mr. Benny there.

"When you've been in the city, the Nelsons have always kept an eye on me. Besides, the season is over, and there's no one else here."

"That's what I mean."

"Please?"

He grunted. "Okay, a week. Farley can pick you up then."

"Thank you, Father." She hung up the phone as exhaustion overpowered her. She pulled on her nightdress, climbed into bed, and instantly fell asleep to the sound of the rumbling waves.

That night she dreamed of riding the elevator down to the hotel lobby. As she promenaded through the lobby, everyone stared at her with smiles on their faces, and she felt they must be admiring her bob.

Mr. O'Shaugnessy tried to stop her and called, "Miss Devereaux!"

But she ignored him and kept going through the door and out onto the sidewalk into the sunshine.

A man driving by in a truck honked his horn. *A-oo-gah, a-oo-gah.* "Look at those gams!" Everyone on the street gaped at her.

Clair glanced down and realized she had on the pink silk corset with lace trim. Her long legs were bare as birch trees in winter. She awoke covered in sweat, trying to decipher the dream. Did it mean she was exposed, and anyone who saw her would recognize what she'd done?

At dawn, the sun peeked over the bay with a glint of gold. On the edge of sleep, Clair's memories from her dream and the tryst with Mr. X swirled in her mind, billowing there. Upon fully awakening, instead of feeling regret and guilt, she smiled, lingering in bed, reliving the moments. How could God make it a sin if it felt so good? Or maybe it was a sin *because* it felt so good.

Famished, she slipped on her wrapper and padded to the kitchen. Mrs. Nelson's fresh muffins sat on the counter in a blue-and-white Wedgwood bowl. A note told Clair to let her know if she needed a hot breakfast cooked. She took the bowl back to bed and munched on the muffins there, something she had never allowed herself to do before.

She changed into her favorite bathing costume, the sleeveless one with the fitted bloomers. Her father had said it was too skimpy, so she never wore it when he was around. He had said, "It's a disgrace the way young men and women frolic on the shore together."

She ran her fingers through her bob with a smile—she would forgo her swim bonnet. That thick hair had always been a nuisance. Salty seawater soaked it into hemplike snarls that took forever to comb out. What a relief it would be not to have to deal with that!

In season, the cove was always crowded. Today, the smoke-colored clouds in the sky were her only companions. The weather matched her conflicting emotions, and the tangled knot in her stomach twisted tighter.

Out on the promontory, she stepped carefully in her thin booties to avoid the sharp rocks. Wind whipped her body as her eyes scanned the far-off horizon, her mind taunted by thoughts of a life with Farley. She'd never be able to abide him touching her.

She dove into the Atlantic, the water an icy shock to her body. From shallow foam she rose, her feet setting down on soft sand. Water swirled around her. Salt clung to lips that now had been kissed. Sunrays licked her wet shoulders that Mr. X had touched. She swam breaststroke toward the horizon, turning her head side to side, inhaling the briny air.

Soon she fell into a rhythm as if she could swim all the way to China. The frigid water began to numb her mind and body. Over and over, she reimagined the tryst of the night before. She swam farther away from the shore. As a wave passed under her, she wished it could cleanse away her desire for him. The undertow tried to pull her back toward the shore, but she had to stay away from the sandy gravel and hunt for peace in her soul.

As much as Clair tried to shut down her lustful impulses, they wouldn't let her go. What did her future hold? As a tarnished woman, she wouldn't be able to get married like her father insisted. Or would she have to?

31

Clair let herself in the suite. All was quiet; her father must still be at work. She had sent a telegram to Farley telling him not to come pick her up, and she made her way back to town on the train alone. In her room she dropped her valise on the ground, closed the curtains, and stretched out on the bed.

It had been a week, but it felt like an hour. Instead of the memories of her night with Mr. X growing dim, they continued to deepen. She had hoped the respite would erase him from her mind, but instead it reinforced the memory, the lingering tangy scent of him, the simmering touch of his hands tracing the lace of her corset.

She wouldn't ever forget him and the lusciousness of their night together. Never telling another soul, she'd keep the secret memory in her heart, like a picture hidden in a closed locket, to open and remind her that she'd been made love to with an irresistible desire.

She sat on the sofa, pulled her list from her pocket, and studied it.

Reasons not to marry Farley:

1. *His cowlick won't be tamed.*
2. *His roaming hands are sweaty.*
3. *He talks about money all the time.*
4. *He's a terrible braggart.*
5. *He'd never let me go to college.*

She crumpled up the list and tossed it in the trash. If she refused to marry him, her secluded life would tighten its hold on her. She tried to convince herself that marriage to him couldn't be that bad. She didn't really believe it. But if she could talk him into letting her go to Juilliard, then it might be worth it.

If she married, she'd have to give herself to him whenever he reached for her. Perhaps if she had children, she might be satisfied. She'd love them even if they inherited his gruff manner. Maybe he'd be a good father. Fat chance!

Spring was a long way off, and she still had time to work it out.

She recognized his knock on the suite's door and held her breath.

"Clair, are you in there?" Farley's voice rang out coldly.

She was tempted not to answer. However, at some point she needed to face him, so she might as well get it over with.

She walked to the foyer and slowly opened the door.

His cowlick pointed straight up, more pronounced than usual. "I went to the station, but I couldn't find you. Why didn't you look for me? You've been gone for days. Didn't you miss me?" He slid inside, reached for her, and attempted to kiss her. How she wished Mr. X reached for her instead of Farley.

"Don't." She stepped back. He grabbed her waist, and Clair pulled away. "I'm alone. You're not supposed to be here."

"I'm allowed. Your father and I have completed all the details."

With a frown she put a hand on her hip. "What details?"

"The wedding." He grinned at her.

"Wedding?"

"Your father decided we should wed without delay. The ceremony is in three weeks."

"Three weeks!" She followed him into the parlor. Rain began to pound on the window as loudly as the beating of her terrified heart.

"Aren't you thrilled?" Farley helped himself to a cigar on her father's desk, and lit it. "A small affair with just one hundred guests. More rain is expected. Don't get your hair mussed. Bring an umbrella."

Clair stared at him. "I can't."

"Can't what? Bring an umbrella?"

"It's too soon." She sat in a chair. "We said spring."

"There is concern about the market, and he insists we marry right away."

"What's happened?" She hadn't read the paper while she was gone.

"Don't worry your pretty little head. I have plenty of money."

She tried to get a word in with no success. "Farley—"

"We make a good team, you and I. In a year, we'll buy a house uptown. You will spend your days with the children."

"But I want to go to college before having children."

He looked at her sideways. "Oh, that's right. I forgot. You can go after we're married."

She didn't believe him. Not one minute more could she be in the same room with him, let alone marry him. She hated to disappoint her father, but it just had to be.

She took a deep breath. "Farley."

Another squall of rain hit the window, and he glanced out, puffing his cigar.

"Farley, look at me." She waited until their eyes met, and said, quite distinctly, "I can't marry you."

He bolted back as if shocked. "You don't mean that. It'll be wonderful. After the reception we're going straight on our honeymoon. Your father has booked us on an ocean liner to Europe."

"I'd rather go over Niagara Falls in a barrel!"

Farley blinked at her. "I've never thought of that."

He can't really be that stupid. "You need to go." She walked to the foyer and opened the door.

"But I just got here."

She put her hands on his chest and pushed him out the door. She paced the suite. After she was sure he was long gone, she grabbed her raincoat and left in search of Winnie. Clair had made up her mind. She'd find out who Mr. X was, no matter what. She just had to see him again.

Clair stopped at the Macy's candy counter. "Two scoops of nonpareils, please."

"Certainly." The man behind the counter handed her the bagful.

"Have you seen Winifred today?" Clair took out a candy and sucked on it.

"No, ma'am."

She rode the escalator up to the second floor.

Mr. Smithers approached, peering over his glasses. "Hello, Miss Devereaux."

"May Winifred assist me, please?"

He frowned. "She's not here today. Is there something I can get for you, or may I have one of the other girls help you?"

"I'll check back another time." Clair dared not ask him for Winnie's address at the boardinghouse.

Clair could take a taxi to the speakeasy tonight, but of course it would be closed. She'd read that after a speakeasy had been raided the owner would move it to another location. Rudy had always talked about getting "bigger digs." More likely though, if they hadn't gone to jail, they were both on the lam.

When she arrived home from Macy's, her father sat in his easy chair reading *A Farewell to Arms*. He looked up at her.

She'd better start softly. "I really enjoyed that one."

"Yes, it's a goody."

"Father, thank you for allowing me to stay at the cottage."

He smiled at her. "Did you have enough time to come to your senses?"

"I can't believe you pushed up the date. Three weeks?"

"You two will be very happy." Her father lit a cigar.

She slumped in a chair across from him. "Happy? Never! I can't marry him."

"Why not?"

"I don't love him."

"Love can grow."

She sat up and leaned toward her father. "Really. Did your love for Mother increase over time?"

He looked stunned. "Of course."

"Did it?"

"Yes."

He must think Clair was stupid. "Also, I'm certain he won't ever allow me to go to Juilliard."

Her father puffed on his cigar. "He promised me he would, after the honeymoon."

"I don't trust him, and I say no to the wedding!"

"You have no choice!" Her father raised his voice. "I need you safe and sound, in case something happens to me."

"Nothing is going to happen to you!" She ran to her room and slammed the door.

32

When Anne awoke, it was still dark. Her heart chakra roiled with fire, and she couldn't breathe. From the coffee table, she picked up the rose quartz heart and held it in her hand. *Inhale: one, two, three. Exhale: one, two, three, four, five.* She visualized clear colors in her chest, but all she could see was black, gray, ebony—sorrow colors.

She got up, put the kettle on to boil, made a cup of licorice tea, propped up a pillow, and climbed back into bed. Ever since Sergio broke up with her two weeks ago, her morning rituals had been off-kilter. Sleeping in used to be one of her life's pleasures, but not now. Her body and mind wouldn't allow it. Her heart beat so rapidly each morning she didn't even want to drink caffeine.

She missed him. At least once a day she texted or called him, but he wouldn't respond. She consulted the weather app on her phone. It was eight o'clock New York time, and the weather was already eighty degrees. She pictured him getting ready for work in a lightweight suit over a white shirt, slim canvas Ferragamos on his feet. Which hat did he choose? The Panama, or his straw fedora? Was he thinking of her, too? She resisted the urge to send him a *thinking of you* text.

She dunked the tea bag in her cup and took a sip. She'd come to terms with the reality that she'd really blown it. As a modern woman, why had she been so shallow as to want him to propose? She should have agreed to move there even without a commitment. It would have been better than feeling this miserable. She needed to take it all back, but he wouldn't even talk to her. It wasn't something she could say in a text or an e-mail.

Tears began to well in her eyes. Before, even when they weren't physically together, she always felt grounded, just knowing he loved her and lived in her world. They had talked or texted every day. Now the hours ticked by without him, and her calendar was filled with empty pages, projecting a lonely future without him.

She sat up, pulled a Kleenex from the box, and blew her nose.

Since Anne was awake, she knew she should use her time wisely—write in her journal, practice yoga, or do some art. Even though all she wanted to do was go back to sleep, her body just wouldn't cooperate. She hadn't been able to eat since he left, either. She never weighed herself—she didn't even own a scale—but she could tell by how her clothes fit that she had lost quite a bit of weight.

She picked up her journal and wrote:

Maybe he would have wanted to marry me if—

I was more sophisticated.

I had manicured nails instead of chipped and paint-stained ones.

My hair didn't always look as if a cyclone had hit it.

My feet were smaller. (Even though he said he liked them big.)

This is stupid.

Journaling wasn't doing it for her. Maybe she'd feel better if she did some yoga. She forced herself to get up, spread her mat on the floor, slip the yoga CD into her computer, and lay on the ground. Bending her knees toward her chest, she began to follow the directions the best she could. After a few downward-facing dogs, planks, and child poses, the mojo hit her and she had the urge to create an art piece. She would use her sadness and longing to be deeply loved.

The shoes sitting on the counter reminded her of the joy of dancing with him at his co-op right after she bought them. The shoe painting on the easel still stymied her. No matter which artistic techniques she used, the rhinestones wouldn't shine on the canvas.

Time to start fresh. She laid newspaper on the kitchenette table and from her stash picked out a narrow box, fourteen by four inches, separated into three-tiered niches perfect for found objects. She mixed blue and green paints together, and with a brush slapped on the concoction.

From her knickknack shelf she selected ceramic objects that would stand out from the turquoise: a duck, a pair of lips on a white game tile, and an old-fashioned couple two inches tall—the feathered hat on the woman's head was a study in lovely pastels.

After the box dried, she manipulated the pieces, deciding which squares each piece fit best into. Anne's chest tingled as the assemblage began to take shape. The duck fit perfectly in the top square, the couple in the middle, and the lips on the bottom. She glued them all down. She rummaged through the old jewelry container and found a white heart with metallic lacy edges, silver hugs and kisses, and a teeny arrow.

She adhered the lacy heart above the couple, and the OXO and arrow in the lip section. The whole thing needed something else. She rifled through the charms again, knowing she'd find the perfect thing. *Aha!* There it was, the cupid charm. She tied clear fishing wire through the hole and used a thumbtack to secure the other end of it to the inside top of the square, as if cupid's arrow had shot the man in his back.

Anne stepped back to examine it, grabbed her journal, and brainstormed possible titles:

Shot with a Beau

Cupid's Arrow

Duck! Cupid's Shot His Bow

With a smile she circled the last one. She ruffled through her lace and ribbon basket, picked out some cobalt-blue lace, and used matte medium to adhere it to the outside rim of the box.

Spontaneously, she took a photo of it and sent it to Sergio. She carried the box to her feng shui relationship corner, putting it on the window ledge next to the soap and shampoo. If this didn't make him talk to her, she didn't know what would.

33

After she sent Sergio the photo of the cupid art piece, all he wrote back was *cute*. She hadn't replied. That had been a week ago.

She'd decided to lay low for a while and give him the space he'd requested. She'd barely left the apartment, had turned down coffee with Fay, didn't feel like thrifting or even getting fresh air on the roof.

But last night Fay had sent a text: *I have a surprise. Come over tomorrow at 7 p.m. I won't take no for an answer.*

Anne forced herself to get dressed, wearing a white shift to lighten her mood. Instead she felt as if she wore a black shroud over her entire body and on her head rested a round black hat, the opposite of a halo. The dark circles under her eyes and weight loss might scare her friends, so she applied makeup and practiced smiling in the mirror. It seemed like a long time since she'd smiled. She hoped they wouldn't notice anything was wrong. Lyft car requested, she made her way down to the street.

As Fay opened Bay Breeze's front door, Lucky tried to scoot out, but Anne grabbed him up in her arms. "You snickerdoodle, you."

Fay, in a chartreuse sheath with dangly peacock-feather earrings, closed the door behind them. As Anne stepped into the foyer, the gardenia scent hit her as usual and she inhaled the calming aroma.

She put the wiggly Lucky down and took out a bacon treat for him. "Sit." He sat. "Good boy!" Anne handed him the treat, and he gobbled it right up.

Fay laughed and hugged her. "That little Houdini dug a hole under the fence last night, and we couldn't find him anywhere. Finally, a neighbor two blocks away called. Lucky had shown up in his yard. We should have known—he's the guy that gives giant cookies to Lucky when we walk by his house. Hey, have you lost some weight?"

"Maybe a little. What's the surprise?"

"Hold on to your knickers." Fay led the way into the library. Candles were lit, and a centerpiece of rosemary branches and pine cones ran down the sideboard. Champagne glasses gleamed in the light. Beside them, a bottle of Dom Pérignon chilled in an ice bucket.

"You told me we were having a spot of tea."

Paul hobbled in with his cane, singing, "There she is, Miss America!"

Anne gave him a hug and sang back to him, "With those cataracts, you can't see me anyway. How are you?"

"Fair to middling." He eased himself into his chair, and Anne sat close by.

Lucky jumped in her lap and oinked toward her coat pocket, looking for more treats. She handed him one with a laugh. "You sound like a pig."

George came in, nodding hello to Anne, then set down a tray on the sideboard filled with appetizers: escargot, spring rolls, asparagus wrapped in prosciutto. Sergio would have approved of this spread.

"Honeykins, please open the bottle?" Fay asked.

George popped the cork. It flew across the room and bounced off a window. Lucky jumped up and started barking. George poured the drinks and handed them out.

Fay beamed at him with a nod.

He raised his glass and said, "Please join me for a toast to the incredible Fay."

Everyone lifted a glass.

"She has agreed to be my bride."

Anne felt as if she'd been sucker punched. "Blimey!"

"What?" Fay asked as she clinked her glass with Anne and took a sip.

"Congratulations!" Anne managed a smile.

"We'll marry next month at the courthouse and have a reception at Bay Breeze afterward."

Paul's eyes twinkled. "Don't you want to have the ceremony here, too?"

"No, thanks." Fay smiled at him.

Paul looked at Anne. "Sylvia was so lovely coming down the staircase at our own wedding. She'd said she hoped you would do that someday, too."

"And when will that be?" Fay teased.

"Not sure." Anne smiled and held back tears. No one seemed to notice.

Fay sipped her champagne. "I want you to be maiden of honor."

Anne felt as if she might throw up. "That's nice."

"Nice? Bloody nice? What's wrong with you?"

"Nothing." Anne couldn't spoil the moment by confessing that Sergio had broken up with her. "I'm just not feeling well. I'm sorry. I need to go home." Anne took out her phone and started to call for a Lyft.

"I'm sorry. Can we get you something?" Fay asked.

"Would you rather lie down here for a while?" Paul frowned.

Anne put her hand on her forehead and closed her eyes. "No, thanks."

"I'll drive you." George offered.

"That's sweet of you, but I'd rather go on my own." She didn't want him to see her cry. And that's what she did all the way home.

34

A week to the day after her visit to Bay Breeze, she started to send Sergio a text, but he beat her to it. *I've got news.*

Her heart galloped, but trying not to seem too eager, she set her timer for five minutes. After it dinged, she called him. "What's your news?"

"I went by the shop today. The closed sign was still up, but I peeked through the crack and the lights were on. I knocked, but no one answered."

"That's hopeful."

"I'll keep checking. How are you?"

"Okay," she lied. "How are you?"

"Great."

"Listen, Sergio. I've changed my mind. I'll move to New York even without a commitment."

Sergio paused. "Let's switch to FaceTime. We should see each other for this."

"No, my hair's a mess." She didn't want him to see she'd been crying.

"Come on. I've seen it messy before. So is mine."

She wrapped a scrunchie around her hair, relented with a sigh, and switched on FaceTime. "Okay."

"I'm sorry I hurt you." He looked as if he hadn't slept in ages.

Dark circles rimmed his sad eyes, and he'd skipped his morning shave.

She ached to touch his face. She loved him even more than the last time she'd seen him. "As I said, I take it all back. I'll move there without an engagement."

"It won't work. I'd know what you really want is to get married. That cloud would be hanging over my head and keep me from feeling at ease in my own home."

"I release you from even thinking about it."

"It's not that simple. I'd still know that's what you want. I do miss you, though." He kissed his fingers and touched the screen.

She reached out and placed her hand on her screen also. "Miss you, too."

He nodded, and his sparkling brown eyes filled with tears.

"Your big 4-0 is next week. How are you celebrating?" Trying to be cheery, she forced a smile.

"Not sure yet."

She swallowed. "Want some company?"

"Maybe." He shrugged.

"Do you want me to come, or don't you?"

"It depends."

"On what?"

"You not trying to seduce me."

She laughed. "I can't promise you that."

"Then don't come."

She couldn't tell if he was kidding or not. "Okay. I won't then." She shouldn't have replied so swiftly. Confused and on the verge of tears, she said, "Bye." She wanted to say *I love you*, but somehow it didn't feel quite right. She hung up and turned off the phone.

~

That afternoon, Anne's door buzzer rang. She got out of bed and answered it. "Hello."

"It's me, Fay."

Anne wasn't up to seeing her. "I'm kind of busy right now."

"I have a check for you. I'll just come up for a minute."

Anne was relieved; she really needed to pay some bills. She buzzed Fay up.

At the door, Fay handed her a mocha and a paper bag. Her eyes scanned the messy room. "Are you okay? You haven't answered any of my texts."

Anne cleared a space at the kitchen table, and they sat down. "I've been working." She opened the bag and put the blueberry scone on top of it. "Thanks for the drink and the scone. Want a spot of tea?"

"No, I had some on the way over." Fay ran her hand through spiky hair streaked with turquoise highlights. "You rushed out so fast the other night we didn't have a chance to talk about the wedding."

"Right. Okay." Anne tried to drum up enthusiasm.

"You could wear your green dress, or I'll buy you a new one if you wish."

"It's your wedding, whatever you decide. If you want me to wear a new dress, I'll pay for it myself. What else do you need me to do?"

Anne hoped she wouldn't have to throw one of those god-awful bachelorette parties. "Should I give you a shower or bachelorette party or something?"

Fay guffawed. "Are you daft? Of course not!"

Anne picked up her cup and set it back down.

Fay eyed Anne and looked around the room again. "Are you sure you're okay?"

"You know how I get when I'm on a roll, I don't take time to straighten up the apartment or shower." Anne hoped she didn't stink.

Fay nodded slowly but didn't look convinced. "What have you got for the gallery?"

On the kitchen counter, Anne displayed *Waiting for a Ring, Finding Her Way,* and *Duck! Cupid's Shot His Bow.* "This last one isn't for sale yet."

"These are fabulous!" Fay said. "Very romantic, and a different direction for you."

"And here's one I'm doing with the picture." Anne brought out the photo and the unfinished flapper collage and set them on the table.

"Interesting. Have some mocha, you haven't even tasted it."

Anne took a tiny sip and pointed to the easel with the shoe painting. "Here's one I'm stuck on. Can't get the rhinestones to appear shiny."

"Keep working. If you use your instincts, I know you'll figure it out."

"You're so good at reminding me." Anne smiled. "Heart, not mind."

Fay took a bite of scone and pushed it toward Anne. "It's delicious, try some."

Anne compelled herself to pick up a piece and chew on it.

"How're you holding up financially?"

"Pretty good."

Fay took an envelope out of her bag and handed it to Anne. "Here's your check. The buyers of your *Political Diva Series* were thrilled."

"I'm glad you were able to keep those three pieces together." The pieces included assemblages of Eva Peron, Imelda Marcos, and Madame Mao. All of these ambitious, self-absorbed women had helped catapult their husbands' careers to the top of the political heap.

Anne set the envelope on the table. "This will really help."

"Shall I put a word in for you at the museum?"

"I doubt I'd be any good at teaching."

"You'd be aces. They might be looking for someone who is adventurous in their own work. I'll check in with them."

Teaching wouldn't be the answer to those empty days on Anne's calendar. Maybe she shouldn't have quit valeting after all. She had to sign that new lease soon and would need to increase her income.

"Paul has finally agreed to have his cataracts removed."

Anne nodded. "I'm glad. When's the appointment?"

"In a fortnight."

"Need any help?"

"We've got it covered. How're things with Sergio?"

"It's over."

"Over!" Fay sat up straight. "I knew something was wrong. Why didn't you tell me? What happened?"

"I realized it might be foolish of me to move to New York without a commitment, like you'd said. I thought he was going to propose, but instead he broke up with me."

"I'm so sorry." Fay pouted her red lips. "Are you speaking?"

"A little, but it's painful. His big 4-0 is coming up next week, and I'm thinking of visiting him."

"Is that a good idea?"

"I'm not sure. I miss him so much, but being with him might make me too sad."

"Is it worth the hurt?"

Anne shrugged and held back tears. "Being without him makes me sad, too."

"I suppose the Italy trip is off. I know how much you were looking forward to it."

"Of course it's off."

"Go alone."

"Yeah, because that wouldn't be horrible, visiting one of the most romantic places in the world by myself. Not to mention it costing too much." Anne looked down and started to cry.

"Do you think maybe you should go talk to someone?"

Anne raised her eyes. "You mean like a shrink?"

"They're called therapists. They can be very helpful."

"How do you know?"

"From experience. When I moved here, I was going through a bad breakup and needed some help. She was wonderful. I could refer you."

Astonishing. Fay always seemed so strong and together. "I'll let you know."

"So, are you going to visit him?"

Anne shook her head. "I haven't decided yet."

35

Miraculously, her father had found a dressmaker who could create a wedding gown on short notice. From the limousine's back seat, Clair examined the rain dripping down the window. Her fingers played Chopin's "Funeral March" over ivory lace; satin pooled at her feet.

Clair would prefer to be a spinster than marry Farley. No matter how much she pleaded with her father, he told her that if she didn't go through with it, he'd set up a guard at their suite door forever.

She gave her father an evil eye as he drew the tulle veil over her head and arranged it around her shoulders. Even as she stood there in the gown, she wondered for the thousandth time how she could escape.

Despite everything, her father appeared handsome in his tuxedo, his hair slicked back and gleaming. She speculated how Farley would look in his tux—the expensive one he'd insisted on buying for today, even though he already had perfectly good ones.

She closed her eyes and imagined marrying Mr. X instead. In her daydream, his pressed tuxedo accentuated the length of his tall, firm body, and his smile was a magnet, pulling her down the aisle to him. He held out his left hand to her, without a ring on it. His eyes were welcoming and warm, due to the passions she knew he held for her. She wondered if the feelings she had for him would diminish over time—maybe even snap, break, and let go, like her string of pearls.

The chauffeur glided the limousine up in front of the church. Soot covered the towering Gothic building as if foreboding her future life. Her father opened the door, holding an umbrella for her. Shaking her head, she stayed put until her father lost his temper. "Come on!" he said gruffly.

She stepped out, draping the gown's long skirt over her arm to keep it out of mud-filled puddles. At least she didn't have one of those god-awful trains. There was nothing she could do about her *peau de soie* shoes.

Her body heavy as lead, she trudged to her fate. She only wanted the day to be over—and especially the night. Imagining what it might be like with Farley made her queasy. She knew she had to submit to him, her husband. Maybe tonight he'd glut himself and nod off as soon as they got to their room, leaving only a gooey stain of his greasy hair oil on the pillowcase next to hers.

She'd considered asking Aunt June for some guidance, but since she'd never been married, she probably wouldn't be able to help. Mrs. Schmidt, her next-door neighbor and chaperone, continued to be bedridden with one malady after another, her bronchitis having developed into pneumonia. Besides, Clair would have been too embarrassed to ask.

In the church foyer, someone handed her a lily of the valley, stephanotis, and gardenia bouquet, and Clair held on tight. The pipe organ began to play Wagner's "Bridal Chorus" and she sang along in her head the dreaded "Here Comes the Bride." Suddenly it hit her that she couldn't go through with it. She turned to hurry back out the door, but her father forcefully grabbed her arm. "It's for your own good," he said, blinking wet eyes at her.

She submitted to his firm grasp, step touching along beside him into and down the aisle. Lo and behold, who did she see turning toward her at the back of the congregation but Winnie and Rudy! Clair smiled at them. Their names hadn't been on the guest list.

Winnie wore a conspicuously large hat three times as big as her head, filled with lace, feathers, and silk flowers. Rudy winked at her as she passed, sporting a gray pinstriped suit with his trademark white carnation decorating the lapel.

Across the aisle, on the groom's side, three large men she'd never seen before sat with crossed arms in dark suits. The other pews were filled with her father's business associates, clients from the brokerage firm, and Odd Fellows Lodge members, many of whom she had met for the first time at her coming-out ball.

Step touch, step touch.

Bea, seated with her parents, waved with a sad smile. Clair's father had told her that Bea's parents kept her under lock and key, with no marriage prospects in sight.

Step touch, step touch. The odor of candle wax permeated the air.

Mr. O'Shaughnessy and his family took up an entire pew, and all grinned as she passed by. Dr. Johnson nodded at her. Aunt June turned to her from the front row with sorrowful eyes.

Farley in his tight tux waited for her, a stuffed penguin in a museum. Red-faced, sweat seeping from his brow, his hands fidgeted like they did right before he reached for a cigar.

At the altar, her father let go of her arm and sat next to Aunt June. Clair pivoted to escape, but Farley grabbed her hand with his sweaty one and glared at her. Resigned, she exhaled and stood quietly beside him, but she pulled her hand from his.

The priest nodded and began to sermonize, but she didn't hear much of what he had to say. On and on he droned, until finally he asked her to repeat after him.

"I promise to be true to you in good times and in bad, in sickness and in health. I will love you and honor you all the days of my life." She nearly choked on the words.

In a resounding voice he added, "You will obey your husband.

You will obey your husband." He caught Farley's eye for emphasis.

Beside her, Farley began to weave back and forth. Clair turned in horror, just in time to jump out of the way, as he keeled over and fell forward on top of the priest. Farley hit his forehead on the altar, and brass candlesticks tumbled to the marble floor with a crash.

A communal gasp rose from the congregation. Her father and Aunt June leaped to their feet.

Aunt June held up her skirt and stomped out the burning candles before the altar cloth caught fire.

Clair's father laid Farley on his back, crouched beside him, and yelled. "Farley! Farley!"

Clair helped the priest up, and he stumbled to the pulpit.

Dr. Johnson ran up the aisle. "Someone call an ambulance!"

Aunt June pulled smelling salts from her bag and wafted them under Farley's nose, but that didn't revive him. A purple eggplant of a mound had already started to form on his forehead.

"Out of my way." Dr. Johnson pushed Aunt June and Clair's father aside and checked Farley's pulse. "Dear, dear, dear."

The priest began to orate, "All kneel and let's pray. Our father, who art in heaven . . ."

The congregation ignored him and continued to hover and talk.

After a few minutes, medics rushed down the aisle. Soon they had lifted Farley onto a stretcher and carried him out of the church, with Dr. Johnson following.

"We'd better go to the hospital, too." Her father carried his top hat in his hand as he headed up the aisle. "Come along, Clair."

Relieved that she didn't need to marry Farley today after all, Clair glanced up at the Jesus statue above the altar with a nod of thanks.

Aunt June stepped up to the pulpit and put her arm on the praying priest's shoulder. "Let me say a few words, please."

He acted flustered but stepped back. She faced the church.

"Friends, Farley will be fine. Let's move to the reception hall and enjoy the repast the caterers have prepared. That's what Leland would wish us to do."

Clair pulled back her veil and followed her father up the aisle.

"Bad luck." Mr. O'Shaughnessy shook his head as she passed by.

At the back of the church, Rudy and Winnie stood waiting.

Her friend giggled from under her hat. "Too bad, toots!"

Rudy leaned over and took Clair's hand. "Dodged a bullet there, gal pal."

"At least for now," she said, and tried not to smile.

36

A wail woke Clair. She threw on her wrapper and ran to the parlor. "Goodness gracious me! It's freezing in here." She rushed to shut the open window. Outside, gray clouds filled the sky. The leaves had fallen off the maple trees long ago.

"Gone." Her father hunched over in his chair, took a handkerchief from his smoking jacket pocket, and blew his nose.

"What's gone?" She knelt in front of him and put her hands on his shaking knees.

"Gone. All gone."

"What's gone?"

He didn't answer. She'd never seen him cry before. It couldn't be on account of Farley and the wedding fiasco. That had been a month and a half ago. Farley had been released from the hospital a few days later, and resumed coming over every evening. Within no time, to her chagrin, the men started to make new wedding plans.

Clair had tried to reason with Farley. "Wasn't your accident God's way of telling us we're not supposed to wed?"

"Don't be silly. It was only a little spill." Farley had put his hand on his still-black-and-blue forehead.

Last week, after the devastating stock market crash, he had stopped coming. When her father called Farley's hotel, they said he'd checked out. She was mightily relieved, but it seemed odd that he would leave without so much as a goodbye. He always seemed to have access to cash, and with her father's business acumen, she had assumed he had foreseen the crash and had cashed in all the stocks he managed. But she might have been wrong.

A knock sounded at the door. Had someone heard her father howl?

He put his hand on her arm. "Don't answer it," he whined.

Another knock followed. She tried to ignore it, but it grew louder.

She stood. "I should get it."

Her father shook his head and grabbed her hand. What had gotten into him? She pulled away, stepped into the foyer, and opened the door.

"Your father, please." Mr. O'Shaughnessy slid his foot over the jamb, holding an envelope in his hand. His tall body filled the whole doorway.

Clair paused. "He's unavailable. May I give him a message?"

"There's the matter of the bill." He looked down at her.

"What bill?"

"The hotel bill."

"What about it?"

"It is past due."

"I'm sure he'll take care of it right away." It didn't make any sense. Her father always boasted that he paid every bill in full at the end of each month.

But things had been so strange lately. The kitchen had forgotten to deliver their breakfast, and three times she had to call down to remind them. Even Mr. O'Shaughnessy frowned at her when she walked by, instead of giving her his usual smile and nod.

Now he stared at her coldly. "Your hotel bill has been in arrears for quite some time. I told your father if he didn't pay by today, you had to go."

The *stocks*. That must be what was gone. The truth hit Clair like a pail of cold water. "But I've lived here my whole life."

His eyes softened. "Sorry, Miss Devereaux, but the hotel owners say it can't be helped. You aren't the only ones."

She swallowed, eked out a smile, and took the envelope. "I'm sure Father will pay you directly."

"I hope he can." Mr. O'Shaughnessy stepped back.

In a daze, she closed the door and wandered back to the parlor. Tears continued to slide down her father's face.

"I'm cold." He shivered.

It had begun to snow. The fire had gone out in the grate, but when she tried to start a fire, there was no fuel. She wrapped the sofa blanket around him, pulled over the hassock, and sat down in front of him. "Did you lose it all in the crash?"

He moaned, "How will we survive?"

She took his hands in hers. "Answer me. Is our money all gone?"

"I'm sorry." He put his head in his hands.

She placed her hand on his back for a moment and then stepped over to his desk. In the top drawer she found the account book. Since she was ten, it had been her job to open the bills, fill in the checks for him to sign, and do the sums in the bankbook. About a year ago, though, he had told her it was unladylike and took that role back from her. She thought nothing of it at the time. Now in a bottom drawer she discovered a pile of bills and glanced through them quickly, realizing they were all past due.

It all began to make sense—the hotel staff's attitude, Farley's disappearance. Her father must have lost Farley's investments, too.

Her father began to moan again, "What are we going to do?"

She grabbed his cash envelope from the drawer and put it in her purse. "Let's go!"

The cab dropped them off at Aunt June's apartment. Clair helped her father up the steps and knocked on the door.

Aunt June opened it wearing an apron. "What a surprise!" She smiled at Clair, then saw her father wrapped in the blanket. "Oh, dear me, Leland."

"Hello, June." He lifted his glassy eyes toward her.

"I didn't know where else to go," Clair frowned.

Aunt June took one arm and Clair the other, and they led her father across the oriental carpet that flanked the hardwood floor and sat him on the sofa. Clair stirred the fire in the hearth.

"It's gone. It's all gone." Her father shook his head. "What are we going to do?"

"You are here now." Aunt June spoke softly. "Everything will be okay."

"Thank you, June." He stared at her. "You have always been so kind."

She put her hands on her hips and raised her eyes to the ceiling. Then she closed the floral drapes, helped him lie down, and covered him with the blanket. "Close your eyes, and soon you'll be in the arms of Morpheus."

She led Clair into the kitchen, put the kettle on, and whispered, "How long has he been like this?"

"Since early morning. I'm sorry to barge in on you." Clair sat at the dinette. "Mr. O'Shaughnessy told us we had to leave immediately. Turns out father hadn't been paying the bill."

Aunt June nodded, and her eyes softened. "You are always welcome here."

"But there's not enough space." The apartment had only one bedroom and a bath.

"You're family. We'll make do. Where's Farley?"

"Apparently he flew the coop last week."

"Good riddance!" Aunt June set cups on a tray and sat down across from Clair.

"Can his investments all really be gone?"

"I'm afraid so. He must have lost it in the market like so many others."

"But he always said it was important to diversify." Clair's eyes filled with tears. "What about the properties?"

"He must have sold them off a while ago." Aunt June paused. "He suggested I sell this apartment, too, and let him invest the money in the market, but I declined."

Clair sighed. "You saw it coming. I know he made other investments in the market for you, though. Is that all gone, too?"

"Never you mind. Everything will work out." Aunt June patted Clair's hand, stood, and took the boiling kettle off the stove, pouring it. "Check on your father while I finish the tea."

He had fallen asleep. From the table beside the sofa, Clair picked up a silver-framed daguerreotype. The older girl appeared to be a younger version of her aunt, and the child of about ten looked similar, but with more delicate features. Both had large doe eyes, with the curls of their lips in wry smiles. The younger one must be her mother! Odd Clair had never seen this picture before. She'd been to the apartment hundreds of times.

Her aunt came into the room and started to set up tea. Clair swiftly replaced the photo, planning to study it later. *Pshaw!* All the pictures of her mother had *not* burned up in a fire. Clair glanced at her father. He had probably not even loved her, and now the money was gone. He was a liar! Perhaps there were other secrets he was keeping.

37

The next morning, Mr. O'Shaughnessy allowed Clair into the suite to sort through their things.

"Thank you, Mr. O." She hadn't called him that since she was a girl.

He smiled sadly. "Do you need assistance?"

"No, thank you. Aunt June is sending over a man to pick up a few boxes." Clair could only take the minimum.

"Feel free to leave whatever you can to help pay the bill. I'll check on you in a little while." Mr. O'Shaughnessy closed the door behind him.

Shaking her head, she sat at her father's desk, studying the bills again. He had been too agitated to come with her, and the idea of clearing out his things overwhelmed her. Holding the rose paperweight, she rubbed her fingers over the smooth glass. He had tried to keep her like that rose under glass, perfect and unchanging. She had bucked at his restrictions and insisted on whirlwind adventures, but now that was all over.

She sighed. Of course she couldn't take the piano. She crossed to the bench, sat down, and played the Chopin piece one last time. Tears ran down her cheeks like the rain the music implied. She finished playing the notes softly at the end, closed the cover, and ran her hands across the carved wooden front. "Goodbye," she whispered. "Thank you for the years of pleasure." Opening the bench, she straightened her sheet music and put it in the "keep" crate.

She picked up the mantle clock. Even though its incessant chimes annoyed her, she had a yen to take it. Leaving the fragile Waterford candlesticks, she carefully wrapped the clock, a photo of herself at eight, and a cupid figurine in newspaper and put them in the "keep" crate, too.

In her father's closet she pulled clothes from the rack and laid them on the bed. Returning for more, she spied Mr. LeRue's painting hidden in the back.

"Egad!" She'd forgotten all about it. Even though it had only been a few months, it seemed like years since her coming-out ball. She set the painting on the dresser and stood back to inspect it. Still hideous—the pink dress with crisscrossing black lines made her skin crawl.

But as she studied it, she realized that Mr. LeRue had been trying to do something modern. A few weeks ago, Aunt June had taken her up some stairs to a photographer's gallery, where he displayed his wife's modern flower paintings. The bold turquoise, purple, and green colors were so welcoming, Clair wished she could dive into them and take a swim.

She left the portrait in the closet to help with the bill, but she doubted it would bring in much. Perhaps someone would buy it for the canvas.

She threw most of her father's clothes in another crate and put it in the foyer. In her room, she tossed her most fancy shawls, hats, and shoes onto the bed to leave, and picked through the armoire, choosing her most practical outfits. She couldn't resist keeping the pink corset and fringed dress at the bottom of her trunk, and folded all of her keepers on top. Rolling her jewelry into a silk slip, she piled it in her valise along with her hidden makeup and beauty products.

The full crates were soon stacked by the door.

In the stuffy parlor she raised a window, and blaring city noise filled the space. She sat at her father's desk once again and began to sort the contents, throwing out pencil nubs and stubby erasers. The bills, all official-looking papers, fountain pens, and ink went into the keep pile. She picked up a box of cigars and hesitated. Maybe he'd quit that stinky habit—a luxury he could no longer afford. But she put them in the crate so at least he could enjoy these last few.

Mr. O'Shaughnessy knocked on the door and stepped inside the foyer. "Ready?" he called.

Clair wiped her eyes. "Almost. I need another few minutes."

He turned and left.

An envelope poked out from under the desk blotter, and she pulled it out. Strange. It was addressed to her. She opened it to reveal her father's stationary, his initials *LLD* embossed at the top of the thin blue paper, his penmanship scratchy.

Dearest Clair,

If you are reading this, I am gone. I am ruined, but you are not. You still have your whole life ahead of you. I waited too long to sell off before the crash. I couldn't resist the lure of the market and possible riches. Greed was my downfall. I've lost everything.

Her eyes filled with tears as she continued reading.

I couldn't face your aunt and the others I had advised. I truly believed those investments were solid. I never meant to deceive them.

I rue other mistakes I've made and apologize for never having the nerve to tell you the truth about your mother. Aunt June will explain it to you. Tell her I have always been sorry.

Clair paused. She wondered what the truth was—and what it had to do with him calling her mother a tramp.

Cash can be found in my closet safe. The combination is written on the back of the top desk drawer. This money should tide you over for a while. You'll have an easier time without me. When Farley returns, marry him, and have a good life. Sorry I couldn't protect you from all this.

Raffie, you have always been my best girl.

Love,

Father

Clair reread the first line. Where would he have gone? A horn honked outside, and she glanced at the open window, the one that had been wide-open yesterday morning.

He had been contemplating suicide!

Oh, no. Would he try again? Aunt June was at school teaching, and he was alone in the apartment. Her hands shaking, folding her father's note, Clair quickly put it back into the envelope and pushed it in her purse. She took out the desk drawer, wrote the combination on a slip of paper, and attempted to open the safe hidden in his wardrobe. Her hand fumbled on the first try, but she was successful on the second. Inside she found the cash, counted it, and folded it neatly in her purse, too.

38

What a horrible flight. Anne had forgotten to bring a book to read. She tried to sketch in her journal, but the flight was too bumpy. She'd eaten seven bags of peanuts, read the in-flight magazine twice, and tried to watch *Frozen* on the tiny TV screen five seats forward. Finally she gave up and listened to music on her iPhone instead.

Two days ago she decided she didn't have anything to lose and found a cheap flight on Jetblue. She considered just showing up at Sergio's, but instead, on her way to the airport this morning, she'd sent him a text: *Surprise! Happy Birthday. On my way. Boarding. Plane gets in at 4:00.*

When her plane landed, she checked her cell to see his text. But since she'd listened to music most of the flight, her phone had run out of juice. He probably would meet her at the baggage claim as usual.

She anticipated the ride into town with glee. Last time in the back of the town car she had thrown her velvet coat over them, and they'd fondled each other all the way to his place. When they got upstairs, he pulled her inside and kissed her long and deep. She clung to him as he carried her down the hall and into his bedroom with the view overlooking Central Park as twinkle lights had begun to blink on. He threw her on the king-size bed and ravished her for hours, exactly what she had wanted. Would he be all over her again this time?

Now she rode the escalator down into the baggage area, but she didn't see him. Instead, among the row of black-suited drivers, one held a sign that said: *Big Foot*. She laughed, held up her foot, and pointed to her shoe.

"Mr. Parmeggianno asked me to tell you that he will meet you at his place later."

Disappointed, Anne followed the driver to his car. The June sun vibrated down on her while they rode into the city, and she began to get nervous. She'd taken a big chance by coming to New York unannounced. What if he had made other plans?

Nearing his co-op, clouds had begun to fill the blue sky. She tried to smooth her frizzy airplane hair. Out of her backpack, she removed the lace-doily collaged birthday card she'd made and smoothed it out on her leg.

At Sergio's building, the driver handed her suitcase to the doorman.

"Welcome back, Ms. McFarland."

Anne tipped the driver and followed the doorman inside. "Mr. Parmeggianno is still out and asked that you go on up."

He must be at work and would probably be home soon. Anne rolled her suitcase into Sergio's bedroom, which smelled of his honeysuckle aftershave. She tamped down her hair in the mirror, pulled it up into a scrunchie, and hung her coat in the closet.

In the kitchen, she flattened out his birthday card again and leaned it against the bowl with the pearls. A Coke can sat on the counter. That was curious—Sergio hated sodas. Thinking how meticulous he was, she tossed the can in the recycling bin.

She tried to recharge her phone on his desk, but another cell, with a sexy Kate Spade black lace cover, was plugged in. That certainly wasn't his phone. A lump formed in the pit of Anne's stomach.

Oh, God! Had he already found someone else?

Anne resisted the urge to rip the black lace phone out of the cord.

She looked at the elevator entrance. Where was he? Should she bolt?

Instead, she took a deep breath, sat on the leather couch, and grabbed a magazine from the coffee table with Taylor Swift on the cover, sporting the cutest short haircut. Anne started to flip through the pages. *Wait a minute.* She closed it and studied the magazine cover. Why did Sergio have *Glamour?* He was into fashion but wasn't the type to read a strickly women's magazine.

The elevator stopped, and the door opened to the sound of Sergio's laugh and a female voice. Anne grew hot. She ran over, wadded up his birthday card, stuffed it in the trash compactor, and stepped on the squish button. Had he forgotten she would be here? No, he had sent the car.

She stood up straight, grounded her feet, and clenched her fists, ready for a fight. Sergio moved toward her with a grin, removing the delectable fedora she had bought him at Goorin Bros. for Christmas. His hair had been cut quite short, making him look like a GQ model.

Beside him, a petite woman about his age smiled at her—straight dark hair draped to her waist, perfectly applied makeup accentuating large eyes, and spike-heeled boots on her tiny feet.

"You must be the famous Big Anne." The woman rushed toward her, reached up, and placed air kisses above each cheek. "I've heard so much about you." She let Anne go, then took a Coke from the kitchen fridge as if she owned the place.

"All good, I hope." Anne tried to keep her composure.

"Not really," Sergio teased.

"We just came from the Chinese exhibit at the Met, high fashion juxtaposed with Chinese costumes. Incredible. You must see it." The woman hurried toward the bathroom. "*Un momento.*"

Anne walked away and sat on the couch.

"I'm glad you are here, *amore*." Sergio sat beside her and leaned in for a kiss.

She backed away and crossed her arms. "So, just who is . . ."

The woman returned and sat on the other side of Sergio, snuggling up on his arm, showcasing flawlessly manicured nails. Anne hid her paint-stained hands in her armpits. She'd been working on his card until the last minute.

"Who are you?" Anne finally blurted out.

"Anne, this is Bella, my sister."

39

Bella slept in the guest room. After Sergio's breakfast frittata, he and Anne rode down to the lobby with her.

"*Ciao*. I'm so glad I got to meet you." Bella kissed Anne on both cheeks.

"Me, too." Embarrassed that she had imagined Bella was a rival, Anne kissed her back.

Sergio put Bella's Louis Vuitton luggage in the town car trunk and hugged her. "I thought I'd be spending my birthday all alone, and you both showed up to surprise me."

"I'm glad I could come, even if it was for only two nights," Bella said out the window. She waved as the town car cruised down the street.

As Sergio and Anne rode the elevator up to his place, he pulled her close. "Thanks for coming."

"What shall we do today, birthday boy?" she asked. Were they back together?

He kissed her lips. "I've missed you so. How about another birthday surprise?"

"Okeydoke. It's right inside." Back in the kitchen, she dug his card out of the trash compactor, laid it on the counter, and tried to straighten the wrinkles out of it. She held it up to him with a laugh. "Here's your surprise."

"Not exactly what I had in mind. But it will do, since it is an Anne McFarland original. What happened to it?" He took it with a smile, ran his fingers over the lace doily, and leaned it against the bowl.

"I tried giving it a distressed look." She paused. "I have a confession to make. When I saw Bella's things here yesterday, I was afraid you'd started seeing someone else."

"*Non c'è modo.*" He shook his head and put his hands on her shoulders.

"Are you sure you aren't playing the field?"

"How could I? You are on my mind all the time. It would take me forever to find someone else I love as much as you."

That knocked the wind out of her—in a good way—and she couldn't speak.

He pulled her close, but then let go. "Are *you* seeing someone else?"

"No way!" She laughed. "I told you, I don't care if we ever get married. I just want to be with you."

"I'm sorry I hurt you, but let's not talk about it now. Bella's gone and we are alone, so how about a different birthday surprise?"

"Maybe."

He lifted her up in his arms. "Come on. Hey, have you lost weight?"

"A little."

"I'd say a lot. Were you dieting?"

"Not really." No way would she tell him how distraught she'd been about the breakup.

He carried her into his bedroom. They were definitely back together. But what did it really mean?

∽

Later, Anne lounged on the couch wearing Sergio's velour robe. "I'm excited to go to Rudy's tonight."

"Don't get your hopes up. It's seedy. Choose a matinee for this afternoon while I get you a 'pop'."

She laughed and picked up the copy of the morning *New York Times* Bella had left strewn on the coffee table. "What are you in the mood for?"

"Anything but *Cats*."

"How about *Hamilton*?" she asked.

He handed her a Coke on ice and sat beside her. "I can't get tickets for under a million dollars on such short notice."

"Is that too much?" she teased.

"I'll take you next time you come to town."

He said *come*, not *move*. He must not be convinced she didn't care about the engagement anymore. What could she do to let him know she was serious about moving here without it?

She handed him the paper and sipped her Coke. "You decide, but let's not go to a musical where little girls sing off-key in sober tones about something they shouldn't even know about."

He scanned the listings. "*Avenue Q*?"

"No way. I hate the idea of puppets talking dirty. They're puppets, for God's sake!" she laughed.

"I've got it! *Beautiful: The Carole King Musical*."

"Really, you'd go to that with me?"

"Of course."

"I'm warning you. You'll need to hold me back from singing aloud." Her mom and Aunt Tootie would play Carole King's songs over and over again.

He laughed. "I'll take my chances." He opened his phone and hit a few buttons. "Done! We'll go by the antique shop first."

"While you're in the shower, I'll write a letter to the shop guy."

"Great idea. Then get ready."

Anne neatly folded up the newspaper and set it on the coffee table. She ripped out a piece of paper from her journal and wrote:

Dear Sir:

Remember me? I'm the one who bought the rhinestone shoes. In the bottom of the box, I found a pearl necklace. Please contact me to return the pearls.

Sincerely,

Anne McFarland

She wrote her cell number, folded the note, and put it in her coat pocket. From her suitcase she donned jeans and a black lace blouse, and put on the pearls and her coat.

Sergio, in a sports coat and jaunty plaid cap, took her hand, and they made their way, arm in arm, down the sidewalk and into a cab.

At Timely Treasures, drapes were drawn like theater curtains. The closed sign had been replaced by one that read: *Reopening Soon!*

"Look!" Anne yelled. "Someone *has* been here!" She spotted a crack between the curtains and peeked inside. "There's a light on, and something just moved!"

"I told you someone had been here."

She knocked on the door and waited, but no one answered. Disappointed, she fingered the pearls and knocked again. "Let's wait a few minutes."

Sergio put his hand on her back. "We'd better go, or we'll be late for the show."

Finding no mail slot, she stuck the note under the door.

At Times Square, the crowds had begun to gather. Anne checked out the giant ads as the big-screen TV scrolled ticker-tape news at the bottom: *A judge ordered the army to redo part of its environmental analysis for the Dakota Access pipeline.*

Sergio and Anne made their way to the historic Sondheim Theatre on West Forty-Third Street. Inside the lobby, photos of past performers decorated the walls. Anne peered closely at them and stopped to inspect a black-and-white picture of a voluptuous girl wearing a gigantic frilly bonnet and another taller girl in a shorts outfit. "These are the same girls from the shoebox photo!"

"The flappers? It couldn't be. That's too much of a coincidence."

"It might be. I believe in serendipity. Aren't those the rhinestone shoes?" Anne pointed at the tall girl's feet.

Sergio leaned in and studied them. "Could be."

Anne could tell he didn't really believe it and wished she could prove it to him somehow.

40

Beautiful turned out to be one of Anne's favorite musicals ever. The actress playing Carole sounded just like her. Anne caught herself lip-syncing many of the songs, and tears pooled in her eyes during "Will You Still Love Me Tomorrow?"

Afterward, outside the theater, a cool wind stirred and rain began to fall. She started to back up under an awning and slipped on the slick sidewalk. Sergio caught her elbow, and she sang out loud, "I feel the earth move under my feet! I feel the sky tumbling down."

The other people exiting the building stared at her.

Sergio laughed. "Let's go, Carole. I'm starved."

Anne smiled. "I've heard that before. Is Rudy's far?"

"No. But we'll take a cab. You wait here."

Soon they were heading downtown in a big checkered taxi.

"Do we have reservations?" Anne brushed wet drops off the shoulders of her coat.

"They don't take them."

As they approached the restaurant, the "Rudy's Bar & Grill" neon sign blinked on. A wooden facade had been built over the brick building. A kitschy sculptured pig in a red vest and bow tie smiled with a wave.

Sergio and Anne got out of the cab. A velvet rope cordoned off the entrance, and a sign said: *Closed for a Special Event.*

"Can't we go in and just take a look?" Anne begged the short, skinny bouncer.

He shook his head. "Sorry. It's a VIP reception."

"But I found a picture of some flappers . . ."

"Excuse me." A girl in a very short dress and very high heels pushed Anne aside and gave her name to the bouncer.

Anne looked at Sergio, and they stepped back. "Can you get us in?" she asked.

"I'll try."

The bouncer unleashed the rope for the girl. As she opened the door, music blasted out.

"Any chance you can find us a table?" Sergio smiled at the bouncer and tried to hand him a hundred.

He held up his hands and shook his head. "Sorry."

"But my friend is working on some . . ."

The bouncer frowned at him. "Doesn't matter."

Anne didn't want to embarrass Sergio, otherwise she would have pushed right past this scrawny guy. She could take him on any day.

Sergio walked back to her. "Sorry. I can get us in another time." He pushed a number on his cell. "*Ciao*. It's Sergio. Any reservations open for tonight?"

She could hear a male voice on the other end, but couldn't make out the words.

Sergio laughed, hung up, and hailed them another cab. "We're all set," he told her as they settled into the back seat. "Pasta is specialty of the house."

"Perfect. I'm warning you, I'm in a slurping mood. Pootie and I used to have contests to prove who could inhale the most noodles the loudest."

"Bella and I used to do that, too!"

"No way." Anne punched him gently on the arm.

"Way!"

"I'm louder."

"No, I am."

In no time, they arrived in front of an old apartment complex: no sign, no nothing. The building blended in with many on the street except red geraniums bloomed in a window box.

Sergio spoke into the intercom. "*Ciao*!" A buzzer let them in, and they ascended the dark stairs.

"Where are we?" Anne asked.

"A secret kitchen for locals."

She squinted at him. "I've never heard of such a thing!"

"Speakeasies were secret. You've heard of them. And besides, you aren't a local."

"At least not yet," she mumbled.

"What?" he asked.

"Nothing." She shook her head. Hopefully at dinner they would talk about her moving to New York.

They hiked up two floors, and he knocked on the door of Apartment 22.

A hefty Italian in an apron and tall chef's hat ushered them inside. "Sergio! Pergio! It's been a long time!" The men exchanged bear hugs.

"Cousin Connie. This is my girlfriend, Anne."

So they *were* back together.

"Ana! *Benvenuto*." Cousin Connie squeezed her, too—an embrace so strong she could hardly breathe. He ushered them into a room filled with empty tables covered in red-checkered cloths. Straw-covered wine bottles on each table held lit candles with dripping wax. A mural of an Italian vineyard graced one wall. Garlic permeated her senses as he led them down a narrow hall and into another room. This one with three tables must have been a bedroom at one time.

"Best seat in the *casa*! Or should I say, in the *appartamento*?"

Their small table next to a window looked down over a garden. Twinkle lights blinked on around it as the sun began to set. A Scottish terrier slept among the greens.

Connie delivered a bottle of Chianti, poured it for them, and left.

"Are you and your cousin close?" Anne asked.

"No. We don't see each other much."

"I don't get to be with Pootie often, either, but we are very close."

"Women are different."

"That's for sure." Anne smiled. "Where's the menu?"

"Connie doesn't use one. It's either pasta or pasta."

"Pescatarian option?"

"I'm certain of it. Spicy or not?"

"Of course, for me the more garlic, the better. If we both have it, we can still kiss."

"That's important." He took her hands and leaned toward her. "I am sooo glad you're here."

"Me, too. Happy birthday." Anne nodded. She wanted to ask him if he had decided if she could move here with him, but she'd wait and see if he brought up the topic first.

Connie seated two other couples at the tables in the room. He left and returned to deliver bread to Sergio and Anne.

"What type of pasta do you have tonight?" Sergio asked.

"Mushroom *Fantastico*."

"Spicy and spicy." Sergio pointed to each of them. He chatted with his cousin, and Anne leaned back in her chair. Sergio seemed at ease in this unusual eatery; he spoke Italian using big gestures that matched Connie's in size.

They sipped their wine slowly, and each ate a piece of melt-in-your-mouth garlic bread.

Sergio leaned across the table and took her hand again. "I've never met a girl like you."

She swallowed the bread she was chewing. "I've never met a guy like you."

"I need to ask you something. Please come to Italy with me. You won't be sorry."

But when they returned, would she just go back to San Francisco? "I need to check my finances."

"I have miles saved up. I'll pay for the flights, our accommodations, and meals. As I've told you, every artist needs to see Italy. Please come."

Connie delivered their pasta. Sergio twisted the noodles around his fork, and so did she. Hungry, she longed to inhale it fast but took her time and slurped as loudly as possible. He laughed and noisily sucked a big mouthful of noodles in.

The people at the other tables gaped at them.

"I was the loudest!" Sergio yelled with his fist lifted toward the ceiling.

"No, I was!" Anne put her hand on her hip.

"No, I was!"

A man from the next table leaned over. "She was!" He raised his glass at Anne and turned back to his frowning wife. Her pinched mouth made her seem like a reincarnation of Mrs. Astor.

Anne stuffed a piece of garlic bread in her mouth and stared at the woman.

Sergio put his hand over his eyes.

The man laughed, used a bit of bread to soak up some of the sauce from the edge of his plate, and stuffed it in his mouth, too.

His wife glared at him. "Take me home." She stood up and strode off.

He shrugged, took another bite off his plate, got up, and followed her.

A few minutes later, Connie slid a check next to Sergio. "Cousin, you need to go."

"But we haven't had our tiramisu yet," Anne pouted.

Sergio looked at the other couple in the room. They turned their heads away.

"Okay. Sorry!" Sergio left cash on the table and helped Anne put on her coat.

"I didn't mean to get us kicked out."

Sergio laughed. "It was worth it! Connie will forgive me."

"I doubt it."

"He will. We're family. I want to get home early anyway."

"Why?"

"I need time to convince you to come with me to Italy this summer." He pulled her to him and landed a big garlicky kiss on her lips.

41

It had been a few months since Clair and her father had moved in with Aunt June. Fortunately there had still been no word from Farley. The days had shortened, and the cold nights lasted longer. Thanksgiving and Christmas had come and gone without the usual decor and festivities.

Clair's father continued to lie on the sofa and brood. Early on, Dr. Johnson had made a house call. He opened his black bag, examined her father, and shook his head. "Time and rest is all he needs." But that had been ages ago, and her father still hadn't recovered. Aunt June and Clair had a silent agreement not to spend precious cash on the doctor just to receive the same instructions.

They had also decided it best for her father not to learn Clair had found the letter. His pride would be damaged if he found out they knew he had planned to take his own life. She had begged her aunt to divulge her mother's secret, but all she said was, "I promised your father years ago I'd never tell you."

"What happened to that photo I saw the first night we were here?" Clair asked. "It seems to have disappeared."

"Your father doesn't like to be reminded of her, so I put it away."

"May I see it?"

"Of course. It's in the top bureau drawer. Look at it whenever you wish." Aunt June patted Clair's arm.

Clair had asked him questions that might release the secret. However, whenever she mentioned her mama's name, he would frown and not say a word. So she left the topic alone. She didn't want him to get more upset.

After breakfast, Clair kissed his cheek, his gray hairs scratchy on her lips. "Out for a stroll. I won't be long."

"Isn't that frock too fancy?"

"No, Father." For her outing today she needed to look respectable. She had cobbled together a drop-waist dress with lace trim at the bodice and skirt hem, and had even put on her knotted pearls. Memories of that night with Mr. X kept her from selling the repaired necklace, but she knew she might need to soon.

Clair had to take care of the family now. Before the holidays, enrollment had dropped and Aunt June's school had let her go. During the day they sat in the apartment and played Authors, their favorite card game, unable to get her father to join in. At night they didn't light the apartment, to save money.

They had all begun to lose weight. Aunt June had a deep cough that shook the bed and kept Clair up at night. Aunt June said they'd get by, but Clair knew if she didn't do something, it was only a matter of time before they ended up in a breadline, too.

She had vowed to find Winnie today in hopes she could help her get a job. Clair had been by Macy's several times in search of Winnie, but she hadn't been there.

Clair trod down the flight of stairs in front of the apartment to the sidewalk. A group of men crowded around a Model T trapped in the mud, attempting to push it out.

Strong winds pushed cold gusts from the harbor onto Manhattan. It had poured for five days and nights straight. Even though she wore her long coat with the fur collar, Clair was still chilled. Draping a woolen shawl over her head, she continued on her way. She quickened her pace, gingerly avoiding puddles from last night's rain. Clouds rolled in, covering her with more darkness. Another storm was on its way. The tip of her nose felt frozen, and she could see her breath. She kept walking, even though the pavement under her thinning boots was cold on her feet.

A whiff of chestnuts from a nearby stand caused her stomach to rumble with hunger. It had been days since she'd eaten a decent meal. How she longed for fresh eggs—poached, broiled, or baked, simmering with butter.

She made it to the shoe-shop window as the owner raised the aluminum cover. Every chance she got she stopped by to admire the silver shoes for a few moments. As she passed the business next door, the nice young Italian barber waved at her, and she smiled and waved back. He probably didn't even remember her. The bob had begun to grow out.

She turned, and a tall man in a hat came toward her on the sidewalk. Could it be Mr. X? She kept walking toward him with a vigorous heartbeat, but then as he got closer he nodded at her, and she realized it wasn't him at all. Over the months she had imagined seeing him everywhere.

Clair took a shortcut down an alley and rambled toward the Waldorf. A tabby snarled and skittered across her path, chasing a mouse. The cats, too, were hungry.

At the hotel, Mr. O'Shaughnessy stood at the entrance. Clair hid in the shadows across the street and gazed up at the window of their old suite. She wondered who lived there now, imagining her comfortable bed, the spacious parlor, and her fingers gliding over the ebony-and-ivory keys. Had the new residents kept the piano? She had resented being a caged bird then, but now she longed to go back to that life. All the luxuries she had—all the food they could eat—caviar on toast for breakfast if she wished.

"Got a penny?" A dirt-smudged hand flew toward her.

"No, Nook." She gave him a wistful smile. "I'm sorry."

She started to pass him, but he hurried along beside her. "Would you like a penny for your thoughts?" He grinned.

Slowly she recited, "I'm thinking it 'twas a bright night. Or I'm thinkin' the moon had shone not right."

"Good enough." He pulled a coin from his pocket and handed it to her.

She shouldn't take it, but she did; every cent counted these days. "Thank you."

He bowed low and blew her a kiss.

At Macy's, Clair sighed as she passed the candy counter, riding the elevator up to the employment department on the top floor. A woman sat behind the desk with a pencil sticking in her hair. Clair took off her coat and straightened her cloche hat.

"Hello," Clair told the woman. "I'm looking for my sister. I went to the address we had from her last letter, but she's moved, and nobody there knows where she's gone. She had said she worked here, but none of the staff have seen her today. Would you please be so kind as to give me her address?"

The woman shook her head. "I don't think we give out that type of information."

Clair ran a handkerchief under her watery eyes as if catching a tear.

"But I came all the way from Chicago with some sad news. Our papa passed away."

The woman frowned. "I'm sorry. I'm new here, and as I said, I'm sure it's against our policy." She looked at the door and smiled. "However, under these circumstances, I'm sure Macy's would make an exception. What's your sister's name?"

"Winifred Waters."

The woman shuffled through a pile of note cards and pulled one out. "Oh. She doesn't work here anymore."

"Can you give me the home address written there?"

The woman nodded, pulled the pencil from her hair, wrote down the address, and handed the slip of paper to Clair.

On the way out of the office, Clair crossed paths with Mr. Smithers. He glanced at her with a surprised look on his owl-eyed face. Clair smiled back at him and sashayed by. Maybe she could be in the movies, too.

Out on the sidewalk, she studied the address. It was too far to walk. She rode a bus to a nearby street, walked the rest of the way, climbed the steps, and knocked on the door.

A gray-haired lady answered and looked Clair up and down. "We don't got any rooms available."

She smiled at the woman. "I'm looking for Winifred Waters. Is she here?"

The landlady pointed to the staircase. "Last door at the end of the hall."

Clair passed over the hooked rug and glanced into the parlor, where a trio of ladies played cards and another knitted on a faded sofa. Clair felt their eyes on her back as she ascended the stairs. She knocked on the last door.

"Boy, am I happy to see you!" Winnie squealed, giving Clair a hug and drawing her in. Simply furnished, the small room had an unmade single bed, a nightstand, and a dresser piled with stacks of movie magazines. "How did you ever find me?"

"Told Macy's personnel department that I was your long-lost sister."

"Well, you are. I've missed you so!" Winnie quickly pulled up the chenille bedspread and began to untwist the white rags from her hair, letting the curls bounce down to her shoulders. Instead of the emaciated appearance of most people on the streets, Winnie's body, wrapped in a torn robe, had increased in size. "I've been to the Waldorf looking for you, but no one there would tell me where you'd gone."

Tears filled Clair's eyes. "We've fallen on hard times." She dropped onto the edge of the bed, breaking down in sobs.

"There, there." Winnie held Clair while she cried.

After a minute, Clair pulled away. "I'm sorry."

"If you can't cry on my shoulder, whose can you cry on?" Winnie pulled a handkerchief from her pocket and dried Clair's tears. "Better? I've got just the thing to cheer you up."

"A cup of tea?"

"Something much better." Winnie gave her a devilish grin.

Clair raised her hand. "Dear me! Not alcohol. That would make me feel worse."

"Not booze." Winnie opened her nightstand drawer, took out a small paper sack, and handed it to Clair.

Clair put her hand inside, pulled out a chocolate disk with white sprinkles, placed it on her tongue, and closed her eyes. The nonpareil melted in her mouth. She swallowed and opened her eyes. "You're the best friend a girl could ever have!"

"Such a good friend I even crashed your wedding." Winnie giggled.

Clair helped herself to another candy. "You're not the only one who crashed."

The girls broke out in hysterics. It felt so good to laugh again.

"Was he okay?"

"He was fine. Only a big bump on his head."

"A big bump on the big lump."

They broke out in laughter again.

"We were supposed to set a new date, but then he disappeared."

Winnie smiled. "We didn't need that bluenose anyway!"

Clair nodded. "What happened to you the night of the raid?"

Winnie hugged herself. "We used Rudy's exit plan. He grabbed me, and we slipped out the back way."

"Didn't the police realize he owned the speakeasy?"

"Yes, probably, but you know that Rudy." Winnie grinned, rubbing her fingers together and nodding. "He knows people, and cash is king."

Clair got the picture. "Do you remember a tall young man from that night?"

"Who?"

"My pearls broke, and he helped me gather them up. Did you see him?"

Winnie shook her head. If she probed too deeply, Winnie would get suspicious and Clair would be too embarrassed to share the details of what they had done that night. She changed the subject. "I'm sorry I cried so much."

"This should cheer you up, too." Winnie picked up her purse from the floor, rummaged through it, and offered Clair a few bills.

"I can't take that!" She pushed it away.

"Let me help."

"You can. Help me get a job."

"Work? You?" Winnie's eyes widened.

"Yes, a real job, something steady. Do you still have acquaintances at Macy's?"

Winnie laughed. "We didn't exactly part on very good terms."

"I'm sorry." Clair frowned. "Did Mr. Smithers fire you?"

"Nothing like that." Winnie put her hands on her hips. "I quit!"

"You did?"

"I'm getting ready for my debut." Winnie raised her head up.

"You're going to be a debutante, too?"

"No, silly! At Rudy's place."

"But I had assumed it had closed down."

"No, at the new Rudy's! Opening tomorrow. After the raid he decided to go legit. It's a real classy joint like he always said he'd get. It used to be owned by a theater company that did Greek and Shakespearean dramatizations. They left the back room filled with all sorts of crazy costume and set pieces we can use, even abandoned the Singer sewing machine."

Clair smiled and ate another nonpareil.

Winnie continued, "I've made up a dance routine. And, of course, designed a fabulous costume with a fancy hat. Rudy says I'll knock 'em dead."

Clair knew about Winnie's hats and hoped this new one wouldn't fall into the audience and really kill someone. "Congratulations!"

"Maybe Rudy will hire you. We could use some help making costumes."

"But I don't know how to sew." A tailor had always repaired Clair's wardrobe.

"It's a cinch. We'll teach you. Rudy probably can't pay much. Not until the crowds start coming in. What fun it would be to have you there! I'll talk to Rudy. Come down tomorrow. You can stay for my debut, too. Like I've always told you, I'm going to be a big star!"

Clair would be relieved to have a job, but she could never tell her aunt and father she worked in a speakeasy-type business, even a legitimate one.

42

Clair stared, astounded at the theater's lofty marquee: *Rudy's Rollicking Review! Featuring Varinska the Vamp, Rudy's Cuties, and introducing the Wonderful Winnie Waters. Acrobats, contortionists, and more . . .*

No secret password was needed to get inside this building. Clair entered through a marbled lobby and into the cavernous theater space. Winnie hadn't been fooling. This place *was* posh; rows of plush seats sloped down toward a real stage with burgundy velvet curtains.

A pianist in the pit played an introduction to "Puttin' on the Ritz." Clair knew this tune by heart, and her fingers ached to feel the piano keys.

"Hello?" Her voice rang out as she walked down the aisle toward the music.

The piano abruptly stopped.

She found her way down to the pianist.

"May I help you?" The man's vibrato voice resonated in the key of D.

"I'm looking for Winnie."

"Not here yet." He shook his head.

Clair frowned. "She told me to meet her here at ten this morning."

"She'll be here soon. You can wait for her downstairs in the dressing room." He tilted his head to the left of the stage.

"Thank you, kind sir." Clair smiled at him.

"Don't mention it." He stood and bowed. "Mordecai at your service."

Clair tried not to stare. He stood about Nook's height, but with the features of an adult male. He must be a midget like she'd seen at the circus. It was a miracle that his small hands could play so well. Glancing down, she noticed blocks tied to the piano pedals.

She nodded and walked off as Mordecai played and sang, "Jeepers creepers, where'd ya get those peepers! Jeepers creepers, where'd ya get those eyes?"

Clair laughed aloud. She yearned to join him in song but instead found her way backstage and descended a flight of stairs. She stood in the grimy basement's doorway. There were cigarette butts in glass jars, peanut shells on the floor, cobwebs in the corners, and clothes piled on the floor. The odor of kerosene permeated the space.

Across the room, a girl rocked her feet up and down on a treadle sewing machine. One of her hands expertly moved a wheel while the other guided fabric beneath the machine's arm.

A dark-haired young woman wearing horn-rimmed glasses looked up from her hand sewing. "Clair?"

She had no idea who the woman was.

"Clair! It's me, Bea." Her voice had a high squeak.

"I didn't recognize you." Clair couldn't believe it. The girl who had been a flapper looked mousy in her dark suit and glasses.

"What're you doing here?" Bea walked over, put a hand on her hip, and squinted through her glasses.

"Winnie asked me to help with costumes."

"Are you sure?"

"Certain." Clair nodded. "And what are *you* doing here?"

"My folks and I didn't see eye to eye."

Clair wasn't shocked. "That's too bad."

"I heard you've had troubles, too." Bea pointed to the sewing-machine girl. "Meet Dominique Swan."

"Bonjour, new recruit!" She saluted Clair. "Didn't I see you at the old Rudy's?"

"Possibly." Clair recalled Dominique dancing with Mr. LeRue. Clair wondered where he had landed, but didn't dare bring up his name. Maybe later she'd ask about him and try to slip a description of Mr. X into the conversation.

"We'd better get a wiggle on. We're on a tight schedule. Sit." Bea put her hand on the bench.

Clair removed her gloves, put them in her coat pocket, hung her coat on a rack, and sat next to Bea, who handed Clair a piece of material. Clair laid it on her knee and ran her hands over the sash. The smooth satin reminded her of the pink corset, the one she'd worn that night with Mr. X.

Bea dumped a spool of thread, a packet of needles, and a heap of red sequins on the table in front of them. Clair had no idea how to get started. Bea sewed beside her, dark head bent over a long cape. Clair, too embarrassed to ask for help, picked up a needle and thread. It wiggled in her hand as she tried to poke it through the hole.

Winnie clomped down the stairs and jumped into the room. "Ta-da!"

That girl really knew how to make an entrance. With her voluptuous body, curly hair, and frilly frock, she resembled a pint-sized Mae West.

She kissed Clair, picked up the sash, and studied it. "Oh, no! You haven't even started."

"Sorry. I have no idea where to begin," Clair whispered in her ear.

Winnie glanced at Bea. "Please teach her how. I've got to rehearse." Winnie pranced with her arms outstretched and admired herself in the dusty oval mirror displayed on a stand in the corner. She mouthed the words to a song.

"Okay, here, I'll show you." Bea sighed loudly and adjusted her glasses. "Hold the needle up to the light. Lick the thread and slide it into the hole. Cut it and knot the end." She picked up a sequin. "Put your hand under here. Hold the sequin and poke the needle through. Don't prick yourself. These are tiny but sharp. Make sure to use your thimble."

"I don't have one." Clair felt her face turn red.

Dominique stopped her treadle and blinked at Clair.

Winnie pranced over to a basket sitting on the table and pulled out a thimble. "Here, use mine." She tossed it to Clair and returned to the mirror.

Clair observed carefully as Bea sewed the sequin to the band. She handed the cloth back to Clair. At first it was challenging, but Clair finally got the hang of it. It felt good to be doing something constructive with her time, plus the meditative rhythm of the in and out movements was relaxing.

After a while, the sparkle of the sequins began to hypnotize her. She gazed up and watched Winnie practicing her steps. They were more like gallops than the struts that Clair assumed were called for. Head down, looking at her feet, Winnie pushed her arms as if swimming a breaststroke. It might look better if Winnie held her head erect and moved one arm at a time—right forward, then left forward.

Clair didn't want her friend to think she was criticizing her, so she held her tongue. Clair visualized her own body doing it that way: her long arms reaching toward the audience as if giving an invitation—an invitation for what, she wasn't sure, but definitely something secret.

Winnie noticed Clair staring at her and shimmied. Clair laughed, bowing her head back to her sewing. The thread ran out, so she tied it in a knot and leaned down to break off the ends with her teeth. Bea shook her head and handed her a pair of scissors. Clair cut above the knot and started anew. After missing a few times, she managed to get a new length of thread through the needle and sewed on a new line of sequins.

She peeked back up at Winnie. With both hands on her hips and her body at an angle, Winnie threw each foot out wildly. Her stiff-legged kicks didn't go very high. Clair instinctively knew that if Winnie bent her back leg, it would give the illusion that her other leg flew up higher. Clair had the urge to jump up and show her friend how, but she didn't dare.

Winnie turned. "Is the sash done?"

"Almost." Clair decided to be brave. "Maybe when you kick your leg, you could try bending the other knee?"

"What?" Winnie scrunched up her nose.

"Like this." Clair stood and demonstrated.

Bea and Dominique watched with smirks on their faces.

Copying Clair, Winnie bent her back knee and kicked—and her other foot did go up higher! She grinned. "You're right!" She practiced step touches, kicking with her back knees bent.

Clair sewed on the rest of the sequins and knotted the thread. "Done." She rose and handed it to Winnie.

Bea squinted at the zigzaggy rows and loose loops, but Winnie shrugged.

"Never mind. No one from the audience will even notice." Winnie held it around her waist.

Clair secured the snaps at the back. "It seems a bit snug. Are you sure it's not too tight?"

"It's fine."

Feet tromped down the stairs, and two more girls came in. The petite one had short raven-black hair, and the other had auburn hair and a freckled face.

"Hiya, the rest of Rudy's Cuties! Meet Clair." Bea said.

The dark-haired one looked Clair up and down. "I'm Olga. What type of act do you do?"

"No act. Just sewing."

"I should say so. I'm Henrietta." The other girl took off her cloche hat and laid it on the table. "Rudy said half hour to places."

"Clair, hang up the clothes after each performance and hand them out like this." From a rack, Winnie gave black-and-white costumes to the four Rudy's Cuties: Olga, Henrietta, Bea, and Dominique. They slipped on the bloomers, helped each other zip up their blouses, and strapped on their black shoes.

"That's easy." Clair would also do some tidying up when she had time.

A pair of identical twin girls wandered in.

"This is Ping and Pang, our Oriental contortionists."

"Pleased to meet you," they said simultaneously, and nodded at Clair.

The sweet things seemed to be about five years old. They sat on the ground in their white silk outfits. Legs splayed out, they faced each other, clasped hands, and stretched back and forth. Clair would definitely start with sweeping the floor first.

A muscular man in a tight-fitting leotard with a little skirt lurched in. "Who's this luscious creature?" He dangled his arm over Clair's shoulders.

She hunched and closed her eyes.

Winnie pushed him away. "Back off, Henry."

"Yur just jealous." He stumbled away.

The Cuties took turns putting their makeup on in a mirror surrounded by lights.

"Darlinks!" Varinska sauntered in.

Olga rose from in front of the mirror, and Varinska sat down. She appeared older without her makeup.

Rudy rushed in, looking dapper in his tuxedo. He grinned at Clair. "Hi, gal pal. Welcome to the new Rudy's."

"I appreciate you taking me on."

"I never can say no to Winnie." He grinned at his girlfriend and looked back at Clair with a frown. "It's on a trial basis, you understand."

Behind his back, Bea rolled her eyes at Dominique.

He clapped his hands. "We have a decent matinee crowd. Places! You're going to be a big hit."

The cast ran up the stairs sounding like an earthquake.

Rudy pointed to a handwritten poster on the wall. "Gal pal. Make sure to read the rules."

Clair looked at Winnie expectantly, but her friend handed her a torn skirt. "You'd better mend this. I'll go up for the opening number and come get you to watch my act. "

Clair silently read:

Rudy's Rules

1. *No alcohol*
2. *Don't eat in costume*
3. *No wearing costumes in public*
4. *Always be decent*
5. *If you can see the audience, they can see you*
6. *The show must always go on*

Easy enough. She sat back down and picked up the skirt, but had no idea how to begin.

"Miss Devereaux!"

She looked up and there stood Mr. LeRue in the doorway, wearing a royal-blue velvet suit. His toupee sat crooked on his head.

Oh, dear God! She cleared her throat and pointed to her own hair.

Mr. LeRue turned his head, moved to the mirror, and promptly straightened the pompadour with his fingertips. He seemed dashing in a flamboyant blue jay kind of way.

"I'm sorry to hear your family has fallen on hard times," his voice drawled.

Was he being sincere? "We're getting by."

"You don't look any the worse for wear. How's your father?"

"He's doing the best he can. How've you been?"

"Tip-top!"

From above, Mordecai's piano played, and she heard rhythmic click, click, click sounds, too. She looked up.

"Tap dancers." Mr. LeRue put his hand on his hip, pointed his toe, and snapped his foot up and down.

"Are you in the show, too, Mr. LeRue?" she asked.

"Call me Andre. Dear me, no! I design the sets, props, and costumes."

"I thought Winnie did that."

Applause could be heard from above.

"She dabbles a bit. But I'm the one with the vision." He put a narrow hand on his chest.

"Really?"

"Why yes! Rudy has given me carte blanche."

Clair doubted that very much.

Even though Mr. LeRue was being nice to her, she still didn't trust him. There always seemed to be trouble whenever he was around.

43

Clair straightened Winnie's feathered bonnet and tightened it under her friend's chin. "Are you sure you have to wear this? It might fall off."

"Of course, I want to wear it." Winnie pouted with a nod as the top-heavy hat precariously teetered.

"Have you practiced with it onstage?" Clair asked.

"No. It's a surprise." Winnie inspected herself in the mirror and straightened her bonnet, but all of a sudden, her rosy cheeks turned pale. "Uh-oh. I'm feeling woozy."

Varinska came in. "Only stage fright."

Winnie's face broke out in a sweat. "What do I do?" she moaned.

"Breathe, darlink, breathe." Varinska shrugged, lit a cigarette, and went out the back door into the alley.

"I'm thirsty."

Clair handed Winnie a cup of water.

She took a sip with shaky hands and plopped down on the bench. "I can't do it."

Clair wished she had some smelling salts just in case. She looked at the rules. "Yes, you can! Rule number six—'The show must always go on.'"

She blotted Winnie's face with a handkerchief and grabbed her hands. "Look at me," Clair said. "You've aspired to this your whole life. Now take a deep breath."

Winnie inhaled.

"Let it out." Clair wasn't sure what to say next, so she let her instincts guide her. "What is your favorite flower?"

"Roses."

"Mine, too!" Clair smiled. "What color?"

"Yellow."

"Mine's pink." Clair softened her voice and spoke slowly. "Now close your eyes. Smell the intoxicating aroma of yellow roses. Breathe with me. In and out, in and out."

Winnie's breathing slowed, and after a few minutes, she opened her eyes and smiled at Clair. "I'm better now."

"Are you ready to go upstairs?"

Winnie nodded. Clair put her hand on the small of Winnie's back and guided her up. From the wings, they watched Ping and Pang lean back in their white leotards, put their feet on top of their heads, and roll around and around in somersaults. They exited behind the curtain. Winnie and Clair had to step aside to make room for them.

From the other side, Rudy came onstage carrying a microphone on a long cord, his rhinestone bow tie gleaming. "Ladies and gentlemen! Let's give our Chinese contortionists, Ping and Pang, a big hand!"

Their pigtails flying, the twins sprinted back onto the stage, took deep bows, and ran off again. No two girls could be more adorable.

"Next up, we have a special treat for you. First time ever onstage, a big round of applause for the Wonderful Twinkle Toes, Winnie Waters!"

The band played her introduction, and Winnie shook her head. "I can't do it," she whispered to Clair.

"Yes, you can. Inhale the roses." Clair tightened the hat's bow beneath Winnie's chin.

Winnie closed her eyes and inhaled and exhaled a few times, then turned toward the stage. "I'm ready."

The band repeated the introduction, and this time Winnie stepped onstage. Kick step. Kick step. Her steps should have hit with the drum's top hat but were off by a beat. Her voice was off-key, too. "Yes sir, that's my baby."

Center stage, Winnie faced the audience and kept singing.

Someone in the audience yelled, "Boo!"

Oh, poor Winnie!

Winnie froze and Clair's hands flew to her face. After a few beats, Winnie curtsied hello like she'd practiced, but her hat fell at her feet and the audience tittered.

Winnie stared at her hat. Then she looked out at the audience, shimmied, and leaned forward, giving the crowd an eyeful as her voluptuous breasts practically fell out of her costume. The men hooted and whistled.

One in the back yelled, "Take it all off!"

Winnie's face fell and she looked as if she might cry. Clair longed to run out there, put her arm around Winnie, and hurry her offstage. But Winnie turned and punted the hat in one fell swoop, like a football, into the wings toward Clair.

Winnie's mouth broadened into a smile, her eyes brightened, and she continued to sing. "Yes sir, that's my baby. No sir, I don't mean maybe. *Doo doo doo doot doot doot doo doo.*" She moved her arms back and forth, hamming it up.

This time the audience wasn't laughing at Winnie but with her. She took another bow. The red sequined sash ripped from her waist and fell to the floor. She got another round of laughter and Clair joined in, too. Winnie continued her routine to the very end and then skedaddled offstage. But immediately afterward, she danced back onstage and performed another chorus as the audience continued to applaud.

That girl couldn't sing or dance particularly well, but Clair realized making it in this business wasn't about talent but guts and gumption.

"Bada bing!" Rudy came onstage. "Yes sir, that's my baby! Ain't that Wonderful Winnie a dame?" He took and raised Winnie's hand as she curtsied again.

The crowd stood on their feet, clapping and hollering with pleasure as Rudy escorted her offstage and handed her over to Clair.

"Oh, yes. Leave them wanting more, dear Winnie," Clair whispered in her ear.

Arm in arm, Winnie and Clair watched Varinska's gypsy finale, with a repeat of her speakeasy act. Clair was still mesmerized by the act, but it seemed a bit out of place in this gorgeous theater.

During the final curtain call, each act came out and bowed, but when Winnie returned to the stage, the audience jumped to their feet in loud applause. The whole cast joined hands, bowed in unison, and began to sing "Jeepers Creepers," pointing to people in the audience. Clair almost dashed onstage to join in the fun.

After the curtains closed, Rudy said, "Everyone take off your costumes and meet me upstairs for notes in fifteen!"

Clair followed the cast downstairs and helped Varinska out of her costume and into a satin robe with a marabou collar and cuffs, one of Andre LeRue's recent creations.

"Andre, this genius." Varinska ran her hand down the smooth fabric and gave him a wry smile. She lit a cigarette and slid out the back door with Henry, the acrobat.

Clair began to mend the ripped sash. The chorus girls threw their costumes on the floor, put on wraps, and made their way back up to the theater along with Ping and Pang.

"Come on, Clair. Join us!" Winnie called as she started up the stairs.

"Let me finish this one last stitch. I'll meet you there." Clair tied a knot, cut off the ends, and laid the band neatly next to Winnie's hat. She hung up the costumes as fast as she could and hurried up the stairs, not wanting to miss anything Rudy had to say.

Clair relaxed back into a cushioned seat next to Winnie, and Andre slid into a chair on the other side of her. The theater smelled of cigarettes, stale perfume, and body odor.

From the stage Rudy checked his clipboard and looked up with a squint. "Please turn off that spot and turn up the houselights." He paused. "Thanks. Folks, I have good news and bad news. We are sold out for tonight."

The group whistled and applauded. Clair couldn't believe she was sitting in a real theater as part of the group.

Varinska strolled in and sat in the front row.

Rudy continued, "The matinee was okay, but tonight we need to wow them. I've put all my dough into this, and if we don't make it, all of us will be out on our ears."

"We'll make it, Rudy!" Bea called, and the others chimed in, too.

Rudy continued, "Winnie, good save. The crowd loved you, but rule number four is 'Always be decent.' No vulgarity in my theater."

"It was all in fun." Winnie squeezed Clair's hand.

The whole group nodded their heads.

"Just don't get carried away." He glanced at his clipboard. "Henry." Rudy looked around and yelled, "Where is Henry?"

"He had to leave, sir." Mordecai folded his hands in his lap.

"Where'd he go?"

"He didn't say."

"He's fired."

The room grew quiet.

"I told you, nobody leaves until after tonight's show is over. Now we need an acrobat. Ping and Pang, can you add some flips to your act?"

Ping shook her pigtails. "No, we do contortion. Somersault, yes, feet on head, yes. Always foot or hand on ground."

Pang ticked off on her fingers, "Contract says: 'No jumping, flying, or flipping.'"

Varinska blew smoke from her cigarette. "Darlinks, I have something can help you jump."

"Get it." Rudy ordered.

She sauntered down the stairs while everyone waited. It was taking her ages. Maybe she had gone to Transylvania to get it. She came onstage with a funny-looking stick in her hand and handed it to Rudy.

"Mac brought on boat to Ellis. Used to hop all over even vhen big waves. One day, *boing* over railing." Varinska lifted her graceful hand, raised it up, and dropped it to demonstrate.

"Show us how it works." Rudy tried to hand it to her.

Varinska meandered toward her seat and threw back her head. "Not me."

Winnie ran up onto the stage. "Let me try it. I might be able to add it to *my* act." Drawing her skirt aside, she took it from Rudy, put her feet on the metal pedals and her hands on the top bars, and tried to hop like a bunny. But it wouldn't budge.

"It doesn't work." Winnie scoffed.

"Needs lighter body." Varinska looked at the group.

"Who else? Ping? Pang?" Rudy waved at the twins.

Their pigtails flew as they shook their heads.

Nobody volunteered. Clair began to formulate an idea.

Andre nudged her elbow. "Why don't you try it?"

She stood up. "Rudy, I might know someone."

"You do? Is he an acrobat?"

"Of a sort. He can jump higher than anyone I've ever seen."

"We need him for the eight o'clock show. Can you get him on the horn?"

"He doesn't have a phone." She shook her head.

"Then go find him, gal pal!" Rudy yelled.

Clair rushed out of the theater in hopes that Nook was still on the corner outside the Waldorf.

44

Clair rushed through the alley door into the dressing room.

"Did you find the acrobat?" Winnie yelled, sticking a Baby Ruth in her mouth and tossing the wrapper on the floor. The other girls stared at Clair with expectant eyes.

"No, I wrote down the address and asked the fruit vendor to send him to me right away." Out of breath, Clair poured a drink of water from the pitcher.

Winnie asked. "Will he come?"

"Sure hope so." Clair shrugged. She had considered going home to tell her father and Aunt June she'd be home late, but she knew it would be too hard to get away.

Andre flitted down the stairs. "An hour till curtain."

Winnie retied her kimono sash and practiced her shimmy in front of the mirror. "I'm nervous. Rudy says there's a Hollywood scout in the audience again tonight."

"It must be that Clifton Marshall." Bea smiled and looked at herself in the makeup mirror. The chorus girls twittered in a corner.

"Any last-minute mending?" Clair asked the group.

No one spoke up, so Clair used the time to straighten the costumes on the rack and dust the full-length mirror. She'd wait to tackle the floor tomorrow.

Varinska took a puff of her cigarette and tilted her head back, indicating that Bea should vacate the makeup mirror. The gypsy sat and pulled a flesh-colored diamond-shaped patch from between her eyes.

"What's that?" Winnie asked Varinska.

Bea put a hand on her hip. "They're called Frownies."

Clair nodded. She had seen them advertised in the magazines.

"Keep vinkles avay." From beneath her silk robe, Varinska pulled her rabbit's foot on a cord from around her neck, dabbed it into talc, and powdered her face. She drew exotic points off the edge of her eyelids with a pencil and applied red lipstick. "Vith lights on stage I look younger."

"It's like magic." Winnie giggled. "How old *are* you?"

Varinska gave her a sideways glance. "Ancient. Take care, darlinks. Hard life. You one day be dried fig like me."

"No! You are gorgeous." Clair smiled at Varinska. "And so talented. How did you learn to perform like that?"

Varinska turned her body around to the table, facing the girls on the bench across from her. She took a worn scarf from her pocket and removed a colorful deck of cards.

She spoke in her slow accent. "In old country, traveled in *vardo*, cart, shaggy black pony pulled it. Everything fit inside." She shuffled the cards. "At stops, Papa played violin and Mama vould dance." Varinska pointed to herself. "Pass hat for people coins. No coins, tiny hands—money, jewelry, vatches." She wiggled her fingers. "Help self. Ve'd hurry, move on to next town. Mama sick, I took over dancing. Night, fire light, vere best times. Close to nature vas our vay."

"What happened to your parents?" Winnie pursed her lips.

"Mama died, then Papa. Burned him in *vardo* as custom." She shook her head, all the sorrow in the world in it.

Clair and Winnie locked eyes.

"How did you survive?" Clair asked.

Varinska raised an eyebrow. "Tell fortunes."

Winnie clapped her hands with excitement. "Tell me mine!"

"Don't do anymore."

"Please?" Winnie begged.

"Vell for you, darlink, I vill." Varinska wiggled her fingers again. "Give me something or von't verk."

Winnie handed her a coin. Varinska laid it on the table, held Winnie's hand, and traced a line on her palm.

"Vear heart on elbow. See beeg man, little boy."

Winnie giggled. "That's funny. What else do you see?"

Varinska ran her finger along another line. "Love." She touched an arched curved line. "Long life."

Winnie smiled. "Clair's next."

"Could consult cards." Varinska raised an eyebrow, nodded to her cards, and held out a hand.

"I don't have a coin to spare." Clair shook her head. Did she really want to know her future?

"Anythink vill do."

Clair pulled a button she'd found on the sidewalk from her pocket and handed it to Varinska.

She set it aside and nodded. "Ask question."

Clair swallowed. Did she dare ask about Mr. X? "Will I see *him* again?"

Winnie scrunched up her nose. "Farley! That's a waste of a question."

Ignoring Winnie, Varinska shuffled the cards and shifted them upside down on the table. "Cut them." She looked at Clair.

The chorus girls and Ping and Pang gathered around to watch as Clair split the pile in half.

Varinska closed her eyes and raised a hand over the cards. "Vill see him?" Her low-pitched tone wavered as she repeated the question. "Vill see him? Vill see him?"

She opened her eyes and stared at Clair. Then Varinska flipped a card over and pointed to it with her polished fingernail.

The card had an upside-down man on it. Clair knew it had to do with death. Her stomach felt as if bats were flying around in it.

Varinska continued. "The Hanged Man—mysterious man. Trapped. Can't get to you."

Clair was disappointed.

"Someday he vill return."

Clair suppressed a smile.

"I hope not." Winnie giggled.

Varinska glared at her with an evil eye. "Cards tell truth." She flipped over a card, paused, then turned over another. "Never before vitnessed these two together."

"What does it mean?" Clair leaned forward.

"Shhh! Moon and Empress." Varinska flipped over another card and an eyebrow shot up. Was she trying to hide an expression of surprise, or was it danger?

"I'm not sure vhat mean today." She shook her head, returned the button to Clair, and gathered up the cards.

"Will you understand tomorrow?" Clair asked.

"Von't vork that way." Varinska shrugged.

"Are you sure? Then let me try another." Clair pointed to the deck and handed back the button. "Will I ever learn my family secret?"

"One more card." Varinska closed her eyes and turned over another card that had a long stick with leaves sprouting from it. "Gardener. You must dig deep."

"How?" Clair reached for Winnie's hand.

"Dig. Very deep." Varinska replaced her cards in the scarf and went out the back door.

"But how am I supposed to do that?" Clair called after her.

Andre came down the stairs. "Half an hour till places. Clair, there's someone here to see you."

She looked up, and Andre pulled a boy in front of him.

"Lookin' for me, miss? I got your note. Everything okay?"

Clair ran over. "It is now!" She put her hand on his back and called, "Everybody, this is Nook. The lad I told you about."

"Hip hip hooray!" The girls and Andre all cheered.

Nook gave a shy wave, and his ink-smudged face lit up with a gap-toothed grin.

Andre inspected Nook. "Help me clean up this ragamuffin before we show him to Rudy."

"Hey, what's goin' on?" Nook squirmed while Clair spit-bathed him as best she could with a handkerchief.

"I've got a job for you."

Winnie found a Shakespearean costume in the back room, complete with a puffy white shirt, velvet doublet with gold braid, and breeches.

"Aren't these girlie clothes?" Nook complained.

"No. Never you mind." Clair rubbed a missed smudge on his cheek.

Andre helped dress him.

Winnie held up a codpiece.

Nook sneered at it. "What's that fer?"

Andre grinned at Winnie. "That won't be necessary."

"I should say not." Clair laughed and brushed back Nook's hair with her hands. "You are very handsome!"

Rudy came in. "Ten minutes till places! Everybody, we've got a full house. Did the acrobat arrive?"

"Here's Nook." Clair put her hands on the boy's shoulders.

Rudy shook Nook's outstretched hand and handed him the pogo stick. "Sorry, young man, no time to practice onstage. Andre, take him outside and see if you can teach him how it works."

Andre escorted Nook out into the alley as Varinska slipped back through the door.

Rudy walked over to her with a frown. "Do I smell booze on you?"

"Dr. Johnnie's Health Tonic. Have sore throat." She coughed and sauntered over to the costume rack.

Rudy shook his head.

"It's almost places," Clair whispered, grabbing Varinska's costume. "I'll help you. Hurry!"

Winnie picked up the red band and started to wrap it around her waist, but it fell apart in two pieces. "Darn it, Clair, I thought you fixed this," Winnie grumbled. The other girls, who were putting on their costumes, glanced over.

"I promise I did." Clair examined it closely. "I don't understand. It appears as if someone snipped right through it with scissors. Who would do such a mean thing?" She looked around. None of the performers would do anything like that.

Clair's eyes landed on the open alley door. Andre? Could he be trying to get back at her all these months later for not allowing his painting to be shown at the ball?

Winnie stamped her foot. "But without the band, that trick won't work. My act will be ruined, and it's all your fault."

"I'm sorry, but I'm certain I fixed it."

"Don't get your knickers in a bunch." Bea's high squeaky voice grated.

Varinska smoked her cigarette.

Clair held back tears. "I'll come up with something."

She rummaged through the remnants and plucked out a black ribbon too short to go around Winnie. Then she came across a silver swathe of satin that seemed about right. She draped it around Winnie's waist and tied it into a big bustle-like bow in back.

"*Violà!*" Clair smiled.

Winnie turned her back to the mirror, shimmying her behind, waving the big bow back and forth. "It's perfect. Even better than the other one." She gave Clair a big hug. "I'm sorry I got mad."

"That's okay."

"Places everyone!" Rudy clapped his hands as he came in. "Good luck. Wow them!"

This time Clair viewed the entire Rollicking Review from the wings. Rudy's Cuties tapped in first, their phony-baloney smiles all teeth. Andre's lone claps from the back of the theater prompted the audience to do so also. The girls did look cute in their Peter Pan–collared white blouses with black bloomers that hit the bottom of their knees. Their tap shoes clickety-clacked along. Clair moved her feet and hands copying them.

Next Ping and Pang somersaulted in. They rolled up, did handstands, and walked in a circle. Then they faced each other, set their feet on top of their heads, and clasped fingers to each other.

Before Winnie's entrance she closed her eyes, inhaled a few times, and whispered to Clair, "Smelling yellow roses!" Then Winnie wiggled onto the stage. "Yes sir, he's my baby!" She repeated all the matinee mistakes but emoted like a pro, pretending to be surprised each time. The audience clapped loudly, and she received another standing ovation.

As Nook *boing, boing, boinged* onto the stage in a zigzaggy fashion, Clair clutched her hands together under her chin, certain he would fall. He stopped in the center and sprang the contraption off the ground as high as it could go toward the catwalk. Next he did a flip, landed right side up on the stick's point, and teetered there for a moment until it stopped.

His big eyes told her he was as shocked as the audience that leaped to their feet in applause. Nook's grin grew wide, and he jumped off with one arm held over his head. Then he hopped back on the stick, bounced his way off the stage, and planted a kiss on Clair's cheek.

"Hey!" She wiped it with her sleeve.

"Sorry, miss. I'm just so happy, I couldn't help myself."

45

Anne studied the Italian collage tacked to the wall above her daybed. She'd made it ages ago, after Sergio had invited her to join him in Italy the first time. The collage was a process piece, not something she would put in a gallery. Made from magazine travel pictures, it included hand-painted plates from Siena, a bottle of red wine, a couple walking hand in hand under a bougainvillea-covered trellis. That could be Sergio and her in a few weeks if she agreed to go.

She sang along to the Italian song mix he had sent. "*Volare! Wo-oh. Volare! Wo-o-o-oh!*"

It had been three weeks since she'd returned from New York. They communicated every day through text and FaceTime. He was booking flight reservations in the morning, and she had to decide whether she would join him or not. Even though he wanted to pay for the trip, she had saved enough for her incidentals, like museum passes and such.

It was the perfect opportunity, but she was frightened what would happen when they returned. After a trip like this she'd probably feel even more connected to him, and living apart would be even more excruciating. But she really wanted to go.

The itinerary included Milan and Florence, then a visit to his *nonna* in Tuscany. Anne worried that his grandmother wouldn't like her. He did say she spoke English. Was she as sophisticated as Sergio and Bella?

Anne had seen an interesting article in the *San Francisco Examiner* that morning about a wealthy donor restoring the Roman Colosseum. She searched her coffee table until she found it:

> *Diego Della Valle, CEO of Tod's, has given $33 million toward restoring the world's most famous monument, the Colosseum, shifting responsibility for Italy's preservation from gridlocked government to private philanthropists. Over three years, thirty restorers used soft bristle brushes and water to scrub the travertine back to its original ivory.*

And she couldn't even keep her bathroom tiles clean.

> *They have also so far restored one of the manually operated elevators that lifted animals up onto the stage.*

She shivered, imagining the cheers of an enormous crowd as a ferocious lion jumped off the elevator. *The lion roared as Sergio ran out from underneath a columned archway in full gladiator regalia, his olive-oiled muscles shining in bright sunlight. Wielding a shield in one hand and a sword in the other, he pushed the lion farther and farther back until it fell down into the elevator's trapdoor.*

She texted Sergio: *Will you take me to Rome, too?*

He called her right away. "Ah, the Eternal City. I can fit that in the itinerary. I'm warning you though. It's *molto romantico*!"

"That's what I'm hoping for. I read about the Tod's Colosseum restoration."

"Yes. We are blessed. Fendi funded the Trevi Fountain redo, and now Bulgari is financing work on the Spanish Steps. Hopefully the scaffolding will be down when we're there. Last time I asked my hotel clerk when it would be done, and he said, 'I do not know. Even the pope does not know.'"

She laughed.

"Will you join me, please?"

"I have one question first." She took a deep breath and paused. "When we get back, am I moving to New York with you or not?"

"Let's wait and talk about it when we are there."

"Are you sure we can't discuss it now?"

"I don't want to." He sounded very definite.

"Let me think about it. I'll text you within the hour." She hung up and studied the article photos again.

She snipped out the iconic Colosseum shot from the street, one of the inside where the stage would be, and an inset map. She glued them all to construction paper. Visiting Rome would be *fantastico*.

Standing up to stretch, she glanced at the rhinestone shoes sitting on the counter and pictured herself tap dancing down the Spanish Steps like in an old Shirley Temple movie. She googled the Spanish Steps and Trevi Fountain, printed them out, and added them to the collage, too. Across the top she wrote with a sharpie: *The Eternal City, Molto Romantico.* She paused, then added, *Let's Go!*

She took a photo of it, sent it to Sergio, and tacked the original onto the wall above the daybed next to the other collage, in hopes they'd give her romantic dreams.

46

Finally, Anne was in Italy with the love of her life! How lucky she was to have her own private tour guide: proud, knowledgeable, and gracious. How could she help but fall even more deeply in love with him than before? The one thing that kept it from being perfect was that she still had no idea what would happen to their relationship when they returned to the States. Would Sergio want her to move to New York or not? She tried to put it out of her mind, but it was hard.

In Milan, he had to work for a few hours each day, but that was fine because she got to explore a bit on her own. She took the Cathedral's elevator up to the roof and snapped photos of the scary gargoyles. Human-like demons, dragons, dogs, and even one that resembled a duck—all with their mouths open as if they were screaming.

She also visited the high-end designer shops where the price of one blouse was more than she'd spend on rent in an entire year. But the next day Sergio dropped her off in a section of town that had vintage shops to die for. There she bought a red lace blouse that only cost as much as one day of rent.

In Florence, they had strolled along the Arno, visited the Palazzo Vecchio, and perused the Uffizi Gallery, including the *Birth of Venus*.

Now Sergio opened a final door for her. "And here you'll see the number one Florentine attraction, one of the most amazing masterpieces ever made by man."

Anne and Sergio walked down the wide hall to the viewing room. Even with an early reservation, it was already crowded. She glanced up at the marble face of David looming above a plethora of teenagers, with their backs to the sculpture, waving selfie sticks and taking pictures.

Sergio and Anne waited for the group to leave, then got a closer look. Astounded by the perfection of David's body, she hankered to climb up and rub her hands along his smooth marble muscles—only because she was an artist and wanted to understand how the sculpting had been done, of course.

She motioned to Sergio. "Stand in front of him."

Imitating David's pose, he stepped back, turned his head, and lifted his left hand above his shoulder as if holding the slingshot's pouch.

"How's this?" He copied the sculpture's serious expression.

Anne snapped a photo. "*Perfetto*."

She took a few more pictures and gave Sergio a mischievous grin. "To make the resemblance better, would you pose naked?"

"*Sì!*" Sergio laughed and started to take off his shirt.

"No, no. I was joking!" Anne turned as another noisy tour group moved toward them.

She chose a photo and typed in her phone: *My own David next to the real marble giant-sized one.* Pushing the button, she posted it on Facebook.

Sergio held out his hand. "Let's not miss our train. Next up: *Roma,* the Eternal City."

~

A driver picked Sergio and Anne up at the train station in Rome and sped toward their hotel. With the faster traffic, louder horns, and pedestrian-filled sidewalks, the energy here seemed even more rapid than New York's. By the time the driver dropped them off, the sun had begun to dip beyond the horizon, but it was still scorching hot.

Sergio checked them in to their Relais & Châteaux hotel.

"You go on up, I have an errand to do," he said.

She followed the bellman up to the quiet air-conditioned room, a respite from the hustle-bustle of the busy city. A bouquet of red roses, cobalt-blue delphiniums, and tall gladiolas was displayed on an entry table. The bellman set the bags down and she tipped him, hoping she'd given him enough.

At the window she studied the rooftop view of a domed church. "Not bad." She snapped a photo and posted it. The morning's photo of Sergio with David already had seventy-five likes.

The large bed with the carved wood headboard, gold-and-scarlet pillows, and white coverlet looked inviting. Entering the bathroom, she screamed.

Sergio rushed in carrying some shopping bags. "Are you okay?"

"This bathtub is practically as big as my whole apartment."

"You'll live." He laughed. "Hurry, put on your jeans, we've got to get going."

"But I stink and need a bath." She stared at the tub.

"You'll stink more later. You can take one tonight. The city is waiting."

"But if it's the Eternal City, it will wait for us forever."

He smiled, pulling out boots, leather jackets, and gloves from his shopping bags.

"What's all that for?"

"When you drive a Vespa, you are wearing a Vespa." He put on a jacket and turned as if he were a model. "They see all of you. It's part of your look. It's about style."

"But it must be a hundred degrees out there." Anne frowned.

"It's for your own protection."

"Protection?"

"You'll see."

They dressed, walked the few blocks to the scooter rental, and went inside, where Sergio made the transaction.

He rolled a royal-blue Vespa out to the street and patted the back seat. "Hop on!"

"This is going to be fun!" She slid onto the leather.

"Avoid any sudden movements, and don't try to help me by leaning to the side. Enjoy the ride."

"Okay."

"Put this on." He handed her a helmet.

"It's a retro bowling ball!" Anne tugged the silver-metal-flecked helmet on her head.

He strapped his black helmet on and pulled the guard over his handsome face.

"May the force be with you, Darth Vader," Anne laughed.

He jumped onto the Vespa. She held onto him as he hit the gas and sped off into traffic. They bounced out of a pothole and she feared they were going to slide over, but he kept the scooter stable. Her heart raced as he drove down the white line between rows of cars. She closed her eyes as they almost bashed into a florist truck.

"Slow down!" she yelled.

He didn't seem to hear her.

They twisted and turned up and down the hills, zipping in and out of traffic like a human video game. She hoped she wouldn't lose the spaghetti she'd had on the train.

Sergio glanced in the rearview mirror and sped right through a red light.

Anne screamed. "Oh my God! You just broke the law."

"Rules are meant to be broken!" he shouted back to her.

He pulled the Vespa off onto the sidewalk and continued along until he stopped in an area packed with tourists.

She carefully slid off the seat and tried to calm her wobbly legs. "I can't believe how fast you were going. What's the speed limit?" She removed her helmet and fluffed her hat hair.

"There isn't one." He shook his head and attached their helmets to the back of the Vespa. "It's such a pleasure to drive without needing to check the speedometer."

"You drove as if you really were a Star Wars character." This was a side she'd never seen of him. In fact, she'd never ridden with him before. They'd always taken a Lyft, taxis, or town cars, and she'd done the driving while they were in Michigan.

"Let the *Roma* tour begin."

"I need a minute. Water, please."

He bought an *Acqua Panna* bottle from a kiosk and handed it to her.

She drank some water and gave the bottle back to him. "Okay. Ready."

Sergio finished the bottle, tossed it in a can, and took her hand, and they wove through the crowd. The sound of running water could be heard.

He lifted his arm. "Here we have the *Fontana di Trevi*: Italy's largest and most famous Baroque fountain, which stands eight hundred and fifty feet high and sixty-five feet across. Notice the Corinthian pilasters . . ."

"It's stunning!" Anne pointed to the Neptune-like god. "There's Oceanus in his chariot. And I recognize Abundance and Salubrity. Or is it the other way around?" Anne crisscrossed her arms.

"That's right, the snake is drinking from Salubrity's cup."

"What does *salubrity* mean, anyway?" Anne snapped a photo, making sure to get the cascades as they flowed into the aqua-green pool.

"Healthful," he responded. "Turn around." Sergio handed her a euro. "Throw this diagonally over your shoulder from left to right without missing."

She gave him her phone. "Okay. Here goes." She turned and tossed the coin into the cascading water.

He clicked the camera on her phone. "*Molto bene!* It landed in the water, which means you'll return to *Roma* someday."

She frowned. "Hopefully not with you driving."

He motioned toward where the Vespa was parked.

"I'm not getting back on that with you."

"*Mi dispiace*. Next stop is not far. I'll try to slow down, but I have to keep up with the flow of traffic."

"The traffic isn't a flow, it's an erupting volcano."

"Come on!" He took her elbow. She reluctantly climbed back on the Vespa, and he gently steered it around a corner, where he stopped.

"And these *dolcezza* are the Spanish Steps."

It was packed with people who stood and sat on the steps.

"Good, the scaffolding is down." She snapped a photo.

He nodded. "They say there are one hundred and thirty-five steps. Should we run up and count them to make sure?"

"Not today." She yawned. "Let's go back to the hotel for a nap."

"How about a gelato first?"

"Now you're talking." She wondered when he would be ready to talk about her moving to New York.

47

That evening, Sergio pulled the Vespa back onto the street and sped up. Anne tried to relish the swerving motion of the motorcycle beneath her body, her chest against his back. Traffic had thinned out from their day excursion. Surface streetlights popped on as darkness fell. Up ahead she could see the Colosseum, its curved wall of arches serene. A full moon had begun to rise above it.

Sergio pulled onto the gravel, drove toward the arena, and parked. There was only one car there. Anne removed her helmet, hopped off, and rubbed her hands along the rough-hewn limestone wall.

Sergio snapped a quick photo of her leaning against the facade.

She blinked at the flash. "Don't post it. I have horrible hat hair." She ruffled her fingers through it.

"No, you don't! *Molto bella*."

"Too bad the Colosseum's closed." She'd read online that it closed at three thirty.

"*No problemo*." He took her hand, and they walked the wall's perimeter until they came to a wooden door. Opening it, he guided her over the doorpost and into the arena.

"Are we allowed to be here?" she whispered.

"But of course." He gave her a mysterious wide-eyed look.

They walked to the center of the six-acre arena that used to hold as many as eighty thousand spectators, and she spun slowly around, looking up at the stands, imagining what it might have looked like during that era. An owl hooted and flew to a square niche high above, into one of the arches.

"This is crazy. All alone in the Colosseum . . ."

"Shhh. Listen." Sergio took her hands and faced her. "Close your eyes."

Inside the deserted wonder, buffered by the thick walls, traffic noise disappeared. The scent of damp sand permeated the air, and she inhaled deeply. Crickets chirped.

Footsteps crunched on the gravel, and Anne jumped.

"*Ciao!*" A burly man with a stern expression came out from behind a pillar. "Sergio, *cugino*."

"*Buona notte*." Sergio gave him a hug.

The man frowned at her. "You must be Anne."

"Yes. *Sì*." She nodded.

"This is my cousin Cornelius, but we call him Cornie."

She shook his hand. "*Piacere*, Cornie!" She tried not to laugh at his name. With that serious face, it sure didn't seem to fit him.

"*Benvenuto*. Enjoying your Roman holiday?"

"*Sì*." Anne smiled.

"I'll leave you two love doves alone."

"Thanks, Cornie." Sergio hugged him again.

"Close the door when you leave. It should lock behind you." He crossed the arena and slipped out the door they had entered through.

"Where were we?"

Sergio took her hands again, and she could hear the silence. He pulled her close and kissed her. She wondered if this might be the right time for them to talk about her moving to New York. But when she opened her eyes, instead of looking at her, he was scanning the top of the building surrounding them.

She tilted her head back. “Look at that moon.”

Sergio began to sing, rocking her.

“It’s a marvelous night for a moondance

With the stars above in your eyes

A fantabulous night making romance!”

He seemed to know all the words. She didn’t and hummed along with him, their voices echoing off the walls.

He kissed her again. “Did you know thousands of spectators would watch as gladiators fought lions to the death? Either one or the other would die.”

The spell had been broken. “Yes, I’ve read all about it.” She recalled her earlier fantasy. Brave Sergio, a gladiator ready to fight to the death: a bald-headed giant, a mangy bear, a ferocious lion. A shiver went up her spine to the nape of her neck.

“It must have been really gory,” he teased.

“How romantic.” Disappointed, she started toward the exit.

“Wait.” He grabbed her hand. “Let’s explore.” He led her between two columns along a pathway and up into the stands.

She could tell there’d be no serious discussion tonight.

48

Sergio steered the Alfa Romeo around another bend and pointed. "There it is!" A white villa appeared on the hill above them.

Nearby leafy grapevines twisted on wooden stakes that lined the rise like baby telephone poles. Sergio turned the sports car right and ascended the gravel road edged by cypress trees. They passed an olive grove, branches ripe with black ovals.

He slowed, parked in front of the villa, took their luggage from the trunk, and led her through the wrought iron gate, where blue wisteria cascaded over an arch.

Anne's Italian hadn't progressed much, and she hoped she'd be able to communicate with his grandmother.

"Sergio!" An old woman, her dove-gray hair swept up into a bun, moved toward them, wiping her hands on an apron.

"*Nonna*!" He clutched her to him.

After a moment they let go. Nonna blinked back tears of love, and Anne saw where Sergio got his big smile.

"Welcome!" Nonna kissed Anne on both cheeks. "Finally, I get to meet you."

"*Salve*." Anne kissed her twice, inhaling a faint vanilla scent.

"Sit, sit, and we'll have a nice chat. Oh, no." Nonna shook her head. "How rude of me. You must be tired from the drive. Sergio, take her upstairs." Her English was perfect.

"Come, *amore mio*." Carrying their suitcases, he guided Anne through the kitchen, redolent of fresh-baked bread, up a back stairway, and down a long hallway to a room filled with light. Anne rushed to gaze out the window. A lake glistened below, and the countryside beyond spread like a tapestry of gold, sienna, and emerald.

Sergio put his hand on her shoulder. "What do you think?"

"It's idyllic. How could you ever leave it?" she asked. Then, sadly, "Oh, that's right, you were shipped off to boarding school."

He pulled her hair aside and kissed the nape of her neck. "If I'd never left, how else would I have ever found you?"

She turned toward him and he enfolded her in his arms. Soon, tired from the drive, they curled up on the soft bed together. Thick walls kept the house cool, but the afternoon sun on Anne's back warmed her as she dove into sleep to the sound of a lark calling its mate.

They awoke, freshened up, and found their way down to the brick patio under an arbor where a fully set table had been laid: lace tablecloth, crystal stemware, and hand-painted plates, just like the ones in her collage. Sergio opened a bottle of merlot and poured the wine. Clinking glasses, they each took a sip.

A striped kitten stealthily walked along the garden wall. Pale yellow as salted butter, it twitched tiny ears that folded up and down. Paws outstretched, the tiny cat glided down the steps toward Anne and stared at her like Mrs. Landenheim's Siamese. Anne had convinced her landlady to wait until after the trip to sign the lease. If Sergio didn't want her to move to New York, she would need to commit for two years when they returned. She'd have to broach the subject tonight.

For dinner, Anne had expected a big bowl of pasta.

"We're having one of Sergio's favorite meals. French fries and hot dogs."

"I know you love french fries, but Mr. Foodie eats hot dogs?" Anne laughed and cringed inside. She would need to be polite and eat one.

"He became an aficionado at his American school."

"Why didn't you tell me that? I can cook hot dogs."

He shrugged with a smile.

A grin spread across Nonna's face. "This one's for you. Tofu." She put one not as pink as the others on a plate and handed it to Anne.

"How thoughtful of you." Anne took a bite and nodded. "Mmm. This *is* delicious." She bit into a fry, crisp on the outside and soft on the inside.

After they'd devoured their meals, Nonna said, "Anne, tell me about your art."

Anne was coaxed into going into detail about her work, showing photos from her cell until they had finished the wine.

"Let's have dessert later," Sergio said. "I'm stuffed." He'd eaten three hot dogs.

Anne started to help clear the table, but Nonna shook her head. "I'll clean up. You two go for a walk before dark."

Sergio led Anne down the hill through an olive grove and some grapevines to a mosaic bench by the lake. They sat close together, embracing in the golden glow.

"Sergio. Are you ready to talk about me moving to New York?"

"Yes." He paused, knelt on one knee, pulled a velvet box from his pants pocket, and held it toward her. "I have something for you."

Her heart sprinted. "Is this what I think it is?" she asked.

"Yes." He nodded.

"Well?"

"Well, what?" he asked.

"Open the box, please."

"Okay." He lifted the lid. A diamond glinted in the twilight.

"Well?" she prompted again.

"Well, what?"

"Don't you have a question?" She smiled at him.

He swallowed hard. Usually so self-assured, his hands shook. For someone who knew what the answer would be, he sure looked nervous. "Big Foot, will you marry me?"

"Of course!" She laughed and kissed him.

He slid the ring onto her finger. "It fits perfectly!"

"Of course it does!" She laughed again.

He pulled her up into his arms, twirled her around, and kissed her. "I love you!"

"I love you, too. And I love this." She held out her hand, studying the diamond's marquise shape.

"I hope you *adore* it, because you'll be wearing it for the rest of your life."

"I do, it's magnificent."

"It was Nonna's. The shape represents a seed, symbolic of a fruitful life together. She had twelve children."

"Twelve! I doubt we'll have that many. And I'm not ready to start a family yet." Anne smiled at him, but for some reason she felt uneasy.

"You will be when the time is right. You'll be a wonderful mother. I hope our children have your smile, your wild hair, and even your big feet. I'm glad you want to move to New York and settle down with me."

She couldn't wait to tell her family and friends the amazing news.

49

"Where are you going?" Clair's father asked for the hundredth time.

"I told you, to my job at the Grimmons Shirt Factory." Clair hated to lie, but she had no choice.

"Isn't that dress a little fancy for work?" he asked.

She wore the same frock every day. "Not at all. We've been told by the management to always look our best." Clair got her coat, hat, and gloves and went to the door.

"When Farley comes back, you won't need to work. He'll take care of us."

Oh, for goodness' sake! It had been months since they'd seen Farley. If he'd planned to show up, he would have done so by now. Besides, she loved her job and was providing for them just fine. Her father would not be able to force her to accept Farley in their lives ever again.

Aunt June came out of the kitchen and kissed her on the cheek. "Have a good evening, dear."

Stepping out into the late afternoon, Clair pulled her coat close around her. Spring had almost arrived, but the leaves hadn't begun to sprout yet, and a chilly pall still hung over the once-glamorous city.

At St. Peter's Mission, the breadline wrapped around the corner. A woman held a baby, and two other children clung to her skirt. A brunette in a fancy hat and fur coat stood in line next to her. At least Clair had been able to help keep her family sustained through her meager pay.

Folks needed a diversion, and Broadway theaters were still packing them in. Rudy's Rollicking Review had done well at first, despite the steep competition. But two months ago Rudy's ticket sales began to dwindle, and the houses were only half-full for most shows. It seemed as if they were destined to close down, but Rudy mysteriously came up with the cash to stage a brand spanking new production.

"Something that will really wow them this time!" he'd said. Encouraged by audience applause during Winnie's number and Andre's pleading, Rudy had loosened up on his decency rule.

Opening night was tomorrow, and Clair had been sewing costumes for the new acts like mad. She only had twenty-four more hours to finish. Every chance she got, Clair watched the rehearsals and silently followed along, feeling the keys under her fingers as Mordecai played. She practiced the dance steps and knew every word to every song, too.

Everyone had at least two jobs except her. Even Nook had been trained to take over another task. To keep him busy and out of mischief, Rudy had dubbed him Chief Curtain Curator in addition to his role as Acrobat Extraordinaire.

She stopped out front and studied the marquee. Rudy's Rollicking Review had been changed to Rudy's Ritzy Review, and Rudy's Cuties were now called the Sophisticated Sallies.

Clair slipped into the dressing room through the alley door. Even though she'd swept the night before, the floor was covered in debris as if someone had dumped and spread trash all around. The cacophony of noise hummed with energy. The Sallies vocalized "Puttin' on the Ritz," Nook coached Ping and Pang on the hopping stick, and Winnie sat in a corner with her eyes closed, breathing deeply.

"Seen Varinska? Clair asked Winnie. "I've got to do a final fitting on her gown."

Winnie shook her head and continued breathing.

Clair ran up the stairs and stepped onstage, a spotlight hitting her. Mordecai struck a chord and played an introduction as if she was a real star. She laughed, twirled her long willowy body in a circle, and curtsied as if to a crowd.

"What'll it be?" Mordecai asked.

"How about 'The Man on the Flying Trapeze'?"

As his fingers began, she floated across the stage, singing louder than she ever had before. Her voice reverberated all the way to the back of the theater: "With the greatest of ease."

Dancing across the stage, she followed Rudy's rhythmic cues in her mind. *Strut, strut, strut it!* This strutting felt so great.

Mordecai clapped his small hands. "Clair, your voice is clear as moonlight."

"Thank you, kind sir!" She curtsied. Hearing someone else clapping, she looked up and spotted Andre high above her on a ladder, adding finishing touches to the new backdrop.

"Lovely—you can really project! You're full of surprises." Andre drew out the last three words.

She could never tell when he was teasing her. "So are you." She pointed at the backdrop, black-and-white piano keys flying every which way. It looked pretty good.

"*Merci.*" Andre swirled his arm and almost lost his balance, but caught himself.

The house lights went up to full. Rudy stood in the back row. "Andre, are the new shoes here yet?"

"No, sir. When I called yesterday they promised they were on their way."

"Call them again." Rudy walked down the aisle and climbed the stairs in front of Clair. "I need to talk to you."

She hoped he wasn't angry with her for taking up precious time.

He frowned. "The new show is almost up, the costumes are

done, and I'm dead broke." His eyes softened. "I'm sorry, but I'll need to let you go after tomorrow."

Her hands flew to her face, and she held back tears. "What about the costumes?"

"The cast can mend their own darn outfits, and hang them up, too."

"I've got other skills, Rudy. I'm good at math and can help with the accounts," Clair begged.

"Sorry." He looked down. "I wish it could be any other way."

The next afternoon, Clair dragged her feet as she walked to the theater, a shawl of gloom surrounding her body. It would be next to impossible to find another job, especially one she felt so fully a part of.

At the theater, a deliveryman stood under the marquee holding a big box.

"Think it's any good?" the deliveryman asked Clair.

"Don't miss it!" She smiled at him. "Shall I take that box?"

He shook his head. "Mr. LeRue needs to sign for it himself."

"Come on." Since the front entrance was still locked, she took him through the alley to the propped open door. "Andre!" she called.

He rushed over, signed for the box, and opened it. "Sallies! They're here."

Olga, Henrietta, Bea, and Dominique squealed and ran over. Varinska glanced over and shook her head.

Andre checked for sizes and handed out the shoeboxes. Ping, Pang, Nook, and Winnie wandered over to watch. As the Sallies pulled the shoes out, they sparkled in the light, and everyone gasped.

"Ooh," Nook said.

The dancers hurriedly slipped them on, clasped the T-straps, and tested them with the time step.

Clair stared. The shoes were the rhinestone-covered ones from the shop window! How she wished she could try on a pair, too.

Rudy came down the stairs. "The shoes! What a relief."

"Yes!" Andre check-marked the air with his finger.

"They cost me an arm and a leg. Gather 'round, folks!"

The entire cast and crew huddled together. Clair thought to herself that this would be the last time she would get to be part of this group. She would sure miss it. Winnie hadn't said anything to her about it. Perhaps she hadn't heard yet.

"This is what we've all been working toward." Rudy studied his clipboard. "Sallies, slow down and milk it! Finish your solo steps, pose, and wait for the audience to consider what they've viewed. They'll clap louder each time, even if the trick wasn't better than the one before. Now get dressed, get up there, and give it all you've got!"

One last time, Clair handed out the costumes from the rack. The Sallies donned their shiny outfits and ran up the stairs sounding like a herd of ponies. Clack, clack, clack went their new taps. The opening song had been nixed, and the Sallies were up first.

Andre followed them up, and a few minutes later he poked his head in the dressing room, hands aflutter. "Where's Mordecai?"

Varinska shrugged.

"Don't know." Winnie turned so Clair could tie the sash.

Andre flew back up the stairs as Mordecai staggered in from the alley reeking of booze. "Yes sir, she's my baby," he sang.

He started to keel over onto the costume rack, but Clair caught him by the arm. "Winnie, help!"

Winnie rushed over and took his other arm.

Varinska frowned. "Vell, he's done it. Vhy got shooed from midget show. Must toppled off vagon."

"What made him do it? Too much pressure with the new show?" Winnie asked.

They heard footsteps coming down the stairs.

"Kvick, put under table." Varinska pulled out the bench. Winnie dragged him under, and Clair covered him up with her coat from the rack. Then they slid the bench back in place and sat down on it. Nonchalantly, Varinska touched up her lipstick.

Rudy stood in the doorway. "It's a full house, Win! How's my kewpie doll? Can I escort you up?"

"I'm fine, Rudy. Fine."

From under the table, Mordecai started to sing again. "Yes sir . . ."

Winnie sang over him as loud as she could. "He's my baby. No sir, I don't mean maybe." She got up, slipped her arm through Rudy's, and walked him toward the stairs.

Andre dashed in. "Rudy, we've got a problem."

"Now what?" Rudy threw his hands up.

"I can't find Mordecai."

"But he was here earlier."

"I've looked everywhere." Andre shook his head.

"We'll be ruined. It's too late to get another piano player," Rudy grumbled.

"I can do it." The words came out of Clair's mouth before she even realized it.

Winnie looked at her friend. "You can? You never told me you played piano."

"I used to occasionally tickle the ivories." Clair smiled. Her heart beat fast, hoping she'd be up to the task.

Rudy shook his head. "Gal pal. You *are* full of surprises."

Andre laughed. "Sure are."

"Clair, get up there!" Rudy yelled.

"Yes, sir." She stood.

Rudy cringed. "Wait! Find something a little more theatrical to wear. Andre, you go up and tell the cast Clair is taking over, and we'll start in five minutes."

Mordecai began to sing again. "Yes sir . . ."

Varinska kicked him under the table.

"That's my baby," Winnie sang to drown him out again, guiding Rudy up the stairs.

Clair found a black sequined gown in the back room, threw it on, and rushed up the stairs. At the piano, she slipped off Mordecai's foot-pedal blocks and nodded at the band members, who were gaping at her. She reached for the sheet music, but it wasn't there. She searched the floor and shuffled through the piano bench, but to no avail.

In tux and tails, Rudy stood before the curtains in the spotlight. "Ladies and gentlemen! Welcome to our brand-new show, Rudy's Ritzy Review. It's going to really knock your socks off. First up, I give you the Sophisticated Sallies."

Clair's heart beat as fast as the hi-hat drum cymbals beside her. Without the music she wouldn't be able to play and they would be ruined, all because of her. She just couldn't let her friends down.

"The Sophisticated Sallies!" Rudy glared down at her and gestured toward the orchestra pit.

Clair placed her hands on the keyboard, took a breath, and closed her eyes. She hit a few bad notes with a cringe, but then her fingers took over and automatically knew the right ones to touch. Her maestro had once told her she didn't need sheet music at all, and to her surprise, she realized he had been right. Her heart knew the right notes to play.

She opened her eyes as the Sallies tip-tapped onto the stage. It was hard to tell them apart. In identical blonde bob wigs with silver half-moon caps, each still wore a white blouse but now with sequined shorts. Clair's fingers had no problem keeping up with the dancers, especially when they started to sing "Puttin' on the Ritz." Their voices harmonized beautifully.

The new shoes dazzled Clair's eyes! The routine used the same steps, but this time hoops were added. The Sallies twirled them in their arms and on their legs, then posed in synchronized fashion. By the second chorus, she relaxed into the melody and enjoyed the rhythm of the music.

The show flew by. To tighten the show, Ping and Pang and Nook's acts had been combined. The twins did their contortions sweetly in their new lime-green leotards. Nook, in a matching leotard and black sequined bow tie, hopped around the girls on the stick. Due to invisible elastic, the top hat actually stayed on his head as he did his flips.

Winnie made everyone laugh as usual in her even more giant hat and kelly-green dress. If she grew any stouter, Clair would need to let it out soon. Rudy never seemed to mind. All he'd say was, "That's more of her to love."

With this new show, Bea and Dominique each had a solo act, too.

Bea sis-boom-bahed onstage in a Cleopatra costume, complete with a gold asp headband over a veil—her made-up eyes peeking out, wide and mysterious. She danced as if a hieroglyphic goddess, moving her head side to side, over to a basket on center stage. Doing a rumba, she pulled a taxidermy snake out, draped it across her shoulders, and flirted, as if she might kiss it. At first Rudy had brought in a real snake to use, but the girls and Andre screamed for him to take it away. Varinska had only laughed.

With Dominique's entrance, Clair began to play Saint-Saëns' *Le cygne*. Turns out Dominique had been a ballet dancer with the Paris Opera. She tiptoed onstage wearing a tutu and pointe shoes, fluttering her arms as if she were a dying swan. She batted her eyelashes, convincing the audience of her regal sadness.

Clair changed the tempo. Dominique ripped off her costume, leaned back, and spun the pasties on her bosoms. Then she turned and twirled the tassels on her bum faster and faster in a hypnotizing fashion. The audience's eyes—men and women alike—nearly popped out of their heads. Clair chuckled. Even though she'd watched Dominique do this a dozen times, it still made her laugh.

The theater grew dark once more, and Rudy's voice reverberated behind the curtain to a drumroll. "From the far-off reaches of Europe. In darkest of nights, I give you Varinska the Vamp."

Clair's fingers quickly splayed the introductory glissade as the curtains opened and a spotlight hit Varinska center stage. Andre had convinced Rudy to lose the gypsy costume. Now a stunning vision, Varinska's silk shawl had been draped, like a turban, over her long hair. She wore a slinky midnight-blue gown and a sapphire necklace at her throat.

Clair waited for the applause to die down. She focused. This would be a challenge. Every time Varinska rehearsed it, she changed her number slightly. Clair began to play Varinska's signature Hungarian tune at a slow tempo. Varinska sang close to the microphone, her sultry voice alluring. She raised a questioning eyebrow to a man in the front row and swayed back and forth in rhythm. At the end she held her last note as long as possible, and Clair played two alternating keys quietly in the background.

The stage went dark. The clapping and hooting were so loud Clair could barely hear the piano, but she kept playing anyway. Varinska did three curtain calls, the spotlight blinking on and off each time, and at last the applause died down. Clair dreamed that someday she could have just one person feel that way about her, let alone a whole audience.

During the curtain call, when the entire cast opened their arms toward the band, Clair took a bow, feeling as if she'd died and gone to heaven.

Clair quickly changed into her street clothes. No way could she face saying goodbye to the cast. She started to slip out the back door, but Rudy caught her by the arm. "Thank you for saving us. You did a fine job."

"May I return tomorrow, in case Mordecai doesn't come?"

"That's a good idea. But I won't be able to pay you."

50

The next afternoon, Clair entered through the lobby and sat in the back of the theater.

"Sallies, did you see this?" From the stage, Rudy picked up a newspaper, waved it in the air, and read, "While the Sophisticated Sallies looked dazzling in their shimmery costumes, they didn't live up to their name."

"What's that supposed to mean?" Bea squeaked.

"It means you stink!" Winnie hollered. She swatted Nook's shoulder in front of her to stop him from pulling Ping's pigtails.

Clair had read the review that morning. It had said Winnie was wonderful, Nook and the twins darling, Varkinska certainly a vamp, and of course, Bea and Dominique titillating.

Bea crossed her eyes at Winnie.

Dominique stood up. "We'll do better tonight."

"You'd better! Let's get a run-through in before we open the house. I'm changing the sequence of the show. Varinksa, you go on right after the Sallies." He put his hand over his forehead. "Varin-ska!"

"Haven't seen her," Henrietta called.

"When you see her, tell her of the change. Mordecai, Let's get going!" Rudy yelled.

"He's not here." Andre came up the stairs and onstage carrying the hoops. "I've checked everywhere."

Clair started down the aisle. Winnie smiled at her as she passed.

"There you are, gal pal. Glad *you* are here." Rudy pointed toward the piano.

Thrilled to play for the show again, she sat on the bench and played a few scales to warm up her fingers while the Sallies lined up in the wings.

Clair started to play the introduction when the theater door opened and Mordecai ambled down the aisle. "Hello, everybody!" He waved his short arms.

"Where've you been?" Rudy bellowed.

Even though Mordecai smiled broadly, he wrung his hands. "Couldn't get out of bed. Musta had the croup. It came on suddenly, and I had to dash home." Mordecai wiped his forehead with a kerchief. "I'm here now."

Rudy put his hands on his hips and stared at him. "That's too bad, because Clair stood in for you and did a better job than you ever could."

Mordecai's face dropped and he looked at her with forlorn eyes, his lower lip trembling.

Clair felt like a deflated balloon and slowly stood up. "No, sir. Mordecai's skills surpass my own any day. You should forgive him this one time."

Mordecai held his arm out. "I've never missed a performance before. Please, Rudy."

"Please." Clair clasped her hands below her chin.

Rudy scowled. "Okay. But don't let it happen again."

"Thank you, sir," Mordecai croaked, and made his way to the piano.

Clair picked up his foot blocks from the floor and slid them back on the pedals.

"Okay, Clair." Rudy looked at her. "What am I going to do with you?"

"Not sure." She could tell he wanted to keep her on.

Winnie piped up. "She can do the Sallie's routine backwards and forwards. Wouldn't she class up the number?"

Shocked, Clair's breath caught in her throat. Winnie was right; she had done it a thousand times and had even mastered the final time step.

"I don't know." Rudy shook his head.

She might blunder. "I can't do—"

"You can!" Winnie walked down the aisle and laced her arm through Clair's. "There's the original costume we made for Bea before she gained weight."

"Gal pal. What do you think?" Rudy asked.

"Yes! I can!"

"Get ready. We're going to open the house in a few minutes. Places in twenty!"

"But I don't have any shoes." Clair pointed to her old boots.

Winnie grabbed Clair by the hand. "We'll work something out."

They traipsed downstairs. The place was a shambles again. Candy wrappers, street clothes, and newspapers were strewn on the floor.

From above, Mordecai played "Puttin' on the Ritz" and the Sallies tapped away. Winnie came out from the back room and handed Clair a box.

She opened it and tears filled her eyes.

Winnie smiled. "I had them order one extra large pair just in case."

Clair slipped them on, clasped the T-straps, and shifted her feet. "They're a little snug."

"They're supposed to be. They stretch over time."

As Clair took a step, a warm glow ran from the soles of her feet up to her heart and swirled there. It was unlike any previous sensation she recalled. She danced along with the music above. Step, heel, step, heel. Shuffle, hop step. Ball change, ball change. She loved making the sound of the taps. Breaking into a time step, she'd never felt so alive.

Winnie clapped and helped Clair into the costume: blonde wig, silver moon cap, white blouse, black shorts. Her thighs were even visible. She wouldn't think how her father would react if he knew. She was nervous enough already. Hopefully no one would recognize her in the blonde wig.

Clair studied herself in the mirror. The two-inch heels made her even taller. Her height had always been a source of consternation, but not now. The taller you were onstage, the better you looked.

In her costume, Varinska sauntered in, lit a cigarette, and eyed Clair. "Vell, vell."

Winnie giggled. "Clair's our new Sallie."

"Break leg, darlink."

"Thanks."

Rudy yelled, "Places, girls. Hurry up!"

"Varinska. You go on right after the Sallies." Winnie applied makeup on Clair.

"Vhatever." Varinska traipsed up the stairs, and Winnie and Clair soon followed.

Waiting in the wings, Clair walked through the steps. The audience's muffled voices on the other side of the closed curtain could be heard, and her heartbeat sped up.

When the Sallies' music began, Clair stood as erect as a brass candlestick as Rudy had always instructed: shoulders back, head up. As she followed Dominique, Bea, Olga, and Henrietta onstage, Mordecai missed a note, but no one seemed to notice.

Circle this way, now circle that way, Clair recited in her mind, and raised her arms. During the first chorus, her feet in their new shoes, she circled sophisticatedly like the group's name implied. She tapped offstage, following the girls as they grabbed their hoops and shuffled back on again. But when it was her turn, she reached out for her hoop, and it wasn't there! Andre moved his hands back and forth with an apologetic look on his face and a shrug.

Rudy's words rang in her head: *Keep going! No matter what.* She circled an invisible hoop, twirled in synchronized formation each wrist, then each ankle.

After she did her last time step and took her bow, she ran down the stairs, collapsed on the bench at the table, and couldn't stop crying. At least no one else was there. The others must be watching Varinska's act. How could Clair have ever imagined she was Sallie material?

Varinska finished her number and came down the stairs. "Never let see you cry."

"But I'm mortified. The hoop wasn't there as if someone sabotaged me on purpose."

"Who vould do dat?" Varinska shrugged.

Clair raced through the act in her mind. "Andre?" That portrait was so long ago.

"He vouldn't." Varinska handed Clair a handkerchief. "Cry minute, pull together."

Clair dried her tears.

"Always smile like dis." Varinska demonstrated a blasé expression with a small relaxed smile and cool eyes. "Face say: No care in vorld."

Varinska lit a cigarette, stuck it in her ivory holder, and took a drag. "Rough up! Find tender spot, they poke till you break. Show me zat smile until sinks in."

Clair mustered up a grin.

Varinska looked up at the ceiling. "Chin up. Show lovely long neck."

Clair tilted her head back, swallowed, and then said dramatically, "I don't have a care in the world."

"You got."

"Thanks, Varinska. You're the best."

Varinska gave a deep chortle. "Best at vhat?"

"Everything. Dancing, singing, strutting."

"About self. Vhat vord? Con, con . . ." Varinska put red nails on her chest.

"Confidence."

Varinska nodded. "Yes, con-fi-dence. Vith dat can do anything."

"I wish I could be like you." Clair blinked tears off her lashes.

"Darlink. No. Don't vant dat."

"But you're sultry, and your voice is so rich. You have star quality."

Varinska sat next to Clair. "Everyone hass special gift. I'm deep voiced, you soprano, voice like bird or angel. Heard hit notes so high, dead mama can hear in heaven." She pointed to Clair. "Graceful body. Come up vith own act. Be star, too."

Varinska believed in her. Clair put on a true smile.

After the last curtain call, Rudy said, "Good job. Gal pal, take smaller steps so the other girls can keep up with those long legs of yours." He didn't even mention the missing hoop.

51

Anne's studio apartment was messy as usual, with mail overflowing on the counter, dirty clothes bulging out of her open suitcase, and several art pieces in process scattered throughout.

"Ciao, baby! I'm moving to New York! New York!" she sang.

She glanced at the collages above her bed. Their adventure had been dreamy, and she couldn't wait to tell her friends about the engagement and move.

When they had called her mother from Italy, Anne had been disappointed she wasn't more enthusiastic.

Her mother had said, "I'm happy for you. Plus you'll be closer to us here in Michigan and can visit more often."

In her green dress and silver shoes, Anne now knocked on Mrs. Landenheim's door. At the last minute, Anne thought to hide the champagne bottle for Bay Breeze behind her back. Mrs. Landenheim opened the door, and the Siamese threaded itself through Anne's legs and scooted off.

"I'm giving you my notice." Anne smiled.

"Notice to what?"

"Sixty days until I move out."

"What? No!" Mrs. Landenheim groaned. Her basset hound eyes seemed to droop even further than usual. "You can't leave! You're my favorite tenant."

Anne couldn't believe her ears. For the past few years, Mrs. Landenheim had nagged her about everything from treading the stairs too noisily, to letting the cat out onto the street, to being tardy with the rent. "I am?"

"Of course. I love the fact you're up there creating."

"You do?"

"Yes, I do! Why are you moving?" Mrs. Landenheim frowned.

"I'm marrying Sergio, and he lives in New York."

"But San Francisco is your *home*."

"Well, I love him and need to be with him."

"I can understand that." Mrs. Landenheim beamed with a starry look in her eyes. "I've got it! Why doesn't he move here? I'll give you the bigger apartment."

"Thank you. But his job is in New York."

"I sure will miss you." Mrs. Landenheim started to cry, shook her head, and closed the door.

Anne blinked back tears. After all these years, the old lady did really care for her. Calling for a Lyft, Anne stepped out of the apartment building, but Mata Hari blocked the way.

Anne jumped over her and turned around. "I've got great news. I'm moving to New York."

"Move! No way!" Mata Hari raised her rickety body fully upright, folded her fists on her hips, and glared at Anne. "You can't move to New York. It is sooo big. The pollution out there is horrible for your skin." She ran her fingers over a wrinkled cheek. "See? Mine is still smooth after all these years from the foggy moist weather."

"But I'm getting married."

"Married. Don't be ridiculous. What for?"

"Because I love him."

"That's no reason. I've told you before: men are nothing but trouble. Since I got rid of my husband, I've been happy and free as a bird." She raised her arms as if flying.

"Here's my ride. I've gotta go." Anne frowned.

She jumped in the car and sat back. Why couldn't her friends be happy for her? At least everyone at Bay Breeze would be.

At the house, she ran up the steps carrying the bottle of champagne.

George opened the door with Lucky in his arms.

"Hi, sweet one. Have you been a good boy?" Anne asked the puppy.

George manipulated Lucky's head to nod *yes*, and Anne gave the dog a treat from her pocket.

Paul wobbled toward her on his cane. "Anne. You look glamorous—and I can really see you this time."

She hugged him. "You had the surgery, huh?"

"It's a miracle!" He chuckled.

The white film was gone from his sky-blue eyes. With George leading the way, Anne and Paul looped their arms together and made their way along the marble floors.

As they entered the library, Anne hollered to Fay, "Get out the champagne flutes!"

"Brilliant." Fay had been positioning gingersnaps on a Haviland plate next to the tea service and cups. Fay's flamboyant dress twirled around her feet like a whirling dervish's as she moved toward Anne.

"I've got my own announcement!" Anne handed Fay the champagne bottle and helped herself to a cookie.

"You're pregnant," Paul teased.

"Not yet." Anne laughed and showed off the ring on her finger.

Fay grabbed Anne's hand. "Blimey. Look at that! Did he get it at a thrift shop?"

"No. It is vintage, though. Been in his family for eons."

"Who's the lucky chap?" Paul sat in his easy chair with a smile, Lucky at his feet.

"Sergio, of course."

"When's the wedding? Will you have it here?"

Anne settled on the sofa next to Fay. "Probably spring. We haven't decided where we're going to have it yet. As you know, my family lives in Michigan, and most of his is in Italy. However, my friends are here, and many of his are in New York. It's very complicated."

"Wherever it is, give us plenty of notice so that we can all be there." Paul nodded his head. "Marrying Sylvia was the best thing I ever did. May we at least host an engagement party for you here?"

"That would be nice. We'll see."

George set a tray with the ice bucket and champagne flutes on the desk. He carefully removed the cork and started to fill the glasses.

"I'm sure going to miss all of you when I move." Anne laughed.

Everyone stopped and stared at her.

Fay yelled, "Blimey! You didn't tell me you had decided to move."

Lucky woke with a bark and did a flying leap into Anne's lap.

"Shhh!" She stroked his back. "Of course, I'm moving to New York. That's where Sergio lives."

"Can't he move here?" Paul asked.

"No, his work's there."

"What about *your* work?" Fay scrunched up her red lips.

"Mine? Living there, won't I be stimulated to grow and make new work?"

Fay continued, "But you've been doing that here. As I've told you, you're starting to make it here in San Francisco. And there's that job opening at the museum you've applied for. Commute back and forth like you've been doing. There are lots of bicoastal marriages these days."

But I want to be with him all the time." Anne didn't even feel like drinking champagne now.

52

For the past three months, Rudy's Ritzy Review had been doing quite well. Many nights they played to full houses. Clair had become part of the Sallies, and she realized on live stages mistakes happened all the time. It felt good, too, to be bringing home more income.

Her father's constitution had improved. He had a new crony at the local coffeehouse, and afternoons they met to play chess there. Aunt June seemed happy to have him gone. Their bickering over the smallest things had increased with his health. "The tea's too cold. Where's my book?" he'd complain.

Clair hummed "Puttin' on the Ritz," donned her cloche hat, and adjusted it in the hall mirror. There was a knock at the door. Her father must have forgotten his key again.

"I'll get it," she called to Aunt June, who was in the kitchen baking bread.

"Farley!" Clair stepped back as he pushed his way inside.

"Clair." He nodded at her and removed his bowler. His droopy mustache had been shaved off, he'd lost his paunch, and the muscles in his upper body had filled out. It had been over six months, and she wouldn't have recognized him if not for the too-sweet scent of his pomade.

Aunt June hurried into the room.

"Hello, June. Leland told me I could find him here. Where is he?"

"At the coffeehouse around the corner. Why don't you go down and find him?" She put her hand on Clair's back.

"I'd rather stay." He pulled a cigar from his pocket and lit it with a match.

Clair took her purse and coat off the hall tree and started for the door, but he caught her elbow.

"Where are you off to?" His grip was firmer and his words more clipped than they had been before.

"Work." Clair tugged her arm away.

"I'll give you a lift." He put his cigar in an ashtray. "We've got a lot to talk about."

"As far as I'm concerned, we have *nothing* to talk about."

He closed the door and stood in front of it. "Tell me more about this job of yours. A seamstress of sorts I've heard."

Clair nodded. "Yes."

"Where is it?"

"Midtown."

"What exactly do you do there besides sew?"

"Help with odds and ends." She kept her voice calm. If she pushed too hard, she'd never get to the theater.

Farley frowned. "A girl of your standing should not be out working."

"Things have changed. Even women do what they can."

June took Clair's hand. "Yes, if it wasn't for her job, we'd have starved long ago."

"I've got to go now or I'll be late." Clair tried again to push past Farley.

He got in close to her, nose to nose. "We need to discuss this further."

"No, we do not!" Clair yelled. "Who do you think you are? Barging in like this and trying to tell me what to do."

"You are my betrothed!" He put his face close to hers.

"Are you demented? That was long ago."

Aunt June stepped between them and put her hand gently on Clair's forehead. "You seem to have a fever, dear. Let's go to our room and you can lie down."

Farley stepped back. "It might be consumption. I'll get the doctor!"

"No need. She probably just needs a little rest." Aunt June guided Clair into the bedroom and shut the door.

Clair's body shook with anger. "If he thinks he can sashay in here and lord it over me, he's got another thing coming!"

Aunt June whispered, "Settle down. Last thing you need is to get him all riled up."

"But I need to get to work."

June shook her head. "You should stay here until your father comes home."

"But everyone at work is depending on me." Clair had been tempted to tell Aunt June the truth about her job but didn't want her to have to keep that secret.

"They'll get along for one night without you."

Clair plopped down on the edge of the bed and started to cry.

"I'm sorry." Aunt June handed her a lace handkerchief.

The front door slammed and June peeked out the door. "Good. He's gone."

Clair stood. "Then I'm off, too."

"You'd better wait. He might be lurking outside."

Clair paced the apartment while June checked her bread and made soup for supper. Thirty minutes later Farley returned with Dr. Johnson.

"Farley tells me you aren't well."

"Oh, for goodness' sake! She's fine," Aunt June grumbled.

Her father opened the door. "Farley!" He shook his hand. "Dr.

Johnson! Why are you here? Has June had a relapse?" He put his hand on his chest.

Farley lit another cigar. "No, it's Clair. She's gravely ill."

Clair squinted her eyes at him. "You bastard!" She clasped her hand over her mouth and looked at Dr. Johnson and her father sheepishly. "Sorry."

Crying, she ran past them out the door. "I've got to get to work."

"See, this is what I was talking about." Farley blocked her way.

Dr. Johnson took Clair's hands in his. "My, my. You certainly aren't yourself."

"Then who would I be?" She smirked through her tears.

"Clair, don't be disrespectful to the doctor." Her father frowned at her.

"Let's go to your room for a little exam." Dr. Johnson escorted her by the elbow, smelling like the witch hazel he had prescribed for her pimples a few years ago. He sat her on the bed and put his black bag on the dresser.

Farley and her father followed them in.

"Gentlemen, you two can go now." Aunt June closed the bedroom door and sat next to Clair. "This is not necessary, doctor. She's fine."

"We need to be sure." He grabbed his stethoscope from the bag.

With his back turned, Clair jumped up and tried to leave the room.

He stood in her way. "Sit down." Using the stethoscope, he listened to her chest through her blouse. "My, my, my. How are you feeling?"

"Angry as hell!" Clair shouted.

The doctor nodded, escorted Aunt June from the bedroom, and closed the door. Clair, alone in the bedroom, ran her fingers over her thighs, then got up and put an ear to the door.

"Is my Clair going to be all right?" her father asked.

"Leland, I have grave news." The doctor kept his voice low, but Clair could hear him anyway. "My diagnosis is that she has what we call 'impulse hysteria' and needs to be confined to complete bed rest."

"Really, doctor?" Her father sounded scared.

"Leland, that's ridiculous." Aunt June always had the voice of reason. "She was fine until Farley arrived."

"I recommend she stay in bed for at least a week, Leland, under your direct supervision."

Clair came out of the bedroom, put her arm through her father's, and managed a smile. "I'm fine, now. I promise." She wished she had heeded Varinska's advice and not let them see her cry.

"Ha! I've discovered what caused this 'illness,'" Farley sneered.

Everyone in the room stared at him.

"She's been performing at a burlesque house!"

Clair's body felt as if it were a chandelier falling onto a marble floor, shattering in a million pieces.

"That's not true!" Aunt June looked at Clair, but when she saw her niece's expression, she sat down on the sofa.

"Here's the evidence." Farley unrolled a scroll in his hand, held it up to the group, and gave it to her father.

Clair's father studied the playbill, handed it to June, and dropped onto the sofa next to her, his head in his hands. "My little Raffie."

"Women are runaway trains. If you don't control them, they'll crash." Farley glared at Clair.

Dr. Johnson shook his head. "This won't do at all. Won't do at all. An upstanding young woman like you performing burlesque!"

Clair stood tall, put her shoulders back, and tilted her head up. "It's not a juice joint or anything distasteful. Rudy runs a clean house!"

She tried to make another run for it. Farley stood in front of the door, and she pounded on his chest. Stopping her, he grabbed her wrists. "See, she's out of control! Let's lock her in the bedroom."

"Don't touch her!" Aunt June put a hand on Clair's back. "Come with me, dear."

The women sat on the bed. Aunt June shook her head. "Lord, what fools these mortals be!"

They listened to Dr. Johnson through the door. "Put four of these drops in water every eight hours and make her drink it. I'll return tomorrow. If her fits don't stop, there are other treatments we can use. One of my other patients never snapped out of it, and we had to send her to a sanitarium."

"I'm sure that won't be necessary," her father moaned. "We'll take good care of my girl. Goodbye, and thank you."

The front door closed.

They let her out of her room, and the four of them—Clair, her father, Aunt June, and Farley—silently drank their soup and bread.

At bedtime, her father pulled the cork from the vial, counted drops into a glass of water, and made sure she drank it down. The reddish-brown liquid tasted bitter, worse than any hooch she'd ever tried, but she denied him the satisfaction of grimacing.

"It's for your own good, Raffie. You need to get better."

"But I'm not even sick." She shook her head, deeply shocked by the day's events.

53

Hot summer rain evaporated off the windshield as Farley steered his Lincoln down the street. His crooked smile didn't seem quite right. A foreboding sense of fear with red swirls of panic flew into Clair's chest, like falling in an elevator after the wires had been cut. She shouldn't have agreed to this drive.

It had been weeks though, weeks of being locked inside the apartment. Weeks at a standstill.

"Please, Father," she had begged. "If not the theater, I'll find somewhere more acceptable to work. How else will we make ends meet?"

"Don't worry. I've found another source of income," her father had told her.

"Where?" she asked.

"Never you mind." He shook his head.

And then the next evening, she saw Farley slip an envelope to him.

That man wouldn't give up.

"Your reputation has been sullied. The answer is for you to marry me."

"It's for the best." Her father frowned.

It felt as if she were a cow being sold. "Never!" she had yelled. She'd rather die than be married to Farley. He seemed obsessed with having control over her.

She thought if she continued to deny him, her father would eventually relent. Instead though, he kept doting on Farley. "Thank you for helping us, son."

Clair had long ago run out of tears. The tincture made her dizzy and sleepy, so after a week she learned to feign swallowing it. As soon as her father left the room, she'd spit it into the now-dead philodendron's pot.

Rudy and Winnie had tried to help. They showed up a few times, but there were strict orders that Clair wasn't to talk to them. Aunt June had offered to help her get away, but Clair declined; if the men found her gone they'd be livid and might take it out on Aunt June.

She had become Clair's constant companion; without her, she really would have gone mad. Attempting to cheer her up, June made afternoon tea, played cards with her, read Shakespeare, Austen, and the Brontës aloud. When no one else was around, Clair performed song and dance routines for her aunt.

That afternoon the doctor had recommended Farley take Clair out for a spin to get some fresh air away from the stifling apartment, and she couldn't resist. As it grew dark, lights across the East River began to twinkle on. Farley drove the Lincoln onto the bridge, and they left Manhattan in a stream of traffic. Lighting a cigar, he inhaled and let it out. The smoke soon permeated the car. So much for the fresh air that had been promised.

"Yes, this bridge is 1,595 feet long. A miracle as the first steel-wire suspension bridge ever built . . ." Farley continued to spew boring facts to her, unaware that she'd stopped listening.

She could barely make it out, but a sliver of moon peeked over the horizon, like the curve of the scimitar sword displayed over her father's desk that she had left in the move. Clair wished with all her might that she could soar up there and stand on it. Some people believed it might be possible to visit the moon someday.

Clair had heard that the moon held the parts of your life that were wasted. Like her mother who had wasted away when Clair was so young. The memory of her rose scent and smooth skin filled Clair's mind. How different her life would have been if her mother hadn't died. Clair would have been loved and protected.

Farley glanced behind him, turned to Clair, and spoke softly. "If you'd agree to marry me, I wouldn't need to do this."

"Do what?" Clair's body shook with fear. The car slowed down and a horn honked behind them. "Pull over before we have an accident!" Clair shouted.

He guided the car to the side of the bridge, put his hands on her shoulders, and pulled her close.

"Let me go! Do what?" It dawned on her that Farley might be planning to take her to a sanitarium.

"With time you'll get used to me."

She struggled to get away, but Farley held on tight, his evening whiskers burning her skin. She shoved him back, put her hand on the door handle, and tried to push it down, but it wouldn't budge. She heaved harder, and this time it opened. She stepped out onto the bridge. Her eyes swept across it, back and forth, gauging which end was closer.

Farley revved the motor, honked, and backed up beside her.

Her shoes scraped along the metal grate as she ran away from him, back toward Manhattan, a string of lights above leading the way.

"Clair! Get back in here!"

She shook her head and tried to pick up the pace, but the full-length skirt Farley and her father insisted she wear restricted her legs from a quick stride. Leaning over, she flipped up the hem and held it in her hands. As a gust of wind swirled around her, her hair unfurled past her shoulders.

"Clair, stop!" Farley turned off the car, got out, and followed her along the grate. Horns honked as traffic passed by on the bridge, casting shadows.

"No!" She shook her head and kept moving away from him along the walkway. Glancing back at him, she saw he was bent over, hands on his knees as if out of breath.

The moon and the bridge's V-shaped vertical lines called to her. She could feel the cold steel seep through her gloves as she grabbed the railing and held on. One foot on top of the steel, she looked down into the murky water. Did she dare jump?

Cars stopped and she heard voices yell, but she couldn't concentrate on the words.

Farley caught up to her and grabbed for her waist. She attempted to kick him off, but he held fast and raised himself up behind her onto the railing, trying to pull her back down.

"Clair!" His voice caught in the wind and blew away.

"Leave me alone!" She yanked her body away, stood atop the railing, and gazed into the river again.

He reached for her and this time she let her body go; gravity pulled them both through the air—down, down, down. Clair pointed her arms forward, straightened her legs, and dove deep into the water that struck her body like a cold bath.

Farley screamed as his body plopped sideways into the river with a loud splat. Had he survived the fall?

She butterflied her arms back and forth, rose to the top, and gasped for air. The briny water smelled of fuel, rotten food, and human waste.

A wave splashed over her in the strong current. She began to sink and slipped off her Mary Janes underwater. By the time Clair returned to the surface, she knew that in order to survive she couldn't panic. She turned onto her back in a floating position like she'd been taught as a child in the cove.

"Help!" Farley's voice flew over the current a few yards from her. "Help! Help!"

His pleas reverberated in her head, and she realized no matter how despicable he had been she couldn't let him drown. She swam against the current toward his calls.

"Help!"

If she was going to save him she had to keep him calm. "It's okay. I'm almost there," she said through chattering teeth.

Seesawing her legs, she finally clasped one of his arms.

"Ow!" he cried. "That hurts."

"Your arm might be broken."

She tilted him back on top of her chest and held him from behind. The current was so swift she wouldn't be able to hold on for long. Farley grew quiet. He seemed to have fainted.

She needed something to hang onto. The nearby docks were too far away for her to carry him to. A shoe, a plastic baby doll, and an apple floated by, bouncing on the strong current. A log came toward them, but as she reached for it, it careened out of her grasp.

She almost lost her grip on Farley, but a tire, practically invisible on the dark water, approached with great speed. She stuck out her hand, managed to grasp it, and held on. With the other arm she readjusted Farley's weight on her body.

Her wet hair draped around them like a mermaid's. She continued to slowly scissor her legs back and forth while trying to hold Farley's head above water. To stay alert she stared at the moon. As long as it was above her, they were still alive. She sang a desperate plea to the orb over and over, "Oh, moon, silver sliver of beauty. Save us!"

She wasn't sure if it had been five minutes or thirty, but her strength was nearly gone when she heard a man's voice call from across the water. "Ahoy there!"

A far-off light slid slowly toward them in the darkness until she could see a skiff.

The man yelled, "Ahoy!"

She gasped for breath and tried to call out. The skiff floated closer, and she could make out two men with knitted caps pulled low over their foreheads. One held a lantern and the other rowed.

"Farley, wake up." She shook him, avoiding his injured arm.

The men pulled alongside them and reached out. The boat tipped on its side as they dragged Clair and Farley aboard, setting them on a slat seat amongst crates of bottles.

"Jingle-brainers! We saw you jump off the bridge."

"You could have died." The other shook his head.

"Yes, she almost drowned, but I saved her." Farley resembled a wet rat as water dripped off his head.

Oh, for pity's sake. "Yes, you are so brave." She glared at him.

One of the men took off his peacoat and wrapped it around her shivering shoulders. "There you go, miss. We'll have you to shore in no time."

The man handed Farley a burlap sack. He covered his back with it and closed his eyes. The other man started to row and land soon came into view. They pulled the skiff onto a small beach between two boulders.

"Wait here," the rower said.

From behind the rocks, the man with the lantern pulled a Ford truck toward them. The men loaded the crates of bottles onto it. One helped Clair into the passenger seat and the other climbed in the truck bed beside the bottles with Farley, and they quickly sped away.

"We'll get you to a warm place soon. Need to drop off the stash at the warehouse first. It's too dangerous to drive through Manhattan with it."

As the truck pulled into the warehouse, a man walked over. "Stowaways?" He laughed gregariously.

"No, sir. Fell off the bridge, they did."

"Glad you were there to save them."

Clair would have recognized that voice anywhere. "Rudy?"

He frowned at her, confused.

She pushed back her damp hair. "It's me."

"Gal pal?" He rushed to her. "Are you okay?"

"I am now."

"Hey! Farley. You boozehound, you."

Farley peeked at Rudy.

"You know each other?" Clair asked.

"Uh-huh." Farley shrugged, a guilty look on his face.

"Sure, he used to come in the speakeasy all the time. Quite the dancer!"

"He did? He was?" Clair gave Farley a wide-eyed stare.

He shrugged again.

Clair tried to run her fingers through her matted hair. "I'm glad your guys came along when they did. We could have died out there."

"That's true. Come on, Clair." Rudy opened the truck door for her. "I'll get you home."

"What about me?" Farley asked. "I've got a broken arm."

Rudy snorted. "Ask the guys to help you when they finish unloading the truck."

Billowy clouds covered the moon. Clair gave Farley a little wave as she climbed into Rudy's tin lizzie. Her icy body had begun to thaw out, and her body ached from the fall. She could smell the river's stink on her.

Rudy let his car idle and turned to her. "Clair, what happened?"

"I can't talk about it now. Please take me home."

"Want to go to Winnie's instead?"

"No. I have to tell Father about Farley's duplicity."

When Rudy pulled up in front of Aunt June's apartment he asked, "Shouldn't I come in with you?"

Clair shook her head. "Better not."

He smiled at her. "We've missed you. You're welcome back to the theater anytime."

"That's good, because I plan to return there very soon." She stepped out of the truck and he drove off.

54

As Rudy drove away, Clair tossed the stinky coat on the stoop. She certainly didn't want the apartment to reek.

She stepped inside, and her father jumped up off the couch and hollered, "What happened to you?"

"Fell into the East River!" Feeling a bit woozy, she held on to the back of a chair and yearned to sit down but didn't want her filthy dress to stain the furniture.

Her aunt ran out of the bedroom in her nightgown. "Oh, my stars and garters! Are you okay?"

"I'm fine."

"No, you aren't. Look at that bruise on your cheek. You must have others, too."

"I'll be okay."

"What about Farley?" her father cried.

"He might have a broken arm is all. Father, I can't believe you were ready to have me locked up."

"Locked up! Leland?" Aunt June gaped at him.

He shook his head. "What are you talking about? Dr. Johnson said a drive would be good for you."

"I believe they colluded to put me in a sanitarium."

"What? I had nothing to do with it."

"Farley isn't who you think he is. Turns out he's been drinking and going to speakeasies for ages!"

"That's impossible." Her father shook his head.

"The man whose workers rescued us from the river recognized Farley. Said he was quite the dancer."

"I had no idea." Her father sat down. "He bamboozled all of us."

Aunt June harrumphed. "Leland, that's it! You haven't always been so perfect yourself. It's time we removed our masks and revealed this masquerade. Clair deserves to learn the truth."

This is what she had been waiting for.

"June, are you sure that's wise?" Her father frowned.

"I'm taking her to the farm this week whether you approve or not!"

"I guess you are right. You usually are." He looked at Clair. "When you learn the truth, please don't think too badly of me."

A few mornings later, white clouds floated above them, schooners in the indigo sky. Aunt June navigated the neighbor's Model T along the dusty rutted country road. They curved over and down small hills and around winding paths. Broad open spaces provided a desolate beauty. A dried-out oak grove spread across a parched meadow, where a pair of emaciated horses attempted to graze. Manure caressed Clair's nose. A windmill had collapsed on its side.

For the last few days, Clair had begged her father and Aunt June to tell her what was at the farm, but she was told to wait and see.

"How much longer?" she asked, stretching her cramped legs. The bruise on her right hip from the fall began to throb again. The one on her forehead had disappeared.

"About another half hour," Aunt June said.

"What was it like growing up on a farm? You've rarely talked about it."

"Early mornings. All those chores: milk Bertha, gather eggs, and in the fall, pick crops. But those sunrises were worth getting up early for—peaceful pink pleasures."

Clair wasn't sure she'd enjoy it much, being so far away from culture. They rode along in silence. She couldn't wait to learn the truth and wondered what had been hidden at the farm. It must have something to do with her mama.

"We're almost there." Aunt June smiled at her.

Clair spread her fingers wide above her head and stretched. They pulled onto a dusty trail, barely wide enough for the car. Soon a faded frame house with gabled windows, a pitched roof, and a wraparound porch came into view. A barn tilted as if a slight breeze might trigger a collapse of boards. The silo had rusted red.

Aunt June pulled over, scattering a few chickens in the yard, and stopped beside a peeling picket fence. Even though the farm looked dilapidated, Clair could tell it once had charm. Rays of sun shone through a giant oak as if coming straight from heaven.

A tall woman came out of the house, a calico apron hanging loosely on her skinny frame. Staring at them, she dipped her hands into her pockets and tossed feed to the clucking chickens.

How curious. Clair had been told that the farm had been deserted years ago. She opened the car door and stepped out. The weedy ground itched her ankles through her stockings.

Aunt June got out of the car, too, and stood beside it. The two older women eyed each other. The stranger looked at Clair with a frown that became a wry smile. Clair followed Aunt June through the gate. Shadows fell on the ground as the tall woman walked down the steps and embraced Aunt June.

"When the money stopped, I hoped you might come." The woman tried to smooth her straggly gray hair. Her large dark eyes remained on Clair, glistening with tears.

Aunt June stepped back, wiped the tears on the woman's weathered cheeks with a hankie, then turned and waved Clair over. "And, of course, this is our girl."

"Of course. You're all grown up." The woman moved to Clair

and with rough hands traced the curves of her face. Clair's impulse was to pull back, but she didn't want to be rude. As she inhaled, a rose scent tingled a trace of memory from inside her. She lifted her own hand and put it over the woman's.

"Who are you?" Clair asked.

"I'm your mother."

Clair shook her head. "No, you're not. She's dead."

"I'm right here. I'm April."

Clair stood with her mouth open, her soul awash with awe at the truth that had always been hidden. She had never considered that her mother could still be alive.

"Mama?" With a weeping breath, Clair fell into her arms.

"Baby," the woman whispered as she held her daughter close. "My baby."

She guided Clair up the steps into the cool, dark house, led her to a worn sofa, and sat her down. June settled in beside her. Clair stared up at her mama. Tinges of her beauty still remained. Caved-in cheeks held a peachy golden glow. Her thin lips tightened into a chipped-tooth smile, yellow as an old lace wedding dress.

April sat on a nearby chair. The contrast between the two sisters was astounding. April's hair had been twisted back into a tight bun, gray as the picket fence, while Aunt June's neat coif was still mostly auburn; April wore a soiled apron, June her Sunday frock. It was their matching doe eyes, though, that revealed their relationship, brown pools of grief. Clair had seen those eyes when she looked in the mirror.

"Why did you stop writing?" Aunt June asked.

"Nothing to say." April shrugged.

"Mama, what happened? Why did you leave? Why didn't you visit?" Clair coughed. Her throat felt as dry as the dirt road.

"Hush, hush," Aunt June whispered. "She'll tell you everything. First, April, may we have some water, please?"

"Of course." She filled glasses from a pitcher on the sideboard and handed them to Clair and June. "Make yourselves comfortable. I've got a lot to say."

The women shifted in their seats, sat back, and drank from their glasses.

"I wasn't like your aunt June," April began. "She always minded and did what was right, reading those thick books, helping the teacher. A selfish child, I coveted what my big sister had—a candy cane, a ribbon, a doll. I understood it was wrong, but I couldn't help myself."

"You weren't that bad," June interrupted.

April put out her hand for silence. "At fourteen I was like a feral cat—wouldn't do my chores, refused to go to school, stayed out past dark. June went to work in the city. Ma had consumption, hacking all the time. Pop struggled to keep the farm going on his own. The day after he found me between the hay bundles with Benny McDabbens, Pop packed me up and put me on a train to June in New York.

"I guess that's what I had wanted all along. I couldn't stand for her to have all that freedom, living in the big city."

Clair could relate to that.

"When I arrived she was teaching school and was engaged to Leland. He was handsome with his sophisticated manners and fine clothes, smelling of money."

"Wait! You were engaged to Father?" Clair stared at her aunt, who nodded.

"He adored you, June. Your beautiful brain, as he called it. But as usual, I couldn't stand for you to have something I didn't."

"You were so young." June reached for April's hand.

"I knew exactly what I was doing. Leland would come to call. We'd sit in the boardinghouse parlor playing cards and singing to the piano. I'd flirt away, but he'd just laugh. Didn't take me seriously.

"That night, you had an emergency suffragette rally and asked me to tell him you were sorry but would see him the next night. I had on that dress, the one with the sweetheart neckline Pop had forbidden me to wear. When no one was looking, I slipped off my shoes and lifted my skirt, showing Leland my ankles. I enticed him up to our room. We snuck up quietly. He couldn't help himself."

June pulled her hand away.

April looked at Clair. "Afterward, he broke off their engagement but didn't tell June the reason why. I didn't tell her either. She was despondent. When she realized I was pregnant, she went to him for solace and it all came out. Of course he did the honorable thing and married me. I moved into the Waldorf with him, had you, and even settled down for a while. I knew he didn't love me, but I didn't really care. I was getting what I wanted. Him."

June dabbed at her eyes with a handkerchief.

"Did *you* learn to love him?" Clair asked.

"I tried, but then Benny came to town and started sniffing around. Because of the attraction I felt toward him I was certain we must have loved each other all along." She shook her head.

"I thought I could have it both ways, be a wife and mother and have Benny, too, but I was wrong. When Leland discovered what I'd been up to, he told me I had to choose." She sighed. "I needed to be with someone I loved."

Clair's stomach tightened. "Didn't you love me?"

"When you get older, you'll understand. I needed the love of a man. So I chose Benny."

Clair couldn't believe what she was hearing.

"Leland said I could have him and sent me back to the farm."

"Where's Benny now?" June asked.

"Gone long ago. Fell down drunk on his corn mash whiskey." April sneered. "By then Ma had died and Pop couldn't keep up the farm. Leland sent money every month as long as I didn't try to see you, Clair, so I didn't have much choice. Besides, your father never loved me. He always loved you, June, even after we were married."

"That's not true!" June waved her hand, tears pooling in her eyes.

"I could tell by the way he looked at you." April turned to gaze at Clair. "And when you were born, he doted on you. He wouldn't go to social events and only wanted to sit at home in the evenings with you. I was stuck, suffocated in that boring blue box of a hotel suite, my beauty fading like a peony. Sure I loved you, but it wasn't enough."

Clair's whole body ached with sorrow. She wondered what she would have done in the same situation. First of all, she would never flirt with someone else's betrothed. She raised her voice to Aunt June. "Why didn't *you* tell me?"

"Your father made me promise to go along with the charade or else he wouldn't let me spend time with you. I tried to do my best. Tried to give you the love and devotion a mother would."

Clair nodded and took Aunt June's hand.

April reached over, put her hand on top of Clair's, and nodded at June. "I'm so sorry. Will you ever forgive me? I recognized how much you loved him."

"I forgave you years ago."

"I have so many regrets."

"I certainly hope so!" Clair pulled her hand away, jumped up, pushed through the screen door, and ran out the gate to the barren field beyond. She couldn't let them see her cry.

She waited until her sobs abated and listened to the quiet. Without the city's rush of traffic or the pounding waves at the cottage, a symphony of sound came to her ears, carried on soft winds. Oak leaves rustled, hens clucked like castanets, a far-off windmill squeaked and banged as if a tambourine, the cow's moo was an oboe.

Clair's mixed emotions darted like the sun as it moved in and out from behind the clouds. Bright one moment and dark the next, fading in and out from happiness at meeting her mother, to deep sadness, to anger. The calm country sounds flowed through her body like the touch of Aunt June's hand on her back.

55

Clair rushed up the stairs and barged into the apartment. Her father was sitting on the couch.

"Father, I can forgive you for allowing Farley in our lives. But I will never forgive you for keeping Mama from me."

Her father wiped his brow with a handkerchief. "I'm sorry. I believed I was doing the right thing."

"You were wrong."

"She didn't deserve to see you."

"By punishing her, you were punishing me, too." Clair stamped her foot.

Aunt June entered the apartment and put her hand on Clair's back. "Settle down."

"I won't. I'm returning to the theater tomorrow. It's where I belong. Father, I never want to see you again." Clair ran to her room and slammed the door.

Aunt June knocked on the door and went in. "I don't blame you for being angry."

Clair crossed her arms and stared at her.

"I never should have gone along with the deception. I hope someday you'll be able to forgive all of us. If you feel you belong in the theater, then by all means return."

"Do you really believe that?" Clair asked.

Aunt June nodded. "Yes, to thine own self be true."

~

Clair stepped through the back door into the dressing room. She had missed the gang. The Sallies practiced their routine in a corner with a new girl who must have been added after Clair left. Winnie sat in another corner doing her breathing exercises. Nook was teaching the girls how to do backflips.

"Look, it's Clair!" he yelled.

Winnie ran to her. "Welcome back, honey."

The Sallies and Winnie surrounded her with hugs as if she was their long-lost sister. In a way she was.

"Look vhat ze kitten dragged in." Varinska took a puff of her cigarette.

Rudy came in. "Hi, gal pal. Quite the adventure you had the other night."

"That's for sure." Clair smiled at him.

Varinska put her head down on the dressing room table and closed her eyes. "No go on tonight."

"What do you mean? We've got a full house! Clifton Marshall is even in the audience," Rudy said.

"I'm ill."

"But it's time for places in fifteen minutes. We'll have an angry crowd." He pointed a finger at the rules. "The show must go on!"

"Not vith me." Varinska took another drag of her cigarette and coughed.

"Then who's going to be my showstopper?" Rudy yelled.

Everyone stared at Winnie.

She shook her head. "Not me."

"But what about your dream?" Clair asked.

"Turns out Hollywood wasn't meant to be my dream after all." Winnie put her hands on her belly. "My performing days are numbered. I'm gonna have more important things to do."

Rudy gaped at her. "What could be more important than performing?"

"What do you think, silly?" Winnie put her hands on her hips.

"Congratulations!" Andre yelled, and everyone chimed in.

"Really?" Rudy's grin widened and he shook his head. "We aren't even married."

"That's the lousiest proposal I've ever heard, but the answer is yes!"

Rudy smacked her on the lips. "I'm gonna be a papa!"

Mordecai stuck his face in the room. "I hate to interrupt this family pleasure, but we need to get this show going."

"Yes." Rudy came out from the spell. "Who's gonna be our showstopper?"

"Me! I've memorized all of Varinska's act." Bea squeaked and tried to raise an eyebrow.

"*Nein.*" Varinska pointed her cigarette toward Clair. "Can stop show."

Clair's chest beat as fast as a baby bird's wings.

Andre swished his hands in the air. "Without a rehearsal?"

Winnie put her hand on Clair's shoulder. "She can do it!"

"Can you, gal pal?" Rudy asked.

Clair swallowed, stood up straight, and tilted her head back. "Yes. I can please the crowd, but in my own way." Her voice sounded surprisingly calm even though she didn't feel it inside. "I've been working on a solo routine for months."

"Ok, gal pal. Sing me a few bars."

Clair began to sing to the tune of "The Man on the Flying Trapeze."

"I fly through the air with the greatest of ease.

Free as a bird, I can do as I please.

They tried to cage me, but I got away.

I'll be free as a bird

for the rest of my days."

She moved her arms up and down and flew around the room.

"Okay. I buy it. Find a costume and come on up!" Rudy turned and climbed the stairs.

"This will be fun!" Andre clapped his hands with a laugh.

"Yes." Winnie followed him into the back room.

"All white! I need to wear all white." Clair shed her clothes down to a slip.

Winnie returned with an armful of shimmering white fabric. She lifted the sheath, slid it over Clair's head, and pulled the pearl and sequin voile material down around her narrow hips. In the mirror, Clair could see the ornamentation barely concealed her womanly parts.

"Look what I found!" Andre held up a pair of boa-feathered wings. "Probably from a Daedalus and Icarus skit."

"Perfect." Clair held out her arms and he slipped them on. Winnie crisscrossed the laces and tied them in back.

Andre found Clair's shoes still in their box and handed them to her.

"Oh, no—the taps will be too loud for my number!"

"Hand them over." Andre found a teeny screwdriver in the toolbox, twisted the screws, and pulled out the taps.

Clair put the shoes on and buckled the straps. She studied her reflection in the mirror. "I need something on my head."

"We've got just the thing!" Andre ran back into the storage room and quickly returned with a two-foot-tall pearl-encrusted headdress. "We made it for Varinska, but she refused to wear it—said it upstaged her." He positioned it on Clair's head. She reached up and ran her hands down the smooth pearls, studying her reflection in the mirror.

"Now this is some tiara." She thought of the one the jeweler had offered to make her. Wonder what her father would say about this one! She loved the heavy weight of it, making her feel like royalty. The chinstrap would keep it snug.

Everyone applauded, Andre the loudest. "Marvelous! As if it were made for you."

Surprised, Clair smiled at him.

He gave her a hug, careful not to bump the tiara. "Good luck."

Clair paused. "And all this time I thought you hated me."

"Hate you? No." He whispered, "You've always been my favorite, but I couldn't let the others catch on."

"But weren't you angry about the painting?"

"That was ages ago. Besides, your father's extra cash paid for my toupee." He patted his pompadour.

"What about the torn sash, the lost sheet music, and the missing hoop?"

"That wasn't me." He shook his head.

"Well then, who?" Clair asked.

"Not me. I have a hunch, though." He stared at Bea.

Bea squinted her beady eyes. Her voice squawked higher than ever. "You always thought you were better than me. Even before our debutante debuts. When you were in the room, all eyes would be on you, not me."

"But I thought we were friends." Tears floated in Clair's eyes.

"It was all an act. When you joined us here I knew you had *it*, even when you were only hanging up costumes. I feared you'd become a star and I wouldn't."

"That's pure green envy." Winnie put her hands on her hips.

Dominique scowled. "Bea, you are such a mean vixen."

The others shook their heads and grumbled.

"After the show we'll discuss this further with Rudy." Andre looked at his watch and picked up the hoops. "For now the show must go on. Places!"

Everyone scurried up the stairs. "Clair and Winnie, come along," Andre called.

"In a moment." Winnie wiped Clair's tears, touched up the smudged makeup, and tested the tiara on Clair's head again.

Varinska stood and nodded approvingly.

"Thank you both for believing in me." Clair managed a smile. "Varinska, I hope you recover from your illness soon."

"Not sick." Varinska raised an eyebrow.

"You're not?" Clair asked.

"Your turn. Besides, Josephine has invited me to Paris, darlinks. *Adieu!*" Varinska waved her cigarette and sauntered out the back door.

Clair ran up the stairs with Winnie behind her.

"Where are you going?" Her father stood on the stairs above her.

"What are you doing here?" Clair tried to push past him as Mordecai began playing the Sallies' introduction.

Winnie put her hand on Clair's shoulder.

"If you go out there, he'll disown you." Farley stood behind her father, arms akimbo.

Clair lost her cool and looked into her father's eyes. "Disown me from what? From gambling away all your money in the stock market, from breaking Aunt June's heart, for lying to me all these years about my mother?"

"Don't talk to your father that way!" Farley roared.

"And Father, after what I told you about what an imposter he is, you're still encouraging him." Clair pointed at Farley.

Her father stared at her stone-faced, but his hands shook.

"And you, Farley, you big phony. Acting all religiously high and mighty, as if you were so pure, when all the time you were drinking and carousing."

"You tell 'em, sister!" Winnie shouted.

Rudy closed the stage door and came down the stairs behind the men. "Quiet. The show's started. Clear the stairs! You two out of here." He pointed toward the alley.

Just then, a group of blue-clad policemen bounded in with their guns drawn.

"Hands up. Nobody move!" a tall policeman bellowed.

Clair raised her arms. *Oh, no.* They must have found out about Rudy's warehouse filled with booze.

The officer stepped forward. "Farley Parker?"

Farley hid behind Clair's father.

Leland pulled Farley out from behind his back and called, "Here he is, officer!"

Farley tried to break free and run up the stairs, but Clair's father held him tight until two policemen grabbed Farley's arms and handcuffed him.

"Farley 'The Fingers' Parker. You are under arrest for murder in the first . . ."

"I didn't do it!" he shouted as they dragged him down the stairs and out the door.

Clair stood with her mouth open.

The tall officer shook Clair's father's hand. "Thank you for the call, Mr. Devereaux."

"It's the least I could do. When I learned he had lied to us, I wondered what else he might have been deceiving us about and felt it best to check in with you."

"Glad you did. We've been searching for the owner of that Lincoln left on the bridge. You'll never believe what was in the trunk."

"What?" Clair asked.

"A body, strangled." The officer bunched his lips together. "Turns out he worked for the mob. Has been linked to a string of other murders."

"Oh my God!" Clair shivered, recalling what Farley said on the bridge. "He might have been planning to kill me, too."

Her father gave her a hug. "I'm so sorry. You'll never be able to forgive me."

Loud applause could be heard from above as the Sallies took their curtain call.

Rudy called. "Clair. You're on. Get on up there. It's your turn to show them what you've got!"

Her father smiled at her. "You'd better get up there. Good luck."

Clair nodded, passed by him, and started up the stairs but returned and kissed him on the cheek.

Winnie took her hand. "Let's go, doll. I'll be there watching you in the wings."

56

Her heart pounding, Clair waited for her cue. *All the world's a stage, and all the men and women merely players.* Well, she'd played for others all her life: the perfect daughter, the debutante, the downtrodden. Now it was time to do what she'd always wanted. But what if everyone laughed at her, or worse yet, booed her offstage? They'd almost done it to Winnie the first time she'd performed her solo. Feathered wings soft on Clair's arms, pearl headdress secure on her head, she closed her eyes and imagined embodying a white dove empowered with the voice of peace.

The stage was pitch-black, and Rudy's voice boomed over the microphone. "Ladies and gentlemen. We have an unexpected pleasure for you this evening. The debut of the Songbird of Broadway."

In silence, with outstretched arms Clair glided onstage in her rhinestone shoes. The spotlight lit up and followed her as she gracefully circled the wooden floor. On a diagonal with a figure-eight pattern, she swept forward, floating her arms up and down. She stopped center stage, spotlight hot on her body, sequins sparkling and pearls glimmering. She wore a wide-eyed look of innocence.

Fragments of audience members could be made out, a glint off a bald head here, a reflection of eyeglasses there. In the heat of the moment, thoughts of Farley disappeared from her mind.

Clair nodded to Mordecai, who had received Rudy's message to play the "Man on the Flying Trapeze." Slowly Mordecai began to play the melody. In perfect pitch the made-up lyrics soared out of her, like a rainbow of colored sequins arcing all the way to the back of the theater.

"I fly through the air with the greatest of ease.

Free as a bird, I can do as I please.

They tried to cage me, but I got away.

I'll be free as a bird

for the rest of my days."

She sang as if taken over by an otherworldly spirit. She was no longer herself, or even a bird, but a winged immortal being with a voice from the heavens, Nike the strong, winged goddess of Victory.

Clair's arms swirled in a windmill motion, slowly at first, then gradually picking up speed. She imagined flying up and above the audience. She struck poses—curved, smooth, graceful. Holding each, she counted to ten in her mind. The moves were innocent at first, then with a dip of her shoulder sensual, until finally they became sexual in nature with a rotation of her hips in a circular fashion, one way and then the other. She could sense the crowd's eyes gazing at her with desire.

If it hadn't been for that one night with Mr. X, she'd never have known how to move her body this way. And she was grateful to him for opening up her seductive passions.

She circled the stage several more times and trilled her finale, arms wide, holding the last note for what seemed like an eternity. Bright lights cast a shadow of her wings behind her, making her appear fifteen feet tall. Before she exited, she soared downstage, put her fingers to her lips, and blew a kiss to the crowd.

In her fantasies she never had imagined performing in front of a crowd that insisted on multiple encores. With pride and a desire to do it all again, she felt what it was like to captivate an audience and be a star.

After the show ended, after the cast gathered round with congratulations, after she thought she couldn't feel any higher, she stepped out into the alley, where the crescent moon vibrated.

"Hello," a deep voice said.

Her gloved hands flew to her pounding chest. Had Farley escaped from the police?

A man wearing a fedora and an overcoat walked toward her from the shadows.

"You scared me." Clair breathed a sigh of relief.

"I'm sorry." His blue eyes shone as he came closer. "I've been hoping to see you again."

Mr. X!

"Me, too." Her voice trembled as she looked up at him. He was more handsome than she had remembered.

"Can we go somewhere to talk?"

Still shaken up from revelations of Farley's crimes, she couldn't talk of that now and would probably be wary of any man for a long time. However, she still wanted to say yes to Mr. X. She had so many questions to ask him but paused. "No. You're a married man."

"Married? I'm not married. What gave you that idea?"

"I noticed a ring on your finger that night. Afterward."

He frowned. "Is that why you ran off?"

She nodded. "Yes."

"I had been widowed for two years. I still hadn't been able to take off my ring."

"I'm sorry." Clair couldn't believe how foolish she'd been.

"If it's any consolation, I took it off the next morning. With you I realized it would be possible to find someone else to love. Please, I'd really like to talk with you. How about a cup of coffee?"

"But I don't know you."

He gave her a sideways smile. "You didn't know me that night either."

She laughed and held out her hand. "I'm Clair Devereaux."

"Yes, the Songbird of Broadway. What a performance!" He clasped her hand. "I'm Clifton Marshall."

She stepped back in surprise.

"*The* Clifton Marshall? From Hollywood?"

He chuckled a deep-throated laugh. "Yes. Every few months when I've come to New York in search of talent, I've kept my eyes out for you."

"You have?"

"Your act tonight was the best I've witnessed in years."

"You're only being kind." She shrugged nonchalantly to hide her elation.

"I mean it. Please have that coffee with me, or maybe even breakfast?"

Lots of breakfasts, she thought. "Thank you for keeping me safe from the police that night. And for . . ." She paused.

"For what?"

She grinned at him. They both laughed. With a questioning look, he held out his arm.

She took it. "Let's go! We have a lot of catching up to do."

57

Anne gazed out the window of Sergio's co-op. So high up, she felt removed from it all. The snow had stopped. The bare maple trees in Central Park below resembled stick figures. Back in her San Francisco apartment, her body had been immersed in life. She had been here for a month and had figured by now she'd be into a rhythm of some sort, but instead her mind remained discombobulated.

Tomorrow she'd fly back to San Francisco, finish packing up, clean the apartment, and give the keys back to Mrs. Landenheim. All her furnishings were sold, and a buyer was lined up for Tweety. Anne would cram a U-Haul truck with her "keepers" and begin the long cross-country drive. In New York she'd look for a job and start her new life.

Her first week staying in New York had been exciting. Sergio had taken the week off, and they visited her favorite museums: the Met, the Frick, and the new Whitney. On days when the weather allowed, they walked through the park. They'd gone to see *Hamilton* and the Alvin Ailey Dance Theater. Every night he had taken her to a different restaurant or cooked a gourmet meal at home.

Week two, Sergio returned to work and his hours were long. Many nights he had late client dinners. Occasionally she joined him in these meetings, dining alongside strangers she didn't have anything in common with—corporate buyers wearing stylish, tony black fashions.

She found she preferred to stay home and binge-watch *Orange Is the New Black*.

She might do that tonight because he wouldn't be home until late.

In the last few days, a freak autumn snowstorm had taken over the city, and she felt like a prisoner. It was so quiet in his apartment.

A blank canvas sat in the corner of the living room—Sergio had bought her brushes and new paints, but she hadn't even opened the packages. Nothing had inspired her.

She'd tried. She had doodled in her journal, flipped through old magazines, and even sat on a bench and sketched in the park. Even though they'd put down a tarp, she was still afraid to sully his pristine penthouse.

Her muse wasn't here!

She picked up her journal and wrote:

I miss –

My cozy apartment.

The trolley running by.

Mrs. Landenheim's cat hissing at me when I go to pet it.

Looking for Mata Hari on every doorstep.

Being able to visit Paul.

Anne sighed. She'd get used to it here. The sun shone on her through the window as a break in the weather appeared. She slipped on boots, grabbed a parka, and headed out the door. On the street she exhaled puffs of steam. The geraniums in the building's window boxes had died. The snow had begun to melt to an icy slush. Little streams ran in the gutters.

Hurrying along the sidewalk, huddled deep in her parka, she pulled the hood down over her head. She slipped and slid on the icy sidewalk, catching herself on a trash barrel before she fell. Ugh! This was one of the reasons she had moved from Michigan.

She hopped on a bus and headed toward Timely Treasures. Last week when she went by, it still hadn't reopened. She stepped off the bus, turned the corner, and her heart sprinted. The shop's curtains had been raised and the lights were on. In the front window a man struggled, trying to dress a mannequin.

Anne rushed across the street. The bell announced her entrance, and the scent of beeswax and lemons greeted her like it had over six months before.

"May I help you?"

Anne hurried to the window.

It was the same man who had sold her the shoes—his hair slicked back, wearing a white shirt with a vest over it.

Huffing, he smiled. "Please."

She held the mannequin while he tugged the beaded sheath down over the mannequin's slim hips. Together they turned it to face the sidewalk.

"Thanks! I couldn't have done it without you. Wait a second." He held up his finger, ran out onto the sidewalk, and raised an arm. Anne followed his instruction and reset the mannequin's arm. The man gave her a thumbs-up.

The shop had been transformed. Man Ray photographs hung on the walls, plush pillows adorned a brocade sofa, a furry white rug covered the floor.

"Remember me?" Anne smiled at the man as he came back through the door.

He studied her. "Of course! You're the one with the black velvet coat. How did the shoes work out for you?"

"Perfectly. I love them. Where have you been? I've come looking for you." She tried to keep from sounding irritated. "Didn't you get my note?"

"Sorry about that. I had a family emergency."

Now she was the one who was sorry. "Oh, I'm sorry to—"

He cut her off. "Did you find my surprise?"

"The pearls? You put them in there on purpose? Why?" She wished she had them with her. They still sat in the bowl on Sergio's counter.

"I knew they'd look lovely on you. Your tall frame and large feet reminded me of my godmother who owned them."

"Winnie or Clair?"

"How do you know about them?" An antique chair crackled as he dropped into it.

"From the picture you left in the bottom of the box."

"What picture?"

"The one under the tissue paper."

He frowned, clearly bewildered.

"You mean you didn't leave it in there?"

"No." He shook his head.

She sat on a chair next to him, searched through the photos on her phone, and showed him the picture. "It's a bit grainy."

"I wonder how that got in there." He squinted and pointed. "That's my grandmother Winnie and my godmother, Clair. They were great pals. Performed burlesque together. Boy, the stories they told. What a hoot." He shook his head.

"At Rudy's, right? It says so on the back of the photo." Anne showed him the photo of the writing on the back of the picture.

"Rudy's was a speakeasy run by my grandfather. After it got raided, he opened a theater—later he married Winnie. I lost them both a while back. Clair quite recently." He sighed.

"I'm sorry."

"That's why I closed the shop. Her house sold, and I had to clear everything out. Fortunately, I had a place to move the best things to." Tears filled his eyes.

Anne handed him a Kleenex from her backpack. "That's sad."

"It was time. She was over a hundred. Quite a performer in her day. The rhinestone shoes were hers, too."

"Really?"

"Want to see her scrapbook?"

"I'd love to."

He ambled into the back room, returned with a tattered album, and sat back in the chair beside Anne. "By the way, I'm Roland Rowlankowski. Everyone calls me Row." He extended a hand.

"I'm Anne McFarland. Pleased to meet you." They shook.

He opened the scrapbook on his lap and pointed to a photo of two doe-eyed girls, wry smiles on their lips. "That's Clair's Aunt June and her mother, April. Here's a picture of the three of them together." The women stood in front of a dilapidated farmhouse. "Quite a story there. April abandoned Clair when she was a child to be raised alone by her father. Later in life Clair and her mother became reacquainted, but it took ages for her to be forgiven."

Anne sighed. "How very sad."

He nodded and put his fingers under another photo. "Here's Clair's father. He had one blue eye and one brown one."

"Really? I've never heard of that."

"Yes, it's very rare."

Row turned to a picture of chorus girls in a line, their arms linked together.

Anne pointed to their feet. "Are they wearing the rhinestone shoes?"

"Yep." He nodded. "Can you tell which one is Clair?"

"The tallest?" Anne put her finger on Clair's image.

"With the biggest eyes. Here's another good one." He turned the page to reveal a yellowed newspaper clipping with Clair in a pearl headdress and feathered wings. The caption said: *Songbird of Broadway a Soaring Success!*

On the next page, Clair hung in the air above stage in a crescent moon. That caption said: *It Must Have Been Moon Glow.*

Row put the album in Anne's lap, and she turned another page. "Who is this?" She pointed to a tall man with light curly hair standing next to Clair in front of a Spanish-style home flanked by palm trees.

Row smiled. "For some reason she'd never divulge, Clair called him Mr. X."

Anne laughed. "Really?"

"He was a talent scout for a Hollywood film studio. Took Clair out there and put her in a few films, but she soon became homesick. She always said, 'New York is my home. Where I can be my best.'"

"How did she know?"

"She told me she simply *followed her heart*."

Anne's started beating fast. The words from the past really spoke to her.

58

Later that night, Anne led Sergio to his couch. "We need to talk."

"Sounds serious."

"It is." She hugged him, then took his hands. "It's not that I don't love you, I do. But I can't move here."

"Why not?" He frowned.

"Staying here with you the first week or so was fun, but lately I've felt out of sorts." She paused.

"Go on."

She hoped he'd understand. "My muse isn't here with me."

"What can we do to get her here? I told you we could clear out the guest room. Or I'll rent a studio for you."

"That's sweet, but it's deeper than that. New York feels too lofty. San Francisco is my soul place. Where I can be my best."

"Oh, Big Foot. I don't want to lose you."

"I don't want to lose you, either." Her eyes filled with tears. "Can't we just continue our coast-to-coast romance after we're married?"

"I'm not sure." He shook his head. "I doubt it."

She pulled off the ring and handed it to him.

He slipped it back on her finger. "Keep it for now."

They held each other while they cried.

~

Before Anne opened her eyes, a bleating horn warned her it was foggy outside. She reached for Sergio, but of course he wasn't there. He had been in her dream, the scent of him, her fingers entwined in his dark curly hair, the smooth sheets below her. For the hundredth time she wondered if she'd made the right decision. She sighed and looked at the ring on her finger.

Fortunately, when she'd returned from New York six months before, Mrs. Landenheim hadn't yet rented out the apartment and gladly accepted Anne's newly signed lease. Now she looked around: the knickknack shelves filled with found objects, canvases and boxes stacked against the wall, vintage magazines piled high. Several new pieces were in progress. This was where she was supposed to be. Living among her inspirations in the city she called home kept her juices flowing.

She clambered out of bed, started the coffee, and rolled out her yoga mat. Since returning from New York, she practiced almost every day. Her body had become more flexible, the poses came more easily, and she felt more grounded. In classes she still felt like a klutz, but she'd learned to not care what others thought and only tried to do her best.

The fog lifted as she climbed out onto the rooftop. Dew glittered on her green garden. She tried to pull up a carrot, but it wouldn't release from the ground. It must not be ready yet. She tugged out some weeds and discovered a few vivid red strawberries hidden beneath scalloped leaves. The feel of damp soil on her hands soothed her. She picked the tiny dots of color, along with some mint sprigs. Smiling, she rinsed them in her kitchen sink, threw them in the blender along with a banana, and made a breakfast smoothie.

It was delicious.

Before she left for work she had to finish the shoe painting.

She'd promised to get it to Fay in time for the Gallery Noir installation tomorrow, but Anne still couldn't get the rhinestone shading just right.

She imagined a young Clair wearing the shoes onstage and remembered Fay's advice: *follow your heart*.

Anne closed her eyes, inhaled, and suddenly it hit her. Why not use the real thing? She rummaged through a basket for jewel-encrusted remnant she'd bought ages ago at an antique mall. She found it, held it up to the light, and admired the rhinestones.

She pulled them off the sheer fabric, and, using tweezers, picked up each rhinestone one by one, dunked its base in glue, and adhered it to the canvas. With an energy rush, consumed by the act of creation, she worked until each shoe was completely covered. Sighing happily, she took a photo of the canvas and messaged it to Fay and Sergio.

Last night she had set out the magazines and empty shoeboxes on her classroom tables at SFMOMA. Now she gathered up the box of found objects: buttons, seashells, beads, and faux pearls she'd selected from her stash.

She couldn't wait to share them with her students.

ACKNOWLEDGMENTS

First, I want to thank provocateur Judy Reeves for leading me onto this story's bridge, enticing me to jump in and keep swimming until I had a finished draft but standing by to rescue me with a lifeboat.

My gratitude goes to my cohorts at San Diego Writers, Ink for their support and for writing beside me, especially Kristen Fogle and Kim Keeline and Room to Writers John Van Roekel, Danielle Baldwin, and Linda Salem. I'm grateful to Tammy Greenwood and group members Robin Kardon and Dina Koutas for responding to my first typed draft. I'm appreciative to editor Marni Freedman for coaching suggestions on Clair early on and to Jennifer Silva Redmond for expert content and line editing. Jennifer Coburn, thank you for pushing me to go beyond my social-media comfort level and to Indy Quillen for my beautiful website.

Brooke Warner, Crystal Patriarche, Cait Levin, Julie Metz, and others at She Writes Press (SWP), I'm indebted to you for providing hybrid publishing opportunities, guiding me through the journey, and educating me to be a savvy authorpreneur. A big shout-out goes to my SWP sisters, in particular Leslie Johansen Nack.

I'm eternally grateful to my fellow Point Loma Book Club members Pat Fitzmorris, Marti Hess, Lisa Laube, Carol Leimbach, and Patti Wassem for cheering me up and on. To Tanya Peters for being here when I need you most, thank you. To my siblings Todd Greentree, Sandy Greenbaum, and Leslie Zwail, it's a blessing to have you always in my heart. Thank you to mis amigos Andy Hein for coffee chats and giggles when Clair began to show her true colors. Many hugs go to Phil Johnson and Seth Krosner for your friendship and confidence in me. To Dottie Laub, thank you for showing me how to buckle the straps on my own silver shoes and for urging me to keep Anne a modern woman. Leslie Meads, thank you for your fantastic party planning and for hysterically laughing with me during that burlesque show. To yoga teachers Lisa Hampton and Banoo, I appreciate your calm voices that remind me to breathe, stay flexible, and be in the moment. To all the dance instructors I've had over the years, thanks for your patience and inspiration. My gratitude goes to Jerry, who encouraged me to follow my creative path. Thanks to Lucy, my beagle-basset, for demonstrating how to relax.

Lastly, I am thankful to the readers who have written reviews, followed me on Facebook, and hosted me at their book club events. Because of you I kept writing.

ABOUT THE AUTHOR

photo credit: Chris Loomis

JILL G. HALL is the author of *The Black Velvet Coat*, an International Book Award Finalist for Best New Fiction. Her poems have appeared in a variety of publications, including *A Year in Ink, The Avocet,* and *Wild Women, Wild Voices.* On her blog, CreaLivity, she shares personal musings about the art of practicing a creative lifestyle. She is a seasoned presenter at seminars, readings, and community events. In addition to writing, Hall practices yoga, tap dances, and enjoys spending time in nature. Learn more at www.jillghall.com.

SELECTED TITLES FROM SHE WRITES PRESS

She Writes Press is an independent publishing company founded to serve women writers everywhere. Visit us at www.shewritespress.com.

The Black Velvet Coat by Jill G. Hall. $16.95, 978-1-63152-009-9. When the current owner of a black velvet coat—a San Francisco artist in search of inspiration—and the original owner, a 1960s heiress who fled her affluent life fifty years earlier, cross paths, their lives are forever changed . . . for the better.

Portrait of a Woman in White by Susan Winkler. $16.95, 978-1-938314-83-4. When the Nazis steal a Matisse portrait from the eccentric, art-loving Rosenswigs, the Parisian family is thrust into the tumult of war and separation, their fates intertwined with that of their beloved portrait.

The Great Bravura by Jill Dearman. $16.95, 978-1-63152-989-4. Who killed Susie—or did she actually disappear? The Great Bravura, a dashing lesbian magician living in a fantastical and noirish 1947 New York City, must solve this mystery—before she goes to the electric chair.

Beautiful Garbage by Jill DiDonato. $16.95, 978-1-938314-01-8. Talented but troubled young artist Jodi Plum leaves suburbia for the excitement of the city—and is soon swept up in the sexual politics and downtown art scene of 1980s New York.

Start With the Backbeat by Garinè B. Isassi. $16.95, 978-1-63152-041-9. When post-punk rocker Jill Dodge finally gets the promotion she's been waiting for in the spring of 1989, she finds herself in the middle of a race to find a gritty urban rapper for her New York record label.

The Sweetness by Sande Boritz Berger. $16.95, 978-1-63152-907-8. A compelling and powerful story of two girls—cousins living on separate continents—whose strikingly different lives are forever changed when the Nazis invade Vilna, Lithuania.